Finding
MR. SUNDAY

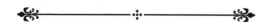

DICK WARD

Cover design by JR Designs and Nu expression. Book design by Nu expression, Winston Salem, NC.

IBSN 978-0-692-19126-2

ACKNOWLEDGEMENTS

This book would not have been possible without the help of many people. The research for this book was augmented by the staffs of many historical associations and societies who took their time to give me excellent information. There were too many to mention by name herein. But I must extend a sincere thanks to Jon Lane, Curator of the South Pass City Historic Site in South Pass City, Wyoming, who graciously shared his time during my visit there. I also thank Carol Hanner, whose editorial talent and guidance kept me on track. Also, thank you to my dear wife Betty, who tolerated my constant ordering of books and other research materials and long hours at the Mac.

DEDICATION

To Betty, my partner, my best friend, and loving wife of many years: There is no other like you. To my beautiful and talented daughter Kelly: You stole my heart the minute I first held you in my arms. I love you both. You two have made my life complete.

Finding
MR. SUNDAY

CHAPTER ONE

1865

W ill Sunday watched the Missouri sun settle below the tree line and almost immediately felt the chill of early fall. Yellow leaves from the river birches guarding the creek drifted down in the light breeze. He stoked the campfire and shoved a pan of side meat closer to the flames.

He removed a Henry rifle from its scabbard, unbuckled the gun belt that held his Remington Army revolver and placed the two within reach as he reclined lazily on his saddle and bedroll.

It had been a good day on the trail, he mused as he watched the daylight sour to dusk. Jefferson City couldn't be more that fifteen or twenty miles. By tomorrow evening he could enjoy a hot bath and a good meal.

The campsite had been a stop for many a traveler, he thought as the breeze hushed the day and the creek gently rippled. He could hear his horse and the two pack mules crunch the grass down by the creek. This is the outdoors he remembered so fondly. No carriages clattering down the street, no teamsters yelling, no celebrants weaving down the sidewalks.

His reverie was shattered as the big bay lifted his head and whinnied loudly. He stood up quickly and looked into the fading light. Riders were approaching at a slow pace, coming from the direction of the trail he had left not long ago. He reached for the Henry and levered a cartridge into the chamber.

"Yo' the fire. We ain't meanin' no harm," someone shouted.

He could make out two riders who had stopped their horses well away from the campfire.

"Can we git down?" said the same voice.

"Come in closer," he answered.

Will kept the Henry pointed in their direction. The riders dismounted and walked toward the fire, leading their horses.

They were a scruffy pair, one tall and skinny, the other short and fat. The horses were thin tired nags.

"Be obliged if we could sit a spell," said the fat one.

Will knew right away these men were not his kind of people. They were the kind that needed to be watched closely. Stay sharp, he said to himself.

But, he thought, he had the Henry rifle and the revolver nearby and had complete confidence in his skill with both. He backed up, watching them intently, keeping the Henry in his hands.

"Come and sit," he said to them.

"Why, that's mighty kindly. Mind we make some coffee?" said the fat one.

"Help yourself," he said.

"Burt, stake 'em horses and bring 'at grub sack," said the fat one as he handed the reins to the skinny one, who moved quickly to the order and led the two horses away.

With some difficulty, the fat man sat down across the fire from Will. The man scratched his face with dirty fingernails and took stock of the camp, eyeing the gear and two wooden crates stacked to one side. His eyes settled on the Henry rifle the lone camper was holding.

"Ya ain't gon' need that. We friendly. Just need a little rest, that's all. Then we moving on," he said.

Will moved the barrel of the Henry a little to one side, pointing it away from the stranger, then sat.

In the better light he could see the fat man wore homespun pants and a coarse wool frock coat. A pot belly concealed most of the belt that held up his dirty pants.

He had a fat face, little pig eyes, and a droopy mustache that topped off his tobacco-stained whiskers. If he had a neck, it was hidden by the extra chins.

"You a big fella, ain't you?" said the fat one. "Look young, though." He paused for a response but got none.

"Names Hurley. That's Burt gittin' the coffee," he said. "Where you headed?"

"Independence. Then on to California in the spring. Planning to stop in Jefferson City for a couple of days to clean up and have some decent food. Give the animals a good feed and let them rest up. I left St. Louis about a

2

week ago," said the young man.

"Yeah, us, too. Come up the Mississippi to St. Louis from down South. Bad place, the South, now the war's over," he said as he shook his head. "Ain't nothing but hungry folk, carpetbaggers, and Yankees all over the place."

The man caught himself. "No offense meant."

The pig eyes watched the young man closely for a reaction.

"Boat were full of damn foreigners. We get to St. Louis and they's even more of 'em. Ain't no work. And people dying in the streets with the cholera. Sure's hell won't going to stay in 'at place."

"It's bad," Will said. "The older folks that were around when the last epidemic hit in '49 say this one might be worse. And thousands of people died then. You'd think in all those years they'd know what's causing people to die. I'm happy to leave that part behind."

"You sho' right," said Hurley.

Burt came back to the fire with the grub sack. He withdrew a battered coffee pot and a small bag of coffee and stepped to the creek to fill the pot. On returning, he poured some coffee into the pot and placed the pot on a flat rock. Using a stick, he pushed the rock into the edge of the flames. He sat down beside Hurley, scanned the campsite, and looked at the crates.

"You freight'n?" Burt asked, gesturing at the wooden crates on the edge of the campsite. "Saw that bay and them mules. We mule handlers, me an' Hurley."

A toothy grin split Burt's face.

Burt was absurdly thin and tall. His long arms stuck out beyond the sleeves of his coat, and his pant legs rode high, revealing the tops of worn brogans. He wore suspenders over a dark shirt and a once-black bowler hat. His large eyes and teeth seemed out of place on his hatchet face. He sat there with his legs drawn up looking like a grasshopper about to hop.

"No, I'm not in the freight business. Those crates are gunsmith tools and supplies. A few books. I was raised by a gunsmith, and he left me those when he died. I worked in Tom's gun shop since I was a little boy."

The skinny man's face didn't show comprehension; the odd smile remained in place.

"The tools are mostly of sentimental value because they belonged to

3

Finding Mr. Sunday

Tom. Some of those books might be hard to come by out West."

He saw no reason to tell these strangers any more than that. He had probably said too much already, he thought.

Hurley cocked his head. "A gunsmith, you say? Is that what you gonna do out West?"

The young man paused a moment before answering.

"Maybe. May study law. May learn the cattle business. I don't really know yet. I hear the West is full of opportunity."

"That it is, that it is," said Hurley. "Least ways, you can git shed o' all this war misery."

Will wanted these fellows out of his campsite. He was uncomfortable with the amount of interest they showed in the crates. Maybe if they had their coffee and some food, they would leave his camp sooner. He knew he could not sleep with these two so close.

"That's a fine-looking belt and holster you got," Hurley said as he pointed to the outfit. "Where'd you get 'em, if you don't mind me askin'?"

"They were handmade for me by a man who did leather work for Tom. Belts, holsters, and such. He made my boots, too. He took a lot of pride in the detail of his goods," Will said.

Hurley leaned over and looked at the boots the young man wore.

"Right purdy," said Hurley.

"Is that coffee nigh done, Burt? Po' me some if it is," Hurley ordered.

"Be ready soon. Be ready soon," said Burt.

He nudged the pot a little closer to the fire.

Hurley spit a wad of chewed tobacco toward the fire and wiped his mouth with the cuff of his shirt and the back of his grimy hand.

Shortly, Burt rattled around in the grub bag, found a tin cup, poured coffee from the pot and handed the cup to Hurley. Hurley took a noisy sip.

"Damn, 'at's hot. Why didn't you tell me, fool?" said Hurley.

Hurley shot a mean look at Burt, who looked wounded by the comment. Will was beginning to see that, despite his coffee-making skills, there was something not quite right about Burt.

"There's some side meat in that frying pan there," said the young camper. "I've got some bread and cheese. Not much, but you are welcome to it. I can restock when I get to Jefferson City."

4

Dick Ward

The two men almost jumped at the pan. Will laid the Henry aside and pulled the bread and cheese from his grub sack. He tore a small portion from the loaf of bread and handed the rest to Hurley. He broke off a bit of cheese and handed what was left to Hurley. Hurley took most of the bread and cheese for himself and gave the rest to Burt.

They ate without speaking. The two men stuffed their mouths and chewed hungrily between gulps of coffee. It wasn't long before they were finished. Hurley sopped the grease out of the frying pan with the last of the bread.

"Mighty good. Mighty good," he said. "Wish I had me a jug of whiskey. Be fine then."

He burped loudly and wiped his hands on his pants, reached into his coat pocket and pulled out a bag of chewing tobacco and began stuffing the pieces in his mouth. He rolled his tongue to position the wad and began chewing.

The uneasy camper was immediately angry at himself for being so careless. The stranger could have easily shot him had he reached for a pistol. A bad lapse in judgment like that could have gotten him killed.

He finished his meager dinner and poured water from his canteen onto his hands and wiped them on a cloth. The two travelers looked at him with curiosity. He knew what he did must have seemed strange to these fellows. He needed to get these men on their way.

"You going to take them mules west with you?" asked Hurley.

"I don't know yet. I'll be in Independence six or seven months before I leave for the West. I'll have plenty of time to decide what I am going to do. I'd like to talk with some folks that have been out West."

He set the cloth aside, keeping a keener eye on the two than he had earlier.

"I'm going to California eventually, so I need to learn more about that part of the trail, the best way, and such. Why do you ask?" he said.

"I hear tell Injuns will eat a mule. Won't eat no ox. I ain't never been west, though. That's what I heard," said Hurley. "A mule lasts better'n a horse but not like no ox. Them split hoofs make it easier for an ox. They slow, though."

"I didn't know that," Will said. "But there's a lot I don't know about going out West. I plan to learn, though. I'm a quick study."

There was a bit of silence. Maybe if he said nothing more they would leave.

Finding Mr. Sunday

"Gonna be chilly tonight," Hurley said through the mouth full of tobacco. "Colder up in these parts. But we got a nice full moon coming up."

He spat to the side.

"Be pretty riding tonight. When I was a young'un, I'd hunt all night on a night this. I could about see as good in full moonlight as daylight. Hunt coon, possum, deer. You a hunter?"

"Some. Small game mostly," Will said. "We had a cabin on the river outside of St. Louis. We spent as much time as we could up there. Did more fishing than hunting. But I can dress a rabbit or a deer if I need to. A full moon night was always fun, especially down on the river. Catfish would really bite then."

"They always do on a full moon," said Hurley.

Again, no one spoke for a moment. Hurley leaned forward with both hands on his knees.

"Well, we gonna go on up the trail, put in a few more miles," said Hurley.

Burt turned to Hurley with a surprised look on his face, his big eyes momentarily even bigger.

The camper was also surprised by the abrupt announcement but was glad to hear it.

"Burt, get all 'at stuff together. Rinse 'at pot in the creek," said Hurley as he pushed himself off the ground. Again, Burt jumped to the task.

"Appreciate the vittles. Sure good of you," Hurley said as he shot a stream of tobacco juice into the fire.

"Glad I could do it," said the camper as he stood with the Henry in his hands. He kept a close eye on the pistol in Hurley's belt.

Burt came back from the creek with the grub sack over his shoulder. Hurley looked around the campsite one last time and turned to join Burt. Then he turned back toward the young man.

"You mind yo'self on this trail, boy." His pigs eyes narrowed. "Ain't everybody as nice as me and Burt."

He chuckled and walked into the darkness, his fat behind keeping time with his pace.

That poor horse, thought Will as he watched the fat one struggle into his saddle.

The sound of the horses faded in the direction of the trail. He added more wood to the fire, relieved they were gone.

Good riddance, he thought. He was still angry at himself for his earlier mistake. You couldn't survive out West being that careless with strangers, he thought. He moved the gun belt closer to his bed roll, took off his boots, and covered himself with the blanket.

He wondered if he should move to another spot to sleep, an old trick he'd read about somewhere. He gave it some thought and decided he was too comfortable where he was.

He looked up at the night sky and watched thin clouds veil the stars briefly, then move on. He thought of Caleb. Three years gone now. And Tom, dear Tom. How he missed them both.

That part of his life was gone forever. There would be very little familiar to him from now on. It was somewhat frightening to the eighteen-year-old. But at the same time, he found excitement in the unknown.

He pulled the blanket under his chin and closed his eyes. Another day tomorrow, he thought.

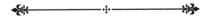

He bolted upright from his bedroll, wide awake from a tattered sleep. He didn't know what woke him. The fire had died quite some time ago, and he could feel the damp mist in the air. He scanned the area, trying to focus in the pre-dawn gray.

Forms began to take shape as his eyes adjusted to the low light. He could see the bay and the mules grazing calmly nearby. The wooden crates were stacked just as they had been when he went to sleep. Nothing seemed out of place.

He yawned, then stretched, still scanning his surroundings. He put on his boots, walked to the edge of the woods, and began to relieve himself. He watched a few leaves drift to the ground and shivered in the cool air as the warmth of the bedroll left him. If he broke camp soon he could get to Jefferson City earlier than he had thought yesterday.

Lightning exploded inside his head, paralyzing him with intense pain. His body seemed to float in the air. He knew no up or down. He felt a crushing jolt as if he had been slammed to earth by some unseen force. He tried to cry out but could make no sound. His mind went to a terrifying place. He tried to wake up from the nightmare but fell deeper into a dark swirling pit. A great warmth washed over his body. He sighed peacefully and let go.

Hurley and Burt rushed out from the woods.

"You got 'em, Hurley! You got 'em!" said Burt.

"Couldna missed," said Hurley. "I was only about ten yards from him. He never saw me."

Hurley came out of the wood line, stepped closer, and stared down at the still body, the rifle in his hand. Burt followed Hurley and stood beside him.

The impact of the bullet had knocked the young man backward, and he was lying face up. His fingers twitched then became still. Blood flowed from a wound near the top of his head, a couple inches above his hairline. It ran through his thick blond hair down into a growing pool at the back of his head.

Hurley squatted close, trying to hear or feel a breath. He stood up and looked at Burt.

"He ain't going nowhere," said Hurley.

He began to walk away, then turned, reached down and yanked a boot from one of the downed man's feet.

"Damn," he said, "I been hankering 'em boots since I seen 'em. Oughta' knowed they'd be twice my size."

He tossed the boot to Burt. "Here, you take 'em. He don't need 'em anymore."

Hurley walked over to the wooden crates, took out a knife, and pried the top off of one of them. The crate was filled with straw. He shoved his hand down in the straw and felt around. His tiny eyes opened wide, and a smile came to his face.

"Just what I thought," he said.

He pulled a long muslin-wrapped bundle from the crate, tore off the wrapping, and held up a shiny new Henry rifle. He put the Henry down, reached in the crate, and pulled out a rectangular bundle wrapped in the same manner.

Unwrapping it, he found a polished walnut wood case. He lifted the top of the case and saw a nickel-plated Smith & Wesson pocket pistol, .32 caliber with ivory grips and ornate engraving. There was also a box of rimfire cartridges in the case.

"Get 'em mules and load 'em up, Burt. Damn if we ain't going west with money in our pockets," he said with a big smile.

CHAPTER TWO

1852

S t. Louis stretched seven miles along the Mississippi River and three miles inland from its banks. The population increased daily as German, Irish, and English immigrants spilled from the endless stream of ships that docked at the wharf. The acrid smell of iron ore furnaces mingled with that of fresh baked bread, animal waste, and the refuse of humanity.

Wagons, carriages, drays, and conveyances of every kind crowded the streets. Teamsters shouted and cursed their way to passage. Steam whistles from the boats blended with those of the railroad engines and added to the cacophony.

Carpenters, masons, and hod carriers worked side by side building brick and stone structures to replace the wooden buildings that had burned in the great fire of '49. In the three years since, new buildings had risen in every direction.

Men and women, dressed in their latest finery, strolled merrily past invisible beggars and homeless children. All the glory of a new spring was lost amid the dirty streets and barren walkways.

The bell on the front door of the shop tinkled as the door opened. A tall, sturdy man entered, leading a young boy by the hand. The man was clean-shaven and dressed in plain but neat attire. He moved with a confident and purposeful stride. The boy was a handsome little fellow with cotton-colored hair and blue eyes, wide with wonder as he took in the contents of the shop.

They crossed the oiled wood floor and stepped to the front of one of the glass-topped counters. It was filled with pistols of every size and design, from a small-bore single-barrel Philadelphia derringer to a large-caliber Colt Dragoon revolver. There were new pistols and well-oiled used pistols, as well as handcrafted holsters and gun belts. The walls behind the counters were lined with cabinets holding assorted rifles and scatterguns.

A pleasant-looking man stepped through the open door behind the counters. His dark hair was graying at the temples. He had on a well-worn leather apron and was wiping his hands on a cloth. He nodded at the man, then smiled broadly at the boy.

"Good morning," he said. "How can I be of service?"

"I am looking for Tom Peyton," said the man.

"You have found him," said Tom.

He came from behind the counter and stepped closer to the visitors.

"I'm William Sunday, Mr. Peyton. You may not remember me. I was a mite young when you and your father left Petersburg. I am Joshua Sunday's son." William extended his hand to the shopkeeper.

"Well, well," he said as he shook William's hand. "That was a long time ago. I'm surprised you even remember me."

Tom looked William up and down. His eyes narrowed, and his memory whirred.

"Yes, I remember now. Joshua Sunday had a young son when we left Virginia. That was back in '25."

"That was me," said William. He smiled warmly at Tom.

"Joshua and Pap were good friends. They used to go fishing together in the Appomattox River. Your father had a blacksmith shop on Plum Street. The Sundays were often guests in our home as were we in theirs," said Tom.

"That's right," said William. "Our families were close."

Tom turned to the boy and bent low. "And who is this handsome young man?"

"This is my son, Will," William said.

Tom stuck his hand out to Will. The little boy looked up with a disarmingly sweet smile.

"Well, hello, Will. Good to know you," said Tom.

Without hesitation, Will took Tom's hand and pumped it as a well-mannered adult would.

"Hello, sir," said Will.

Tom turned to William. "How is your father, William? Well, I hope?"

"I'm sorry to say Pa and Ma are both gone. Pa passed on about two years ago and Ma within six months of him," said William. "I miss them. They were all the family I had."

"My condolences," said Tom.

12

"Thank you. Pa and Ma mentioned your name often over the years, ... even talked about visiting St. Louis some day. I think the years just came too fast, same as they do for all of us."

He paused a moment.

"They both spoke highly of you and your father. I couldn't come to St. Louis without looking you up, despite all the years that have passed."

"I'm glad you did. We don't hear from home folks much anymore," said Tom.

"Does your father still work in the shop? People back home still carry his rifles," William said with a smile.

"He worked every day right up until he passed. I'm sorry to say I lost him last year," said Tom.

"Then my condolences to you, Tom," said William.

"Thank you. Are you planning to stay in St. Louis?" asked Tom.

"Just passing through. We'll be here a few days, go on to Independence, then head west from there. I'm already signed up with a wagon train."

He absent-mindedly stroked his son's head.

"I want to look at outfitting prices here. Just to educate myself. Someone told me you'd pay more if you waited 'til you got to Independence. 'Course I don't know if that's true or not. But it won't hurt to know what the market's like," said William.

"Well, you two are in for an adventure. Do you have time to sit and visit for a while?" said Tom. "I'd love to hear about Virginia, your plans and all."

The invitation was heartfelt and genuine.

"Yes, I'd enjoy that," said William.

Then he caught himself.

"But you're in the middle of a work day. We don't want...."

"No, no," Tom interrupted him. "Let's go in the back. We'll be more comfortable. Caleb can watch the front for me. This time of day we won't have many customers anyway. Besides, I've got a little treat for Will."

"All right," said William. "Come on, Will. Let's go see what's in back."

Hand in hand, they followed Tom through the door leading to the rear of the shop.

They entered a large room that was brightly lit with gas lights. Two work benches dominated the space along with assorted cabinets, bins, and shelving. There were lathes, grinders, polishers, drill presses, and a number of other tools, including a massive rifling machine. A collection of hand tools hung on a rack near the benches. Despite the many pieces of equipment, the shop was clean and orderly.

There was a desk in one corner of the room with a comfortable-looking leather chair pulled up behind it. In front of the desk was a sitting area with a low table surrounded by several stuffed chairs. A nearby large cast iron stove made the area look homey and inviting.

At one of the benches, two men sat on stools across from one another. One was a gray-haired man wearing eyeglasses and the other was a boy who had the build of a lumberjack and looked to be still in his mid-teen years. Several pistols lay on the bench in various stages of assembly. Both men looked up as the three entered the room.

"This is Caleb and Penn. Fellows, these are some friends from Virginia. Caleb, would you mind watching the front for me? I'm going to visit with these folks for a while."

The two men smiled warmly and greeted the visitors. The younger of the two stepped from the stool and headed to the front of the shop, his muscled body moved with surprising grace.

"Sure, Tom," said Caleb. He ruffled Will's hair and smiled broadly as he headed to the front.

"Let's have a seat over here," said Tom, gesturing toward the desk and chairs.

Tom walked around to the desk and removed a small tin container from one of the drawers. He brought it to Will and opened it. It was filled with quarter-sized colored wafers. The boy looked at them curiously.

"Go ahead. Take one. Just bite off a piece and tell me what you think."

Will picked up a wafer, bit into it and chewed. His eyes widened in delight.

"Do you like those?" Tom asked with a smile.

"Yes!" Will said, nodding his head up and down.

"They are called hub wafers...flavored candy. One of my little weaknesses. Take some and enjoy them," said Tom.

Will carefully picked out several, climbed into a chair, and began to nibble away at the wafers.

Dick Ward

"Have a seat, William," said Tom. He retrieved a pipe and a tobacco pouch from the desktop and sat in a chair facing William. He filled the pipe slowly and lit it. A cloud of fragrant tobacco moved slowly across the room.

William's tall frame filled the chair. He sat with his hands clasped in his lap, his brushed stove pipe boots flat on the floor, his good posture still evident even as he sat.

"So, you have decided to go West, have you?" said Tom.

Tom had a presence about him that made others feel comfortable. His ready smile immediately put them at ease. He leaned his head forward when others talked, the kind of man who picked up on every word. William was already beginning to feel a kind of kinship toward Tom.

"Well, Tom, things seemed to happen all at once. Pa died, then Ma. My wife Maizey was about to birth our second child when Ma died."

Tom looked at William. He noticed William's eyes were an unusual color of blue, like blue and white English china.

"She come down with a fever a few days after we buried Ma. She had chills, wouldn't eat. Too weak to get out of the bed. The doctor couldn't tell us what the fever was from. Just told us to give her cool baths and keep her quiet and comfortable."

William paused. Tom could see the lingering grief shadow the man's face.

"The fever wouldn't go away. Then the baby started coming. She had a terrible time of it, and the baby was stillborn. Maizey didn't even make it another day."

Tom could see the big man's eyes glisten as he talked. Losing a wife and a baby was a terrible experience for any man. He knew the pain of losing a wife.

"I'm sorry, William. I know what you are going through," said Tom. "I lost my wife to cholera in the epidemic of '49. I wish I could tell you all the pain goes away eventually, but it doesn't."

William took a deep breath and continued. "I owned a farm outside of Petersburg. Grew wheat, corn. Had a few cattle, some hogs, chickens. Nothing big, mind you, but we always had enough to sell some and make a little cash money. We were never going to be rich, but we weren't going to starve, either.

"When I lost Maizey, I don't mind telling you, it hit me hard. Will too.

15

Finding Mr. Sunday

Hadn't been for Will, I don't know what I'da done. The farm just wasn't home without Maizey. I didn't want to stay on there.

"Years ago, when I was little more than a pup, I had a hankering to go off... you know...over the next rise, so to speak. Just to see what was over there. Guess it was just young man's blood. But I put that feeling to rest when I met Maizey.

"Since the mid '40s there's been talk among some of the local folk about going west. Some did leave when they found gold in California in the late '40s. I didn't think much about it, even then."

William shifted his position, crossed one leg over the other and faced Tom more directly.

"But with Maizey gone, that old hankering came creeping back. I got to thinking about it seriously."

William paused a moment, studied his calloused hands and looked up at Tom.

"There's a lot of unrest in the South now, Tom. They're arguing about slavery, states' rights, this compromise, that compromise. I don't know what the future holds. It all bothers me."

William paused and inhaled deeply.

"I finally decided to do it. I sold everything. The house, the farm, the animals, all of it."

William raised both hands, palms out as if surrendering to an inner struggle.

"And here we are."

He placed his hand on Will's knee and gently squeezed. The boy smiled up at him.

"I was worried all this would be too hard on Will, but he's done fine."

There was a long pause as Tom waited politely to be sure William was finished.

"Sorry, Tom," said William.

He stirred a bit in his chair. "I didn't mean to go on so."

"No, no. Don't apologize. Thanks for sharing your story. There are a whole lot of people heading west nowadays. For one reason or another. Not a week goes by that we don't see a story in the newspaper about it. If I was a little younger I'd give it some strong consideration myself," said Tom.

Dick Ward

"I don't mind telling you, it's a long haul, William. But I hear the trip is getting easier every day. And let me tell you, California is an amazing place."

Tom shifted in his seat and puffed on his pipe.

"I was in the Army in '46 during the war with Mexico. Went from there to California with Kearney and caught a bullet in the ribs. I was laid up for quite a while, didn't know if I'd make it.

"In '48, they told me I could be discharged in California with travel pay, or I could come back home with the troops. I decided to get discharged and spent some time seeing the country before I came back home," he said.

He looked off for a moment; the recollection warmed him.

"I don't regret it. If I hadn't been married I would've stayed. But I did okay while I was there."

He winked at William and chuckled at some private thought.

The two men caught up on mutual acquaintances, Virginia politics and the like. The conversation was warm, easy, and enjoyable. They could have just as easily been sitting on a front porch in the warm Virginia spring, enjoying a glass of lemonade.

Young Will, however, was getting a little restless.

"When did you say you were leaving for Independence?" asked Tom.

"We'll stay over the weekend and leave on Monday," said William.

"Good! Would you be my guests for a meal tomorrow night? I can tell you about California. I don't live far from here. Mrs. Cleary, my housekeeper, is a fine cook. And I know she would enjoy meeting you. I have to warn you, though, she might try to steal Will. She has a few grandchildren and loves little ones," said Tom with a laugh.

"You're mighty gracious, Tom. We'd like that," said William.

"Where are you staying?" asked Tom.

"At the Monroe House, at Second and Olive," said William.

"I know it well. I'll meet you there with a carriage at six tomorrow," said Tom.

"Looks like Will there is ready to be off," said Tom as he smiled at the boy.

"He has had a long day," said William. "I should get him fed and in bed."

"Then let me walk you out," said Tom. He led them into the front of the shop.

"It was a pleasure seeing you, William. I'm truly honored that, after all these years, you would go to the trouble of looking me up. I'm looking forward to your visit."

He turned to the boy. "Will, I will see you tomorrow night."

He patted the boy on the head and shook hands with William.

"Thank you, Tom. We'll see you at six tomorrow." said William.

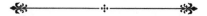

Mid-afternoon the following day the front door of the shop opened abruptly, and William Sunday rushed in. It was obvious that something was wrong. Tom was behind a counter.

"Tom, there has been an accident. Will has been hurt!" he said, his voice somewhat unsteady.

Tom said as calmly as he could, "Tell me what happened."

William took a deep breath and began.

"We went out to Benson livery about a mile north of here. We were talking to the owner about wagons, yokes, and so on. There was a fellow there buying two young mules. They were green, and he had his hands full trying to keep them calm. He was leading them out to tie them to his wagon when one of them broke loose and ran toward us kicking and bellowing.

"I grabbed Will and yelled at the mule, and that's when it happened. The mule shied away from us, but when he turned away he kicked both back legs in the air. He caught Will as I was lifting him up off the ground. He broke one of Wills' legs and tore into the flesh."

He drew an audible breath.

"We took him over to City Hospital. They've stitched the cuts and set his leg. They gave him morphine, and he's out right now. They said he would be out the rest of the day. A nurse is watching him now."

"Good Lord, William," said Tom. "Is there anything I can do?"

"I don't know, Tom," said William as he paced the floor, visibly shaken.

"The doctor said he should heal up in due time, but he can't travel for at least four weeks. Even then, it's going to be awful hard on him to be in a wagon going over a rough trail. I don't know what I'm going to do just yet."

18

Dick Ward

William ran his hand over the top of his head as if to smooth his hair.

"He can't stay in the hospital for four weeks," William said. "The hotel room is no fit place for him. People coming and going at all hours. I'm going to have to find another place for him to stay. I was hoping you might refer me to some place."

"No, sir! I wouldn't hear of it. You bring that boy to my house," Tom said.

He stepped closer to William and put his hand gently on William's shoulder.

"Mrs. Cleary will take care of him. She would love to do it, and she'd be the perfect one to do it. I'm home every evening by six, and I'll help out, too. I have a room for him and a place for Mrs. Cleary to stay while she cares for him. At least until we know what you are going to do."

"Tom, that's asking too much of you. I appreciate your offer but ..."

"Nonsense," Tom said. "I insist. I want that boy to be in good hands. This city can be hard on people, especially if you don't know who to trust. I won't take no for an answer, William."

"Are you sure, Tom?" said William. His gratitude was palpable.

"Of course, I'm sure. I wouldn't have it any other way," Tom said.

He could see the relief on William's face.

"I'll take you up on the offer, then. I'll bring him to your house when he is ready to leave the hospital. Tom, I can't thank you enough."

"It's settled then," said Tom. "I'll tell Mrs. Cleary about this, and we'll get things ready."

William, humbled by the generosity, took Tom's hand in both of his. "Tom, thank you. Thank you."

Two men carried little Will into Tom's home on a litter. William followed, carrying Will's belongings.

"Put him in here," said Tom. He pointed to the doorway of a small bedroom off the main hallway.

Will had been in the hospital for four days, and the doctors thought it safe to move him to Tom's house. He looked pale and drawn, with dark circles under his eyes. They put him in the bed, placed his head on a pillow and

Finding Mr. Sunday

covered him.

"He is drowsy from the morphine," said William. "He's talked a little over the last few days, but he slept most of the time. I told him earlier where he was going, but I am not sure if he remembers our visit to your shop."

He bent down and pushed Will's hair back on his forehead.

"Will, do you remember Mr. Peyton? We met him at his gunsmith shop."

Will looked up as Tom leaned toward him, but the boy's expression did not change.

"Hello, Will. It's good to see you again. I'm sorry you got hurt. You're going stay here with me for a while, and we're going to take good care of you," Tom said in the most gentle voice.

The front door opened and closed, and a short, plump, gray-haired woman came down the hall, placed some parcels on the floor and moved to the side of the bed, making a space between William and Tom.

"This is Mrs. Cleary, Will," said Tom.

The woman looked down at Will. The expression on her face was one that could come only from a mother. Her eyes softened, and a smile filled her round face as she placed her hand gently on Will's cheek. Her voice was soothing and sweet.

"Hello, Will. I am glad to meet you, lad. Mr. Peyton's told me all about you. But he didn't tell me how handsome you are," said Mrs. Cleary in her Irish accent.

She lightly rubbed Will's cheek with the back of her curled fingers.

" I'll be a-taking care of you, darlin'. I told Mr. Cleary he'd see me when he sees me. I'll be staying in the room next to you. Day or night, I'll not be afar from you, Will."

She withdrew her hand and turned to William, putting her hand on his arm.

"And you'd be Mr. Sunday?"

With the same gentle tone she said, "You needn't worry, sir. I brought three boys into this world, and they're fine strapping men this day. I've been through this before. I'll love him like he's my own, I will."

"I know you will, Mrs. Cleary. I'm so grateful for what you and Tom are doing. I'll never be able to repay you," said William.

Mrs. Cleary turned to Tom.

"Sir, I'll put on some coffee, then come back and stay with the lad while you two visit in the parlor."

She headed down the hall to the kitchen.

"She's a fine lady. Never a harsh word. She's been with me since before my wife died. She took care of Pap, too. I don't know if I could do without her."

Mrs. Cleary returned. Will looked up at her, gave a little smile, and closed his eyes.

William and Tom went into the parlor for coffee and conversation.

Sometime later William looked in on a sleeping Will, kissed his forehead, and left to return to the hotel.

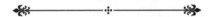

The smell of brewing coffee, bacon, and fresh-baked biscuits welcomed Tom to the kitchen. The pleasant room always seemed to promise a good day.

"Good morning, Mrs. Cleary," said Tom as he poured coffee into a thick mug. "I was about to go in and check on Will. How is he this morning?"

Mrs. Cleary, wiping her hands on an apron, wrinkled her forehead in concern. Her cheeks were rosy from the warm kitchen oven.

"I'm not sure, sir. He's not had a good night. He's sleeping now, but he seems feverish to me, he does. When he wakes I want to check his bandage and look at his leg. I'm a bit worried, sir."

"Let's take a peek, then," said Tom.

They walked quietly into Will's room. Tom touched Will's forehead. The child was hot, his lips dry and cracked. He moved about restlessly and mumbled incoherently.

"You're right, Mrs. Cleary. This boy has a fever. Put some cool cloths on his head. I'll get the doctor here as soon as I can."

He left the room and went immediately out the front door.

Not far away, William Sunday stood staring out of the window of his hotel but seeing little. Bad things just seemed to be happening to those he loved, one after the other, he thought. What had he done to deserve this? What had poor Will done to deserve the pain he must be going through?

21

Finding Mr. Sunday

Then he caught himself. The good Lord doesn't punish people that way. In life, you just have to take the bad with the good. There just weren't many good things happening lately.

He had not slept well since Will was injured. He was worried about his son, but he felt his injuries would heal in due time. Tom, God bless him, was a Godsend. And Mrs. Cleary was just what Will needed now. He took great comfort in their help and was overwhelmed with gratitude.

Will's injury certainly created problems he had not counted on. There would be many unplanned expenses. The hospital and doctors must be paid, and lodging and living expenses for an extended stay in St. Louis would be considerable. He had some cash, but much of it was earmarked for outfitting the trip west and capital to get a homestead going once he got there.

A four-week delay meant he would miss the departure time for the wagon train. Another could be found, but a later departure would increase the possibility of bad weather once they got into the higher elevations. If he missed leaving this spring altogether, he would have to wait many months, possibly another year or so.

Out of all of this, his main concern was to do what was best for Will. He was unwilling to depart with a child who was still recovering from injuries. It would simply be too hard on Will. He would just have be patient and see how things developed. He had to stop worrying about what he couldn't control, he told himself.

He put on his coat and headed for the Peyton house.

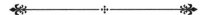

Mrs. Cleary answered the door.

"Ohh, Mr. Sunday. I'm so glad you're here," she said.

He could see the worry in her face.

"What's wrong, Mrs. Cleary? Is Will all right?"

He stepped past Mrs. Cleary and started down the hall at a quick pace. He looked down at his sleeping son and was further alarmed. He touched the boy's head.

"Why, he's burning up!" he whispered.

"Yes, sir. Mr. Peyton has already gone for the doctor. He got a fever in the night, he did. But I'm sure the doctor will be here soon. You sit with him, and I'll get you coffee," she said. She patted his shoulder and left the room.

Tom and the young-looking doctor arrived almost two hours later. It was obvious he was tired. Dark circles underlined his eyes, his faced was unshaven, and his suit was rumpled. He took off his jacket and bent to attend Will.

"I'm sorry. I have been working most of the night, and we were very busy. I got away as soon as I could," the doctor said as he touched the boy's face.

He began a careful examination. As he unwrapped the bandages covering the wound, his expression changed immediately. He shook his head, somewhat breaching his professional armor.

"The cuts caused by the mule's hoof are festering. These wounds are not healing as they should," said the doctor.

His tone was soft but matter of fact.

"We'll have to remove the splints, then lance the wounds, clean them thoroughly, sew them back up and re-splint his leg. It's going to be hard on him, but it has to be done.

"He will have to be sedated again, and he'll need constant medical attention for several days. I'm afraid he has to go back to the hospital immediately. He is going to be a very sick little boy for a while. I'll make the arrangements."

He touched the boy's cheek again and gave a sigh. Without further delay, the weary doctor put on his coat and left quickly.

Will was moved to the hospital, and the necessary procedures were started immediately. William and Tom waited in a small room off the main corridor of the hospital talking quietly. Both men knew that Will was in considerable danger, but neither discussed his concerns. Instead they made small talk, keeping an eye to the doorway for any word on Will's condition. Eventually, a man stepped into the room.

"Which of you is Mr. Sunday?" he asked.

"I am," said William as he stood to greet the man. He was older than the young doctor who had visited Will earlier. He didn't waste time on formalities.

"I'm Dr. Lester, Mr. Sunday. I must be honest with you and tell you your son is quite ill. We lanced and drained the wounds, then flushed them with a vinegar solution. There was dirt and other matter present in the wound."

His manner, though not entirely insensitive, was deliberate and straight-forward.

"I put in new sutures. I re-splinted the leg but only temporarily so we can have complete access to the wound. He is still sedated, and we must keep him that way for a while," said the doctor.

"Is he going to be all right?" said William.

The doctor answered without hesitation.

"I won't know for a while, maybe several days. I don't think we have hindered the mending of the bone, so the main concern is the wound. We have to watch him closely."

The doctor paused for a moment, and his tone softened somewhat.

"I am sorry I can't be more positive right now, Mr. Sunday. In any case, his recovery will take some time. You can see him in a few minutes," he said.

The doctor nodded to William, then left the room. The two men stood for a moment. Tom turned to William and put his hand on his shoulder.

William, his hat in his hand, turned pale as he stood there in front of Tom.

"William, I know you are worried," Tom said softly. "So am I. But let's pray for the best. You are not alone in this. I will do anything I can to help. We will take it as it comes. Now let's go see Will."

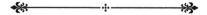

The next two days seemed to drag on forever for William and Tom. Will was sedated most of the time, but on a few occasions he acknowledged his father's presence. Caretakers checking on Will gave William reassurance, but that did little to lessen his worries. Tom visited a couple of times each day.

On the morning of the third day William walked into the hospital room and saw a nurse leaning over Will. He rushed to Will's bedside, afraid that his son's condition had worsened.

He looked down and saw that Will was drinking water. On a tray beside the bed were a bowl of cereal and a container of milk.

"Mr. Sunday," said the nurse cheerily. "Look who is with us this morning?"

"Hey, son."

He looked down at Will. He was afraid he might weep. "How are you feeling this morning?" he said.

"Poppa!" Will's face lit up, and William could see right away that his son was better.

"My leg hurts," said Will.

"I know, son. It is going to hurt for a while. But it's going to get better," said William.

"The fever is about gone, Mr. Sunday. I think he's going to be just fine," said the nurse. "He told me he was hungry, and that's a good sign."

William sat down in the chair by the bed. He felt like he could breathe for the first time in days. As his son ate the cereal, William watched, looked upward, and silently thanked God.

A month later Will was sitting up in bed at the Peyton house, his splinted leg stuck out before him. He thoroughly enjoyed being the center of attention in the household. He was eating well and talking incessantly. He was a little fussy about his confinement as any normal little boy would be.

William spent most of his day with Will but slept at his room each night.

"When can I walk, Poppa?" asked Will.

William looked at his son, pleased to see the sparkle in his eyes and the color in his cheeks.

"Well, son, it's going to take time before you can walk the way you used to. You'll have to learn to walk on that leg a little at a time. Those new crutches will help a lot. After a while you'll get to where you won't need a crutch. Then, if you keep walking steadily, your leg will be as good as new."

"Are we going to stay here?" Will asked. "I like it here."

"I know you do, Will. They are good and kind people. But I'm not sure how much longer you can stay here. We'll just have to see how things work out," said William.

William knew he had to make some decisions soon. He knew the current

Finding Mr. Sunday

arrangement could not continue indefinitely. He could see that Tom was very fond of Will, and Mrs. Cleary doted on the boy. He himself had developed a close relationship with Tom and looked forward to their talks together.

The more he got to know Tom, the more he liked his steady, positive character. He had developed a great respect for Tom, even though he had known him for a short time. The last thing he wanted was to take advantage of Tom's generosity.

The next evening William and Tom sat in the parlor as they had for many evenings. Will had fallen asleep, and Mrs. Cleary had gone home to spend the evening with Mr. Cleary. Tom sat in his favorite chair and puffed his pipe. There was a lull in the conversation, and William shifted in his chair and leaned forward, his elbows on his knees and his hands interlaced.

"Tom, I want to thank you for all the kindness to Will and me. I will never be able to repay you. I don't know what I'da done without you. But we can't continue to be a burden to you and Mrs. Cleary.

"I've given a lot of thought to what I should do, and I'm going to put off the trip west. I'll find a rooming house where we can stay and get some kind of job until next year. Will should be able to travel by then. California can wait."

Tom listened and puffed his pipe slowly. He looked off in the distance and was silent for some time, absorbing what William had said. He tapped his pipe in the bowl on the table beside his chair and scraped the pipe with a small knife. He turned to look at William.

"William, there should be no thought on your part about repaying me. I helped you and Will because it was the right thing to do. And I'm glad I did. Will is a fine boy. He's smart beyond his years.

"He may have had a hard time of it so far, losing his mother and all. But he sure doesn't show any ill effects from it. I've enjoyed having him here, and I will have to say, I've grown very fond of him. He surprises me every day. I sometimes forget he is a little boy."

He paused and refilled his pipe from the tobacco box but set the pipe aside.

"This is a hard town, William. But I'm sure you can find something to do here, and you can get by until next year. It won't be easy. Not on you and certainly not on Will. I know you have been put in a difficult position.

"I think I've come to know you, and I know your first priority is Will. You are a good father, and I know you love your son. But a rooming house is no place for a small boy, even for a short time. If he is here in my home, we can take care of him while he heals and give him a safe place to stay."

William shifted in his chair and was about to say something, but Tom continued before William could speak.

"Just hear me out for a minute, William."

His voice was soft and reassuring.

"If you choose to go to California, the trip is not that long, really. Unless something unusual happens you can get there in three of four months. The trails are so much better than they were in the '40s. From what I read in the paper, there are bridges, ferries, army forts, and trading posts along the way now.

"You can even get a letter from west to east now. The paper prints some of them regularly. There's also a steady stream of people headed from west to east now. Not thousands, mind you, but enough to bring news."

He paused a bit and leaned closer to William.

"Here's what I propose. Leave Will here with me. You go on west. When you get to where you are going, write me a letter and tell me where you are. I'll see that Will gets safely to you. I'll bring him to you myself. I'd kind of like to see that part of the country again anyway.

"I just hired another gunsmith at the shop, and Penn is fully capable of running it. Caleb is a fine employee, too, and I can count on him. Will can have plenty of time to heal, and he will be close to some of the best medical care available."

William sat staring at Tom, saying nothing for a moment.

"Tom, you would do that?" He fumbled for words.

Tom could see that his suggestion had made an impact on William and that he might warm to the idea.

"Leaving Will would be hard on both of us. He's so young, and he's been through so much. I don't know, Tom."

"He's a strong boy, William. He likes it here. You see how well he and Mrs. Cleary get along. Sure, he'll miss you, and you'll miss him. But I think it will be best for him in the long run. He is your son, and I don't want to

Finding Mr. Sunday

come between you two. I'm just trying to help," said Tom.

"You should just talk to him about it and see how he takes it. You might be surprised. It might be eight months or more before you two can get together again, but he is young and resilient. We'll keep him busy, see that he gets his leg back to normal, even get him some tutoring while you are gone. It's you that will probably have the hardest time."

William sat there, taking in every word, trying to work through the idea.

"Tom, you've done so much already. I appreciate everything, and it's just...well... I just need time to think this through. The idea of leaving Will never entered my mind, and, believe me, that needs a lot of thinking. Let me ponder on it. I've got a lot to sort out."

"Of course, William. I know it's not an easy thing to decide."

"I can see now why my folks thought so highly of you and your father," William said as he stood up to leave.

"You've given me a lot to think on. I'm going to check on Will, and I'll see you tomorrow. Good night, Tom."

"Good night, William."

William sat in the chair by his bed, unable to sleep. He thought about Tom's offer. It made a lot of sense. He could still leave for California despite a somewhat late departure. He could avoid a prolonged stay in St. Louis, which would save some of his resources. Further, he knew he could not give Will the quality of life he wanted for him during a year delay.

But could he stand to be without Will for almost a year? What would that do to Will? He had already been through a lot for one so young, although he could see nothing but a happy little boy. He knew from personal experience, though, that a person could bottle up a lot on the inside. Was this the case with Will? Or were the young truly much more resilient, as Tom had suggested?

Was Will too young to even know how he would feel about being separated? Maybe he was underestimating his young son.

Before he could make up his own mind about going or staying, he needed to see how Will would react to the idea. Only then would he make up his mind.

The following day William was sitting with Will in his bedroom. Tom had acquired a small wooden chair with arms and a matching stool that made sitting easier for Will and provided a prop for his leg. Will was already standing with the aid of crutches and walking around the bed.

"See how I can walk, Poppa?" said Will proudly.

The young boy walked a few steps and turned around.

William was amazed at the boy's intense desire to resume walking. But then, Will had always amazed him, charging into life with a neverending enthusiasm, walking early, talking early, and showing a thirst to learn everything. He knew Will was an exceptional child.

"You are doing a good job, Will. Pretty soon you will be walking on your own. But remember the doctor said not to rush it. We have to make sure that bone knits well before too much weight is put on it," said William.

"I know, Poppa. If it hurts too much, I stop," said Will.

"Good. You are a smart boy. Will, why don't you sit in your new chair. I want to talk to you about something important."

William bent to help Will get in the chair.

"No, I can do it, Poppa."

Will backed into the chair and eased his leg onto the stool.

"I see that you can," said William with a smile.

"Will, you know before you were hurt, we were headed out West. We were going on a long trip to start a new home in California."

"Yes, a wagon train."

"That's right. We were going with a lot of other people on a wagon train. And when we got there, we were going to build a new house and have a new farm. Remember?" he said.

"Yes, and I was going to get a pony," Will said.

"You're right," William said, chuckling.

This boy never forgets anything, he thought.

"Well, when you got hurt we had to put off our trip because it would be to too hard for you to travel with a broken leg."

"Yes. But I could go now, Poppa," said Will.

"No, I don't think so, Will. I know you feel much better now, but the trip could be three or four months long. And even if you rode most of the way in a wagon, it would be very hard on you... Your leg might not heal right. We would't want that, now would we?"

"No," said Will, shaking his head.

"Well, you and I may have to stay here in St. Louis while your leg heals and leave next year."

"Good. I like staying here with Mrs. Cleary and Tom."

"Well, Will, we would probably have to stay somewhere else, I'm afraid."

William watched as the expression on Will's face changed.

"I don't wanna stay somewhere else," Will said with a disappointed look.

"I know you like it here, Will. And that is one of the things I wanted to ask to you about. Tom and I talked about another idea.

"What if you could stay here with Tom and Mrs. Cleary while I went ahead to California and got our house started? I would come back to get you. Or Tom could bring you out to California to join me once things were ready. He has said you could stay here right where you are. They would continue to take care of you just like they have been doing."

He watched Will's face to gauge his reaction.

Will sat still, absorbing what his father was saying but showing no emotion.

"How long before I would see you, Poppa?" asked Will.

"It would be at least eight months, maybe a year. You are almost five now. You would be nearly six when we got back together. That might seem like a long time for someone your age, and I suppose it is."

He reached out and put a hand on his son.

"When we see each other would we have a house in California?" Will asked.

"Well, I'm not sure, but I can promise you we will have one started, maybe even finished by then," he said.

"And my pony?"

Will's face brightened.

"Oh no, son. I want you to help me pick out your pony. But we'll do that as soon we can in California," said William.

They spent the rest of the day visiting. Will walked periodically, even venturing into the hallway. If he was disturbed by the conversation, he hid it well.

Dick Ward

When Tom got home that evening, he came in, as was his habit, to talk with Will. Tom found Will to be quite the talker. Will was especially interested in the gunsmith shop and asked Tom many questions about what he did during the day.

Tom said, "I know you like the shop. How would you like to come to the shop and spend some time with me during the day? I'll talk to your father about it, but I am sure he wouldn't mind."

Will's face lit up at the thought.

"Can we go tomorrow?" he said with excitement.

"Well, not tomorrow. But as soon as I talk to your father. Provided he has no objections, I'll arrange for a carriage to take us there."

"Oh, good, good," said Will.

He paused and wrinkled his brow in thought.

"Is it okay for me to stay here?" Will asked out of the blue.

"What? Why, of course it is, Will. We like having you here."

"For a long time?" Will asked.

"You are welcomed to stay here as long as you want to. Why? You do like it here, don't you?"

"Oh, yes, I do," said Will. "Poppa said he may go to California without me but come back to get me."

"Yes, we talked about that. I told your father that if he wanted to go west this year we would be glad to have you as our guest while he was gone. Then he could come back to get you. Or you and I could go to California to meet him as soon as he is ready for you."

"Would I stay here in this room... and Mrs. Cleary would be here?"

"As long as you like."

"Would I go to school?"

"Yes, but at first I would have someone come here to teach you until you can walk well again. Then you can go to school."

"I can read," said Will.

"I would not be surprised at that," Tom said with a chuckle. "How would you feel if your father was away for a pretty long time?"

"W-e-l-l-l," Will said, pausing. "I would miss him. But he will come back."

"Yes, and we would keep you busy with learning to walk again, going

31

to school and church. And we can visit my cabin down near the river. You could even come down to the shop after school some days, if you wanted."

"I do!" said Will.

"We would like to have you here, Will. But that's up to your father to decide."

"I know," said Will.

"He is going to be here for dinner soon. Are you hungry?" said Tom.

"Yes!" said Will, who seemed always ready to eat.

Later, Will sat proudly at the dining table, pleased that he could join both William and Tom for the evening meal. He was not his talkative self this particular evening. But during a lull in the conversations he addressed his father in a matter-of-fact tone.

"Poppa, I think you should go to California and build our house. I will stay here and work in Tom's shop and go to school."

Both men were a bit surprised. They looked at each other across the table, each with a trace of a smile on his face.

"When you are ready you can come and get me. We can get my pony here, and I'll ride to California with you."

William, Tom, and Mrs. Cleary all sat in the parlor of the Peyton home following a very special breakfast.

"Mrs. Cleary, that was quite a meal," said William.

"Thank you, sir. A man should start a long journey with a full stomach," she said.

This was the moment William had been dreading for the last few days. He wanted to be strong for Will.

"Mrs. Cleary, you're an angel from heaven. Thank you so much for what you are doing for Will and me," said William.

"It's my pleasure, sir. And I don't want you to worry about Will. We'll take good care of him."

"I know you will." William stepped close to her and gave her a warm hug. He turned to Tom.

"Tom, I'm not that good with words. I don't know how to thank you properly for all you have done," he said.

"What you just said is good enough," said Tom.

He shook William's hand.

William knelt in front of his son. He barely managed to control his tears.

"Will, I know you will be a good boy. You always have been. Listen to Tom and Mrs. Cleary. Study hard and keep using that leg."

He had to stop talking and take a deep breath.

"I will, Poppa," Will said.

Tears were filling the young boy's eyes.

William wrapped his young son in his arms and pulled him close.

"I will do my best to see that we are together again as soon as possible."

He held his son's face in his hands and looked into his eyes. Will could still see his father's blue eyes through his tears.

"I love you, Will. I love you." He stood up, turned quickly, and walked out of the front door.

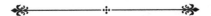

"Happy Birthday, Will!" said Tom. He, Will, Mrs. Cleary, and Caleb sat around the table after having finished a very special dinner. In front of Will was a tremendous cake decorated in white and yellow icing with six birthday candles burning brightly.

"Now make a wish," said Mrs. Cleary.

Will took a big breath and blew out all the candles, and everyone clapped.

"I'll help you slice it, Will, and you can pass the plates," said Mrs. Cleary. "I hope you made a very special wish."

"I did Mrs. Cleary. I'm six now, and Poppa should be coming to get me soon."

Everyone at the table fell silent.

"And when he comes we are going to get a pony and go to California," said Will with a big smile on his face.

"Let's have our cake now, Will. I think there might even be a few special gifts for you," said Tom.

For eleven months Tom waited for word from William. Nothing. After six months, he initiated his own efforts to find him. Several times he enlisted

Finding Mr. Sunday

representatives to check all available resources in Independence and other departure points in an effort to find some record of William Sunday. Nothing.

Tom hired a private detective to follow the trails all the way to San Francisco. Coach service was available part of the way, but no record of William Sunday was found on their passenger lists or for the lists for boats and ships that might have been used on certain legs of the journey west.

Will had not ceased asking about his father. Now, almost a year after William's departure, Tom found himself at a loss to explain to Will why his father had not returned or been in contact.

One evening Will stood in front of Tom's chair and out of the blue asked "Tom, why hasn't Poppa come back?"

Tom, sitting in his favorite chair, took both of Will's hands in his and looked him in the eye. He could feel the boy's pain.

"I wish I could answer that question. I honestly don't know why we haven't heard from your father."

He could see the little boy's eyes begin to fill with tears.

"I know it hurts you that you haven't heard from him. If there was any way in the world he could be here right now, he would be here. I just know this ... and this is what you need to remember forever and ever ... Your father loves you more than anyone or anything in this world. Wherever he is, that love he has for you is alive and well. You remember that, Will. You hear?"

Tom was near tears himself as he saw the heartache in the little boy's face.

"Yes ... yes ... I hear you. I will remember," said Will as tears streamed down his face.

Tom pulled the boy close to him and wrapped him in his arms.

CHAPTER THREE

1865

Gitty up, Buck. Any slower and you'd be goin' backwards. Go on, durn you!" he yelled.

The farm wagon rattled down the main street of Linn, Missouri, scattering several chickens and waking the hound dog that was napping during guard duty at the general store.

"Get out of the way," yelled the driver at a man leading a cow down the middle of the street.

Neither the mule, the man, nor the wagon was used to such recklessness. But all survived intact as the wagon came to an abrupt stop in front of the sheriff's office. The cloud of dust that had been chasing the wagon finally caught up to it, dusting the farmer and his passenger.

"Sheriff! Sheriff!" yelled the farmer. "You better git out here."

A gray-haired man on the far side of fifty stepped out on the boardwalk in front of the small office. He was putting on his hat and slipping a suspender over a shoulder.

"What in the hell's got you so riled up, Horace? I ain't seen you this excited since that old mule of your'n stepped on your foot," said the sheriff with a laugh.

"In the back of the wagon, sheriff," said Horace as he set the brake and jumped off the wagon.

The sheriff's smile quickly faded as he stepped off the boardwalk.

"I think I got a dead one ... leastwise he's a poor 'scuse for a livin' one."

Sheriff Wilkes hurried over to the side of the wagon and looked down at the body of a young man lying on a bed of loose straw. The man was bootless, wearing a shirt, pants, and socks. His blond hair was covered in dried blood as were the back of his neck and the collar of his shirt.

"Found him down on Wilson's Creek where that campsite is. You know the one in that bunch of river birches. He was lying near the edge of the woods. Big pool of blood. Two fellers helped me load him. Looks like he may have bled out."

The sheriff leaned over the side of the wagon for a closer look.

"Naw. He's still breathing. I don't know for how much longer, though," said the sheriff. "Go over and see if you can find Doc Stanton. If he ain't already too much in the bottle, get him over here."

People gathered around and stared down at the man in the wagon. A few mumbles flowed through the group.

"He looks like a goner to me," said an older lady in a bonnet and shawl. She pulled the shawl tighter to her shoulders as if the thought chilled her.

"He ain't dead yet. Now everybody just step back and give the doc some room," said Sheriff Wilkes.

A couple of people shuffled their feet, but no one moved much.

Sheriff Wilkes looked up and saw Horace coming across the street, trying to coax an older man to hurry along.

"He's not going anywhere, dammit," said the older man.

He took his time getting to the wagon.

Doc Stanton looked as if he'd had a rough night. He wore a rumpled gray jacket and striped wool pants. His collarless shirt was open at the top. A few days of gray whiskers covered his face, and he smelled like rye whiskey and cigar smoke.

With pale, trembling hands he reached down and gently turned the man's head toward him for a better look. He lifted one of the man's eyelids and peered into his face.

"He's alive. Some of you boys bring him to my office. Support his head. And don't be jerking him around like a side of meat."

He walked toward his office, leaving the carrying to the men standing around.

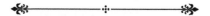

"He's a big one," said Doc Stanton. "Put him on that table, and all of you get on with your business. Sheriff, you stay here a while."

Sheriff Wilkes watched as the doctor put some water in a pot, opened the door to the stove, threw in some small sticks of wood, and opened the draft on the stove pipe.

Dick Ward

Doc took a pair of scissors and cut off the man's bloody shirt. He studied the clotted mass on the man's head, poured water on a cloth and cleaned dried blood off the man's neck, then dabbed gently around the wound. He pulled a trumpet-like tube out of a drawer, placed one end on the man's chest and put his ear to the other end and listened, then examined the man's hands, arms, and face.

"Well, he's been shot in the head as anybody can see. I can't tell how deep the bullet went. I don't want to poke around the wound too much, or he'll start bleeding again. My guess is he has a deep scalp wound. He took one helluva blow from that bullet. His heartbeat is steady, and he seems to be breathing all right," said Doc Stanton.

"You think he's gonna live, Doc?" asked Sheriff Wilkes.

"Damn'd if I know, sheriff. He's in a coma now. If I'm wrong and the skull has been penetrated he might not ever wake up. Or he could wake up tomorrow and just have one helluva headache.

"Best thing to do is to keep him warm and as still as possible. Which means you gotta find someplace for him to stay and somebody to take care of him. He can't stay here, and I can't babysit him."

"Hell, Doc, I don't know what to do with him," said the sheriff with a little annoyance.

"By the way, sheriff, this fellow is not your ordinary saddle bum. I don't know who he is, but somebody is likely going to miss this young man and come looking for him," said Doc Stanton.

"Why do you say that, Doc?"

"Well, first off, other than a little road dirt, this man is clean. He's young. He's healthy. He's got good teeth. His hair is well cut. He has a few days of whiskers, but he probably shaves every day when he's not on the road. That shirt I cut off of him is no cheap general store shirt. And those pants are high-quality wool you find in a men's clothing store or a tailor shop."

"That's pretty sharp of you to notice all that, Doc," said the sheriff.

"I'm a drunk, sheriff, not an idiot," said the doctor. "Now, I'll stay with this young man for a few hours, but you better get to making other arrangements."

"You got any suggestions, Doc?" asked the sheriff.

"Why, hell, I don't keep up with such things. It's all I can do to bring babies in this world, sew up knife wounds, and maintain my drinking."

Sheriff Wilkes wasn't sure if the doctor was joking or being serious.

"Wait a minute, sheriff," the doctor said, pausing a second. "What about Mrs. Daniels, the Nelsons' widow daughter out on their old orchard on the west of town? Took care of old man Morris when he busted his leg painting the church. Worked at the Sanitary Commission in St. Louis during the war."

"Mrs. Daniels," said the sheriff. "You're right. She just might do it."

"My guess, it'll take some convincing," said Doc Stanton.

"Well, all I can do is ride out there and see if I can talk her into it."

"Don't be gone too long," said Doc.

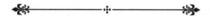

Sheriff Wilkes turned his dun horse off the main road onto the lane that led to the Daniels' farm. Apple trees, planted in neat, well-tended rows on both sides of the lane, were heavy with ripening fruit. The air was sweet with the smell of fresh apples.

As he rounded a curve in the road, he saw a white frame farmhouse. The front yard was fenced in by a white picket fence. Chrysanthemums lined the front of the fence and the porch, showing off their fall colors. A sitting porch across the front held two rocking chairs that beckoned. There was another smaller house at the edge of the orchard that was equally well tended.

In back of the larger house was a big red barn. Beside it was a shed with a large roofed area extended out on both sides. Under one side, a wagon loaded with apples was pulled up to tables. One worker unloaded apples, while others separated them into baskets.

A large yellow dog began barking and trotted toward him, wagging its tale in welcome. A woman wearing work pants, a flannel shirt, and a leather apron walked toward him. He dismounted and tied his horse to a hitching post. He was not surprised that Mrs. Daniels wore pants. She tended to do things like that.

"Good afternoon, Mrs. Daniels," said the sheriff.

He tipped his hat as she walked toward him.

"Why, hello Sheriff Wilkes," she said pleasantly. "We don't get to see you out here very often. Are you wanting some apples?"

Mrs. Daniels' youthful face could hardly be improved upon, but her sweet smile made the effort. Her shining brown hair trapped gold highlights from the sun, and her radiant brown eyes returned some of it to those lucky enough be in her presence.

"I'm sure gonna' get some soon, Mrs. Daniels. You know Mrs. Wilkes will dry up a bunch of them like she does every year. Her winter pies hold our marriage together," he said, laughing.

Mrs. Daniels smiled warmly at the remark.

"But today I just need to talk to you," he said.

She could hear the tone of his voice turn serious.

She pushed a loose strand of hair from her eyes. The grace and simplicity of the motion struck the sheriff. The moment was worthy of capturing for eternity, he thought.

"All right. Let's go sit on the porch. Can I get you something to drink? In a week or so I'll have cider to offer you, but not yet," she said.

"Water will do just fine, ma'am," he said.

She left to get the water. The yellow dog walked beside him to the porch, hopeful for a scratch on her head.

He sat down in one of the rocking chairs and looked out on the orchard. The rows of apple trees, the fence, the flowers, and the well-kept yard created a scene an artist would envy. A man could find his own sanctuary just sitting in this rocker, he thought.

"Here you go, sheriff," said Mrs. Daniels as she handed him a glass of water.

"Thank you, ma'am," he said.

He took a drink of water and turned to her, thinking how to make his pitch.

"Just before noon today Horace White brought in a young man he found near the trail at Wilson's Creek. He'd been shot in the head and left for dead. Whoever done it even stole his boots. He's with Doc Stanton now."

He paused a moment, mentally wincing at his own bluntness. He took another sip of water.

"Doc says he thinks the bullet grazed his head, but his head is one clotted

39

mess. He don't know if the bullet went in his skull, and he's afraid to disturb the wound for fear he'll start bleeding again. He's already lost a lot of blood."

Mrs. Daniels wrinkled her forehead in concern as a pained expression tried in vain to mar her beauty.

"My lord, sheriff, do we know who it is? Is he going to live or do we know yet?" she said.

"Well, you know Doc. He says either he will or he won't live. And he doesn't know. Says he's in a coma now and we just have to wait and see.

"As to who he is, we don't know. But Doc says he's not your ordinary saddle bum. Says he was too clean and well dressed. Says he thinks somebody will come looking for him. He's a big man, Mrs. Daniels, but I doubt if he's even twenty yet."

Neither spoke for a minute.

"I was hoping all that killing and robbing was over. We had enough of it during the war. Not the soldiers, mind you, but those raiders like Quantrill and Anderson. There's no telling how many innocent people they killed and robbed," she said.

"Yes, ma'am," he said. "Problem is we don't have any place to keep him or nobody to look after him. Doc says he won't do it."

He let the comment age a moment.

"I was kind of hoping you might consider doing it, Mrs. Daniels. He may not last long, but we can't just put him in the livery. We don't have a hotel. I know you helped Morris when he fell painting the church."

She stared straight ahead and started the chair rocking slowly. A pleasant squeak from the chair filled the break in conversation.

"Yes, I did," she said after a while. "It was the right thing to do... and I also knew Mr. Morris was going to heal and be all right. We don't know if this man is going to live or die, who he is or what he is. I might be taking on more than I can handle.

"As you can see we're right in the thick of harvest. I've had to hire extra help this year as it is. I even had to ask Mr. Samuels to help us. And that means we'll have to help him when his crop of late apples comes in."

"I know. I truly hated to ask you," he said. "But we didn't know who else to turn to. There's nobody else, nobody with your experience."

Dick Ward

Neither of them spoke for a moment. Mrs. Daniels continued to rock slowly back and forth, hand in hand, surveying the scene in front of her.

After a long pause she took in a deep breath, sighed, and looked at the sheriff.

"Well, sheriff, I guess the Lord must have sent you out here for some reason. Here's what I'm willing to do. I'll follow you back to town in the wagon and decide when I get there. Let me talk to Mary Nel, Maggie, and Ish."

She got up from the rocker, walked to the shed and began talking to a girl and an older Negro couple. Mr. Samuels stood nearby and listened to the exchange. Shortly, Ish, the Negro male, left the shed and went into the barn. His wife, Maggie, went into the house with Mrs. Daniels.

In a little while, Ish emerged from the barn driving a farm wagon pulled by a mule. The wagon bed was covered with loose straw.

He stopped the wagon near the back door to the house. Mrs. Daniels and Maggie came out laden with pillows and blankets and loaded them into the wagon. Ish got down from the wagon, and Mrs. Daniels and Maggie climbed aboard.

"Let's go, sheriff," Mrs. Daniel said.

She took the reins and headed the wagon down the road. Sheriff Wilkes mounted his horse and followed them, a smile on his face.

"It feels good to get out in the warm sun, doesn't it, Maggie?" said Mrs. Daniels, who never wore a bonnet.

"Why, I was just thinking the same thing, Miz Kate. Won't be long 'fore that old winter gets here. Might as well enjoy the sun while we can," said Maggie.

"Miz Kate, you sure you up to taking care of another wounded man? Didn't you see enough of that during the war? I worry about you, child," said Maggie with concern in her voice.

"I appreciate that Maggie. I'm not sure why I am drawn to taking care of others, but I am. Maybe I just got used to it. Besides, it makes me feel good. Truth be told, I don't know if I do it for them or for me. But I don't suppose it matters either way."

She clicked the mule and gave the reins a gentle ripple.

As they pulled up to the doctor's office and went inside, the smell of coffee filled the small room, and the doctor was piddling in one of his cabinets, arranging assorted bottles. He turned as they entered.

"Mrs. Daniels," he said, nodding politely.

He knew Mrs. Daniels was not one to put up with too much of his usually brusque manner.

"Doctor Stanton," she said, nodding back.

Without hesitation she walked over to the table and bent over the young man. She looked at the wound for quite a while, then settled her eyes on his face.

Despite his somewhat sallow color and the dark circles under his eyes, she could see that he was a good-looking young man. She had seen many young men like him trying to hold on to life. Regardless of how many she saw, her heart was pained when she looked at their faces. They all looked so helpless.

Doc Stanton was right. He was no saddle bum. But looks could tell you only so much about a person. What would she be getting herself into? There was Mary Nel to think of, too. What if he was the wrong sort? There were so many questions.

But despite all her concerns, she had a feeling about this one. Some inner voice told her this young man needed her, as much if not more than all the others. A strange calm overtook her as she looked at him. Yes, I was meant to help this man, she decided.

"The wound has good clotting. He survived the trip into town earlier, so I think he can survive the trip to the farm," she said as she turned to Sheriff Wilkes.

"Sheriff, if you will get some help, we'll get him in the wagon. I brought some blankets and pillows to make him comfortable. We'll need some help getting him into bed when we get to the farm. Ish can help, but he can't do it by himself," she said, looking to Dr. Stanton.

"I had some experience with men in comas when I was at the Sanitary Commission. I know he can't be given anything until we know more, but it might be good to have something for pain when he wakes."

Doc was happy she would care for the young man, but he didn't let on.

"Hold on a minute," he said.

He opened one of his cabinets and sorted through a few bottles, selected

42

one and handed it to her.

"That's laudanum," he said. "I'll ride out in a few days and check on him if he ain't dead."

In a few minutes the sheriff came in with three other men.

"I've got a litter you can use. It ought to hold him. Someone may have to support his feet, though," said the doctor.

He disappeared through a door and returned with a folded canvas litter.

"Make sure I get that back, sheriff," he said.

With a great deal of care and no small amount of difficulty, the man was loaded onto the litter and taken to the wagon. Mrs. Daniels made sure he was cushioned as much as possible on the straw and the blankets.

"Maggie, would you mind riding back there with him? And try to keep his head as still as possible," she said.

Maggie climbed into the back of the wagon and sat beside the man. They slowly headed back to the farm with the sheriff and two of the men following closely behind.

Sheriff Wilkes, Ish, and the other two men took the man from the wagon into a spare bedroom in Mrs. Daniels' home. They carefully removed him from the litter and placed him on the bed. Mrs. Daniels covered him with blankets.

"Thank you, gentlemen," said Mrs. Daniels. "Sheriff, when he comes around I'll send word."

"Yes, ma'am," the sheriff said. "And I do appreciate what you are doing. I hope he lives."

After the men left, Mrs. Daniels turned to Ish.

"I think that is as comfortable as we can make him. Let's leave him be for a while. I'll ask Maggie to keep an eye on him while we finish up for the day."

"All right, Miz Kate," said Ish. He looked down at the man lying in the bed and shook his head sadly. "It's a shame somebody do something like this. He's just a young man."

"I know, Ish. It breaks my heart," Kate replied.

43

Finding Mr. Sunday

Just after dusk, Kate, Mary Nel, and Maggie sat down to a dinner Maggie had cooked. Mr. Samuels joined them. Ish was watching the man in the bedroom.

"You going to have a lot on your hands, Mrs. Daniels, with both the harvest and taking care of that boy," said Mr. Samuels. "That boy might not ever wake up. But you need somebody there if he does."

"You're right, Mr. Samuels. We're all going to have to help out. With your kind help, I think we can keep up with the harvest."

She passed him the bread and gave him a smile.

Mr. Samuels seemed to always take the opportunity to remind Kate of the challenges she faced in running the orchard. It probably had something to do with his wanting to buy her out. An offer that she consistently declined. She changed the subject.

"Mary Nel and Maggie, I will be asking you to take turns with me and Ish minding our guest. He's in a coma now, but there's a strange thing about comas.

"At the Sanitary Commission, we had men to come to after a few days in a coma and tell us they could hear us while they were out. Not everything, but bits and pieces, certain voices and so on. They said it made them know they were still alive.

"From that, we learned to talk to all coma patients. Sometimes we'd sing to them and, if we had time, hold their hands awhile.

"So when you are sitting with this man, talk to him, sing to him, hold his hand. Do what you can do to let him know he's still alive. You never know, it just might help him."

"What do I say to him, Momma?" said Mary Nel.

She looked at Mary Nel. Sometimes she was surprised at the beauty of her own daughter. Her shiny hair lay softly on her shoulders and cascaded down her back. Her complexion was clear and radiant. Her full lips and perfect teeth complemented eyes that all but begged one to linger.

"Oh, I don't know, honey. Tell him about yourself, what you like to do, about books you have read, what you'd like to do when you grow up. Most anything. He just needs to hear your voice."

"All right, Momma."

There was a little trepidation in her voice, but her firm chin and upright

44

posture reflected the determined nature that ran in the family.

After the meal, Mrs. Daniels went into the room where the guest was lying.

Ish was sitting in a chair beside the bed. His gray head was bent reading the Bible.

"Ish, I will take over for a while. Any change?" she asked.

"No, Miz Kate. He just laying there. I can see he's breathing, though," replied Ish.

"All right, you go on and eat. And thank you, Ish. I know you don't have to do this, but I appreciate it." She gave Ish a warm smile.

"Remember, you have to talk to him some."

"Yes'm," he said. He got up to leave the room.

She looked down at the young man's face. He had a good facial structure with high cheekbones, a strong brow, and a well-shaped nose. She could see through the light whiskers that his skin was clear and unmarked. His breathing was smooth and regular.

Mary Nel came into the room.

"Mary Nel, would you get me a bit of butter in a spoon, please?"

Mary Nel went to the kitchen. She seldom questioned her mother when asked to do things as she had learned her mother always had a sound reason for her requests. Besides, she was happy to help her mother in any way she could.

Mary Nel returned with the butter.

"His lips are cracking," she said. "Let's try a little of this."

She touched her fingertips to the butter and spread a small amount on the man's lips.

When she was finished, she handed the spoon back to Mary Nel.

"That should help," she said. "I think it would be a good idea for us to move his arms and legs every once in a while, too."

She moved his arms, bending them at the elbow and straightening them several times.

Mary Nel watched as her mother gently lifted the man's legs and bent his knees.

"He doesn't look a lot older than I am, Momma," Mary Nel said. "How old do you think he is?"

45

Finding Mr. Sunday

"Well, I think he is probably four or five years older than you are. Maybe nineteen or twenty," she said. "I need to tend to a few things before bedtime. Then I'm going to move a rocker in here and stay with him for a while tonight. Do you suppose you could watch him until I can get back in here? It won't be long."

"Yes, Momma. What if he wakes up?" she asked.

"Well now, that would be wonderful if he did. He is not going to bite you, honey. I'll just be in the kitchen, and you can call me if you need me."

"All right, Momma," she said.

"Remember, talk to him," Mrs. Daniels said as she left the room.

Mary Nel sat in the chair her mother had just vacated. She was at a loss as to what to say to the man.

"Well, I guess I should tell you my name. It's Mary Nel. Only one "l" because my middle name is Nelson. That was my mother's name before she married my father. He died in the war.

"I'm fourteen, almost fifteen. I go to school in town, but I will be finished soon. I've had all the subjects taught there, and I've read all the books they have. Mostly now I read books to the little ones while Mrs. Miller is teaching other students.

"I love to read. Whenever we go to Jefferson City, Momma lets me buy some books. Last time I bought The Old Curiosity Shop. Some of my favorite books are by James Fenimore Cooper, like The Pioneers and The Prairie, but I can't find some of his that Momma told me about that I really want to read."

As she talked, her fear of being alone with the stranger subsided somewhat, and she found herself rambling on. Then she remembered she should touch his hand. Cautiously she laid her hand on one of his.

"Oh," she said. She had not expected his hand to be warm. She was a little uncomfortable at first but then curled her fingers under his hand and applied a little pressure. She was surprised at the softness of his hands.

"Momma said I should hold your hand. She said you may be hearing what I say and that it may help you." She paused.

"My mother knows a lot about caring for people. We lived in St. Louis during the war, and she helped take care of wounded soldiers while Father was away at war. I don't know how she did it, caring for all those poor men.

But my mother is a very strong woman."

She heard someone and turned to see her mother coming through the doorway carrying a rocking chair.

"Well, I see you have been talking to him and holding his hand. See, that isn't so bad. And I know you helped him. You can sit here a while with me if you want."

"Well," she said, "I'm kind of tired now. But I will watch him tomorrow if you need me to. I don't mind."

"That will be good," she said.

Mary Nel got up from the chair and moved it so her mother could put the rocker in its place.

"Momma, I hope he is going to be all right," said Mary Nel. "He looks like a nice person."

"So do I, dear. So do I," she said with a sigh.

"Good night, Momma."

She kissed her mother's cheek and left the room.

Kate moved to the side of the bed and moved the young man's arms and legs a few times, covered him, then sat down in the rocker.

She reached for the oil lamp and turned the wick down. The warm yellow glow reminded her that it had been a long day. She retrieved a comforter from a dresser drawer and sat down again, covering her legs. As she stared down at the young man's face, many questions ran through her mind. She eventually put her head back and closed her eyes. It wasn't very long before she was asleep.

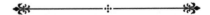

Mrs. Daniels awoke with a start. Her neck ached, and she turned her head slowly to ease the pain. She got up, checked on her guest, and saw that he was still breathing evenly. She could tell, however, he had not moved in the night. She went to her room and attended to her morning ablutions, put on her work clothes and went into the kitchen just as Maggie came in the back door.

"Morning Miz Kate. You all right this morning?" asked Maggie. "Don't you tell me you stayed up all night with that young man. Now you can't go missing your sleep, Miz Kate. You got to get your rest, child."

She walked over and put her hand on Kate's arm. Maggie had all but raised her and knew her better than anyone. Kate knew she could never fool her nor would she ever try.

"I got some sleep, Maggie," she said as she patted Maggie's hand. "Not as much as usual, but enough. He didn't move during the night, but his breathing is still good. Maybe you can watch him some today. I'm going to ask Ish to watch him as soon as breakfast is over. Is he at the barn?"

"Yes'm. He's getting the mule hitched and wagon ready to pick first thing. Mr. Samuels said he'd be here early this morning. Bringing Silas to help today. That'll make up for Ish being here at the house," Maggie said.

Maggie loaded kindling in the fire box of the kitchen stove and started a fire. She opened the reservoir at the end of the stove and filled it with water.

She went to the flour cupboard and sifted flour into a large bowl. She tossed in a bit of salt and baking soda as she stirred the mixture with her hand. She went to the back porch and returned with a container of buttermilk and a handful of lard. It wasn't long before she had a dozen biscuits ready for the oven.

Kate went to the pantry, unwrapped a side of bacon, and started cutting thick slices.

"Mary Nel brought in a nice basket of fresh eggs last night. I'll get them going just before the biscuits come out."

As she spoke, Mary Nel came into the kitchen. Her shining brunette hair picked up the light of the lamps.

"Good morning, Momma," she said as she kissed her mother's cheek. "I didn't hear you go to bed last night. You didn't sleep in that chair all night, did you?"

"I'm afraid I did, honey. I didn't intend to. I just fell asleep," she confessed.

"I told her she can't be doing that, Miss Mary," said Maggie.

"Maggie is right, Momma. As hard as you work you need your rest. I will sit up a while with him tonight. You need to go to bed early."

"Are you sure, Mary Nel?" asked Kate.

"Yes. I kind of liked talking to him. I didn't think I would, but I do. I don't know what I would do if he woke up," she said.

Dick Ward

"Well, I doubt he will wake up and immediately jump out of bed. You'll probably see some movement, or he might try to speak," said Kate.

"If he wakes up," said Maggie. "Poor child."

"Oh, let's all hope and pray he does. I don't think that will hurt anything at all," said Kate.

Ish came in through the back door. "I could smell them biscuits and that bacon almost to the barn. Make a man mighty hungry."

"You can sit right down, Ish. Everything is about ready," said Kate.

He sat down as the table was loaded with bacon, eggs, biscuits, honey, and fried apples.

"Let us bow our heads," said Kate. "Dear, Lord, thank you for this meal. Bless those who prepared it and bless this household. Allow us to use this food for the nourishment of our bodies as we use your love for the nourishment of our souls. Please lift up the stranger who is with us, and by your hand may he rise up and be made whole. In Christ's holy name we pray. Amen."

"Amen," the others chorused.

"Ish, once you get the wagon out into the orchard and the pickers started, would you please come in and sit with the young man? I want to show you how to exercise his arms and legs before I leave the house. I'll come in later today and watch him while I fix the noon meal," Kate said.

"Yes'm, Miz Kate. He any better this morning?" asked Ish between bites.

"No, about the same. But I've got great hope. His breathing is strong, and I do believe his color is a little better," she said

Later, Ish sat beside the young man's bed. His large frame filled the rocker, and his big calloused hands gripped the arms. He knew he should be talking to him as Miz Kate had asked. He, too, found it a bit awkward at first.

"Young man, my name is Ish."

His voice was deep and resonant.

"That is short for Ishmael from the Bible. He was Abraham's first son. I was the first born in my family, too. You probably think I was a slave, but I never been one. Neither has Maggie. We come here free people more than thirty years ago.

"Come to work for Mr. Nelson and Miz Ida before this orchard was

49

started. Hired me and Maggie both. Told me he couldn't pay us much, but he'd share what he had and what he earned. And he did, too. Every year he paid us like clockwork. Finest folks I've ever known," he said, nodding his big gray head up and down.

"Treated us with respect, like we were partners all along. Built us a house soon as he finished his. Gave me the land mine is on. I helped him plant every tree in this orchard, and I planted every one since he gone. God didn't make no better people.

"Miz Ida died just before the war started, and he died in '63. That's when Miz Kate came home from St. Louis. After her husband was killed. Poor child lost her father and her husband in the same year.

"She came home with a broken heart, she did. She just like her folk. Kind, honest. She's family to me and Maggie. Maggie about raised her. We both glad she back home. She's a determined one, she is. Got this place rolling again. Mr. Samuels, man who owns the orchard down the road, so jealous he want to buy her out," he said, laughing.

"I don't know if she's happy, though. Still not over losing Mr. Daniels, I suppose. Seems lonely to me. Sometimes I see her just staring off into the yonder while she rocking on that porch.

"Least she got Miss Mary. Miss Mary, she a fine little lady, too. Full of spunk just like her momma. Smart as she can be. Some young man going to get a good lady one of these days down the road.

"Lord never blessed me and Maggie with no children. Makes me sad to think about it, but not much a man can do about such things. My Maggie is sweet as a rose. Loved her from the first time I saw her. She was as thin as a rail then, but she didn't take no foolishness. Little thing would set you straight in a minute, I tell you. But I couldn't live without my Maggie. No, sir."

He rested his voice for a while. Then he went to the table where a pan of cool water and cloth had been placed. He dipped the cloth in the water, rung out the excess and began to gently wipe the young man's face. He touched the man's lips with the cloth and quickly pulled the cloth out of his line of vision and stared at the young man. He could have sworn he saw the young man move his lips ever so slightly, a small twitch.

He touched the cloth to the young man's lips again, very gently, and lifted the cloth to watch. Sure enough, it happened again. The lips moved, very slightly, but they moved. He thought he could see a slight change in the young man's breathing.

"Son ... can you hear me, son? I know you can. You can move your lips. I just saw you."

He paused and watched the man closely. He wanted desperately for the man to respond to him. He began to exercise the young man's arms and legs as Kate had instructed.

He raised his voice slightly.

"You stay with us, son. You stay with us. You gon' to wake up. You hear me? It won't be long now."

He touched the man's forehead and rubbed gently. He watched for any other movement or response but saw none.

He settled back in the chair, his excitement subsiding. Doubt began to creep into his mind. Had it been his imagination or had the man actually moved his lips? No. He was sure of what he saw. Somewhere deep inside, he had a good feeling about what had just happened.

This boy was going to come out of it. He just knew he would.

CHAPTER FOUR

1862 - 1865

ST. LOUIS

Will and Caleb were at the vacant lot where Tom had built a shooting range many years ago. The lot was a few miles from the shop in an area that was uninhabited, as the land was too wet for development. Will was practicing his fast draw with his favorite pistol.

His pistol was high up on his hips as he had been taught to wear it by Caleb. That minimized motion and allowed him to start the cocking with his thumb and aim at the same time. The barrel should be an extension of the hand, like a finger, he was taught. Learn to point and shoot, no eyeballing the sights.

He scanned the row of targets fifty feet in front of him and mentally counted from one to three. On three he whipped the revolver from the holster with blurring speed and fired five shots, moving from left to right, thumbing the hammer each time. All five of the paper targets showed fresh bullet holes dead center.

"'Attaboy, Will. Perfect shooting. You keep practicing, and you'll be good as me some day," Caleb said, laughing.

Will turned to look at the man who had become his mentor, teacher, and best friend. He saw a tall, solidly built man whose physical strength was matched only by the kindness of his heart. Caleb always seemed to be in a good mood and loved to challenge Will at every endeavor.

"Hah! You know I'm as good as you are already. I just need to practice my speed," said Will. "If powder wasn't so scarce right now I'd be faster than I am. But that's okay, I've got plenty of time. Besides, do you know any other fourteen-year-old who can outshoot a twenty-five-year-old?" he said.

"Well, I guess not. But I also don't know any fourteen-year-old who's been shooting rifles and pistols almost every day for five years, either," said Caleb. "Besides, you've had the best teacher in Missouri."

Finding Mr. Sunday

Will grinned. "Well, I guess I have to give you that. Being able to shoot almost every day is one advantage of being raised by a gunsmith."

"Speaking of which, we better head on back to the shop," said Caleb. "Tom wants to leave early tonight since he and Penn are going to the armory in the morning."

It was their job to test-fire the guns after they had been repaired. Years ago, Tom and Caleb did the test-firing together and brought Will along to watch.

Gradually, however, Tom had allowed Will to shoot, first rifles, then pistols. Over time, as Tom grew comfortable with Will's shooting abilities and Caleb's penchant for safety, the test firings had fallen to Caleb and Will.

Tom had a great deal of trust in Caleb to be a good influence on Will, and for good reason. Caleb took his self-appointed role as a teacher to Will very seriously. He'd taken to Will early on, and a strong bond had developed between the two.

Caleb also recognized that Will was an exceptional boy, a quick learner, and full of self-confidence. Caleb tried to set a proper example for Will in all aspects of his life.

Caleb Stewart was somewhat of a local celebrity. In addition to being an excellent gunsmith, he was an excellent shot with pistols and rifles. Few shooters could match him with a pistol. A crowd would often gather at the lot just to watch him shoot.

He was also an amateur boxer with a winning record. Between his boxing and his shooting, Caleb had become a bit of a showman, and it was obvious that he loved it.

He spent countless hours teaching Will to shoot rifles and pistols. He was amazed at how fast Will developed his shooting ability. Although not quite fifteen years old, the boy had speed and accuracy that astounded even Caleb.

Caleb also taught Will to box. Will had gone with Tom to watch Caleb fight when Will was around ten and had developed a keen interest in the sport. Tom would not allow Will to fight, but he did allow Caleb to teach Will the sport. Over a few years, Will had become quite the fighter, sometimes giving Caleb a challenge.

"I'm going to miss you, Caleb," said Will as they started back to the shop.

"The camping, the shooting, the boxing. I won't know what to do while you're gone."

"Oh, you'll stay busy, I'm sure," said Caleb.

"When do you have to leave?" asked Will.

"I have to leave in ten days. Word is we're leaving in a month to join the 8th Missouri so we have to be ready," said Caleb.

"Wish I was going with you," said Will. "I think I would be a good soldier."

"I'm sure you would, Will. But I'm glad you won't be going, at least any time soon," said Caleb.

"Hello, boys," said Tom as they walked into the shop. "Everything go all right with the test firings?"

"Yes, sir," said Caleb. "I'm afraid I got some real competition from Will here. The boy is a getting too good for me."

"I've been noticing that," Tom said.

Will smiled broadly.

Tom looked up from the workbench at the tall, handsome boy that Will had become. Hard to believe how much he had grown in ten years, Tom thought. The leg injury had hardly been a bump in the road for him. He was a well-behaved boy, hard-working, an excellent student, an avid reader. And he'd already seen Will turn the heads of more than a few young ladies.

"Son, do you have reading to do tonight for Professor Pentross?" asked Tom.

"Yes, sir. I've almost finished Ivanhoe. We are going to talk about that tomorrow. It's really fascinating."

Professor Pentross, a retired professor from St. Louis University, was tutoring Will in the classics three times a week. Will had excelled in literature far beyond the material that was offered in public schools. Will knew that Tom would like him to study law, and the tutoring would put him on the right path.

"In that case, let's leave shortly since I have to get an early start in the morning. Caleb, do you mind cleaning up by yourself today?"

"No, sir. I'll be glad to," said Caleb.

"We're sure going to miss you being around here, Caleb. For a lot of reasons," said Tom. He looked at Caleb with affection.

Finding Mr. Sunday

Caleb was orphaned at an early age and had come to Tom as an apprentice when not quite fourteen years old. Though he was a resident of the children's home until age eighteen, Caleb spent most of his time with Tom. Tom treated him like a son and had grown very close to the young man.

"Thank you, Tom," said Caleb. He quickly turned away and started cleaning the shop.

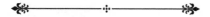

"You're mighty quiet tonight, Will. Is anything wrong?" said Tom as they were having their evening meal.

"I was just thinking of Caleb leaving to fight in the war," Will said.

"I know you are going to miss him. He's been like a big brother to you since your days on crutches."

"I'm just worried that he won't come back. He could get shot, maybe even killed. I couldn't bear that, I don't think," said Will.

Tom put down his fork and looked at Will. He knew Will had never gotten over the fact that his father had gone west ten years ago and never returned. In all that time not a word had been heard from him.

"Son, nobody wants someone they love to go to war. It's a shame our country has come to this. Caleb has strong feelings about preserving the United States as one country. He is doing what he wants to do. He is a brave young man. All we can do is pray he comes back safe. I know that doesn't keep you from worrying about him. Nothing I can say will do that."

"Yes, sir," said Will.

Tom could see the worry in the young man's eyes. They seemed to cloud over when he was worried. He had seen it before when six-year-old Will had asked repeatedly why his father had not come back to get him. He'd had no answers for the boy. After a while the questions ceased, but Tom knew the disappearance of his father haunted the boy.

"Will, I know it won't make his leaving any easier, but would you like for us to take him to his regiment to see him off?" asked Tom.

"Maybe," Will said. "But he might not want us to do that. You know, he might be bothered by us being there when he leaves."

"You are right. I'll talk to him and see what he says," said Tom.

The next day Will sat before Professor Pentross. He was a small gray-haired man with long sideburns. He dressed very carefully and carried himself with the dignity and decorum one might associate with his station in life.

Peering over his glasses Professor Pentross said, "Well, well, young man. What did you think of Ivanhoe?"

"It was all right, but I ain't sure I would read it again," said Will.

Professor Pentross seemed to jump a little in his seat at the response. Will wondered if he had said the wrong thing. Professor Pentross removed his glasses and studied the boy for a minute or so.

"Son, I must share something with you. From all I can gather you are a very bright young man. You have an excellent scholastic record. You are polite, kind, and considerate of others.

"You are fortunate to be raised in a wonderful home by a very kind and giving man who spares nothing in his effort to secure your happiness, to educate you, and to see to your future success."

He paused for a minute as he continued to gaze at Will.

"My job is to enlighten. To teach you the value of learning, not for the mere sake of learning, but so that you can better yourself in life through knowledge and reasoning others may not possess.

"If I am successful in doing so you will leave my tutelage better prepared to find your place in the world. You can continue with your education. You can study law. You can do anything you want.

"So while we are working together you must take yourself away from the gunsmith world, away from the world of your companions, and look at this as an opportunity to look — and go —far beyond your current world. I expect you to begin, right here and now, to better yourself in every regard."

Will could tell by the tone of the professor's voice that a valuable lesson was coming.

"So from time to time, I will consider it my duty to provide what I call life advice when I see the need to do so, in addition to the tutelage."

He paused to make sure he had Will's mind and eye.

"Yes, sir," said Will.

He swallowed as he waited for the professor to speak.

Finding Mr. Sunday

"As to your use of the word "ain't," allow me to offer this. Many people in this world confuse poor language skills with ignorance. Now, you are certainly not ignorant, and it would behoove you not to give that impression."

Professor Pentross leaned over, placed his hand firmly on Will's hand, and spoke with emphasis.

"Learn to speak properly. And do so. Always. Consistently. That will set you apart from others in this world," he said. "Promise me you will do that, young man."

"Yes, sir," said Will solemnly. "I promise."

Will would remember that moment for the rest of his life. He made a vow to himself always to speak correctly, to learn as much as he could about as many things as possible, and to apply the knowledge he received.

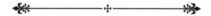

It was the last boxing practice before Caleb had to leave. They tried to practice two or three times a week at the gun shop in a rear corner they had fixed up for that purpose.

"Okay, big boy, let's see what you have learned," said Caleb. "It will be a while before we can practice again, so I'm going to be tough on you tonight."

"Aw, you always say that," Will said with a laugh.

They started slowly, circling and landing light blows.

"I want to see how well you do defensively tonight," said Caleb. "Keep your hands up and watch me carefully."

Caleb picked up the tempo of the sparring. Will was doing well, evading the blows Caleb tried to land. Caleb faked a left, stepped inside, and landed a healthy right on the side of Will's head.

Will shook his head as his eyes watered and he felt the sting of the sharp blow.

"You got in a lucky one," said Will.

"No, you were not watching me carefully," said Caleb.

Once more Caleb landed a solid blow, much to Will's annoyance.

"Watch me, Will," warned Caleb.

Caleb could see Will was getting frustrated. He had been trying of late to teach Will to stay calm, despite what happened in a match. He knew Will had a tendency to get angry, which caused him to get careless.

Caleb faked a move again and popped Will a good blow that was harder than usual. Then another, before Will could recover.

In a matter of seconds, Will let go a flurry of blows at Caleb, swinging wildly but having little success landing them. The harder he tried to land punches, the more Caleb out-fought him.

"Don't get mad, boy. I'll sure whip you then," said Caleb.

With that, Will lost complete control, swinging blindly, burning his energy on wasted attempts to get at Caleb.

"Don't lose it, Will," said Caleb. "Don't lose it."

That sent Will over the edge. Now he no longer cared about strategy; he just wanted to hit Caleb.

Caleb let him go on for a minute or so, then stepped inside and landed a blow that sent Will to the floor. Will scrambled up, now seething, and charged Caleb.

Caleb got in close and wrapped his arms around Will in a move that prevented Will from swinging. Will struggled to get loose.

"Will, stop!" Caleb yelled. "Stop. You have lost your temper again."

Will, with tears in his eyes, stopped struggling.

"Will," said Caleb. "I wasn't doing defensive boxing. I was trying to get you to lose your temper, and you fell for it."

Will began to calm down.

"You can't lose your temper, Will. Ever. That is the lesson I have been trying to teach you for the last year. You are a good fighter. But you have a problem with getting mad in a fight."

He hugged the boy close.

"You know I love you, Will, and I never want to hurt you. But you must learn that lesson. Not only in boxing, but in everyday life. Promise me, Will. Promise me you will learn to control your anger," said Caleb.

"I will. I will, Caleb," said Will.

"All right," said Caleb. "That is enough for tonight."

He put his arm around Will, and they headed home.

Finding Mr. Sunday

Caleb, Tom, and Will stepped out of the carriage at the gate of the arsenal and walked to the gate. A burly sergeant in a blue uniform stopped their progress.

"Hold it up, gents," he said as he held up his hand. "What is your business here?"

Caleb spoke up. "I joined up in December and was told to be here today."

The sergeant looked him up and down. "You going to make a fine soldier, son. You know how to shoot a rifle?"

"Yes, sir. I think I can handle one," said Caleb with a sheepish grin.

"He's the best shot in Missouri!" said Will enthusiastically. "One of the best gunsmiths, too."

"You a gunsmith, son?" asked the sergeant.

"Yes, sir. Small arms … rifles, pistols."

"Corporal Rogers. Over here," the sergeant called out.

A young soldier stepped up to the group.

"Yes, sergeant."

"Take this man over to 8th Missouri," said the sergeant.

"Yes, sir," said the corporal.

"Son, when you get to the group, you tell them Sergeant Burns said for you to see Sergeant Mullins. When you see him, tell him you are a gunsmith," he said to Caleb.

"I will, sir," said Caleb.

"Good luck, son," said the sergeant.

"Thank you, sir," said Caleb.

Caleb turned to Tom and extended his hand.

"Tom, I hope there will be a place for me when I come back," he said, smiling.

"As long as I have a business, you will have a place there, Caleb," said Tom. He dropped Caleb's hand and hugged him closely. "God be with you, Caleb."

Caleb turned to Will, who was fighting back tears with only slight success.

"Will, you are a great friend, and I am going to miss you. There is something special about you. I don't know what it is, but you got something about you nobody else I know has. Don't you forget it, you hear?"

Caleb took Will in his arms and hugged him closely. Tears welled up in his eyes. He turned abruptly and began to follow the corporal.

Will stared at him through his own tears, trying unsuccessfully to blink them away.

"Bye, Caleb," Will called out with some difficulty.

Caleb turned partly around, looked at Will, pointed his finger with his thumb up, winked, and said, "Don't ever miss, Will."

The war years passed slowly, painfully by. Missouri was torn by raiders and marauders. There were shortages of every commodity. Poverty increased, and businesses ceased to exist. But Tom's gunsmith business thrived on government contracts to refurbish and rebuild rifles and pistols. Employees were added to meet the volume of business. Tom, Will, Penn, and the additional gunsmiths worked long hours, often well into the night.

But despite the added business, Tom insisted that Will continue his sessions with Dr. Pentross. The studies expanded to include humanities, works by Plato and Aristotle, readings in law and the sciences. Will was fascinated by it all and worked hard to keep pace with the readings. He never disappointed Professor Pentross.

Will thought of Caleb every day. He had never felt so lonely. Caleb had been his touchstone, his companion, the brother he'd never had. Tom was there, of course, and gave him encouragement and comfort.

But he didn't push him the way Caleb had done. He didn't challenge him. Caleb had made him be the best at whatever he did. He did so to the point that Will himself strived for nothing less than the best from himself.

"I'd sure like to hear from Caleb," said Will over dinner one evening. "It has been over two years since he wrote. Mr. Adams told me his son said that Caleb's company had gone with 8th Missouri all the way down to Mississippi."

"The mail service is bad, son. I doubt if any of the boys have time to write

61

anyways," said Tom. "With any luck the war will be over soon. I don't think the South can hold out much longer, son. Richmond is about to fall, and I hear Lee is bottled up near there."

"I hope so," said Will. "I worry about Caleb all the time."

"I know you do," said Tom. With that he began to cough, and he coughed repeatedly for a minute or two.

"Tom, I'm worried about that cough. It's getting worse," said Will.

"Awww. It's just a reminder of that bullet I took in California back in '48," said Tom.

"But it's been going on for a couple of years, and you haven't done anything about it," said Will.

"I know. I'll see Doc Roberts when things slow down a bit. But all he will do is give me an elixir."

"You've been working too hard. You hardly get a good night's sleep anymore," said Will. "I think I'm going to tell Professor Pentross that I am going to stop our sessions for a while. I can go in to the shop early, and you can get some rest in the mornings."

"No, Will. You are just starting to read law. That is too important for you to miss," said Tom.

"I know. But that's something I can read on my own. I can read Blackstone's work by myself. Besides, I think I would be better served reading American law under an attorney. I dearly love Professor Pentross, but he is really slowing down. He seems very tired in the mornings and falls asleep often."

"Well, let's continue for a while longer. Maybe you can slow down before summer. When the war ends we will be back to a normal workload," said Tom.

"All right, Tom. I won't argue with you. But you promise me you will slow down some," said Will.

"Promise," said Tom.

One afternoon in March, Tom came into the workshop after completing some errands. Will had arrived earlier and was working on a pistol.

"Hello, Tom," said Will, keeping his eyes on his work.

"Hello, son," said Tom.

There was a different tone in Tom's voice. Will looked up at him trying to decipher the reason.

"Are you feeling all right today, Tom?" Will asked.

Tom averted his eyes before replying.

"I'm just a little slow today," Tom said.

Indeed, there was weariness in his voice.

He sat down at the bench and picked up one of the tagged pistols that needed repairing. The afternoon passed with very little said between the two.

When they arrived at home that evening, Tom said to Will, "Come sit with me for a minute. I need to talk to you."

Will could tell by the tone of Tom's voice that this wasn't going to be one of their regular chats. All afternoon he had known something was bothering Tom.

Instead of sitting in his favorite chair, Tom sat on the sofa next to his chair.

"Come sit over here, Will," Tom said.

Will settled his tall body beside Tom and looked at him with anticipation. He knew this was not going to be good news. He sat down, and Tom put his hand on his arm and looked directly into his eyes.

"Will, I'm sorry to be the bearer of bad news. Late this morning I received notification that Caleb has gone missing."

Tom watched Will's face, ready for what he knew would come.

"Over a year ago. They didn't know who to notify, so we're just now finding out. They have no idea where he is," he said softly.

Will's breath seemed to catch in his throat. He felt lightheaded and fought to find his voice.

"Is he dead? Is Caleb dead?" Will said in disbelief. "That can't be."

"They don't know, son. We need to face up to that possibility. But he could be a prisoner. So many men are unaccounted for, we just have to pray for him. That's all we can do now. I'm trying to find out anything I can, believe me. All they have done so far is to verify the original message."

Will sat in silence.

"I am sorry, Will. I know how close the two of you are," said Tom.

Tears filled Will's eyes, and he shook his head slowly from side to side.

"I knew it. I knew it when he left he wouldn't come back. Just like

Finding Mr. Sunday

Poppa." Will's voice failed him as he began to sob.

"We don't know that he won't come back, Will. We don't know," said Tom. "Records, orders, mail, they are all a mess right now. You just have to have hope he will come back."

Tom put his arm around Will's shoulders. He could find no words of comfort. He sat there feeling the young man's body shake with grief.

"He won't," cried Will. "He won't."

Will bent and put his face in his hands. He sat like that for a minute or so. The crying stopped, and he was still. He sat up and wiped his eyes with the back of his hands. He stood, touched his hand to Tom's shoulder, walked down the hall to his room, and quietly shut the door.

"It's finally over, Will," Tom announced as he came into the shop. "Lee surrendered, and that's going to mean the end for the rest of the South. Thank God, too. I was afraid you were going to have to go."

"I wish I had been able to go," said Will. "Now I can't."

Tom sensed a trace of bitterness in his voice.

"Will, I know you feel bad about Caleb. But your going and perhaps getting wounded or killed would not have changed anything. You would have been just another one of the hundreds of thousands who died on both sides fighting for what they thought was right.

"Will, I lost good friends in the war. Men that I lived with and fought with day in and day out. The only consolation I could find was to live my life as best as I could, the way they would have wanted to live their own.

"So the best tribute you can make to the memory of Caleb is to be the best man you can for the rest of your life. And live life to the fullest. He would have traded his life for that certainty if he'd had the opportunity. I'm sure of that. Please remember that."

"Yes, sir," said Will.

"Doctor, is he going to be all right?" asked Will.

Dick Ward

He was in the parlor talking with Dr. Roberts. Tom lay in his bedroom, gravely ill. He had taken sick without warning shortly after the war ended.

"Son, his heart is very weak. That cough he's had for so long has caught up with him."

"But he is not an old man, Doctor," said Will.

"I know, Will. But that chest wound added many years to his life. He may have had a weak heart all along. We just don't know. It's not in our hands anymore. I'll check on him tomorrow, son."

The doctor closed his bag, touched Will's shoulder, and walked down the hall and out the front door.

Will couldn't imagine life without Tom. His memory of his real father had faded long ago, and Tom, as far as he was concerned, was his only father. The one who was always there. The one who gave him constant encouragement. The one who reminded him over and over that there were no limits to what he could do.

He went back into Tom's room and looked down at the kind face he loved so dearly. Tom's gray hair lay back neatly. His face was mapped by the wrinkles of time. Even in sleep he looked tired. His breathing was rough and irregular. Tom stirred and opened eyes.

"Hey, Tom," said Will. "How are you feeling?"

"Tired, son. I am so tired," said Tom.

"Well, you need to rest as much as you can. Can I get you anything?" asked Will.

"No," said Tom weakly. "Can you sit a bit, Will?"

"Of course, Tom," replied Will.

He sat on the edge of the bed close to Tom.

"Haven't felt like talking much lately, Will," Tom said. He coughed, then inhaled deeply.

"You're a good person, Will Sunday," he said. "I want you to know how proud I am of you and the fine young man you've become."

"Thank you, Tom," he said. "But you know you are the reason for all that. You have been all the father a person could ask for."

"And a pleasure it has been, son," said Tom, smiling weakly.

"Son, there is something I want to say. You've learned a lot about guns in your short life. You are better with a gun than any person I have seen. And that includes Caleb.

"But I am not sure that I have taught you the most important thing there is to know about guns." He paused and caught his breath.

"And that, son, is when to use one. Am I making sense, Will?"

"Yes, Tom. You are."

"Promise me you will always remember that," said Tom as he labored for breath.

"I will, Tom," said Will.

Tom closed his eyes. Will reached for Tom's hand and held it in his own. He said a silent prayer as tears filled his eyes.

Two weeks later Tom was laid to rest.

The nightmare that had haunted him since childhood had come true. Everyone he loved was gone. His mother, his father, Caleb, and now Tom. He was completely alone for the first time in his life.

Grief is a cruel companion. He found it hard to sleep or to eat. He woke from fitful sleep each morning only to be bludgeoned by reality. He went to the shop in a daze and tried to work away the emptiness.

He went home to Tom's big house, but that made him feel worse. He went to the cabin for a while, only to find himself sitting on the porch, reliving memories of Caleb, Tom, and better times.

He had no idea what to do with his life. Of course, he'd had some thoughts about his future, but then they were only open-ended musings. Should he stay here in St. Louis and go on to law school as Tom had wished? A career in law might be fulfilling. But was he ready to commit to that?

He could probably continue to run the shop, though only Penn was there now. But did he really want to stay in St. Louis? Fate had brought him here, but he doubted it could hold him for the long term.

He knew he was not in the best frame of mind to be making decisions. He felt his self-confidence flagging for the first time ever. And that realization shook him.

Hold on, he thought. You had better wake up. There is no one to give you advice, no one to push you anymore. Just you. And you are supposed to be so smart, supposed to be mature for your age.

So you better get on with life. Now is the worst time for self doubt. Even if you don't embrace reality, you surely must accept it.

Enough! Whatever is to be, you're going to make the best of it, he told himself. Just like Caleb and Tom would want. Most important of all, he could not lose confidence in himself. Never.

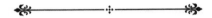

"Will, I know it hasn't been long since Tom died. I am sorry to have to ask you to come here so soon after. But as executor of Tom's estate, I have a legal responsibility to discharge my duties," said Mr. Evers.

He looked at Will over the top of his glasses.

Mr. Evers spoke to Will from behind a large walnut desk befitting the successful lawyer he was. His heavy frame filled the large chair and seemed to overflow onto the desk. His clothes were tailored to hide his girth but fell somewhat short of the task.

Will had given no thought to an estate. He had never talked to Tom about money, what he owned, the business side of the shop, or any other such matters. Mr. Evers unfolded several sheets of paper and glanced down at them. He cleared his throat as if to get Will's full attention.

"This is Tom's will. He had me draw it up a few years ago," he said. "Son, you are Tom's only beneficiary. There is no one else. That means everything Tom owned he left to you. Everything. And his estate is quite substantial."

Will was overwhelmed. He sat there unable to say anything. The last few weeks had all but drained him emotionally. Mr. Evers continued to peer over his eyeglasses, watching for some reaction from Will.

"He owned the entire building his shop was in, not just the shop. He owned several lots in town. Good ones. He owned his home and all its contents. He owned the cabin outside of town. He and his father ran a successful business for nearly forty years.

"I don't believe he ever told anyone else, but Tom told me he made some money in the gold fields when he was in California in the late forties. He never said how much.

"Tom was a generous man in many ways, but he did not spend much of his wealth."

Mr. Evers paused for a moment, then looked directly at Will.

Finding Mr. Sunday

"Will, Tom's estate is valued at well over $100,000. That's a lot of money. For anyone, but especially for one just shy of eighteen years of age."

Will sat, open mouthed, staring at Mr. Evers. He couldn't fathom that much money. Tom had given him a weekly allowance and paid him a small amount each week for his work in the shop. His clothes and living expenses were taken care of by Tom. He had never really wanted anything. Money was not something he thought about. It hadn't needed to be.

"You haven't said anything, son. Do you understand all that I have been saying?" asked Mr. Evers as he tried to get even closer to his desk.

"Yes, yes, I do, but all that money I never thought … it never occurred to me …" stammered Will.

"I understand it is a lot to take in," said Mr. Evers.

They both sat in silence for a moment.

"What do I do with all that money?" said Will.

"Some of it, as I said, is in property. You have to decide if you want to keep or sell it. That's all up to you. I will help you, of course, with whatever it is you wish to do."

He leaned back in his chair, which protested loudly. He put his hands on the edge of the desk and looked off somewhere in the distance, then turned to Will.

"Tom told me all about you, Will. He was very proud of you. He said you were a special kind of person. You have your whole life in front of you. You have both the ability and the means to do anything you desire.

"If I were you, I wouldn't stay in St. Louis. I would go west. Leave the war-torn misery, the disease and violence behind. That's where the opportunity is now.

"You can leave your money here where it's safe. We managed Tom's money for years. We'll send you whatever you need whenever you want it. If you want it all sent somewhere else we can do that, too. My firm will see to your wishes."

"I need some time to think, Mr. Evers. I don't really know what I'll do just yet. I appreciate your willingness to help. Tom trusted you, and I feel that I can also. I'll be back in a while and talk with you."

"That's fine, Will. Take all the time you need. I have authority to provide any funds you need in the meantime. I'll just need your signature on a few things."

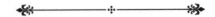

The loneliness was numbing. The empty house, so long a place of comfort and warmth, was little more than a warehouse of memories. Will found himself walking the streets of the big city. There was no comfort in others. Everybody seemed lost in their own worlds, closed and distant.

Will thought long and hard about his future. He had no one left in St. Louis. Mrs. Cleary had moved some years ago to be with her son in Philadelphia. Penn was in his seventies and worked only half days. Business had slowed considerably since the war ended.

He had little reason to stay here. He would turn eighteen within weeks. He had no financial worries. He was free to go where he wanted. He knew this place was not for him any longer.

And he sensed something pulling at him or perhaps beckoning to him.

There was value in Mr. Evers' advice. He'd always enjoyed the stories printed in the newspapers about those who had ventured west. Tom certainly had enjoyed that part of the country. The railroad went much of the way already, and work was underway on a cross-country route. But no, he didn't want to take the railroad, at least not all the way.

He wanted to see the country. Feel it. Taste it. Sleep in the open air. There were still wagon trains headed west, he knew, just not as many as before.

He knew he could take care of himself. He had to. It was just him now.

That is what he would do, he decided ... go west.

He met with Mr. Evers, who agreed to manage the liquidation of the business and properties and established an account and process by which Will could withdraw funds and receive drafts. Will provided Mr. Evers with money that would see to Penn's needs for as long as he lived.

He spent several weeks mulling his trip west. He finally decided he would leave St. Louis and head to Independence. There he would spend the fall and winter educating himself on the trip, learning what he would need, finding the best equipment, and choosing a wagon train to join.

At least that would take him from this city into a new world.

He intended to take very little with him from St. Louis. He put together

Finding Mr. Sunday

an assortment of tools Tom had given him, some books, and a small group of rifles and pistols to take with him.

He went to Tom's favorite livery stable and purchased a beautiful bay riding horse that was the right size for his big frame and had the temperament for the trail. In addition, he bought two well-trained pack mules to carry his books, tools, and weapons.

A well-known outfitter provided him equipment and good trail clothes that went well with his favorite custom-made boots.

He left for Independence just as the leaves began to turn. The more he put the city behind him, the better he felt. He didn't look back.

CHAPTER FIVE

1865

LINN, MISSOURI

Miz Kate, I saw this boy move his lips when I was wiping his face. I swear I did. I believe this boy's going to wake up any time now. His color is better, and he is breathing fine," said Ish as Kate came in around noon.

Kate had just come in from the apple shed and began washing her hands.

"Well, Ish. That may be a good sign. I've seen it before, and it meant nothing. But sometimes it means he may be coming around. Have you been talking to him and exercising his arms and legs?"

"Yes'm," he replied. "I even told him he's gonna wake up. Maybe he heard me. I got a good feeling about this boy, Miz Kate. You mind I said that now."

"I hope you are right, Ish. We'd all like to see that. After you've eaten, Ish, let's bathe him and change the linen. Maggie is on the way in from the orchard, and we'll have lunch ready in just a while," she said.

Mary Nel poked her head in the door.

"Any change, Momma?" she asked.

"Ish said he moved his lips. We'll have to see if that means anything, honey," she replied.

Shortly, everyone sat down to a plate of ham, potatoes, pickles, and cheese with biscuits, honey, and cool buttermilk.

"I don't believe I have seen apple trees so loaded down with pretty fruit in all my life, Mrs. Daniels. What kind of magic do you put on those trees?" said Mr. Samuels.

"Oh, just plenty of love and hard work," said Kate with a proud smile.

"I can't for the life me get that kind of crop from them trees of mine. Course we grow different apples, but still, your crop beats mine ever' year," said Mr. Samuels.

Despite his smile it was evident that the fact bothered him more than a

Finding Mr. Sunday

little.

"Ish and I are going to bathe our guest and change the linens, Mary Nel. After we are finished I am going to sit with him until late afternoon. Would you come in early and get cleaned up? I'll see to supper while I'm keeping check on him. After that, you can stay with him a while before bedtime. You might want to read to him some tonight."

"That's a good idea, Momma," said Mary Nel.

They bathed the man with warm water and soap. Kate very gently cleaned the wound and removed more of the clotted mass.

"He's a handsome young man. Be a shame a man like that don't wake up," said Ish.

"Oh, let's have positive thoughts. I truly believe he will wake up," said Kate. "I have a better look at the wound now. It looks like the bullet grazed his scalp very deeply. Sometimes a deep graze like that causes some swelling inside the head, and that can be a problem. But that doesn't always happen."

"Well, Miz Kate, if you don't mind, I'll go on out and get on those apples. Maggie is working at the shed, so call out for her if you need anything," said Ish

Kate sat down in the chair by the bed and began to talk to her patient.

"Well, young man. You are stuck with me this afternoon. We're in the middle of the largest apple harvest we've ever had. Oh, I haven't told you, we own an apple orchard. My parents started it many years ago. I hadn't planned to run it, but then we can't always choose what we want to do in life.

"I didn't think I would like it. But I do like to see the trees green up in the spring, blossom, and grow the apples from tiny little nubs to beautiful fruit. I like the pruning, the grafting, getting the young seedlings started. Even the harvesting is not so bad.

"I especially like taking them to market. We take wagon loads into Jefferson City every few days. Oh, and we make cider, too. The sweet kind, of course. Now, my father use to make what he called his set-aside cider. But that was for him and a few close friends. I believe Ish continues the tradition." She chuckled.

"We'll finish the harvest in a couple of weeks or so, and I'll get it all sold.

We keep some here for the local trade almost up to the dead of winter. In the meantime we try to keep our farm going.

"We raise a few pigs for meat and a few milk cows. We grow corn and wheat. The town of Linn has a mill, so we have no shortage of corn meal or flour. We also have beehives near the orchard, and we get lots of honey each year.

"As I look at you, I can't help but wonder who you are and where you came from. There are a lot of men on the move now, sort of lost since the war is over. You don't look like one of those, though.

"Most young men in this part of Missouri are farmers. But looking at your hands I can tell you're no farmer. They are soft, like my husband's were. He was a bookkeeper by trade. He worked in St. Louis up until the war.

"My guess is you were on your way to Independence and someone shot you, robbed you, and left you for dead. There are so many scoundrels about these days.

"Anyway, I'm looking forward to getting to know you. I think you are going to come out of this fine. Any day now.

"I am going be stepping in and out for a while so I can fix the evening meal. You just rest now."

She reached over and gently squeezed his hand, then left to go to the kitchen.

Later, Mary Nel came into the kitchen looking refreshed from the day's work. She had tortoise shell clips in her hair. It was sometimes hard for Kate to believe she was going to be fifteen on her next birthday. But right at that moment she looked like a fully grown woman.

"Is there anything I can do to help you in the kitchen, Momma?" she asked.

"Everything will be ready in a little while. Are Maggie and Ish going to join us tonight?" Kate asked.

"Yes, I heard Maggie say she was going to bring over some loaves of bread she baked last night. They went in a while ago, so I expect they will be here soon."

"I know they are tired. I've never seen such a good harvest," said Kate.

"We will need to take more apples into Jefferson City soon. Mr. Samuels said he and Silas would be happy to do it for us if we need him to," said Kate.

"That might be a good idea. I would hope that Mr. Samuels would represent us well. Though he might fail to mention the apples are ours," she said with a chuckle.

"That's possible. I know it's wrong to say anything bad about anyone, but I wish he would not keep asking about buying the orchard," said Mary Nel.

"Oh, that's just the way he is. I don't think he means any harm. Who knows, one day I might just take him up on his offer."

"What? Momma, you wouldn't," Mary Nel said with surprise. "What would we do then?"

Kate pulled out a chair, sat down, and picked up a cup of tea she had been drinking. She tilted her head to one side and seemed to look far away.

"You never know. I love this place. But don't you ever wonder what else is out there? You know, is this it? Or are there other things in store for us?"

Mary Nel stepped behind Kate's chair and put her hands on Kate's shoulders. Kate reached up and grasped her daughter's hand with her own.

"I know you probably don't believe this, but I'm still a young woman. I'm hopeful I will live a long time."

"You are young, Momma," said Mary Nel as she squeezed her mother's hand. "Sometimes, especially when I'm reading books, I think I would like to go somewhere else, seek adventure. I know that sounds frivolous, but I wonder about places I haven't been to or seen yet. So I know how you feel."

They both sat silent for a moment, each savoring her own thoughts.

"I hear Ish and Maggie coming. Time to get back to real life. I'll go check on our guest, then we'll eat."

She got up, went into the bedroom, and looked at the young man. Something made her look harder. Had his arm been in that position earlier? She couldn't remember. But something tugged at her mind. She didn't know what. She smoothed the covers and returned to the kitchen.

After the evening meal, Mary Nel had a book with her and was preparing to sit and read to the young man for a while.

"Mary Nel, are you going to sit with the gentleman tonight?" asked Maggie.

"Why, yes, Maggie. Why do you ask?" she said.

"Well, sweetie, you sat with him, and Miz Kate sat with him, and Ish sat with him. I want to do my part and help, too. Why don't you let me take a turn this evening, and you and your momma can get some rest. No use any one person getting worn out. If we all help that won't happen. Would that be all right with you, honey?" she asked.

Before she could answer, Kate spoke up.

"That's a good suggestion, Maggie," said Kate. "Mary Nel, you have been working nonstop since school closed for harvest. And she is right, we should all take turns."

"That is all right with me, Momma. I'll do whatever is needed. And I admit I am a little tired this evening."

"It's settled then," said Maggie. "I'll stay with him for a few hours."

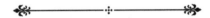

Maggie sat in the rocking chair by the bed. She looked down at the young man and touched her hand to his forehead.

"Least you don't have the fever. That's good. The fever's a bad thing," she said.

"Well now, Miz Kate said I should talk to you some. Seems like you may be able to hear me. So I'll start by telling you my name is Maggie. Now my real name is Magdalene from the Bible. And I bet a fine-looking man like you was raised by folks who read the Bible. I hope so anyway. We all ought to know about the Lord and his magnificence.

"One thing I'm gonna sure do is pray for you. I been praying nearly all my sixty years, and the Lord's been good to me. Gave me a good man in Ish. Gave me a fine family to work for, and we been happy to be with them for such a long time.

"You know I raised Miz Kate. Took care of her as much as Mrs. Nelson did. From the time she first opened her eyes. She's a fine lady. Been through a lot, she has. But she's a strong woman. Would of raised Miss Mary if she'd been here, but Mr. Daniels worked in the city.

"This harvest is about to kill me this year. I don't know why, but I feel mighty tired by the time the day is done. I guess I'm just getting a little too old for all this work. Ish, though, he don't miss a step. Keeps up with those young ones like he always did.

"Miss Mary was going to read to you tonight, but I thought I should take a turn with you. She reads all kinds of books, Miss Mary does. She's as smart as a whip, that girl. Pretty as she can be. Just like her momma. Anyway I'm going to read to you from my favorite book — the Bible. It's always a comfort to me, and maybe it will make you feel better."

She began to read from the book of Psalms, starting with Psalm 23. Her voice was soothing in its softness and warmth. Her spirituality shone through the words like sunshine on a foggy mountain. After a while, she put her head back and slept a sleep of peace and bliss.

The next morning when everyone came into the kitchen, Maggie was humming as she laid out the hot biscuits, ham, eggs, and potatoes. Ish looked at her with a big smile on his face.

"What you so happy about, girl? You couldn'a had too much sleep last night. You came in way after midnight and was up before dawn."

"Oh, I slept plenty," she said. "Fell asleep while I was reading the Good Book. Got here early this morning and checked on our guest. If he's in a coma you'd be fooling me. Just looks like he is in a peaceful sleep. I expect him to open his eyes any minute."

"He kind of looks that way, doesn't he? Let's hope there is some truth to that," said Kate.

"Do you want me to stay with him awhile this morning, Momma?" said Mary Nel.

"I think that's a good idea. I'd like to take Mr. Samuels up on his offer to take a few loads of apples in to Jefferson City today. So I need to get him started. I want him to get some more baskets, too, because the local folks are starting to come. Maggie, it would be helpful if you just stayed at the packing house today. We can finish grading those on the wagons before Mr. Samuels leaves."

"I'd be glad to, Miz Kate."

"Mary Nel, do you think you can wash our guest's face and give him a bit of water like I have been doing? This afternoon Ish and I will give him another bath and change the linen."

"Yes, ma'am," she replied. "I can do that."

Following breakfast, Mary Nel took a pan of warm water and a cloth into the room. She dipped the cloth in the warm water and began to wipe down the young man's face.

"Good morning to you. It's Mary Nel. I trust you had a good night's sleep. Yes, I said sleep. We have decided you are just resting from your terrible experience and that you are going to wake up soon, very hungry.

"It is a good thing you are not out today. The weather is colder than it was a few days ago. The apples must know it is their time because they all seem to be ripening at once.

"I'll be happy when the harvest is over. I just don't know if I could be an apple farmer. I know Momma says she likes it, but I think she is secretly getting a little tired of it. She went through it year after year when she was younger, so I can understand why.

"But what would we do if we didn't raise apples? I can tell you. I would like to travel. Go to far away places. Meet new people. See more of this beautiful country. Now the war is over, things might get back to normal.

"Maybe I can talk Mom into a little trip somewhere, like New York or Philadelphia. Oh, that would be nice! I think she would like to do that as much as I would. She needs to get away for a while. Since my father died she just goes to Jefferson City and church. I know she misses him terribly. So do I. I can't tell you how much it hurt when we lost him.

"He was a sweet, sweet man. Very gentle and quiet. He and Momma met when she was going to school in St. Louis. I can't talk too much about it because I get so sad. I will never forget my father."

She stopped talking because she was, in fact, about to have one of those sad, tearful moments that came when she thought of her father. She didn't want to do that in front of this stranger, even if he was incapable of hearing her.

She sniffed and took a deep breath to regain her composure.

"I think I will read to you now," she said.

She reached for her book and pulled the chair closer to the side of the bed. As she did so she looked into the young man's face. At first, she thought her eyes were playing tricks on her. She thought she had seen movement behind the man's eyelids as if he had moved his eyes from side to side in his sleep. She looked again, and his eyes were still.

She began to read aloud from Cooper's The Pioneers. She pronounced each word precisely and read in a manner that would have pleased even Professor Pentross had she been his student.

She read with feeling, adding life and flavor to the words as would a great storyteller. There wasn't a trace of little girl in her strong and pleasant voice.

She paused from her reading and looked carefully at the young man, wishing that the eye movement had been real and that he would suddenly wake up and talk with her. She just knew he would be easy to talk to and would have much to say. Remembering her mother's counsel, she put her hand on his and applied a gentle pressure.

She was startled and inhaled sharply. Had he squeezed her hand? Was she imagining things?

"Can you hear me?" she said loudly, excitement rising in her.

She felt the pressure again. This time there was no mistaking the sensation. He was squeezing her hand.

She lifted his hand in the air, his elbow still resting on the bed, and wrapped his hand with both of hers. The pressure was still there.

"Are you going to wake up? Please! Try to say something. My name is Mary Nel. I know you can hear me!"

She looked into his face. His eyes were moving just as they did before. "Uhhh."

There. She heard it! A low moan as if he was trying to speak. It came again. This time louder.

"I knew it! I knew it! Stay with me, you hear? I'll be right back. I've got to get Momma."

She rushed out of the room and ran to the back door.

"Momma! Momma! Come here! He squeezed my hand, and he is trying to talk."

Kate ran quickly and followed Mary Nel to the bedroom.

"He squeezed my hand and moaned. I could see he was moving his eyes, but he has not opened them," Mary Nel said excitedly.

"Can you hear me, son? Come on now, wake up. You can hear me, can't you?" said Kate as she grabbed his hand and began rubbing it briskly.

"Uhhhh," he moaned.

Kate could see his eyes were moving beneath his eyelids.

"Open your eyes, now. Open your eyes," said Kate.

Just then Ish and Maggie came into the bedroom and stood just inside the room.

"I told you, Miz Kate. He's going to wake up. Now you just wait and see. That boy going to be fine," said Ish.

The young man moved his head slowly from side to side and tried again to speak. His eyes flickered open, and he looked at the ceiling. He closed and opened them again, trying to focus. The moaning ceased as he turned his head slightly and saw the four people looking down at him.

"Can you hear me, son?" said Kate.

The young man looked at her for a moment, coming to his senses, then nodded his head slowly. His eyes darted about the room as he tried to find his place.

"Praise the Lord. Praise the Lord," said Maggie.

Everyone in the room was smiling. Mary Nel clasped her hands in front of her and bounced on her toes.

"Wat-tuh," he said. "Water."

The man swallowed with some difficulty.

Maggie rushed out of the room to the kitchen.

"You're going to be all right now. Just take it easy. You've been out for several days. Just lie there and be still for a while. You are safe. Nobody is going to hurt you," said Kate.

His eyes continued to rove about the room looking for a familiar face.

Maggie returned with a cup of water and handed it to Kate.

She lifted his head, and he drank from the cup, slowly at first, but then with more vigor.

"Easy now. You can have more, but let's not drink it all at once. A little at a time."

He coughed a little, and she laid his head gently back on the pillow.

He looked around the room, taking in the scene.

"Can you see us clearly?" asked Kate.

He nodded his head slowly, looking from face to face.

"Yes," he squeaked.

"Water," he said.

"All right, a little more," said Kate

This time he tried to raise his head on his own.

Finding Mr. Sunday

"A-h-h-h," he said.

A pained expression came to his face, and he lowered his head back on the pillow and closed his eyes.

"Your head hurts, I know. Don't put your hand up there," said Kate gently.

"In a little while, I'll give you something for that, but just water for now. I think we can try some soup a little later. Just be still for a while," said Kate as she patted his shoulder.

"My name is Kate. You have a head wound, and we must be careful not to disturb it," she said.

"Arm...can't move."

He turned his head to look at his right arm.

"Can you move your fingers?" she asked.

She watched as the fingers on his right hand moved only slightly.

She pulled the covers from his feet and watched his toes.

"Try to wriggle your toes for me," she said.

She watched as he wriggled his left toes. His right toes moved very little.

"Can you move your right toes again?" she asked.

Again, there was very little movement in his right toes.

"Very gently try to pull your left leg up and bend your knee," she said.

He slid his left foot back and bent his knee, not considerably, but enough for Kate to see that he could move his left leg.

"Now, try the same with your right leg," she said.

The only movement was a slight tilting of his toes. She watched as he struggled to move his leg. His heel remained on the bed.

"Arm ... leg ... can't move ..." he said looking to his right.

He lifted his left arm and moved his fingers slowly but adequately.

"Don't worry. Sometimes it takes the muscles a little time to recover. We'll worry about that a little later," she assured him.

But she was concerned. She had seen this before. Sometimes, the use of the extremities came back gradually. Other times, the damage was permanent.

The man closed his eyes and seemed to grit his teeth in frustration.

"Do you want to rest some now?" asked Kate.

"No, talk," he said.

"As long as you feel up to it. Let's start with your name," she said, smiling at him.

"Will ... Will Sunday."

"Well, Will Sunday. As I said, I am Kate. This is my daughter Mary Nel, and this is Maggie and Ish. You have been here since your accident, and we have been taking turns keeping an eye on you."

She watched him look at the others, and he moved his head slightly in acknowledgement.

"What ... happened?" he rasped.

"Well, you were shot at a campsite near town. And a farmer brought you in. The sheriff asked me to care for you as there was no place for you to stay in town," she said.

It took him a moment to absorb what she had said. He had a perplexed expression on his face.

"Shot? Someone...shot me?" he asked in disbelief.

"Yes, Will. You were robbed. We don't know who shot you. As soon as you feel like it, the sheriff wants to talk to you. The doctor wants to see you, too."

He turned his head and again stared up at the ceiling, closed his eyes for a moment, swallowed, then looked at Kate.

"Hungry," he said.

"I told you," said Ish with a big grin. He stepped up closer to the bed.

"Son, I told them you were going to wake up any time and say you were hungry. You look like such a strong man, I knew you would," said Ish.

The trace of a smile crept onto Will's face as he looked at Ish.

"We're going to get you something to eat, and then Ish is going to help you with a bath. He will give you a shave if you want. That will make you feel much better. Then I think you should rest a while, and we can talk more later." She patted his arm.

He nodded his head, closed his eyes, and seemed to relax. But he opened his eyes and looked at her and the others in the room.

"Thank...you," he said.

"Let's let him rest while we get him something to eat," said Kate.

Everyone left the room as Will closed his eyes.

Later, Kate came into the room with a bowl of soup and some bread on a tray. She set the tray on the table and sat in the chair beside the bed.

Finding Mr. Sunday

"You look refreshed. Do you feel a little better now after your bath and shave?" she asked.

"Yes," he said and nodded his head.

"Ish has a lot of experience with that. He helped my father for a while."

"This… your father's house?" he asked.

"It was. My father and mother have passed, and they left the house and property to me. We have an apple orchard that he started many years ago. We are right in the middle of harvest. We do a little farming, too. Let's try a little of this soup. Can you sit up a little?"

She watched him try to push himself up into a sitting position, but his right arm and leg refused to cooperate. She went around to that side of the bed and helped him sit up.

"My head … aching badly," he said.

"After you eat a little I'll give you some medicine that will help that. It might make you a little sleepy, but that's good," said Kate.

"The bullet grazed your scalp. I don't know how deeply. But your head will hurt for a while. I'll try to manage your medicine so you hurt as little as possible, but we have to be careful not to overdo it."

She returned to her seat, spooned some of the soup, and held it to his mouth. He swallowed it hungrily.

"It's good," he said.

She continued to feed him soup, then dipped some bread into the soup and gave it to him. He chewed briefly, then swallowed. She fed him for a while and put down the spoon.

"I think that is enough for now. I'm going to give you some medicine now, and I want you to get a good night's sleep."

She left the room and returned with a glass containing water laced with laudanum and a small brass bell.

"Here. Can you drink this with your left hand?"

She handed him the glass, and he grasped it firmly and drank the liquid.

"You are going to be fine, Will. It is just going to take time. You need to rest. Here is a bell."

She picked it up and rang it gently.

"If you need anything just ring it. Someone should be near most of the time. If, for some reason, we all have to go out, it won't be for long, and I will tell you if that becomes necessary."

"Thank you, Kate," he said.

He closed his eyes and drifted off to sleep.

Early the next morning Kate checked on her guest. He was lying flat, looking up at the ceiling, and turned to her as she walked in.

"I'm sorry. I guess I should have knocked on the door. I'm not used to your being awake," she said.

She saw a flicker of a smile, then he pushed to sit up the best he could. Again, he struggled because of his right arm and leg.

"Did you sleep well last night?" Kate asked.

"I did," he said. "A little lightheaded now."

"That is the laudanum I gave you for your headache. Is it still hurting?"

"Some. I can manage," he said. "I want to get out of this bed. I can't lie here all day."

"Well, I am not sure that's a good idea. But I will leave that up to you. I would ask, however, that you not try until Dr. Stanton can see you and certainly not until Ish and I are both with you. Does that sound all right with you?"

He nodded. "When is the doctor coming?"

"Silas, one of our neighbors, is going into town today. I asked him to tell Dr. Stanton you were awake and also to let Sheriff Wilkes know. They both want to see you. It's not very far to town, so they both might get here today. I'm pretty sure about the sheriff, but we will have to see about Doctor Stanton.

"In a few minutes we'll bring you some breakfast. Are you up for some coffee, today?"

"Coffee would be good. I really hate, I mean, I am sorry you have to wait on me," he said.

"Don't you worry. You will be up and going very soon. I think Ish was right. You are a strong person." She smiled and left the room.

In a little while, Mary Nel came in with a tray of scrambled eggs, toast, and coffee. He looked up, a bit surprised.

"Momma told me I should knock, but my hands were full, and I didn't want to call out and startle you," she said.

"That's all right," he said. "I am sorry. I forgot your name. Still a little fuzzy."

"It's Mary Nel, short for Mary Nelson."

"Your voice, it seems familiar."

"That's because Momma told us to talk to you and to read to you while you were out. She was a nurse during the war and said that sometimes people in a coma can hear people. So we all talked to you and read to you. Maybe she was right. She generally is.

"Do you think you can eat this, or would you like some help?"

"If I can sit up, I can. My right arm and leg don't seem to be working quite right."

"I know. Mom said that will probably get better with use." She quickly changed the subject.

She heard someone come down the hall, and Ish walked into the room with a big smile on his face.

"Good morning, Mr. Will. How you doin' today?" he asked.

"Better."

He smiled at Ish.

"Momma asked Ish to come in and help you sit up."

"Yes, sir, going to fix you right up," said Ish as he walked around the bed and began to help Will sit up.

"You know you just need to use those muscles. I need to think on that some. Might be something I can do about that."

When Will was in a sitting position Ish adjusted his pillows.

"There. Now that's better," said Ish.

"Got to get to work now. You in good hands, Mr. Will. See you later." He patted Will's shoulder and left the room.

Will began to eat his breakfast using his left hand as Mary Nel watched.

"Mmm. So hungry. Nothing has ever tasted this good," he said as he chewed.

"Was Ish a slave?"

"Certainly not!" said Mary Nel with some irritation in her voice. "Ish and Maggie worked for my grandfather for many, many years. They have never been slaves. They were partners in the orchard and still are. They are family to me and Momma."

Will had a look of surprise on his face.

"I am sorry. I didn't mean to be disrespectful of them or to offend you. I made a poor assumption. Forgive me, please," he said contritely.

"Oh, I am so sorry," she said, her finger tips flying to her mouth. "I didn't intend to sound so mean. It's just that… we are so close to them. I could never think of them as slaves."

"We're even then," he said and smiled broadly for the first time. "Let's start over."

She was struck at how handsome he was, even more so when he smiled. His blue eyes were just as she had thought they would be. She couldn't help but return the smile.

They were silent a moment as he ate his breakfast and drank his coffee.

"Coffee never tasted so good," he said.

"Are you left-handed? You use your left hand well," she asked.

"When I was taught to shoot, I learned to shoot with either hand. So I can use my left hand fairly well," he said between bites.

"Shoot? You mean guns?" she asked.

"Yes. I was raised by a gunsmith. He and a fellow who worked in his shop taught me to shoot. We had to fire the guns we repaired, and that led to my learning to shoot at an early age. It became sort of a hobby for me and Caleb, he was the fellow that worked for Tom, the man who raised me."

"I see. Where are you from, Will?" Mary Nel asked.

He paused as if to get his thoughts together. Mary Nel was worried that he might not remember.

"I was born in Virginia. Went to St. Louis when I was around four and lived there until a while ago."

"Were you coming to Linn when the accident happened?" she asked.

He took a sip of coffee and wiped his mouth with a napkin.

"No. I was headed to Jefferson City and then Independence. In the spring I was going out west. To California."

"California! Oh my, that sounds like it would be exciting. What does your family think of that?" she asked a little wide-eyed.

"I have no family. Just me. I was going to join a wagon train as a single."

"You have no family? None at all?" she asked with a look of disbelief.

"If I do, I don't know about them. It's a long story. I'll tell you about it one of these days," he said and looked away.

Finding Mr. Sunday

"I didn't mean to pry. I'm sorry I'm so nosy, but I tend to be that way," she said.

"It's all right. You have every right to know more about me. I really don't have any dark secrets," he said quietly.

Then he looked up and flashed that magic smile.

"You don't have to worry," he said. "I'm a good fellow. I was raised by a fine, decent man. He made sure I had everything I needed. Went to church almost every Sunday. Finished public school. Studied with a retired professor until not long ago. In many ways, I couldn't have had a better upbringing."

"Well. That's a comfort, Will Sunday," she said and smiled back.

She was delighted to see him beginning to talk more. She noticed he was well spoken.

Just then Kate walked into the room. She smiled at the two of them and put her hand on Mary Nel's shoulder.

"You're looking good today, Will. Eating must agree with you," she said as she laughed.

"Good morning. Yes, it does. Best breakfast I ever had. Thank you, ma'am," he said.

"You seem wide awake and normal to me," she said.

"Yes. Except for my arm and leg, I feel good," he said.

"I bet Mary Nel was asking a hundred questions," said Kate.

"Oh, Momma," said Mary Nel a little sheepishly.

"Not quite. But she had a few. As well she should," he said. "I just told her you have a right to know as much about me as you'd like. You are taking care of me and allowing me in your home."

"I am sure we'll have plenty of time to get to know each other. We're going to be pretty busy for the next few weeks, though. Once the harvest is in we will have to get the place ready for winter," Kate said.

"I wish I could help you. I've seldom been without something to do, whether it was school or at the shop. I'm pretty handy with tools," he said.

Then, as an afterthought, "Or I was."

"You can't let that muscle problem get you down now, Will. Just a day or so ago, we didn't even know if you would make it. Now, you're alive, talking with good sense, eating well. Let's take things slowly.

"You'll get through this. It may take a lot of work on your part. I can see you are not a person to lie around feeling sorry for yourself. You are just going to have to be patient."

She quickly moved the conversation along. "You said you worked at a shop? What kind of a shop?"

"I was raised by a man who owned a gunsmith shop. Tom let me come to the shop every day after school. I learned how to repair almost any type of gun. I was just telling Mary Nel, I learned to shoot very young when we fired the guns we repaired."

"Then you are a gunsmith?" she asked.

"No. I could be if I wanted. I'm not anything yet. I was headed to Independence for the winter and leaving for California in the spring. I was going west to, really, to see what opportunities were there."

"I kind of thought you might be headed west. That's a long way to go to find opportunity. But I think that would be a very exciting thing for a young man to do," Kate said. "Were you going by yourself?"

"Yes."

"May I ask a personal question, Will?"

She continued her probe.

"Yes, of course," he said.

"How old are you? We're just curious, that's all," she said.

"I am eighteen," he replied.

"Well, you certainly are a well-spoken eighteen-year-old," she said.

He chuckled a bit. "I finished public school in St. Louis. Tom wanted me to be well read before I considered a university. So I was tutored by a retired professor from St. Louis University. Mostly in literature but he insisted on my speaking properly and it became a habit."

"It serves you well. Were you going to a university at some point?" she asked.

"Tom wanted me to study law, and I was thinking seriously about that. He died rather suddenly and, well, I just decided to head west and see that part of the country. I can always study there. I just didn't like the thought of staying in St. Louis."

"St. Louis can be a difficult place," she said. "I lived there for some time. But nothing compares to being out where the air is fresh and the water is clean."

Mary Nel had been sitting quietly listening to the conversation.

"Oh my, I was supposed to be helping Maggie this morning. I'm already late, but I hate to miss all this," she said.

"I promise you can ask me anything you want later," said Will with a grin.

She returned the grin.

"Then if you will excuse me, I have work to do."

She left the room and went out the back door.

"She is a very nice girl," said Will.

"Yes. I am blessed. She is smart and very responsible. I don't know what I would do without her. She is the joy of my life," said Kate.

Just then a noise could be heard as someone entered the house. Ish came down the hallway with a piece of iron in his hand. It was about eight inches long, a little over an inch in diameter. The middle was wrapped in several layers of rawhide.

"What is that for, Ish?" said Kate.

"Only way he gonna get that arm right is to work it. He can start by learning just to hold on to this bar. Once he gets his fingers working he can try squeezing it. My bet it won't be long before he can hold it and then be able to lift it. If he don't work that hand and arm, it just be weak forever."

"What a grand idea, Ish. And you are right."

She turned to Will. "Will, you try that and we'll start exercising that leg several sessions each day."

Will's face lit up. Ish laid the bar in the palm of Will's right hand as it lay stretched out beside him.

He tried to close his fingers around the bar with only slight movement of the fingers.

"It's not going to happen all at once, Will. One little bit of progress each day is all we want," said Kate.

Will struggled to clutch the bar. The strain was obvious, but he didn't stop.

"A little bit at a time, Will," said Kate.

Later in the day, just as he finished an ample noon meal, Will heard people coming down the hallway. Kate poked her head around the doorframe and offered a small knock.

"Will, you have a visitor. Dr. Stanton is here to see you."

Will looked up as the doctor came into the room. He did not look like any doctor Will had seen.

"Well, now, son. You look better than you did the last time I saw you. Didn't know if you would wake up or not. How you feeling?" said the doctor.

Will looked up at the man, struggling to sit up more upright.

"Hello," he said. "I appreciate your taking care of me, Doctor. Kate told me you helped me."

"She lied. I didn't do anything but put you in better hands. Let's look at that head."

Dr. Stanton gently moved Will's head one way then the other and examined the wound carefully.

"Humph," he grunted. "Guess that's as good as it should be at this point. Still got a headache?"

"Off and on," said Will.

"Are you eating good, passing water and such?"

A little embarrassed Will replied, "Yes, but I can hardly move my right arm and leg."

"Well, let's take a look," said Dr. Stanton.

He went around the bed and pulled back the sheet. He asked Will to move both his arm and his leg and watched the small movements.

He lifted the leg, felt the muscle, and examined the arm in a similar manner.

"Well, son. I've seen this same thing from a bullet during the war, and I've seen it from an oak chair to the head in a bar fight. My guess is if you work these muscles you will get full use back. I can't say when. Where'd you get that iron bar there?" he said.

"From Ish. He made it for me to work my hand and arm."

"Well I be dam … uh … doggone," he said.

"Use it, as much as you can. And start trying to walk. Don't try without help, though, cause you're likely to fall on your butt at first. But you keep trying and work those extremities as much as you can. You get tired, rest. But keep at it day after day."

Finding Mr. Sunday

Dr. Stanton turned to Kate. "Mrs. Daniels, I don't think I can help this boy any more. What he needs is someone strong to get him walking again and someone to get those arm muscles back working again. I think he is in good hands now."

"I think we can do all that, Dr. Stanton. Based on what I have learned about Will, the only problem we may have is holding him back from doing too much," she said.

"Don't worry about him doing too much. He'll know what's too much. Let him push as hard as he can," said Dr. Stanton.

"Young man, I've got sick people to see. Next time we see each other, I hope it's passing on the street."

He patted Will's shoulder and left the room.

CHAPTER SIX

After Dr. Stanton left, Will lay in bed thinking. He felt better about his prospects for the future. He didn't know how competent the disheveled doctor was, but the assurance that he could regain the use of his extremities gave him some comfort. For the first time he thought about what had happened to him. Who had shot him?

It could have been anybody, he thought. But he remembered that pair that had stopped by his campfire the night before. They looked like a couple of scoundrels, the kind of men who would do such a thing. If he had to bet, he would put his money on those two. Not the skinny one. He didn't seem to have the capacity to do such a thing.

However, the fat one could probably make him do whatever he wanted. Yes, the fat one ... what was his name? ... He was the shifty one. Lazy, inclined to drink ... Yes ... That one probably shot him.

Anger welled up in him at the thought. He felt that same old rage come out of nowhere. He saw nothing for a moment but a wall of darkness. His heart beat faster, and his breath quickened. He could only lie there and wait for it to pass.

In a moment, his head cleared. He'd been a fool to be so careless on the trail. But for someone to shoot him, rob him, and leave him for dead — what kind of a man would do that to another man?

You better let this be a lesson, he thought. You are no longer sheltered from the worst of the world, and you'd better wake up to the fact that there are bad people out there.

He'd never before thought of harming another soul. But if he ran into these people, he would find out if they had shot him. Then he would ... what would he do? He didn't know. This was the first time he ever felt the need for revenge. It was powerful and frightening. It was a part of himself he had never known.

My God, he thought, as he lay there. Not only must I learn to deal with the world around me, I've got to learn to deal with myself within it. Reality is often a rude truth.

Some time later Kate came into the room with a tray of food.

Finding Mr. Sunday

"Are you ready to eat?" she asked.

"I'm starved. I never realized how much I eat," he said, laughing.

"You're a big man, Will. Big men eat a lot. In fact, most men eat a lot, big or small. My husband, Ben, ate a lot, and he wasn't a big man."

"May I ask?" he hesitated. "What happened to your husband?"

She helped him sit up and placed the tray of food on his lap. He began to eat.

"He joined the army in 1862. The 26th Missouri. He could have been an officer, but he didn't want to do that. He said the officers weren't going to win the war." She smiled slightly.

"He was killed in Mississippi in May of 1863," she said softly.

"I'm sorry," said Will. "I didn't mean to bring back painful memories."

"You didn't bring them back, Will," she said. "They are always there."

"I lost my best friend in the war. Caleb. He was a gunsmith who worked for Tom. He started as an apprentice and had been with Tom a long time."

Will paused and looked off in the distance.

"He was family to me. He taught me to hunt, fish, shoot, to box. He was like my big brother. He always had time for me. I still miss him."

"The war was a terrible scar for this nation," she said. "It will take a long time for this country to recover. I hope none of those who died did so in vain.

"Let's change the subject, shall we? I think tomorrow will be a good day for you to start moving around some. You might even want to sit on the porch. The fall air will be a little cool, but with a blanket, you'll be fine."

"I want to do that. The sooner I get up and around, the better," said Will. "I'm working on it already."

The next morning, Kate knocked on the door and found Will sitting up on the edge of the bed.

"Well, look at you," she said with a praising note.

"It took a little doing, but I'm up. A little unsteady, but I can manage it if I hold onto the bed frame with my left hand. Look," he said as he pointed to his right foot.

Kate watched as he lifted the toes on his right foot. There was not full motion yet, but there was perceptible progress.

"And I can move my fingers just a bit more. I can feel them coming back.

I'm eager to try to stand."

"Wonderful, Will! After breakfast, Ish is going to come in, and we are going to get you up and out of this room."

As if on cue, Maggie came into the room with a breakfast tray.

"My lands, look at this boy sitting up. I'm proud of you, Will. You gon' be fine," she said with a big smile. "Let's get you so you can eat. Won't be long, you be eating at the table."

She helped Will get settled and then left the room.

Will began to eat his breakfast.

"You know, Kate, I don't have any boots or much of anything. When will you be going to Jefferson City again?" he said between bites.

"I was thinking about that. I am going day after tomorrow. You can make a list of what you need, and I'll be happy to get it for you."

"I'll pay you back," Will said.

"Oh, we won't worry about that right now, Will. I know whoever did this took everything you had," she said.

"Oh, no, Kate. I have money," he said as he looked up at her from the edge of the bed. "In St. Louis. When you leave, I'll give you the name of the attorney who manages things for me. He'll arrange for a bank in Jefferson City to get the money to me. I'll word a telegram to him with instructions."

"You have an attorney managing your affairs?" she asked with a look of surprise on her face.

"Yes... I...uh...I do," he said.

He sounded almost apologetic. It was actually the first time he had thought seriously about his wealth.

"In fact, Kate, I'm ... well ... I guess you could say I have no financial worries. Tom left me well off."

Neither spoke for a moment.

"I'm sorry, Will. I didn't mean to pry. I was just surprised. Most young men your age don't have an attorney — or need one."

"I guess not. I had to get used to the idea myself. Mr. Evers was a trusted friend of Tom's for many years. Truthfully, he's the one that suggested I go west. But then I've thought about it as far back as I can remember, so the idea wasn't new.

"Tom was in California in the forties, and he talked about the West. My father was headed west when he left me. So I guess it was always in the back of my mind."

"Your father?" she said with a tilt of her head. "I thought you had no family."

Mary Nel must have shared their conversation about family, he thought.

He continued to eat his breakfast and seemed to go off somewhere for a moment or two.

"That's true," he said pensively. "I mean … I think it's true."

He stopped eating his breakfast and set his fork down.

"It's a long story. If you have time, I'll tell you about it."

"I'd like to hear it, Will," she said.

She settled back in the chair as Tom recounted his trip with his father to St. Louis after his mother's death, meeting Tom, breaking his leg and the departure of his father to California.

"The plan was for my father to come back and get me, or Tom would take me to California, one or the other. Poppa left in the late spring of 1852. We never heard from him again."

"Oh, Will. That must have broken your heart," she said with a look of compassion.

"I don't know, Kate. I guess it did. But I know there had to be a reason he didn't come back. My father loved me very much. I can still remember his eyes just like it was yesterday. I've carried that vision of his eyes all these years. They were a special color of blue."

Will said nothing for a moment.

"Anyway. Tom raised me. Treated me like his own son. Tom was a gentle man. Honest, hard-working, well-respected. And he did well for himself. But he had either a bad heart or complications from a wound he got in the war with Mexico.

"Not long after the war ended, he was taken ill and died within a few weeks. He died much too young. It was only a short time ago. I still find it hard to believe he is gone."

A shadow of grief moved over his face.

"So, there you have it. If my father is alive, and I doubt he is, I don't know it. I have no one else."

"That's quite a story, Will. You've gone through so much. I know it can't be easy for you. Did anyone try to locate your father?" Kate asked softly.

"Yes, Tom hired people to search for him. They found no trace of him. He missed the wagon train he had signed up for because of my accident, and no one knows whether he joined another or went with a small group on horseback, or even by himself. There are no records of him."

"Will you try to find him in California?" Kate asked.

"Finding him would be almost impossible. I'm not even sure he went to California. He may be in Oregon or anywhere along the way ... or dead, for that matter."

He had a distant look in his eyes.

Kate could see traces of heartache in the young man's face as he fell silent. She knew the feeling well. Everyone has his own personal pain deep inside, she thought.

Ish came in the door and greeted the two.

"I see you eating well. We don't get you moving, you going to be big as a horse," he said, laughing.

"I'm ready," Will said as his countenance quickly changed.

"First, we going to see if you can stand. Find out what work we got cut out for us. Now, don't you get all riled if you can't do much yet. Don't expect you can, but we got to start somewhere. Got to get you some shoes. Have to kill a cow to get that much leather," he joked.

"Kate's going to get some clothes and boots in Jefferson City. Until then, I'll go barefooted while I'm in the house. I can feel the floor better," he said.

"All right. Let's put your feet on the floor. I'm going to be here by your side."

He sat down to the right of Will and put his left arm around Will's back and under Will's left arm. Then he put Will's right arm around his own neck and held on to Will's wrist.

Ish was no small man, but Will proved to be an armful.

Kate held him from the other side. "I'm going to try to take some of your weight on this side. I can steady you if nothing else," she said.

"Ready? Let's stand up," said Ish.

Will stood up, or more accurately, was pulled up by Ish. It was immediately apparent that his right leg was useless. Without the support of Ish, Will would have fallen. He leaned heavily into Ish with his right leg bent at the knee and his foot resting on his toes.

"Just lean into me. Lean into me. That's the first thing we work on, getting you to stand on your left leg. Just so your right leg's on the floor. Can you straighten it all the way?" said Ish.

"No," said Will as he strained.

"Well, we'll work on that. Just learning to stand first." Ish strengthened his grip on Will's right arm. "Let's try a step. Lean on me and lift your left leg."

Will did as instructed, supported solely by Ish. With considerable effort, he managed a step of a few inches.

"Again," said Ish. Will tried again with the same result.

"Let sit back down, now," said Ish.

They pulled Will back to the bed, and he sat down heavily on the edge.

"I'm a little weak," he said. "Never felt weak before."

"That's to be expected, Will," said Kate. "You'll get stronger."

All three of them sat there for a moment, each of them thinking the same thing. This was going to be a long, tough road.

"I'm going to work that leg for a while. Then you should work on that arm with the bar," said Ish.

Afterwards, Will lay back down, and everyone left the room. He had known he had to overcome some problems to get his health back, but this was bigger than he thought. He had always been one to get up and go and could barely remember the one time in his life when he had limitations.

He reflected on Kate's comment. Yes, the last year had been full of change, and hard, he thought. His grief over the loss of Caleb and then Tom was still raw. And his decision to go west was a drastic change in his life.

And now this. Shot. A cripple. Totally dependent on the kindness of people he didn't know.

Well, he asked himself, what are you going to do, Will? Are you going to lie here feeling sorry for yourself? Whining inside like a kid? Why, Caleb would laugh at me if he were still alive. Even gentle Tom would not have allowed me to indulge in self pity.

No, I'm made of better stuff than that. This is just another bump in the road. I'm young, I'm strong. I'm very fortunate to have what I have and to be with such fine and caring people. I just need to accept this reality along with everything else, and get on with life. No, this isn't going to beat me. I've allowed nothing in life so far to keep me down. And this surely isn't going to, either.

An hour or so later, Kate came in the door with a stranger following her. Will noticed a star was pinned on his vest.

"Hello, Will. I'm Sheriff Wilkes. Good to see you looking better." He stuck out his hand, and Will shook it with his left hand.

"Will Sunday. Glad to meet you, sheriff. Sorry, I've got a little muscle problem on the right side. But these good folks are helping me get straight," Will said.

The sheriff nodded as he looked over at the right arm.

"Will, I don't know if we can find out who shot you, but I'd like to ask you a few questions. We might get lucky."

"Sure. I'll tell you all I know."

"Have a seat, Sheriff Wilkes. Would you like me to leave?" Kate asked.

"That's up to Will, Mrs. Daniels."

"No, I would like for her to be here," said Will.

"Do you remember being shot?" asked the sheriff.

"No. I didn't know what had happened when I woke up here. Kate told me I had been shot."

"We're not sure if you were shot late the evening before we found you or early in the morning. One of the local farmers pulled off the trail and found you at the edge of the woods near a campsite. You had probably spent the night there. A lot of people do because of the creek.

"I went out there after we brought you here, and I saw at least three different shoe tracks around the campfire. Do you recall seeing anybody on the trail?"

"Yes, I do. It took a while for it all to come back to me. There were two guys who stopped at the campsite and had some coffee. I gave them some of my food. They didn't stay very long. They looked like some pretty rough people. I was glad to see them leave," Will said.

"When was this?" asked the sheriff.

"That evening. It was getting dark when they came in, and they didn't stay more than a half hour. They said they were going to go on down the trail. There was a full moon," Will said.

Finding Mr. Sunday

"Can you remember much about them?" said the sheriff.

"They were pretty shabby. One was tall and looked like a scarecrow. I don't think he was all together in the head. He did everything the other one told him to do. Acted kind of childish. Another thing, he wore a bowler hat. Dark gray or black. I couldn't tell. His friend called him Burt.

"The other guy was shorter, fat. A greasy-looking sort with a fat face and small eyes. He was a character all right. I think he said his name, but I don't remember it."

"Hmmm. Didn't see anyone like that pass through town," said the sheriff. "But the roads are full of men now. Going and coming. Linn doesn't offer travelers very much."

"The tall one said they worked with mules and were headed to Independence. They had just come north, too. I remember them saying that."

"Yeah. That's probably where they headed. Course if they were mule handlers they could have been headed anywhere, especially on the trail west. What all did they take from you?" asked the sheriff.

"My horse, two mules, and my saddle," he said. He paused a moment. "That big bay is one of the finest saddle horses you can buy. He'd stand out anywhere. I had about a dozen pistols and rifles in two wooden crates. Some gunsmith tools.

"Of course, they took my money, a little over a hundred dollars. I had a Remington .44 revolver in a custom-made holster, and the boots were handmade, too. You won't see any other like them."

"Were the guns anything special?" the sheriff asked.

"Henry rifles mostly. Some Smith & Wesson pistols, some Remington pistols, an Army or two. Oh, there was one special pistol. An ivory-handled Smith & Wesson .32 caliber cartridge pistol. Engraved. Really pretty pistol. I was going to keep that one."

"Anything else you might remember or want to tell me?" Sheriff Wilkes asked.

"I don't think I left anything out. If I did I'll let you know."

He seemed to take a mental pause, then the look on his face changed. His complexion turned almost red. His jaw muscles rippled. His whole body tightened. He narrowed his eyes into a cold stare somewhere off in the distance.

Then he spoke, "I can't say those men did this to me. But if I ever run into them again, I intend to find out."

He seemed to catch himself quickly, then come back to them. He exhaled and turned to the sheriff, who was surprised at the sudden change in the young man.

The sheriff cleared his throat. "One other question, Will. Why were you carrying rifles and pistols?"

"Oh," said a calmer Will, "I guess I should have told you. I inherited a gun shop and gunsmith business before I left St. Louis. Most of the inventory was sold, but I kept some guns. I was headed west and thought a few extra weapons might come in handy.

"The gunsmith tools were given to me over the years by the man who raised me. They meant a lot to me. Some of those might turn up somewhere. A few of the tools have WS scratched in them, my initials," Will said.

"I see," said Sheriff Wilkes. "That's a lot of good information. Those men you described need to be questioned, if nothing else. I'll send all this down the road to other sheriffs. We'll see if anything turns up. Once you get better, do you intend to head west?"

Kate watched Will closely, wondering the same thing.

"Well, sheriff, it seems like I got at least a couple of reasons to head west now. I just might run into some fellows I know."

He nodded his head slowly as he looked away.

"Now, son. Don't you go hunting those fellows. You're going to find out there are a lot of no goods out there. Best thing you can do is keep your eyes open and make sure you don't trust any man you meet. Don't put yourself in a position where anybody can take advantage of you. Some of these fellows are rotten to the core. They'd shoot you in the back just to watch you bounce off the ground."

Will looked at the sheriff .

"I'm beginning to find that out, sheriff. And I appreciate your advice."

"Now take care of yourself, son. You get to where you can come into town, stop by my office and pay a visit."

He patted Will's shoulder and stood to leave.

"Let me walk out with you, Sheriff Wilkes," said Kate.

Finding Mr. Sunday

Out in the yard, Kate and the sheriff stopped to talk.

"What's wrong with his arm, Mrs. Daniels? If you don't mind me asking," said Sheriff Wilkes.

"I'm not sure. His right arm and leg are of little use just yet. But I've seen this before with head wounds. I'm hopeful he will get the use back. We've seen a little improvement in movement on that side, but he has a long way to go."

"You talk to him much?" he asked, a serious note in his question.

Kate folded her arms in front of her, as if to ward off a chill, and stirred the dirt with the toe of her shoe for a moment.

"Some." She looked up at him. "Dr. Stanton was right. He came from a good background. He is very bright and well-educated for a young man of only eighteen."

"I knew he was young," said the sheriff. "But he don't come across as that young."

"You're right, sheriff. He seems much older than he is."

"Does he come across as one with a temper?" asked the sheriff.

"No. Not that I've seen. I will tell you, though, the look in his eyes when he talked about finding those men was one I had not seen before."

"That's why I was asking. I've seen that look before. I wouldn't want to be on the receiving end of it with a man that big."

"I think he's a fine young man," Kate said as if going on record.

Then her face softened as she looked up at the sheriff.

"He's had a sheltered life so far. He's just waking up to what this world can do to a person. His first lesson was a cruel one. I expect there to be some anger and bitterness," said Kate with a little sadness in her voice.

"You're right."

He mounted his horse.

"You have a good day, Mrs. Daniels."

He tipped his hat and headed out of the yard.

Kate stood in the midday sun, a hand shielding her eyes, and watched the tiny dust clouds come and go as the sheriff urged his horse down the trail. She turned and went into the house.

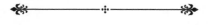

Will was finishing his noon meal. Mary Nel came in to sit a few minutes and retrieve the tray.

"Hello, Will," she said with that perfect smile. "I'm sorry. I've just gotten a chance to come in. But I'll be here the rest of the day."

"Good afternoon, Mary Nel," he said with an equally perfect smile.

"Momma said we had to work on getting that arm stronger. She showed us some things she wants us to try. I'm going to be in the house today, so after a little while will you be up to trying them?"

"By all means," he said. "I need all the help I can get."

He shook his head slowly and rested it on the headboard of the bed.

"I feel like a cripple, but I'm going to get over this thing," he said as he stared down at his right leg.

"Now you mustn't feel like a cripple," Mary Nel said.

She put her hand on his arm for a moment, then withdrew it gently.

"I know it's frustrating. But Momma said she had seen it before. And the fact that you're showing some improvement means you will get everything back if you keep working hard. It hasn't even been a week since you were hurt. And I'm going to help you. We all are."

"I know you are. All of you have been … just … well … I don't know what I would have done if Kate hadn't taken me in," he said.

"Well, we did. And now we are going to work you every day. You might regret being here," she said, giggling.

He looked at her as she laughed and suddenly realized Kate was right. What a pretty girl. Striking even. She must have sensed he was looking at her, and she pushed back a loose strand of hair and colored slightly.

"Here, let me take that tray back, then we're going to go to work," she said.

She came back in a moment and went around to the right side and sat on edge of the bed facing him. She picked up his right arm.

"Momma said almost every waking moment you must try to grasp that bar to build your grip and at the same time try to lift it as you bend at the elbow.

"I know we are a ways from that. For now I'm going to stretch your fingers and work your arm back and forth, bending it at the elbow. Eventually, as you build the muscles back, I want you to resist my pushing your arm back and resist my pulling it back down. Are you ready to try it?" she asked.

"Yes. Let's start," he said eagerly.

She grasped the back of his hand in her right hand and put the other hand under his elbow. She lifted his arm, stretched his fingers back gently, held them with tension for a moment, closed his fist, then pushed his arm, folding it at the elbow.

She repeated the motion several times.

"See, that's the idea. Only this time when I push your fingers back, try to fold your fingers like you're making a fist."

She moved his fingers back very gently.

"Now try to close your fingers and make a fist."

"That's it! That's it! I can feel you closing your fingers. The more you can close them the harder I'll try to keep them open."

They repeated the exercise again and again. After many repeats she saw the effort beginning to show in his face.

"Had enough, Mister Sunday?" she said, laughing lightly.

"No, not yet," he said. "Just a little rest. Then more. I can feel it when you fold my arm back. Just a little."

Will looked at her. She is so pretty she could break a fellow's heart by just walking in a room, he thought.

"Tell me about going to California," she said as she widened her eyes in anticipation.

"What do you want to know?" he asked.

"Everything!" she said as she continued the exercise motions.

"Well, I'll have to admit I haven't thought it all through. I was going to spend the winter in Independence and educate myself. You can go west by stagecoach, partly by train. You can even take a ship all the way around.

"But I want to go on the trail with a wagon train, the old way. I know there aren't that many these days. But I want to see this country. I've looked at some of the maps, and you really see a lot of the country going that way. The trouble will be finding a wagon train with a guide you can trust."

She could sense the excitement building in his voice.

"I don't even know where I want to go in California yet. Maybe Sacramento. Maybe San Francisco. Or even farther south.

"I figured I'd get a good wagon for the trail. I don't know if I'd go with oxen or mules. I'd have to decide that. And take along a good trail horse. Like the one I had. He was a beauty. I'd sure like to have him back."

She was seeing his vision in her own mind.

"Anyway, they've got it down pretty pat what you need to take in the way of supplies. Of course, good guns, like the ones I had, and adequate ammunition. I'd make sure I joined the right train, with a competent leader."

Mary Nel hung on every word, eyes wide open, continuing the exercises almost mechanically.

"You know, every time I think about it I realize what a big decision it is to go that way. But I get excited, and I want to get on with it, just go and take it all in. I know it won't be as easy as getting on a boat. But that's the beauty of it. Seeing this country and having that experience."

She could see the whole idea wasn't just a relocation to him; it was the fulfillment of a deep-rooted dream. And something more perhaps.

"Oh, my. I'm excited for you. It's like a book, an adventure. I wish I could go on a wagon train to California," she said.

"Maybe you will some day," he said.

Then after a pause.

"What do you want to do with your life, Mary Nel?" he asked.

"I don't know. I'm a bit of a dreamer. Probably because I read so much. Sometimes I see myself going to school in St. Louis, meeting someone, getting married, and having a family. Much like Momma did.

"But other times, I'm almost certain I couldn't settle for that. I want to see more of the world than just Missouri. Like you said. But then I'd like to see New York, Paris, London, Rome. I know that may not be what you expected to hear."

"I didn't have any expectations. And I don't see any reasons why you couldn't do all of those things if that's what you want to do," he said.

"I think Momma wishes she had seen more of the world, too. We were talking about Mr. Samuels, our neighbor. He's always trying to get Momma to sell him the orchard. She surprised me when said she might take him up on it one day. She reminded me how young she is, too."

"If you don't mind my saying so, your mother does look young. It's hard to believe she is your mother."

Finding Mr. Sunday

"She married my father when she was just eighteen, and I was born eleven months later."

She colored a bit.

"I think maybe she wanted to start a family early. She told me she was a big surprise to her parents. They had not been able to have children earlier for some reason, but when Grandma was forty-one she had my mother."

"Ah. That explains it," he said nodding his head. "She has plenty of time to do other things if she wants to. I'm glad she has an open mind."

They heard Ish coming down the hall.

"Afternoon, Miss Mary. Hello, Mr. Will. How you doin' today?" he said in a hearty way.

"I'm being outdone by a pretty girl who is stronger than I am," Will said, laughing.

"You might as well get used to that. Won't be the last time," said Ish with a laugh.

Mary Nel smiled at the compliment.

"We've been doing those arm and hand movements Momma told us about," said Mary Nel.

"That's good. That's good," he said. "I been thinking about how to get that leg stronger. I believe if you leaned on a wall in the corner of the room holding yourself up with your good leg and the wall, you could try to put weight on that right leg a little at a time.

"I'll help you get to the corner in a little while to try it, and if you practice standing there every day, we might get somewhere. Miz Kate's bent on finding ways to get you better so we gon' to try everything."

"We sure can. Thank you for all you are doing, Ish. I won't forget it."

"You just get better, Mr. Will. That's all the thanks I need," he said as he left the room.

"I think you should rest now, Will," said Mary Nel. "I'll look in on you later."

"Thanks," he said as she turned to leave.

"Oh, Mary Nel," he said.

She turned back and looked at him, eyebrows raised in a question.

"You hold on to those dreams."

She smiled at him and walked out of the room.

104

Kate came into the bedroom early the next morning to tell Will about the big day ahead.

"Maggie and Ish will both work with you today. I'm going to have to go into Jefferson City earlier than I thought. I'm going to leave after breakfast. If you can make a list of the clothes you want and word that telegram, I can do that for you today," she said.

"Oh, yes. I will. Thank you. I'll put my sizes on the list," he said.

"How is the harvest?" he asked.

"It's coming in quicker than we thought it would. We brought in some helpers from Jefferson City. Mr. Samuels is managing them. I think we will be finished earlier than usual. The biggest problem will be getting it all to market," she said.

"I wish I could do something. I feel like I'm in the way," he said.

"I know you feel that way, and I don't want you to. I think things happen for a reason. You are here, and we're going to do all we can for you."

She stepped closer to the bed.

"And I am glad you are here. You are a fine young man, and we all are enjoying having you here and getting to know you."

He was touched by the words.

"Thank you, Kate," he said.

She smiled warmly at him and said, "You are so welcome. Now we'll have breakfast ready in a little while."

With that she turned, walked out of the room, and gently closed the door.

Soon Maggie brought him a breakfast tray and placed it on the table.

"Thank you," he said. "Maggie, today I'm going to ask Ish to help me get to the porch one way or another. I'll take my arm bar and a blanket, and I'll sit out there. I've just got to get out of this room," he said.

"I know, child. You ain't one to stay cooped up in a room. I can see that," Maggie said. "After you eat your breakfast, I'll get Ish to come in here and see if we can't get you going."

Kate returned to the room a bit later carrying a wash bowl full of water, soap and a towel.

Finding Mr. Sunday

"I thought you might like to clean up a bit so I'll leave this with you," Kate said.

She was dressed for the chilly weather she would face on the nearly half-day wagon ride.

"Do you have that list? And the telegram?" she asked.

"I sure do," he said as he handed her the papers.

"It would probably be a good idea if I read it, in case I have questions?" she asked.

"Certainly," he said.

"Let's see, pants, shirts, boots, belt. This looks about right. Socks, you will need socks." She turned to the telegram.

"Oh, yes, I forgot," he said. "If you see anything else I've missed, you can guess the size and go ahead and get it."

"Hmmm. Will, it's none of my business, but five hundred dollars is a lot of money," she said.

"Well, Kate. I'd rather have it and not need it than need it and not have it," he said. "It will be a few days before I can draw the money. Maybe Mr. Samuels can pick it up on the next trip. I'd rather him carry it than you, anyway."

"That's a good idea," said Kate.

"Kate, if Ish can help me to the table tomorrow morning, I'd like to have breakfast there. Would you mind?" he asked

"We'd love to have you at the table, Will," she said. "I have to leave now. You have a good day, Will." With that Kate left the room.

A little later, he began bathing himself with his left hand. As he touched the cloth to his right arm he felt an involuntary movement, a quick, jerking motion. He felt a tingling sensation in his arm beginning at the bottom of his elbow. At first he was alarmed, then he became excited. Feeling. He had actually felt a sensation in his arm.

He hurried to complete his bath, and Maggie soon returned.

"Ish is getting Miz Kate and Miss Mary off to Jefferson City, and then he'll come help you get to the porch," Maggie said. In the meantime you ready to work that arm, Mr. Will?"

"I sure am," he said.

Maggie began manipulating his arm and hand the same way Mary Nel had done.

"I felt my arm jump this morning, Maggie. Like it had a mind of its own. And a kind of tingling feeling," he said.

"Oh, I think that's a good sign, Mr. Will, a good sign," she said.

They worked on the arm together for a while. Then Will let Maggie rest as he practiced squeezing the bar.

"It's a pretty day out there today, Mr. Will. Sun shining. A little warmer than it has been lately. You're going to like sitting on the porch," said Maggie.

Ish came into the room.

"You ready to go outside, son?" said Ish.

He half pulled and half lifted Will. Will leaned into him as he lifted his left leg. They made it through the bedroom doorway and down the hall to the kitchen. They paused before entering, and Will rested against the door frame.

The kitchen was a welcome in itself. Comforting odors lingered from the morning breakfast. A large black cast iron cook stove, still warm from breakfast, dominated the wall on the left. There was a water reservoir on one end of the stove, and on the opposite end, a firebox with a hinged door.

Three openings on the top of the firebox were covered with black cast iron covers, and a large lifter was placed in the lifting slot of one of the covers. A blue and white coffee pot sat on one of the covers. The white enamel oven door with a wire handle in the middle was browned by many years of baking.

A tin-lined sink with a small pump handle divided white cabinets and a cupboard on the other wall. A breakfast table, surrounded with oak chairs and covered with a red and white checkered tablecloth, occupied one end of the room.

Colorful framed prints of flowers and hand-painted vases reflected a woman's touch and softened the array of frying pans, kettles, and pots that were neatly arranged on the wall and on shelves. The painted milled wallboards were spotless as were the worn plank floorboards.

"So, this is where all the good food is coming from," said Will. "I can see Kate's touch all around."

"Oh, yes, Miz Kate loves this kitchen. Miz Nelson did, too. She called it the heart of the household," said Ish.

Will and Ish maneuvered through the large kitchen to the front parlor. The room was well furnished with a woven wool rug, upholstered chairs, a sofa, and several polished walnut tables. Dark stained shelving on one wall was filled with books, glassware, and vases. There were a number of oil lamps with marble bases placed about the room.

"Let's be careful on this rug," said Ish.

Maggie opened the door to the front porch. The two men managed to get through the door without incident. Maggie steadied one of the rocking chairs as Ish lowered Will into it. Will took a deep breath as he looked around.

"What a beautiful place," he said.

He settled himself in the chair, and Maggie carefully covered his legs with a blanket. He looked out at the white fence, the chrysanthemums, and the orchard. There were apples still on the trees, but the leaves were turning various shades of yellow and gold.

He looked to the left and saw the neat yard, the packing shed, and the big barn. There were several workers unloading apples under the covered work area of the packing shed.

"It looks like a painting," said Will as he took in the scene.

"I forget how pretty it is," said Ish.

"I am going to get some coffee going," said Maggie.

"Me and Mr. Nelson did all of this," Ish said, sweeping his arm in an arc.

"We cut down the trees, planted the orchard. Gathered the stones for the foundations, sawed the lumber, built the buildings, everything — house, barn, sheds, fences. Built my house, too. You can't see it from here. It's behind Mr. Nelson's place on the edge of the orchard.

"Mr. Nelson put his heart in this place. Wanted everything to be just so. He worked from before sunup to sundown. So did Miz Nelson. More than forty years.

"He didn't slow down at all until Miz Nelson died. Then, he was like a lost soul. I think losing her killed him, I do," said Ish with a sigh.

Will listened intently to Ish.

"I thought when Miz Kate came back home he'd get to going again, but it didn't happen. He got sicker and didn't seem like he wanted to get better.

Dick Ward

Sure enough, he didn't. They both buried up on that rise behind the barn.

"I think Miz Kate believes her momma and daddy worked theyselves to death on this place. Some years good crops, some years not so good. All their lives, at the mercy of something they couldn't control."

"Ish, do you think Kate feels the same way about this farm? I mean, like her mother and father did?" asked Will.

"No, sir, I don't. Sure, I think Kate has feelings for the place. But not like her momma and daddy did. Miz Kate's more like most of us. The more in control we are of our lives, the more we like it. Course, you know as well as I do, you never get the control you want."

He chuckled at his own remark, then continued with a more serious tone.

"But I don't think Miz Kate is one to build her life around an apple orchard, where her future is up to the whims of nature."

Just then Maggie came out with a coffee pot and some cups.

"Mmm, that smells good," said Will.

"Well, let me pour you some, Mr. Will."

They chatted a while longer about the apple business as they sipped coffee. Will was always interested in how a business worked.

Ish said, "Well, I've got to get back to work for a while. You sit out here and enjoy the day. I'll look to you a little later. You need me, tell Maggie, she'll come get me."

"Thanks, Ish. I'm fine. I think I could sit here a long time," he said.

Ish went down the steps to the packing shed. His strength and sturdy movement belied his age.

"I like that man, Maggie," said Will. "He's a wise man, too."

"I think he is, too. We been together since we were children, almost. He hasn't steered me wrong yet. I listen to what he says. Don't always do it, but I always listen. Now, don't you go telling him that."

Her eyes gleamed as she spoke of her husband.

"I'm going inside and do a few things. You need me, just call out. I think it would do you good just to sit out here by yourself for a while. We ain't been giving you no peace since you been here."

She patted his shoulder and went inside.

Will felt a light breeze come up. He inhaled deeply through his nose. The fresh clean air brought a crispness to his senses. He felt alive, awake and reveled in the sensation. He watched the leaves on the apple trees dance gently as a breeze curled through the orchard. A hawk floated above, watching for the careless rabbit to come out of the shadows.

Will closed his eyes and thought about his conversation with Ish.

The more in control we are of our lives, the more we like it. Was that what he had said? Will had never thought about that. But that idea hit him hard. He'd never had control over his life and hadn't needed to. He'd left his life up to others, and everything had been fine.

But now, he had very little control over anything, not even his own body. And that upset him. Even angered him. He was angry at himself for letting this happen. Angry at those who had done this to him. He fumed as he sat there.

He took a deep breath and calmed himself. Well, it's time to change. Now. Time to take control of my own life! Whatever it takes. Let this be a lesson. Don't be vulnerable. Don't put yourself at the mercy of anyone. Don't let anyone get the upper hand.

He reached down and picked up the leather-wrapped iron bar and transferred it to his right hand. He had forgotten he was in a rocking chair and was now rocking briskly.

He suddenly realized he had been pushing down with his right leg. Ever so slightly, but he was flexing the muscles of his right leg as he rocked. I'll be, he thought. He pushed harder and harder.

Whatever it takes.

Around mid-morning the next day Kate and Mary Nel arrived home from Jefferson City. They came into his room carrying a number of wrapped bundles and placed them on the bed.

"Hey, Mary Nel," he said with a big smile. "I'm glad you two are back safely."

"We are, but I have decided the two of us should not go to Jefferson City alone again," Kate said.

"Was there trouble?" he asked with concern.

"No, but the roads are full of strangers. I don't know if it's because the war is over and people are still going home or because more people are headed west. But there were many rough-looking people on the trail and in town."

"I think it's a good idea that you not go alone," he said. "Maybe soon, I will be well enough to go with you."

"That would be good," she said.

"Let's see here," she said as she began unwrapping the packages and holding items up for him to see. Here are some shirts, pants, boots, underwear, socks, a belt. I even got you a razor and strap. But wait, there's one more thing."

She stepped back into the hallway and returned holding a crutch. It was a well-made one, strong and sturdy with a padded top, split steamed wood sides and a padded hand grip in the middle. The hand grip was held in place by metal screws and could be moved up or down as needed.

"It is the tallest one I could find," she said with a smile.

"That's just what I need."

A big grin blossomed.

"I was going to tell you both, I was rocking in the chair on the front porch yesterday and found myself pushing down with my right leg. Actually using it some.

"I think my leg muscles are getting stronger. And look…" He held out his right hand curled such that his fingertips touched the base of his palm. "I can't squeeze just yet, but I'll be able to soon."

"Oh, Will," said Mary Nel. "That's wonderful."

"I'm beginning to think you will recover from all this quicker than we thought. It's because you are working so hard at it," said Kate.

"By the way, I am going to ask Ish to move one of the dry sinks into your room. You can put it near the bed and bathe or stand as you get stronger," said Kate.

"I would appreciate that," said Will

"Ish is going to come in before the noon meal and work with me some. After we eat, we're going out to the porch. I believe rocking helps me," he said.

"Soon you will be able to sit with us at the packing house. Ish can bring down one of the rocking chairs," she said.

Finding Mr. Sunday

"I would like to do that," he said.

Will woke very early the next day and bathed at the dry sink. He shaved and dressed himself in his new clothes. He struggled some but was pleased with his efforts. He sat on the edge of the bed with the crutch. If he could grip the crutch better he would be able to stand without assistance. Walking would still be a challenge until his arm was stronger.

He heard someone coming down the hallway and looked up to see Ish coming in the doorway.

"Morning, Mr. Will. Look at you all dressed up this morning. Look like you going somewhere," he said, laughing.

"Oh, I am Ish, I am. It's just going to take me a little longer to get there," he said with a laugh.

"You ready to go to the breakfast table?" asked Ish.

"I sure am," he replied.

Ish helped him up, and they made their way to the kitchen. As he came through the doorway, Kate, Mary Nel, and Maggie looked up at him. They all began to clap their hands and smile at him.

"Hooray!" said Mary Nel with a joyous grin.

He looked at each of their smiling faces.

How could these people have come to mean so much to me in such a short time?

His face lit up, and he sat down.

"Thank you, dear friends," he said. "Let's say a prayer and eat."

CHAPTER SEVEN

They sat at the table in the warm kitchen. Kate was enjoying her morning cup of tea, and Will had just finished reading The Missouri State Times, a Jefferson City newspaper.

"That was the best harvest we've ever had," said Kate. "Mr. Samuels had a big harvest, too. I guess many of the orchards went unharvested because of the war. So apple prices are really high this year."

"Everything is still high because of the war," said Will.

"You see Kate, that room and board I'm paying comes in handy now, doesn't it?" said Will.

Will had insisted on paying for his keep. It had been quite a matter of discussion before Kate agreed to accept it.

Will had spent many days on the porch exercising and working tirelessly getting his leg in shape. He was able to stand and could walk slowly with the crutch and could almost put his full weight on his right leg. He was reinforced each day by the continued improvement and knew he would soon be able to get around without assistance or a crutch.

He hated not being able help, seeing everyone working so hard getting ready for winter. Over the last eight weeks wood had been cut and stacked, hogs slaughtered, hams and bacon set to cure, corn shucked and stored in the crib, and the barn filled with hay.

Apples had been dried by the bushel. The barn and the shed had been repaired, gates and fences mended, and winter clothes brought down from the attic. Thanksgiving was upon them and soon, Christmas.

"We all pitch in, and somehow it gets done," said Kate.

"I can see that. You all work hard and seem to have fun doing it," he said.

It was all new to Will. He had been raised in a pleasant household, of course. But here with the four of them, his sense of family seemed to find new meaning. "Kate, I think I will soon be able to get around by myself. I figure I'll be walking before too long. Slowly, but walking nevertheless," he said.

"I've noticed. It's so good to see you getting better," she said. "You are so eager to get on with your life, and I'm so happy for you. Soon this will all be a bad memory for you."

"It all won't be a bad memory," he said, smiling at her.

Then with some solemnity, he added. "I've met some of the finest people on Earth. Kate, you and Mary Nel, Ish, and Maggie have done so much for me. All of you are the reason I've made the progress I have made. I am truly grateful."

"I know that," she said, "We've been happy to do it."

She smiled.

"As soon as I can, I'd like to accompany you and Mary Nel on your next trip to Jefferson City," he said.

"We'd love to have you. I'll plan on that. I'm going to make at least one more trip before Thanksgiving and another before Christmas," she said.

"I'll be ready," he said with confidence.

Kate got up and poured Will another cup of coffee.

"Will, I hope you won't mind my asking this. Are you still planning to go west as soon as you are able?" she asked.

"Well, at one point I thought that I would get on with the trip as soon as possible. But now, I've had plenty of time to think about that. It's a big undertaking. I don't want to rush headlong into it any more," he said.

"Don't misunderstand me, I am still going. But I'm going to take my time, plan it out. I've made a commitment to myself to manage my life better. To know more about what I'm doing, whatever the endeavor. I don't want anything else to happen because I was naive or unprepared."

"What happened to you could have happened to anybody. You shouldn't blame yourself," she said.

"With all due respect, I disagree, Kate. I was naive. It's quite possible that I might have a lifelong reminder of that with every step I take. I don't have anyone to blame but myself. It won't happen again. I can promise you that," he said with confidence.

"As to when I plan to go west, I'm not sure. By the way, how long do you think you can put up with me as a boarder?"

Kate was a little surprised at the question.

"Shouldn't I be finding someplace else to stay? Jefferson City, perhaps," he asked.

"Well, that's about the only place you could find a room. There is nothing in Linn," she said.

"As to how long you can stay here, I think you should stay here until you are fully recovered. We are a ways from that right now."

He could see a change in her demeanor as she looked him in the eye.

"Will, you must know we are happy you are with us. I like having a man here in the household," she said.

"Can't say I have been much of a man," he said with a little laugh.

"There is a sense of comfort, though, in having someone like you here. Mary Nel enjoys your company. I enjoy your company. I just feel safer knowing you are here in the house with us."

"Isn't my staying here going to be awkward? I mean, won't people talk?" he asked.

"Will, people will always find something to talk about. But I'm beyond caring. I tend to live my life on my terms, and frankly, I'm proud of the way I live. Don't you worry about that," she said.

She placed both hands on the table and interlaced her fingers and was silent for a moment.

Will studied her face. Her shining hair was pinned up, and a few loose strands fell to the side. Her porcelain complexion was tinted by a natural pink glow in her cheeks. Her eyes were clear, a deep brown with flecks of gold.

"I have to be honest. I miss Ben. Still. I was always at peace when he was around. When he left for the war, I had a terrible time without him. When I heard we had lost him, I felt like … like someone had torn me in half, like a rag doll. I sometimes wonder if I will ever be whole again."

Will knew Kate was a strong woman. He saw it every day. Now, though, he could sense she was sharing something deep and personal. He knew she was undergoing a painful moment. They both were silent for a while.

"You must have loved him very much. I know there is a hole in your heart when you lose someone close to you. But I can't imagine the pain you must feel, having lost a husband," he said softly.

"It is hard. I try not to dwell on it. You can see that I stay busy."

She smiled and seemed to look far away.

"He was five years older than I was. I was in boarding school in St. Louis. There was a church social, and Miss Emily, who ran the school, was very particular about knowing our whereabouts at all times. We weren't allowed anywhere without a chaperone.

"Funny thing, I met him over an apple pie. He was handsome, gracious, and a real gentleman."

The sweet memory made her laugh softly.

"He asked Miss Emily if he could visit me the next Saturday, just to sit in the parlor and talk. She had seen him at church before, so he wasn't a total stranger.

"He began to visit me regularly, up until I had a break in school and went home for a few weeks. He surprised me by coming here to see me while I was at home."

Will sat quietly, listening to her memories, not wanting to interrupt.

"My father took a while to like him, but my mother was taken with him right away. I think secretly she thought he had real possibilities as a potential husband. Handsome, educated, employed, quiet, polite. I could almost hear her making the tic marks."

She laughed, then looked up, seeming surprised to find someone else present.

"I'm sorry. I didn't mean to bore you," she said, coming back to the present.

"You are not boring me. In fact, I'm flattered you are sharing those thoughts with me," said Will gently. "I wish I had met him. Someone once told me the only consolation you can get from losing someone you love is to live your life the best you can, for them, the way they would have wanted to have lived theirs."

"I have never thought of it that way," she said. "But I truly believe I have been doing that."

"You are young. You are smart, and you have a lot of life yet to live. I think Ben would want you to be as happy as you possibly can," said Will.

"Thank you, Will. I guess I need someone to tell me that every once in a while," she said.

She got up from her chair and pushed it up to the table.

"I've got a new calf to check on."

She put on her coat and went out to the barn.

Dick Ward

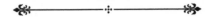

The state legislature had left Jefferson City for the holiday season, but the streets were still crowded. Though smaller than St. Louis, there were many similarities — a busy waterfront, a vibrant trade community, a growing manufacturing center, and a high concentration of immigrants, especially of German descent.

Walking slowly down the sidewalks with the aid of his crutch, Will was again reminded of why he preferred the countryside to the city.

Retail establishments lined both sides of High Street. Kate and Mary Nel were headed to their favorite emporium, but they read every storefront sign, lest they miss something of interest.

Kate had purchased most of the clothing Will needed during previous visits, so Will show little interest in the retail establishments. One shop, however, did catch his eye.

"I have a stop to make, ladies. If it's all right, I'll see you at the hotel later on," he said.

"Good, we want to visit some of the ladies' shops. Don't worry if we are a little late, Will. This is our last visit to town before Christmas." She waved as she turned to enter a millinery shop.

He went across the street into a gun shop. It was about the size of Tom's shop and displayed a wide selection of handguns, rifles, and scatterguns.

"Looking for a firearm, sir?" said the clerk.

"I am," said Will. "In fact, I need several. I see you have a Remington New Army .44 in that case. May I see it?"

"Certainly, sir."

The clerk went to the case and unlocked the sliding door. He lifted out the revolver, checked the cylinder, and handed the pistol to Will.

"That's a mighty fine pistol, sir. Well-made, reliable. That particular one is brand new, never been fired."

Will took the revolver in his right hand. The revolver felt like the handshake of an old friend, familiar, firm, and comfortable.

He turned and aimed the pistol at the far wall. He squeezed the pistol grip. Not quite there, he thought. The .44 caliber required a firm grip when

117

fired.

He transferred the pistol to his left hand. It was equally as comfortable in that hand. Will knew he would have no trouble firing it with his left hand.

He turned back to the clerk. "Is this the only new one you have?" he asked.

The clerk pulled a ring of keys from his pocket and opened one of the cabinets along the back wall behind the counters. He studied the boxes and selected one of them.

"No, sir. I have one other here. Just like that one, brand new," the clerk replied.

"Set the two of them aside, please," said Will.

The clerk's smile was almost audible.

"Is that the new Spencer rifle?" Will asked as he nodded toward a rifle on the wall.

"Yes. That's a .56-50 caliber. Seven shot repeater."

He handed the rifle to Will.

"Twenty-eight-inch barrel?" inquired Will.

"It is. You seem to know your weapons, sir," said the clerk.

"I've had some experience with firearms," he said with a smile.

"I heard Henry is coming out with a new rifle, a 16-shot rifle. Have you heard anything about it?" Will said.

"Yes, sir. We are down for a dozen, but we don't expect them for a few months."

"This will do until then," said Will.

"Yes, sir."

"I'm not one to carry a pistol in my belt," said Will. "So I'll need holsters and a supply of ammunition and caps."

"Sir, are you wanting a double holster? If so, I would have to order it. It would take a few weeks."

"That's all right. I'll pay for it, and you can order it. In the meantime, let me see the left-hand outfits you have in stock."

He was shown a selection of holsters and belts and selected an ornate set in mahogany leather.

The clerk put the order together and wrapped it in a secure bundle.

Will was about to pay the clerk and stopped.

"Wait, I think I'd also like to have a smaller-caliber revolver. Two of them as a matter of fact. A cartridge pistol. What do you have?" asked Will.

"I think I have just the thing for you, sir. You will appreciate the rarity and beauty of these pistols. They are high dollar. But a man with your knowledge of weapons will see the quality right away."

The clerk went to another of the cabinets and retrieved a box. He placed it on the counter top and opened it, revealing two matching engraved pistols nestled in a custom-made walnut case, along with two boxes of cartridges.

"These are matching Moore .32-caliber pistols. Very hard to come by," he said.

Will was familiar with the pistols. He picked one up and liked the feel of the small pistol.

"I'll take them," he said.

Will extracted the cash from his pocket.

The clerk had a big smile on his face as he packed the last purchase.

"Sir, you have purchased some fine weapons. I know you will enjoy them. Check with me in a few weeks. I'll have the belt and holster ready for you."

"Wait. I just realized that I will have a hard time carrying these. Is it possible to have them delivered to my hotel?"

"Why, of course, sir. Where are you staying?"

"At the Union, Jefferson and Water Street. Sunday, Will Sunday is my name."

"Well, Mr. Sunday. We do appreciate your business. We will have those to you very shortly."

After returning home Will asked Ish to help him take his packages to his room. He took several gifts he had purchased and put them under his bed. He unwrapped the guns and placed them on the bed.

"Looks like somebody went to the gun shop," said Ish.

"Yes. I've been around firearms all my life. And frankly I missed having them. I bought a good rifle and several pistols. After I make some adjustments I'd like to fire them. Is there a safe place to shoot nearby?"

"Let me think. All I ever shoot is my old scattergun. Yep, there's a rise a little ways behind my house, and it would be safe to shoot into the bank. You'd need some help getting there. I'll see you make it," said Ish.

"Thank you, Ish. I'll take you up on that when I finish the work on the

Finding Mr. Sunday

guns."

Mary Nel called down the hall.

"We are about ready to eat, Will."

"Coming," said Will.

Will made his way down the hall and sat down at the table. As usual he was hungry. The kitchen, as well as the rest of the house, was decorated with little reminders of the season. After placing the rest of the dishes on the table, Kate and Mary Nel sat down. Following a prayer of thanks, dishes were passed around.

"You did very well with the trip into Jefferson City, Will. All that hard work you have been doing seems to have been beneficial," said Kate.

"It truly has. I'm not nearly as tired as I was at first. My leg is getting stronger every day. My right hand has a little way to go, but it's slowly returning to normal," he said.

"I bought some guns in town today, and I have some work to do on them. Then, if you have no objections, I'd like to do some shooting. Ish said he knew of a place behind his house where I could shoot safely."

"I thought I saw a package that looked like a rifle. Did you buy other guns?" asked Kate.

"Yes, I bought four pistols — two matching pairs — and a belt and holster for the left hand. I ordered a double holster. I don't normally wear two pistols, but I need to practice with both hands to get my shooting skills back. I've really missed shooting. It's always been a big part of my life."

No one spoke for a while. Will could sense Kate might have some concerns with this.

"It is all right that I shoot? I mean, will it bother you if I do?" he asked.

"I understand what guns and shooting mean to you. It is a little hard for me to see the importance of having guns around. You have to understand I was not raised around guns. My father wasn't much of a hunter. Ben actually disliked guns. But if it is important to you, by all means, shoot all you want," she said.

"Well, I won't shoot if you would rather me not. It can wait, I guess. I do feel strongly that anyone going west should know guns, how to use them, and how to respect them for what they are. I know my interest in guns may seem unusual to some, but that's just how I was raised."

120

"And I respect that, Will. So you shoot as much as you want. Really. I have no objections."

Will heard the words, but he could see she was not being totally honest. Something about his shooting or guns bothered her. He decided he would go ahead and work on the guns but would hold off shooting until after Christmas had passed.

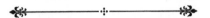

Christmas morning began with a breakfast that could have been served at the finest hotels. The five of them ate a long, leisurely meal, after which they retired to the parlor to enjoy tea, coffee, and a very special eggnog that Ish had made. Everyone exchanged gifts; most were handmade items or purchased sweet treats, nuts, and candies. Will found a beautiful hand painted silk scarf for Maggie and a lambskin vest for Ish. Both were delighted.

Will handed one brightly wrapped small box to Kate and one to Mary Nel.

"I hope you both like these," he said.

He could hardly wait to see their faces when they opened the gifts.

Mary Nel's eyes widened as she took the gift in her hands. For a moment she admired the pretty wrapping, then she slowly and carefully unwrapped the box. She opened the box and inhaled sharply with a brilliant smile.

A small solid gold pendant of a bird in flight hung from a gold chain. The detail of the piece was spectacular, and the bird's eyes were made of rubies.

"Oh, Will!" she said. "It's so beautiful. I don't know what to say. I've never had anything like this."

"Put it on and let's see how it looks," he said, pleased with her response.

She put the necklace around her neck. It looked stunning against her flawless skin.

She got up from her seat and gave Will a warm embrace.

"Thank you, Will. It is the prettiest thing I've ever had," she said, smiling.

"I'm glad you like it," he said with a big grin. "Now, Kate, open yours."

"Yes, Momma, open yours," said Mary Nel excitedly.

Kate unwrapped the box with great care to preserve the wrapping and the bright red ribbon. She lifted the top of the box, and her mouth dropped, and she, too, seemed genuinely shocked.

"Oh, my!" she said.

She lifted out a beautiful broach of gold and gems in the shape of a blossom. The gold filagree was inlaid with small rubies, sapphires, diamonds, and emeralds that glittered in the light as she held it up for all to see. Without question it was a unique piece of jewelry made by a master craftsman.

Kate was speechless for a moment, unable to say anything. She just stared at the piece.

"Oh!" she said, coming back to reality. "I've never seen anything quite so beautiful."

"But do you like it?" Will said with a chuckle.

"It's lovely ... It's ... I'm speechless. Will, you shouldn't have done this ..."

"Nonsense. Without you and everyone else here, I don't know where I'd be now," he said.

"Oh, Momma! It's beautiful! Here, let me pin it on you," said Mary Nel.

She put the broach in just the right spot below the lace collar of Kate's dress.

"Ah, yes, that's exactly where that piece was meant to be," he said with satisfaction.

Mary Nel and Kate seemed to glow with happiness. Will knew he had made the right choices.

The new year came bringing snow and very cold weather. The apple orchard turned to a spectacular forest of lace sculptures. Most days were spent indoors. When the weather permitted Will spent hours sawing and splitting wood, building back the strength in his young body. Other days, he availed himself of the many books in the household.

Mary Nel read from her stack of new books and continued her knitting and sewing lessons with Kate and Maggie. Ish spent time mending harnesses and tack, sharpening tools, and repairing the wagons.

"Ish, do you think we can get down to that shooting spot some time soon? I've worked on the guns, and I'd like to see how they shoot," said Will.

The two of them were in the barn working on one of the wagon beds. The latest snowfall had melted, and the skies were clear of clouds.

"I think so. I see you getting around without that crutch. You might need it, though, to go in those woods," Ish replied.

Ish had worked hard with Will almost every day and deserved much credit for Will's continuing recovery. In the process they had become good friends. Will had learned that Ish was wise in many ways. In turn, Ish had learned that Will was an unusual young man with many talents and an amazing ability to learn new things.

"I haven't said anything more to Kate about shooting, but I'll tell her what we intend to do. I have the sense she doesn't like guns," said Will.

"It's the war done that, Will. She took care of so many men shot to pieces. Mr. Ben dying, too. She's not seen any value to a gun," Ish said gravely.

"I can understand that. I'm not going to try to convince her otherwise. I'd just feel better if I was able to practice some. Especially with my right hand."

"Miz Kate is strong minded. You wise not to try to change her mind. We'll go shooting when you want to, Mr. Will."

A couple of days later the weather was clear and milder than normal. Ish and Will prepared to go shooting. The double holster had come in, and Will was pleased with the workmanship. Will put on the gun belt, and Ish helped him pack the other guns and ammunition in a leather satchel.

They went into the kitchen where Mary Nel and Kate sat at the table working on a dress for Mary Nel. Kate looked up and saw the gun belt around Will's waist, the rifle in his hand, and Ish carrying the satchel.

"Kate, Ish and I are going to be shooting in the woods. Don't be alarmed if you hear the guns."

"All right, Will," she said with a polite smile. "You enjoy shooting. We will have a meal ready when you return. I see you're taking your crutch. A good idea. Going through the woods may be a little difficult."

"Just a precaution. But I won't need it when I shoot."

"Oh, Momma. Can I go with them? I'd like to see Will shoot," said Mary Nel excitedly.

Finding Mr. Sunday

"Not this time," said Kate.

She saw the disappointment on Mary Nel's face and added, "But when Will tells us he is ready, he can demonstrate his skills to both of us."

She patted Mary Nel's hand, "Is that all right with you, Will?

"Yes, ma'am," he said, smiling. "I'll let you know."

He and Ish went out the door. Will had a little smile on his face.

With minimal use of the crutch, Will made it to the embankment. They had brought a grain bag partially full of tin can targets, and Ish set them up in front of the embankment. Will had no difficulty standing or moving about, so he set the crutch aside.

"I want to check the trigger pull," said Will.

He loaded the two Remington pistols and the two Moore .32 calibers. He fired the big Remingtons first.

With his left hand he aimed carefully at the targets about thirty feet away. His first shot was a close miss. He aimed and fired again. This time the can kicked up in the air. He continued to fire the pistol, carefully and slowly, missing only one of the four remaining shots.

Using his right hand next, he aimed the second Remington carefully, squeezed the trigger, and missed the target. He fired slowly three more times, hitting only one can. He knew his right hand was weak but had not anticipated his aim would be off to such an extent. He fired the pistol twice more, missing both times.

"I guess I shouldn't have expected so much. My right hand needs lots more recovery," he said.

"Will, I'm surprised you done this good. You just need more practice, that's all," said Ish.

He reloaded the big Remingtons several times. The more he fired, the more accurate he became. His left hand was deadly accurate. His right was still off and tiring rapidly. He loaded the two .32-caliber cartridge pistols and was pleased with their balance and accuracy. He fired the rifle and missed the targets only a couple of times.

He rested for a few minutes.

"I want to try one more thing, Ish," said Will. "Would you set up six more cans while I load the Army?"

"Glad to."

124

He stepped to the embankment and set up the cans.

Will moved back about fifty feet from the targets. He placed the loaded pistol in the left holster. He stood with his feet slightly apart, both hands down at his side. He counted to himself. On the count of three the .44 seemed to appear magically in Will's hand as it shot forward. He fired the pistol six times at almost the same speed that one could count the numbers. Five times the cans danced in the air.

Ish was flabbergasted and stood there wide-eyed with his mouth open, despite the lingering gun smoke.

"My Lordy," he said, shaking his head back and forth. "I never seen shooting like that in all my born days. Nothing like that."

"I've been shooting a long time. Almost every day since I was nine. I was taught by one of the best shooters in Missouri. It took some time today to get warmed up. But now it feels as natural to me as it always has."

He holstered the .44 and paused a minute, looking at the targets.

"But I shouldn't have missed that one time. And I need to work on my right hand. It's my best shooting hand. It's going to take some time, but with more practice, I'll get it all back," said Will.

"Let's pack up and go home. One of these .44's needs a little work. We'll come back here again soon."

Ish and Will began to clean up the site and pack the weapons.

"Never seen no shooting like that. No, sir," Ish was mumbling to himself.

The practice shooting became a regular event. It wasn't long before his shooting ability was as good as it was before the injury.

Several days later Ish and Will made a trip into town to have some corn ground into meal. The day was cold but clear.

"Ish, would you mind dropping me by the sheriff's office? I want to say hello and see if there is any news on those two thugs on the trail," said Will.

"Sure, I'll head over to the mill. I'm going from there to the general store, and I'll catch up to you," said Ish.

Will, limping slightly, went into the sheriff's office. The office was warm, and the strong smell of coffee greeted Will immediately.

"Well, hello there, Will. Good to see you getting about so well." The sheriff got up from his desk and came around to shake Will's hand.

"I'm about back to normal, sheriff. I'm helping out at the farm with some of the chores, chopping wood and such. Never felt better. Course this right leg is still a little stiff, but it will get back to normal soon."

Sheriff Wilkes gave Will's two guns an appraising look.

"Don't see that much. Most men carry one pistol, and it's in their belt."

"I just got used to a holster early on. Don't normally wear a double rig, but I'm trying to get both my shooting hands back. I practice every day I can."

"I'd keep those handy. We got some bad goings on up at Bonnot's Mill, north of here along the river. Couple of farms hit by some no goods. A bunch of them shot up a farmer and his son last week, stole what money they could find and a horse," said the sheriff.

"They weren't the same fellows I met on the trail, were they?" Will asked. His face clouded over.

"Not that I know of. Most of the law 'round here know I'm looking for those two, and they'd let me know. These fellows are war rabble. Seem to be coming out of the woodwork all over. Specially along the Missouri River. Lots of it going around in the countryside."

"We don't see too many strangers. But you can bet I won't make the same mistake twice, sheriff. We'll keep an eye out," Will said.

"You going to stay at Mrs. Daniels' place a while?" the sheriff asked.

"Until spring probably. She didn't want to accept it, but I pay room and board. They are some of the finest people I've ever known. Ish and Maggie, too. I've grown to like them all."

"They're all the salt of the earth," said Sheriff Wilkes.

"Miz Daniels would be 'specially easy to like," said the sheriff, and he quickly added. "No disrespect meant."

Will was a little surprised at the comment but replied quickly. "She's a fine lady. Never met a woman like her. Tough, smart, hard-working. Highly principled. And she's as kind as they come. Her daughter's just like her, just a bit more spirited. It's going to be hard leaving there. Feels like home."

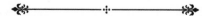

January turned to February, and the weather reminded all that nature often ignores the wishes of mankind and sets its own agenda.

Dick Ward

Will, Kate, and Mary Nel were sitting around the kitchen table, the center of the household and main venue for gathering. Will was going through a stack of printed material and maps, setting some aside and reading others with great interest. Mary Nel picked up some of the papers.

"These maps make California look closer than I know it is. Are they accurate, Will?" she asked.

"Oh, yes," he said. "They are very accurate, according to Mr. Wells. He owns the biggest freight company in Jefferson City. He's been to California several times and said these are the best maps."

Kate picked up one of the maps and studied it closely.

"About how long does it take to get to California by wagon train, Will?" Kate asked.

"About three and a half to four months. Sometimes a little more. Depends on the weather, the cutoff routes you take and where you are going in California," said Will.

"That's a long time to be living out of a wagon. Has to be a hard trip on a body," said Kate.

"I think it would be fun and exciting, Momma. I would like to go some day, maybe to Sacramento or San Francisco," said Mary Nel.

"I think it will be fun and exciting, too, Mary Nel. That's part of the reason I want to go by wagon. I really want to see this country," Will said.

"What about the danger from Indians?" asked Kate.

"There have been a few problems lately. But I was told the Indians are generally peaceful along the trail. They like to trade, like to get food. From time to time they might steal livestock," Will said. "That could change anytime. You never know.

"The biggest problems seem to be disease and accidents. Cholera has been a problem. But that's been a problem even in St. Louis.

"The river crossings are safer now. There are ferries in place, even bridges. Over the last twenty-five years, travelers seem to have narrowed the trail to the easiest routes. I think the best way to have a good trip is to prepare adequately and to find an experienced guide that you can trust."

He put down the map he had in his hand.

"Mr. Wells gave me the name of one of the best guides he knows. He said he was back in Independence until the next spring train. I'm planning to go see him soon," Will said. "When I leave this time, I want to be fully prepared."

"I know this is very important to you, Will. But I don't like the thought of you leaving," said Mary Nel, with sadness in her voice.

The words hung in the air for a moment. Kate got up from the table to go to another room.

As she walked behind Will's chair, she stopped, put her hands on both of his shoulders, leaned down and said, "Neither do I."

She patted his shoulders and left the room.

A few days later, Mr. Samuels paid a visit to the Daniels home. Kate, Mary Nel, and Will sat at the kitchen table enjoying cake, coffee, and tea with their neighbor. They talked about the weather and local news for a while. Mr. Samuels finished his cake and drained his coffee cup.

"A bountiful harvest, eh, Kate?" he said.

Kate knew that when Mr. Samuels addressed her as Kate he was about to get into his heart-to-heart manner. Most likely to talk about buying the orchard, she thought.

"Can we go into the parlor for a chat, Kate?" he asked. "No offense meant to you two. Just a little business talk."

"None taken," said Will.

He looked at Mary Nel, who was trying hard to suppress a grin. They both knew what was coming.

Mr. Samuels and Kate went into the parlor and sat down in two comfortable chairs, a small table and a lamp between them.

"Kate. I've been thinking about the future. For me. For Silas. And about yours, too, Kate. We've had this conversation before, but I don't think you've taken me seriously."

He stopped to take a deep breath.

"You are doing a fine job of running this orchard, and I admire what you have done." He paused.

Kate sat there, knowing what this was leading to and smiling inside. Yes, she had heard this before. But this time there was something a little different in the tone of Mr. Samuels' voice. There was a seriousness she had not sensed before.

"You come back here after you lost your husband, then you lost your daddy. You put your mind to running this place, and you worked a man's day every day and ran your household, too. In fact, I think this place is what has kept you going after all you been through," he continued.

His voiced softened, and he looked at her as a father might.

"But I don't think your heart is in it, Kate. Your mind is, but not your heart."

Mr. Samuels looked as if he wanted to reach out to her and hold her hand.

"Is this really want you want to do for the rest of your life?" he asked.

"You are a still a young woman, Kate. You are one of unusual courage and ability. This can't be giving you all you want out of life."

He reached into his coat pocket and pulled out some folded pieces of paper. He unfolded them and looked down as if reviewing the contents.

"I went to Jefferson City and met with the best land man I could find. He came out the other day, and we walked my property and, I confess, much of yours. And I asked him what he thought your land was worth, and if combined, what all of it would be worth.

"He went back and put a pencil to it. And he sent me his estimate. It's right here. I used his estimate for your land, Kate, but only as a reference.

"I've never really made a dollars and cents offer for your place. We never got that far. And that was a mistake and probably why you never took me seriously."

He paused. "So, Kate, here is a written offer for your place."

Mr. Samuels' hands shook slightly as he handed the papers to Kate.

Without giving her a chance to look at them, he said in his most sincere tone of voice, "Kate, I'm offering you two times what he said your land is worth... Two times."

She had never seen such seriousness in Mr. Samuels' face.

She looked at the offer. It was a lot of money. She had no idea what the property was worth, she thought. But she certainly didn't think it was worth that much. She stared at the papers for a moment, not saying anything.

"I know you won't accept the offer right now. But, Kate, please, don't reject it. Think about it. Talk it over with Mary Nel. Go to Jefferson City and get an expert to look at your place. You'll see it is a very generous offer.

"And don't worry about Ish and Maggie. I'm making them an offer, too."

Mr. Samuels was not one to mince words. He had finished his business.

Finding Mr. Sunday

He stood up and went to get his hat and overcoat from the nearby hall tree. He began putting them on.

"Mr. Samuels, I really don't know what to say. I need some time to think about all of this. It is not just a matter of selling the farm. It presents questions I can't answer right now. Many, as a matter of fact," she said.

"Thank you for coming to visit," she said as she stood and reached for his hand. "I'll be in touch with you."

"All right, Kate," he said. "You take all the time you need."

She walked to the door, let him out, and closed the door softly. She stood there a moment with a thousand thoughts clamoring for attention.

She went back into the kitchen and slid the tea kettle to a hot place on the stove and reached for the tea tin. She could feel the other two staring at her, waiting for her to say something. She ignored them for a moment, fixed her tea, and sat down. She looked at Mary Nel, then at Will.

"Well, Momma. Are you going to tell us what he said? I know he talked about buying the farm, didn't he?" she said with a smile.

Then, both Mary Nel and Will saw Kate had an unusual look on her face.

"Is everything all right, Momma?" Mary Nel said with concern.

"Oh, yes, honey. Everything is fine. I'm just trying to take it all in, that's all," she said.

"All of what?" Mary Nel asked.

"Well, Sweetheart. Mr. Samuels didn't just talk about buying the orchard and farm. He made me a written offer," she said.

"No-o-o. He was serious? Really serious?" Mary Nel asked in disbelief.

"Very serious. He brought in someone from Jefferson City to appraise the orchard and farm," she said.

Then without much pause she added. "And he offered me double the appraisal."

She looked at both of them. "Double."

"That's pretty serious," said Will without thinking.

He had not wanted to say anything. It wasn't for him to comment unless asked, he thought.

"What are you going to do, Momma?" asked Mary Nel.

"Oh, Mary Nel," she said. "I have no idea. He knew I wouldn't accept it. He just asked me to think about it.

"And I'm going to do a lot of thinking. You need to do a lot of thinking, too. Then we'll sit down and talk."

She turned to Will. "You have been through something like this, Will. At some point I would like to hear what went into your decision."

"I'll help you in anyway you need, Kate. I know this is a big decision and one you'll not want to rush," he said.

The following day the air was cold and brittle. Will was getting his gear ready to go shooting. He had been practicing every day the weather allowed. Though he still limped, he no longer needed the crutch. He generally practiced with the Remington Army pistols. His right hand was much improved, and he was better than ever.

Ish came into the door and said a hearty good morning to the three of them. He sat down at the table.

"Coffee, Ish?" asked Kate.

"No, thank you, Miz Kate. I'm full up."

"I had a visitor early this morning," he said looking at Kate. "Mr. Samuels."

"Yes. He said he was going to see you. I should have warned you, but I didn't want to interfere with your business," Kate said.

"When he talked to you all the time about buying your land, I never thought he would say anything to me about mine," said Ish.

"So, I suppose he made you an offer too, then," said Kate.

"Yes'm, he did," said Ish shaking his head. "He sure did."

"He made me an offer I would never believe," said Ish.

"I figured that," said Kate. "He's bent on having this land all right."

"Maggie ain't keen on leaving her home, not for any price. What you gonna do, Miz Kate?" Ish asked.

"I really don't know, Ish. I always thought I'd be here forever. I can understand how Maggie feels," she replied.

"Kate, I wouldn't put my nose in this, but you asked me about my experience in selling Tom's property. I think the first thing both of you should do is go ahead and get another land appraiser in Jefferson City to come out and give you his appraisal. It's just good business, even though Mr. Samuels' offer might sound generous."

"I think that's a good idea, Will. At least we will have a comparison," said

Finding Mr. Sunday

Kate.

"Yes," said Ish. "Let's do that."

Mid morning the following day, Goldie began barking loudly and repeatedly. Normally her bark was more of a greeting to visitors than a warning. But this time it was different. Kate, Mary Nel, Maggie, and Will were in the kitchen. Kate got up and went to front door. Four men on horseback were coming into the yard. Will followed her and saw the four men.

"Kate, I don't like the looks of those men," he said. "They may be trouble. Don't let them come in the house."

There was genuine concern in his voice.

He quickly turned and went to his room.

Kate opened the door.

"Goldie, come here. Come here, girl," she called.

The dog came to her but continued to growl and eye the strangers. She let the dog inside the house.

"Morning, ma'am," said one of the men.

He wore a heavy butternut overcoat, with black coarse woven trousers and a black felt hat. His boots were worn and cracked. The coal black whiskers failed to conceal the sharp, angular features of his face. He held the reins in dirty hands, his fingernails black with grime.

"We on our way to the Missouri. Ain't had nothing much to eat in a while. We was hoping you might spare us a little something."

She looked at the other men. All of them were unkempt, even more ragged and dirty than the spokesman. She knew these men might be dangerous.

"I suppose I could get you something. Tie your horses and wait here," she said.

She closed and locked the front door and returned to the kitchen.

"Maggie, these men are hungry. I don't like their looks, but I don't want to turn them away hungry. Will you help me get together some food for them? I want them to get on their way."

"I'll be happy to, Miz Kate," said Maggie.

She and Mary Nel began to put together plates of ham, bread, jam, pickles, and cheese.

Dick Ward

Will came into the kitchen. He wore his gun belt with the two Remington pistols. Kate looked down at the pistols but continued to prepare the food.

"You are feeding them?" Will asked, a slight tone of disapproval in his voice.

"Yes, Will," she said. "I don't like their looks, but they are hungry. I'm going to feed them and get them on their way."

He gave her a worried look but didn't say anything. Instead he went to the kitchen window that looked out on the porch and observed the men without revealing his presence.

The spokesman and apparent leader was sitting in one of the rocking chairs. The other three were sitting in a row on the edge of the porch and talking among themselves.

As soon as the plates were filled with food, Kate, Maggie, and Mary Nel took the food and some water out to the men. Without a word, the men grabbed the food and began to eat. There was no question they were hungry.

"Gawd, this is good," said the bearded leader.

He held the plate almost in front of his mouth, shoveling in the food. Kate couldn't help notice that he looked her up and down and paid particular attention to Mary Nel.

"Looks like a lot of work 'round here. Where's your man?" he said.

Kate did not like the look in the man's eyes. The comment was at the least disrespectful and bordered on lascivious.

"Oh, he's around," she said.

"Let's go inside, ladies. We shouldn't be out here without our coats," said Kate.

The three of them went inside, and Kate locked the door, leaving the men to finish their food without company. There was more loud talk among the men and regular bursts of laughter. Kate kept an eye on them from the kitchen window.

The men were soon finished eating. The men who had been seated on the porch had stacked the dishes and utensils on the porch and were huddled in the yard chewing tobacco or smoking pipes. Blackbeard had finished his meal and was sitting in a rocking chair, the empty plate in his lap.

Kate went out on the porch and bent to pick up the stack of plates on the porch. She then turned to Blackbeard as he stood up with his plate in his hands. He placed the plate on the stack.

"You men will want to get on your way, I'm sure," she said as she turned toward the front door.

Blackbeard leaped at her as she turned away with the dishes in her hand. He grabbed her from behind with both hands encircling her waist.

She screamed, and the dishes and utensils clattered to the floor. Blackbeard reached to his belt with his right hand, retrieved a large knife and held it near her throat. The men in the yard all turned to see Blackbeard holding a knife to the struggling Kate.

"Be still or I'll cut ya, I sure will."

He held the knife closer to her throat, and Kate stood motionless.

She felt and smelled his stinking breath on her neck.

The men in the yard looked at their leader and began to laugh.

"We gonna have us some fun, boys," said Blackbeard.

"The hell you are!" said Will as he jerked the front door open and stood there with a pistol in his right hand.

All the men froze and silenced.

Blackbeard turned to his right facing Will, still holding the knife to Kate's throat.

"Well, looky what we got here," he said with a grin. "A big man with a gun."

"You hurt a hair on her head, and I'll kill you," said Will through gritted teeth.

Blackbeard looked at the gun in Will's hand that was now pointed directly at his own head.

"You ain't much able to make threats," he said, laughing. "I can cut her throat in a second. 'Sides, I got three boys standing over there that'll shoot you and laugh while you was dying."

"Maybe, but if either one of them makes a move, I'm going to kill you first. I can promise you that," said Will, holding the pistol steadily.

"They ain't gonna move, Will!"

All eyes turned at the sound as Ish stepped around the corner of the house. The double barreled scattergun he held clicked audibly as he pointed it at the three men standing in the yard.

"I figure with both barrels of buckshot I can probably kill all three at once," Ish said with a wry smile.

Blackbeard glanced at the men who quickly lifted their hands in the air. He looked back at Will. Maggie and Mary Nel came up behind Will.

"Get back, ladies," Will said. "I'm about to shoot somebody."

They stepped back out of the doorway and into the house, leaving the door open.

"Now, real slowly. You lift that knife away from her and drop it. Any quick movements and I'll shoot you," Will said.

Will's eyes never strayed from Blackbeard's eyes. Blackbeard look like a cornered rat.

This was a Will that neither Kate nor Ish had seen. His eyes were cold and unflinching. His breathing was steady and deliberate.

Blackbeard looked at Will. Then his eyes cut to the men still holding their hands in the air. He could see both Ish and Will were ready to shoot.

"All right," he said. "All right. I'm gonna drop 'is knife. Don't shoot."

He very slowly moved the knife in a horizontal arc away from Kate's body, then lowered his arm to his right side, the knife pointing down. The knife clattered on the wooden porch.

Kate heard the knife drop. She had been thinking about her best move. She could jump off the porch to the left near where the other men stood or roll to the right up against the wall of the house. Going to the right would put her to the left of Will and safely out of the line of any gunfire.

She spun to the right and flattened herself against the wall.

Her movement momentarily blocked Will's view of Blackbeard, and Blackbeard reached for a pistol he carried in his belt on the left side, butt facing forward.

As Kate moved out of his view, Will saw Blackbeard's intentions. He fired the .44 at almost point blank range, the earsplitting roar magnified by the proximity of the wall.

A hole opened up in the middle of Blackbeard's forehead at the same time the back of his head exploded in a torrent of blood and gray matter. His body was thrown backward by the force of the shot. He came to rest with the lower part of his body staying on the porch and his upper body and what remained of his head resting in the yard.

The ear-shattering sound of the pistol was followed by an almost eerie silence. No one moved or spoke.

"Don't move a muscle!" shouted Ish as the men in the yard stood with their mouths open.

Kate stared down at the body that was leaking dark red onto the brown winter grass. Her hand flew to her mouth. Mary Nel and Maggie rushed out on to the porch and looked at the body, horror on their faces. They both clutched Kate.

Will holstered his pistol. Ish stepped closer to the men standing in the yard. He was the first to speak.

"Take off your overcoats," he said, keeping the shotgun aimed at them.

"No. No, please, Mister, don't shoot us," one of the men cried.

"Take off your coats," Will repeated.

The men removed their coats. Two of them had pistols in their belts. Ish retrieved them, then reached over, grabbed each coat and shook it. One of them was heavier, and he threw it to Will.

"That's probably a pistol in there, Will," Ish said.

Will picked up the coat and extracted a small pocket pistol. He turned to Kate.

"Kate, it's best if you three go inside," he said, putting his hand on her elbow.

"Will, please, no more killing," said Kate as she looked at him through teary eyes.

Will stepped close to her and said in her ear.

"Kate, we're going to make sure they are disarmed, then take all four to Sheriff Wilkes. Don't worry. Go inside and keep the doors locked. Don't open them for anyone. We'll be back as soon as possible."

He moved her gently to the doorway. She looked at him, shook her head sadly, followed the others through the doorway, and shut the door.

CHAPTER EIGHT

Will Sunday stepped from the deck of the steamboat and walked onto the south shore of the Missouri River. Several carriage drivers yelled to him, hoping to gain his fare to downtown Independence. He buttoned his overcoat and approached one of the carriages. "Downtown, sir?" barked the driver as he hopped down to take the leather case Will had in his hand.

"Yes," he said, holding on to his luggage. "To the court house square, please."

He climbed into the worn carriage seat and settled in just as the driver flicked his whip, putting the tired horse to what seemed to be its final test.

He had expected to see a larger, cleaner city. But in the afternoon light, Independence looked dirty, tired, and worn out, struggling to revive itself after the devastating war. As the ride continued out of the river valley, the scars of war pained the eye.

Pedestrians wandered aimlessly through the streets and milled about in front of dilapidated buildings. Strong differences remained among the residents, despite the end of the war. A cloud of bitterness hung over the city, and violence waited patiently in the shadows, ready to emerge at any moment.

The driver stopped the carriage in a part of the city that was closer to what Will had expected to see. Will climbed down, paid the driver, and walked a short distance to a two-story building bearing a single sign advertising rooms.

He opened the door and stepped into a plain lobby with a counter against the back wall, a door to the left and a stairway on the right. The man behind the desk seemed to welcome the interruption to the otherwise slow day.

"A room for two, maybe three nights," said Will.

"Yes, sir," said the clerk.

He paid the clerk for the room, took his key, and climbed the stairs to the second floor. The room was sparsely furnished with a bed, a table, an oil lamp, and a wash stand. Will set his leather case down and removed his overcoat and jacket.

Finding Mr. Sunday

He went to the washstand and poured water from the pitcher into the bowl and proceeded to wash his face and comb his hair. He took a brush from his luggage, brushed his trousers and jacket, then put on his jacket. He reached into his satchel and removed one of the Moore pistols and put it in his belt. He walked down the stairs and out into the late afternoon sun.

Main Street was alive as travelers sought lodging and others a good meal or a good drink. Will threaded through the streets looking for the address on Maple Street where he was to meet Hobs Adams. He stepped inside the tavern and walked up to the bar.

"Evening," he said to the bartender. "You happen to know a man by the name of Hobs Adams?"

"Sure do," said the bartender. "He's that big red-haired man at the table in the corner near the window."

Will walked to the table, looking at the man as he approached.

Hobs Adams was almost as big as Will. His red hair was neatly trimmed as was his bushy mustache. He wore a heavy shirt, a leather vest, and wool trousers stuffed into stove pipe boots. His face was weather-worn and deeply lined. His eyes were a clear blue in the fading light of the window.

He looked up as Will stopped at the table and pulled out a chair.

"You must be Will Sunday," said Adams.

He stood to shake Will's hand. "Hobson Adams."

"Yes, sir," said Will as he felt Adams' firm grip.

"Have a sit down," said Adams.

Will sat down across from Adams and looked closer at the man. Adams looked a man in the eye. That was good. He had a firm but friendly-looking demeanor. Will liked the looks of him right away.

"It's a pleasure to meet you, Mr. Adams. I've heard a lot about you. You come highly recommended," said Will.

"Well, son. A man oughta believe none of what he hears and only half of what he sees," Adams said with a friendly chuckle.

"You're a might younger than I thought you'd be. Come here from St. Louis, did you?" asked Adams.

"Indirectly," said Will. "I've been staying with some friends in Linn for a while. Just east of Jefferson City."

"You plan on going to California by yourself?" asked Adams.

"That's the plan. It might change, but I doubt it," said Will.

"You know with the train and stage coach, a man can mostly go all the way now, without having to take a wagon train. If you're traveling by yourself, you might want to consider that," said Adams.

"Yes, sir. I've thought about that. But I know there aren't as many wagon trains as there used to be, and I don't want to miss the chance to see the country between here and there. You see, I was raised in the city, and I didn't really like it. So the trail route appeals to me," he said.

"Oh, you'll see plenty of country between here and there all right. Over two thousand miles of it. Every kind of country you can imagine. Plains as far as the eye can see, snow-capped mountains, rivers, rain, snow, dust so thick a man can taste it for months. You'll never want to see another sage plant as long as you live. You'll see it all. Sometimes more'n you want," said Adams.

Adams studied Will's face.

"I don't aim to discredit you, son. You look like a strong man. But this trip is about as far away from city life as you can get. Sometimes you're hungry, sometimes you're thirsty, and it's real work for everyone on the train."

"I'm pretty sure I can handle it," said Will a little defensively.

"I noticed a little limp. Is that permanent or did you hurt yourself?" asked Adams.

"Time will tell. A little accident. It's getting better, and it won't affect my ability to make the trip or pull my weight."

Will hid his concern that he might have to live with a limp for the rest of his life.

"Good," said Adams. "I run a pretty tight operation, Will. Everybody pitches in. We have a charter and rules. Everybody agrees to them, or they don't go with me."

He paused to let that sink in.

"It's the only way we can do it. I got the charter here, a list of rules, and a list of supplies you'll need. I got some recommendations on equipment, where to get it and so on. Hiram Young is back in Independence now, and his wagons are as good as they come.

"In addition to a wagon and several teams, I'd suggest you have a good trail horse, maybe two. And a good rifle and pistol. They're on the list."

Will took the papers from Adams and stuffed them in his jacket pocket. As he did so, Adams saw the pistol in his belt.

"I see you carry a pistol. With all the mess going on around here, that's a good idea. Just a word of advice. It's one thing to carry a pistol, but you better know how to use it when trouble comes. And be willing to use it," said Adams.

"Yes, sir. I know what you mean. I can use it well enough," Will said with a smile.

Will liked Hobs Adams. He had an easy way of getting his message across without offense. It was apparent he was comfortable dealing with people.

"Do you have supper plans, Will? I know a good meat and taters place nearby. Least I'm hoping they got some meat. Why don't you join me? I can tell you more about the trip," said Adams.

"I'd enjoy that, sir," Will said.

"By the way, son, I appreciate your manners. I can tell you were raised right. But drop the 'sir.' Everybody calls me Hobs," said Adams.

"All right, Hobs it is," said Will with a smile.

Yes, he liked this man.

It was a full two hours later that they both sat back in their chairs, having enjoyed a simple but delicious meal of cabbage, turnips, and roast beef, fresh baked bread, and butter. Prices were high, but the meal and the discussions were worth the expense. It was apparent the two men enjoyed each other's company.

They had talked of many things. Hobs had told Will a great deal about what to expect on the trip. In turn, Will had taken the opportunity to tell Hobs about himself, his past, and his desire to go west.

"You've got quite a story, Will. I like the way you handle yourself, too. We're gonna get along fine."

"Thank you, Hobs. I'm sure we will," said Will.

"The month of May will be here 'fore you know it. I've got twenty or so wagons lined up already. Probably gonna have around forty or fifty. Not as many folks starting out at Independence as there were. Now most head up farther north to start. But I like the old trail. It's the one I know best," said

Adams.

"You can telegraph me at the address on the handout. Let's agree to keep in touch 'tween now and then. Let me know if you need any help on my end," said Adams.

"I'm going to spend the day tomorrow looking at equipment and finding a couple of good horses. If I think of anything while I'm still here in town, I'll see you before I leave. But I will keep in touch over the next couple of months," said Will.

The two men stood up, put on their coats, and walked to the doorway. They shook hands and parted just outside the door.

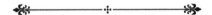

Noise from the taverns and gin mills colored the cool night air. Piano and banjo music poured forth with conflicting melodies and tempos. A staggering passerby going in and out of the shadows seemed more the norm than the exception. Will kept a wary eye as he worked his way along the boardwalk back to the courthouse square.

As he passed one of the gin mills, a tall skinny man came staggering out of the door and stopped just short of running into him. The man was quite drunk and unsteady on his feet. Will stopped to look closer at the man.

Startled, Will took in a quick breath as he recognized the bulging eyes and large teeth. And the derby. Burt! One of the fellows on the trail the night he was shot. The man stood there weaving back and forth, a puzzled look on his face.

Will looked him up and down again. My boots! His beautiful boots were scuffed and beaten up, but there was no mistaking them.

Anger welled up in Will as he stepped to within inches of the man. The rage came to him as he grabbed the drunk by the lapels of his coat with both hands and slammed him hard against the wall of the tavern, knocking off his derby and bringing momentary sobriety to the wide-eyed drunk.

"You! You were on the trail the night before I was shot!" yelled Will.

The man's stinking breath and body odor nearly overwhelmed Will, his face only inches from the other man's face. He could tell the man remembered him.

Finding Mr. Sunday

The drunken man shook his head from side to side. "No. No. Didn't shoot you. Didn't shoot you," he stammered.

"But you remember me, don't you? You're wearing my boots, damn you. And you know who shot me," growled Will.

"Who did it? Who shot me? You tell me, or I'll break your neck. Right now. You tell me!"

Will shook the man and slammed him against the wall again with such force the drunk rolled his eyes, about to pass out. He slumped downward, but Will's firm grasp held him up.

"Hurley! Hurley shot you. In the morning ... you were pissin'." The man began to shake and whine.

"Hurley. I thought so. The fat pig," said Will.

"Where is he? Where's Hurley now?" Will shook the man again as if to punctuate his question.

"Shack Town. Down by the river. He's on a drunk. With the whores and mule skinners," gasped the man.

"Tell me where it is. Now!" yelled Will.

"The old river landing. Tents. Shacks. Big campfire."

Will relaxed the grip on the man's coat. The drunk slid down the wall and settled on the boardwalk and covered his head with his arms. He knew this man was a simpleton, but he was capable of being dangerous if given the chance.

"If you tell him I saw you, I'll find you again. You hear me?" Will said.

"I hear. I hear," said Burt as he covered his head with both arms. He didn't look up at Will. Just sat there without moving.

Will lost no time getting back to the rooming house. He climbed the steps two at a time, ignoring the tightness in his right leg. He went into his room and picked up his leather case. He removed the Moore pocket pistol from his belt and strapped on the two Army revolvers he had brought with him. He checked the caps on each of the cylinders. Then he went down the steps as quickly as he could.

Calm down, he said to himself. Control. You don't need to do anything foolish.

But he was not going to let this opportunity pass.

Outside he saw a driver sitting in the seat of his carriage, his chin on his

142

chest, napping. It was now completely dark outside.

"Hey!" he yelled at the driver.

The driver jumped awake and grabbed the reins as if readying himself for a quick departure, then stopped himself and looked down at Will.

"Yes, sir."

"You know a place they call Shack Town, down by the old landing?" Will asked as he breathed heavily.

"Yessuh, but you don' wanna go down 'ere. They bad men. Robbers, killers. They drunk, too," he said, wide awake now.

Will reached into his pocket.

"Here, five dollars. You take me down there. Wait in the shadows. I won't let anybody hurt you. I'll give you five more dollars when you bring me back here."

The driver's eyes widened at his own good luck. Five dollars was a lot of money. Ten dollars was even better.

"Yes, sir. Yes, sir," he said as he grabbed the money and stuffed it in his coat pocket.

Will climbed up to the passenger seat and sat on the edge of the seat, holding on to the canopy frame.

"Go! Go!" Will said.

He sat back heavily in the seat as the driver hit the mule with his whip.

They went quickly down the street toward the river, past the new landing and onto the weedy and rutted road that led to the old steamboat landing. Banjo music and off key singing could be heard over the sound of the carriage as they neared the camp.

A big log fire cast a glow on the tents and makeshift hovels that surrounded it. The smell of smoke from the fire could not totally block out the stench of cooking cabbage and human refuse.

"Stop here and wait for me. Remember, five more dollars," said Will.

They were fifty or so yards from the camp hidden in the shadow of the woods.

"Turn the carriage around and be ready to leave in a hurry," said Will.

He could easily make out the road ahead. He walked carefully to the edge of the clearing, staying out of the light and surveying the scene. Four or five drunks were around the fire. Some sat cross-legged on the ground, and others sat unsteadily on a large log. Several jugs lay about, and one was being passed around.

Will stood there for a few minutes trying to recognize Hurley without success. Then a man stood up slowly and weaved his way to a narrow space between one of the flimsy shacks and a hut. He stood there in the shadows, relieving himself against the wall of the shack.

Will moved quickly to the opposite side of the shack, walked around behind it, and came up close to the man.

The man was wearing his pants and an undershirt, his suspenders hung down on both sides of his hips. He looked up at Will, trying hard to focus in the dim light. Had he been less inebriated he would have been startled.

"Who the hell are you?" the man slurred as he fumbled to button his pants.

"Easy. Easy. No trouble. Not for you, anyway," said Will.

He spoke softy, not wanting to alarm the drunk.

"I'm looking for a man named Hurley. A short fat fellow, has a face like a pig. You know him?"

The clink of silver dollars could be heard as Will rummaged in his pocked and withdrew several. He held them up to the man who eyed them greedily through foggy eyes.

"Yeah. I know the som'bitch. Come 'ere."

He staggered close to the front of the shack and pointed to one of the bigger shacks across the way.

"He in 'ere. With a whore. He shoot yo' ass, you go in 'ere."

The man looked at Will, and his head moved in little circles.

Will handed three silver dollars to the man. He held out cupped hands to receive the coins and grinned broadly.

"Go on back to the fire. Don't say anything. Just keep drinking and having your fun," Will said.

He watched as the man put the coins in his pocket and stumbled back toward the campfire.

A dirty sheet served as a door to the shack. Instead of walking directly to the doorway, Will walked to one side, completely around the shack, and came up on the doorway from the other side. This way, he could peek into the curtain without presenting a large silhouette to those inside.

Dick Ward

There was a single lamp on a rickety table in the corner and a platform of sorts served as a bed. Hurley, wearing a dirty underwear top and pants, was reclined on the bed leaning against the wall of the shack. A fat, partially clad woman was sitting on the edge of the bed turned toward him.

They passed a bottle back and forth, talking and laughing in low tones. The smell of unclean humanity assailed Will's nostrils. He could not determine whether Hurley was armed or had a pistol nearby. He pushed open the curtain and bent to go in the doorway. He could not stand fully erect as the ceiling was low.

Hurley struggled to sit up in the bed. "Git the hell outta here. This my place tonight," said Hurley in an angry tone.

The woman whirled around and saw Will towering over them.

"Get out," Will said. "And keep your mouth shut."

She gasped loudly, grabbed for her clothes, and covered herself. The forgotten bottle tumbled to the floor of the shack.

He took her by the arm, lifted her to her feet, and pushed her to the doorway. She ran out of the shack clutching her clothes. All the time Will kept an eye on Hurley.

"We're going to share this shack for a few minutes," said Will through clenched teeth.

Hurley's eyes widened in shock and fear as the memory of Will seeped through his drunken haze.

"Yes … it's me, Hurley. The fellow you shot on the trail a while back. You thought I was dead, didn't you?" said Will.

"I ain't shot you. You got the wrong fella. I don't 'eem know you," Hurley whined in his high-pitched voice.

Hurley moved cautiously to the edge of the bed and put his feet on the floor. His pig eyes opened wide as he stared up at Will, who towered over him. Looking up, the memory of Will's size came back to him.

"Oh, yes, you did. I ran into Burt. He told me what happened. I knew one of you shot me. I figured it was you. You wanted to get to those wooden crates," said Will in a now calmer voice.

All of a sudden, Will remembered his promise to himself. There was no rage this time. Something else took its place. It was hard, cold, and deliberate. Almost unfeeling. Anything he did now he meant to do.

145

Finding Mr. Sunday

"No, sir, I didn't ..."

Hurley never finished the sentence.

Will leaned over and slapped him hard in the face. Hurley's head slammed against the flimsy wall, and he slumped to the floor. He lay there whimpering and shaking.

"Get up, damn you," said Will.

He spoke evenly and unemotionally.

He grabbed Hurley by the hair, lifted him up, and threw him back on the bed. Hurley was slobbering and bleeding from the mouth.

Will could not stand to look at the man. This was the man who shot him, tried to kill him, just to get what Will owned. He was an animal, not a man. Will fought the rage coming on.

"Sit up. I ought to kill you, but I'm not going to. I'm taking you to the law in Independence. We'll let them take care of you," said Will. "Get dressed."

Hurley looked up at him. Will could see the contempt in Hurley's eyes. Apparently the knowledge Will wasn't going to kill him emboldened him. Or maybe he just refused to grasp the situation. Hurley didn't move.

Will grabbed him by the hair again with his left hand and backhanded him solidly with his right. He held Hurley in place as he tried to cower and cover his face with his arms.

"Now get dressed. I want to get rid of your stinking body as soon as I can," said Will.

He let go of Hurley. Hurley began to get dressed. He picked up a shirt and started putting it on. He managed to get it buttoned over his fat gut, then slipped his suspenders over his shoulder. Will could see a pair of boots and kicked them toward Hurley. Hurley struggled but finally got the boots on his feet.

He looked around the shack and located his hat. He reached for it, put it on, and picked up his coat from the floor near the table. Will immediately saw a large pistol on the floor where the coat had been. He stepped on the pistol.

"I'll take this," he said as he bent down to pick up the heavy revolver.

He stuffed the pistol in his belt, grabbed Hurley by the arm, and shoved him through the curtained doorway and out into the firelight.

Most of the men around the fire paid no attention to them. The banjo player never stopped playing. Only the man who had pointed out Hurley took notice. Will pushed Hurley ahead of him.

"Head down the road. You run or try anything else, I'll shoot you. You say anything I don't want to hear, I'll hurt you," said Will coldly.

Hurley half shuffled, half stumbled as Will pushed him toward the waiting carriage. He mentally crossed his fingers, hoping the carriage was still there.

Then he saw the carriage. The driver had waited, his lantern turned as low as possible.

"We have another passenger," said Will as he shoved Hurley to the carriage.

"You have any rope or anything to tie his hands?" said Will.

The driver reached under his seat, pulled out his rope tether, and handed it to Will.

Will carefully tied Hurley's hands behind his back, making sure the ropes were tight and the knots secure.

"Get up there," said Will.

He stood close as Hurley climbed awkwardly into the carriage and heaved his body into the seat. Will followed him and sat down beside him.

The man reeked of body odor, and his breath was putrid. Hurley showed only slight signs of intoxication now. The fun was over.

"Do you know where the sheriff's office is, driver?" said Will.

"Yes, sir. In the jail near the square," replied the driver.

"Go there," said Will. "Don't worry about the rough road, just go."

The driver hit the mule with the whip. The mule plunged into the darkness without delay. He knew he was going back to town.

The carriage stopped in front of a brick building not far from the courthouse. Will got down first and helped Hurley down. He paid the driver and walked inside the building, holding Hurley securely by the arm. He remembered he had not searched Hurley since he put on his coat.

There was a counter almost immediately in front of the door. Behind it and to the right and left were several empty tables with chairs. A hallway leading to the cells was on the left side of the lobby, guarded by a door made of metal bars. Several offices were on the right side of the lobby.

A uniformed officer wearing sergeant stripes sat on a stool behind the

Finding Mr. Sunday

counter. He was an average-sized man but had a perpetual scowl on his face that gave him a mean look. He looked at well-dressed and clean Will holding on to the dirty, short, and fat Hurley, then he addressed Will.

"What do we have here?" he said.

The scowl didn't disappear, and the tired tone suggested the policeman didn't want to deal with any problems.

Will spoke. "Officer, my name is Will Sunday. About six months ago I was on the trail headed here. Just east of Jefferson City, I was camped by the trail, and this man and a buddy of his stopped by my camp. I fed them, and they left after awhile. I was carrying a couple wooden crates with personal belongings in them, mostly guns. These fellows took a big interest in those crates.

"That next morning someone shot me, took my horses, all of my equipment, and my cash. A farmer came along and found me the next morning and took me into Linn, Missouri. I was in a coma for a while, and I'm still recovering from the head wound."

"He's lyin' … I ain't shot nobody. I don't 'eem know 'em," said Hurley.

"Sheriff Wilkes in Linn will verify my story. I ran into this guy's partner tonight. He told me Hurley here shot me. The guy's a half wit, but I believe he was telling the truth."

"He's a damn liar," said Hurley. "I don't have no partner. I been breaking mules for Mr. Johns here in town."

"Officer, if I have to, I'll hunt down his partner and bring him in. He'll tell you the truth as long as Hurley isn't present. He's afraid of Hurley," Will said.

"No, you don't need to be hunting nobody," said the officer.

"Did you come to Independence looking for these men, Mr. Sunday?" asked the officer.

"No, sir. I was here to meet with a Mr. Hobson Adams, about a wagon train to California."

"Hobs Adams? I know Mr. Adams. He is the best guide there is. A good man, too," said the officer.

He paused and looked at both men a minute, rolling a pencil in his hands.

"This is all going to have to wait 'til tomorrow anyway. I need to telegraph Sheriff Wilkes and talk to the Captain. Mr. Hurley, you're going to be our guest for a while. Then I'm going to check our files."

"Seems I do recollect us getting something from a sheriff in those parts some months ago."

"You can't put me in jail. I didn't do nothin," whined Hurley.

"Yessir, I can and I am going to, at least 'til tomorrow. You smell like you've had too much to drink anyway. Might hurt yourself being on the streets," said the officer.

"Brody, come up here," yelled the officer.

"Where are you staying, Mr. Sunday?" asked the officer

"At the inn just down from the courthouse. I don't remember seeing a name on the building," replied Will.

"I know the one," said the officer. "You'll have to stay in town until we get this cleared up. Why don't you come about mid-morning tomorrow and see the captain. I'll tell him all about this."

"I'll be here," said Will.

Another officer came into the lobby from the cell area. He was a young fellow, tall and lanky with an easy way about him. He had a ring of keys in his hand and wore a side arm.

"Take this man and put him in lockup," said the desk officer.

"Officer, I didn't search him. I have his pistol here, but he put on a coat just before we left. I'd make sure someone searches him," said Will.

"We'll do that," said the desk officer.

"This ain't right, dammit," yelled Hurley as he was being taken away.

"Shut up," said the young officer. "And come with me."

The young officer took Hurley by the arm and led him to the barred door, opened it, and took him down the hallway.

"Thank you, officer," said Will.

"My name's Williams," said the sergeant.

"Thank you, Sergeant Williams," said Will.

He handed Hurley's pistol to Sergeant Williams. The officer looked up and spoke to Will.

"I don't know where that kind of trash is coming from. City is full of them. Thieves, drifters, and all-around trouble makers."

He shook his head.

"So you are headed west?

Finding Mr. Sunday

BLAM! A shot echoed up from the cell area, and both men jumped at the sound. The sergeant ran to the barred door and unlocked it. Will followed him as he ran past the empty cells to the last cell door on the right. Both men came to a halt at the open cell door to see the young officer standing there holding his revolver.

Hurley lay on the floor, his hand placed on his gut as blood colored his shirt and seeped through his fingers.

"What the hell happened?" yelled the desk officer.

The young officer stood there wide-eyed and breathing heavily, his pistol pointed down by his side.

"He pulled one of those little pocket pistols from his coat and tried to shoot me, but it misfired. I grabbed his arm, but he wouldn't drop the gun so I had to shoot him," said the young officer, who was now visibly shaking.

"Didn't you search him before you untied him?" asked the desk officer.

"No, he said his hands hurt so I untied him first, and he grabbed the pistol from his pocket."

"My God, Brody. You should have searched him before you untied his hands."

Brody stood there as if rooted to the spot, the color gone from his face.

"Go see if you can find Dr. Whisnant," he said to the stunned young officer. "You could use some fresh air. Go on."

The officer bent over Hurley, who was motionless and staring wide-eyed at the ceiling. The blood was pooling heavily under Hurley's back, and rivulets were slowly spreading from the pool.

"The bullet must have gone all the way through," said the officer.

He picked up the small pistol lying near Hurley and held it up to the gas wall lamp and looked at it closely.

"That's my pistol!" said Will loudly. "It's an engraved .32-caliber Smith & Wesson cartridge pistol, isn't it? Hurley stole it from me after he shot me."

The officer looked at the gun, removed one of the short fat cartridges. Then he examined the pistol.

"You're exactly right," said Williams.

"May I see that cartridge?" Will asked.

The officer handed Will the cartridge. Will stepped closer to the gas light and held the cartridge up close to the lamp. He took a small knife from his pocket and scraped at the cartridge.

"I can see why it misfired. These cartridges are corroded. The powder has gotten damp. A Smith & Wesson doesn't misfire very often," said Will.

He picked at the cartridge again, and the bullet came loose from the casing. He scraped powder onto his hand and looked at it under the light.

"Here, Officer, take a look."

The officer stepped closer and looked at the powder in Will's hands.

"The powder is caked. It's gotten wet somehow. These cartridge guns are good guns, but the cartridge seals aren't perfected yet. You have to keep fresh cartridges in the gun. He probably never checked them or didn't know he needed to," said Will.

He handed the cartridge casing and the bullet back to the officer and brushed his hands together to remove the caked powder.

Hurley was no longer moaning and was quite still. His eyes were closed, and his hand had fallen to his side. There was no sign that he was breathing.

"He's out. He's bled out too much to hang on much longer. I don't think a doctor can help him," said the officer.

A couple of officers had come down the hall to see what the commotion was all about. They stared down at the motionless Hurley.

"What the hell happened, Sergeant?" one of them said.

"You'll all find out later. You fellows go on with your work."

After a while they could hear the hall door open and saw Brody coming down the hall.

Officer Brody was followed by a middle-aged, well-dressed man who carried the usual black leather bag.

"I think he is about gone, Doc," said Sgt. Williams.

The doctor knelt beside Hurley and lifted an eyelid. He put his finger to the man's throat. It did not take the doctor long to come to a conclusion.

"Yes. He's dead," said the doctor.

He turned Hurley over and looked at his back. "Shot through. The bullet is probably around here somewhere."

He let go of the body. "Probably need to call Mr. Schmidt and have him readied for burial," said the doctor.

"Oh, God," Brody said, rubbing his forehead. "This will mean my job."

Finding Mr. Sunday

"Maybe not. The man pulled a gun and tried to shoot you. You were careless, yes. But it wasn't murder. But it ain't up to me," said the desk officer.

"Go get Schmidt. Tell him to bring a cleanup man," the desk officer said to Brody.

The doctor left, and Will and Sergeant Williams went back to the lobby.

"You'll still need to come by tomorrow and see the captain. He'll want to hear your story," said Williams.

Will walked out into the crisp night air. The banjo and piano music continued unabated. Laughter and raucous talk poured from the bars along with the smell of cheap cigars and whiskey.

Maybe he should have felt something, he thought. He had just watched a man die. But the death of the man who had tried to kill him did not bother him. It meant nothing. Just like the death of the man who tried to molest Kate. He had felt nothing then. No remorse. No regret. Nothing.

Had he changed in the last six months or so? Or had it always been within him to accept the deaths of these men as justifiable by some internal sense of moral justice?

It didn't matter, he concluded. The world is a better place without those kinds of people.

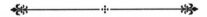

Early the next morning Will visited a horse breeder recommended by Hobs Adams. He purchased two trail horses, a big powerful light bay and a spirited young dark bay. He bought the saddles and tack he would need.

While at the livery stable he saw a beautiful palomino mare about fifteen hands high. She came immediately to Will as he leaned on the fence watching her, her step almost regal, as if she knew she was special.

"Tell me about this mare," he said to the breeder as the horse nuzzled his hand.

"Oh, that's a fine young mare. A Missouri Fox Trotter. I raised her myself. She used to follow me around like a puppy dog. One of the most gentle horses I've ever seen. Took to the saddle right away. Rides like your favorite rocking chair," said the breeder.

Dick Ward

"Is she for sale?" asked Will as he eyed the lines of the young mare.

"Well, I guess everything is for sale at the right price. But I ain't in no hurry to get rid of her. She's got to go to the right place when I do," he said as he scratched his few days of whiskers.

"There is a young lady I know turning fifteen in a few days. She doesn't have a horse, and she'd take to that one. Why don't you give me your don't-want-to-sell price? I can assure you the horse won't find a better home," said Will.

The breeder groaned a bit and eyed the horse up and down like he was the buyer. He shot a stream of tobacco juice a couple of yards, reached up, and stroked the gentle mare. The man was in the business of selling horses, not keeping them, but this was a hard decision. His affection for the mare was obvious.

"I don't reckon I want to part with her. I keep her in here 'cause she likes being with other horses. Guess I shoulda' told you that when you asked," he said.

Will did not let that stop him. That was just the right birthday present for Mary Nel. He imagined the look on her face when she saw the horse.

"Now you know, I'm looking for about twenty of the best mules you can find. The best. I'll pay well for them, too," said Will.

Will gave that comment a few moments to sink in as he stroked the mare.

Then he made an offer for the mare that made the breeder jerk his head toward Will as if he had been slapped.

Will repeated the offer. The breeder spat another stream of tobacco juice and backed away from the fence as if to distance himself from the mare.

"I'd be a fool to turn down that kind of money, he said. "That must be a real good friend you have."

"Good," said Will with a happy look on his face. "Fix her up with the best saddle you got. A real fancy one for a young lady. And all the tack.

"I'm going to leave tomorrow morning. I'll be here the first thing to pick up her and the dark bay. Hold on to the light bay for a little while. I'll pay for all of it now," said Will.

After finishing his business at the breeders he went to the police station to meet the captain. The empty station of the night before was crowded with policemen, and the air was full of loud conversation and laughter as well as the fragrance of strong coffee cooking.

"Captain's in his office. Let me tell him you are here," said the desk sergeant.

The morning desk officer was no doubt a seasoned veteran who wielded not a little authority. Everyone made way for him as he went to the captain's office. He poked his head in the far office and returned in a few moments.

"He'll see you now. Last office," said the desk officer.

He walked to the office door and stepped inside. The office was furnished with a desk and a chair, a couple of bookcases and two arm chairs in front of the desk. A sharp-looking police officer sat behind the desk. He stood to shake Will's hand. His uniform was crisply pressed and as orderly as the officer himself.

"Good Morning, Mr. Sunday. Captain Moore," he said almost formally. "Please have a seat."

"Pleasure to meet you, Captain Moore," responded Will.

"Unfortunate situation last night. I'm sorry you had to witness what was some very poor judgment on behalf of one of our young officers," he said.

"It was a big mistake," responded Will as he sat. "But that lowlife would have surely killed him if the pistol had not misfired."

"I'm sure you are right. He was the type of man that we are having to confront day in and day out since the war ended," said the captain.

"I found the information Sheriff Wilkes sent us a while back. This fellow Hurley fits. Sheriff Wilkes vouched for you in a telegraph message this morning."

"That's good to know, Captain," said Will.

"I have asked my men to keep an eye out for the other fellow. I've also sent messages to the other stations in the city," said Capt. Moore.

"As I told the officer last night, I think the other guy, Burt, is not all there. He's probably smart enough to run, though. I think he works with mules, too, so you might check all the liveries and breeders," said Will.

"Sergeant Williams told me you were a friend of Hobs Adams," said the captain.

"Well, I just met him. But he seems like the kind of man I'd like to have as a friend," said Will.

"He is. He's also one of the best guides in the business. My father owns a freight company here in the city, and he has known Hobs for many years."

The captain reached for a pipe from a tray on his desk, though he did not light it.

"Sets a lot of store in him. I've heard he's not making many more trips west. Been doing it too long, he says. Guess it's hard enough to do it once, never mind many times. "

"Well, if the railroad goes as planned, the wagon trains will be a thing of the past soon. He's probably making the right decision," said Will.

"You are right about that," said the captain.

He then leaned forward with his elbows on the top of the desk, still holding the pipe.

"Mr. Sunday, I understand why you brought this guy Hurley in last night. But it would have been better if you had waited and come to us. You put yourself in a dangerous situation. We would have gone out there to get him," said the captain, showing some irritation.

Then his demeanor softened. He reached for a match, struck it, and lit the pipe. He blew out the match and continued in a more avuncular manner.

"You look like a smart young man with a full life ahead of you. Seem to be educated and from a good family. You're a big fellow and probably just as tough as you are smart. I see you are wearing a couple of pistols, and you're probably pretty good with them," he said as looked Will in the eye.

"Some words of caution. It's easy to get in trouble these days by jumping too fast. You're heading west, and you are going to run up against a lot of situations both on the way and there."

He puffed on the pipe and blew smoke to the side, then continued.

"There are times when you should act immediately, and there are times when you should think things through. Don't let yourself get in trouble by not knowing the difference."

Will was surprised at the comment. He didn't know if it was a lecture, a warning or just some friendly advice from a man who knew more about life than he. He sat there a moment not knowing what to say. He just let his manners guide him.

"I appreciate your comments, Captain," said Will.

His face was expressionless as he responded.

"All right, then. I see no reason to hold you up any longer, Mr. Sunday," said the captain as he stood and extended his hand.

"A pleasure meeting you, Captain," said Will as he shook the captain's hand.

He turned and walked out of the captain's office, through the lobby, and out to the street. He was still hearing the captain's words, trying to decipher each one.

Yes, Captain, he thought, I heard you. But you and I differ on the situation last night. The bastard would have gotten away if I hadn't gone after him. And he's dead now instead of able to kill somebody else.

He adjusted his gun belt, put his hat on, and headed for Hiram Young's place of business.

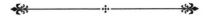

The February weather showed no sign of reneging on the promise of biting cold and frigid mornings. Will rode the bay down the lane to the Daniels farm with the young mare in tow.

As he came in sight of the property he stopped to look at the house, the barn, the shed, and the orchard. He could not help but feel like he was coming home.

He went into the barn, unsaddled the two horses, gave them a rubdown, some water and grain, and put them in the stalls. The two horses seemed to know they were home.

As he walked across the yard heading to the back door, it opened, and Goldie came bounding out barking a grand hello. Mary Nel followed. He could see Kate standing in the doorway with her arms folded against the chill.

"It's about time you got back," Mary Nel said a wide grin on her pretty face. Her hair was tied with a red ribbon and, once again, Will was startled at how pretty she was.

"Hello, Mary Nel," he said as she caught up and turned to walk to the door with him. He added with a chuckle, "I haven't been gone that long."

It felt good to see that he was missed.

"Well, it doesn't seem that long to you because you were busy. I think I've read every book in the house, and there's not a scrap of cloth to be sewn or a bit of yarn to be knitted," she said with a laugh.

"Hello, Kate," said Will as he neared the door.

"Hello, Will. I'm glad you are back safely," she said. She gave him a warm smile and turned to go into the house.

He stepped inside and was greeted with the familiar smells of coffee, the wood fire, and a pleasing hint of lavender from the dried arrangements Kate made.

"I'll put on some coffee. I know you are cold. I can fix you something to eat if you're hungry," said Kate.

Her eyes seemed to sparkle in the light as she looked at Will. He'd missed seeing these two ladies and was glad to be home.

"Thank you, Kate," he said as he removed his overcoat.

"I see you bought yourself two fine horses."

"Yes, I did. I'd like for you and Mary Nel to come with me to the barn after I warm up some," he said with a little grin.

He had his coffee and some cake as they caught up on the last few days. He told them what he had done in Independence but left out the story about Hurley. He decided to tell them later and not spoil the moment. He was eager for Mary Nel to see her birthday present.

"Let's go to the barn and see the horses," said Will.

The three of them put on their coats and walked to the barn. The two horses were in separate stalls. First he showed them the bay.

"He hasn't been broken long. Needs to be ridden more. That's why I brought him here and left the other horse in Independence," said Will.

"Oh, you bought three horses," said Mary Nel.

"Yes. And a lot of mules. And a wagon and all the equipment I will need. The wagon is being built. It will be ready in April," Will said.

"Now, let me show you one of the finest mares you have ever seen."

He went around the side of the stall and led the palomino to the middle of the barn."

"Will, she is beautiful. I've never seen one like that," said Mary Nel.

"She is that," said Kate. "What breed is she?"

"She is a Missouri Fox Trotter. One of the finest you will ever see," said Will.

The mare seemed be aware she was the center of attention and turned her fine head so all could see. Mary Nel touched the horse, and the horse nickered softly.

"I believe you have found a new friend," said Kate to Mary Nel.

"And well she should have," said Will.

Her turned to Mary Nel and handed her the lead rope.

"Happy birthday, Mary Nel," said Will with a huge smile. "She's yours."

Mary Nel's mouth flew open, and her hand went to cover it. She stood there unable to speak.

"Will! Do you mean it? She's mine?" asked a startled Mary Nel.

"Yes, ma'am. She's all yours," he said. "She is an easy rider. And one of these days she will produce some beautiful horses."

Mary Nel turn to Will and gave him a big hug. "Will, thank you. Thank you. She is so beautiful. I have to name her. I'm going to brush her. Right now."

Will and Kate left Mary Nel in the barn with her new horse and went back into the kitchen.

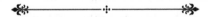

"Well, Mrs. Daniels, I've spent most of the morning looking at your property," said the man sitting at the kitchen table sipping a hot cup of coffee.

He wore a thick wool shirt over canvas trousers and high boots. He had coal black hair and a neatly trimmed mustache.

"It's a mighty pretty piece of property. About as fine as you see these days. And the orchard looks to be in excellent shape."

"Oh, it is, Mr. Mason. We just had the biggest harvest I can remember."

"A good time to be selling produce, I'll wager," he said as he set his coffee cup down.

"It's not really my business, but are you sure you want to sell this place?" he said as he looked up at her.

"No, Mr. Mason, I'm not sure. But an offer has been made, and I just wanted to see what you thought the land was worth," replied Kate.

"I've done some figuring, and here is a price I think you can get." He pushed a paper across the table so she could look at it.

Kate studied the figures for a moment.

"This is for everything, land, buildings, and the house?" she asked.

"Yes ma'am." He shuffled in his chair. "To the right buyer, you might get a little more. But that's a fair price, I think."

"Excuse me a moment, Mr. Mason."

She left the room a moment and returned with Mr. Samuels' written offer.

"Look at this, Mr. Mason. This is the offer my neighbor made just a few weeks ago," she said.

He stared at the paper a moment and scratched his chin. "You say he is your neighbor?" he asked.

"Yes, he owns the big orchard next door. He and his family have been here many years. Before my father even," she said.

"I see," he said, still rubbing his chin.

"Well, Mrs. Daniels. Land has a couple of different kind of valuations. I call 'em head valuations and heart valuations. Most of the time people selling land and property get hung up in heart valuation, for sentimental and other reasons, and think their land is worth more than it is.

"Then there is the head valuation. That's when people look at land for its value, what it will produce or the value of the location, practical assessments, you might say. Most often that is the buyer's perspective.

"But this here's the first time I've seen a buyer offer considerably more than the actual value of the land. In fact, Mrs. Daniels, this offer is about what you might expect to get ten years down the road."

He sat there a moment, looking at the papers.

"Mrs. Daniels, I have no interest in this matter other than to do a good job of appraising your property. And I stand by my appraisal. All I can say is this man wants your land bad. I don't expect anyone else would make an offer this high, good property though it is," he said earnestly.

"I was quite surprised at the offer, too," said Kate. "But I had no idea of the value."

"If you was of a mind to sell, I'd jump on it," said Mr. Mason. "It is a very generous offer."

Kate sat there a moment, not knowing what to say. Then she got up from her chair.

Finding Mr. Sunday

"Let me get your fee, Mr. Mason. I so appreciate your honesty. Excuse me a moment."

Kate left the room and returned shortly with the fee they had agreed upon.

"I'll go back and put my appraisal in good form and send it to you. I wish you the best of luck, whatever you do, ma'am," he said.

"Thank you, Mr. Mason."

He put on his overcoat and thick felt hat. Kate escorted him to the front door.

"Good day, Mrs. Daniels," he said as he left the front porch headed to his carriage.

Kate stood in the doorway and watched Mr. Mason's carriage as it went down the lane. The cool air felt good on her face.

Oh my, oh my, she thought as she closed the door gently and leaned her back against it. This has gotten interesting.

"I'm going to name her Minerva. She is so smart. But of course I can't call her that so I'm going to call her Minnie," said Mary Nel.

They sat around the table having the evening meal. March was in the wings, and a few nice days of weather had teased them into visions of an early spring. But it would be a while before any green shoots appeared.

"I see she loves to be ridden, just as the breeder said," Will said between bites.

"Oh, she does. And she learns everything so fast. I taught her to curtsy like a lady," Mary Nel said, laughing.

"You've spent a lot of time with her, honey. She trusts you now. That horse thinks you are the only person on earth," Kate said.

"Will, I still can't get over how beautiful she is," she said, smiling at Will.

"She will make a fine companion for you for a very long time, Mary Nel," said Will.

"I want us to have a discussion for a minute if we could," said Kate.

Both Will and Mary Nel turned to look at her.

"We haven't sat down for any length of time since Mr. Mason was here. I want to tell you what he said."

She pushed her plate away.

Will and Mary Nel knew that firm look Kate assumed when she was about to turn serious.

"Mr. Mason said Mr. Samuel's offer was extremely generous. Probably what we would get if we stayed here another ten years. He said Mr. Samuels must really want the property badly to make such an offer."

There was silence for a moment as the two of them considered her comment.

"I'm not surprised, Kate. Just the fact that your property joins his makes it more valuable to him. And he knows the orchard is an extremely good one. I also happen to know that Silas is very serious about a young lady in town. He will probably be looking for a home of his own soon."

"How can Mr. Samuels buy our place, Momma? He doesn't look like he has a lot of money," said Mary Nel.

"He's always taken care of his place. But as long as I have known him, he never spent money unless he absolutely had to. Father said he salted his crop earnings every year along with his hams," she said, laughing. "I know he sold a lot of produce to the government during the war, too."

"You can also borrow money to buy land. Not that Mr. Samuels is the borrowing type," said Will.

"Are you going to sell, Momma?" asked Mary Nel as she sat forward with great interest.

She had stopped eating, giving full attention to her mother.

Kate was silent for a moment. She got up and poured some tea in her cup.

"Well, I'm interested in what you think about pulling up roots and moving somewhere else. This is your home, too," she said.

Mary Nel pondered that for a moment. As she did so she seemed very mature.

"I would miss this place. I wasn't very happy when we first came here. But I got used to it. I love living in the country," said Mary Nel quietly. "But Momma, I want to go other places. And do other things, too. Like Will, I want to see this country. Really see it."

Will sat silently. This was a discussion for the two of them, and he felt a little awkward listening to their exchange.

Finding Mr. Sunday

"Momma!" Mary Nel said with excitement in her voice. "Let's go to California with Will. We can go to Sacramento, or San Francisco or … or anywhere out there. If you want to still grow apples, we can start a new place there."

Her eyes seemed to light up at the thought.

Then her cheeks colored as she felt a little self-conscious at her enthusiasm, knowing it wasn't an easy decision for her mother.

Kate looked at Mary Nel warmly and covered her hand with her own. She gave her hand a gentle squeeze and smiled.

"I thought you might say that, but I wasn't sure. I've been giving it a lot of thought since Mr. Samuels made his offer. I know you might be surprised by this, but I have been thinking along those same lines," said Kate, a twinkle in her eyes.

Will, a bit startled by the confession, sat there, wanting to jump up and down at the thought of the two of them going to California with him.

Kate looked at Will. He was staring down at his hands, laced together on the top of the table.

"Well, Mr. Sunday, we've yet to hear from you," she teased. "How would you like to have us along on your trip out west?"

He broke into that huge grin, his eyes lit up, and he looked from one to the other and back again, trying to contain his excitement.

"I can't think of better company," he said.

"Then we better get busy. We have lots to do," said Kate.

CHAPTER NINE

T he April sun fell warmly on their backs as they moved from the house to the two new wagons. Will, Kate, and Mary Nel had spent most of the last three weeks sorting, packing, and finally loading. Kate had deemed some items just too precious to leave behind.

Mr. Samuels had purchased the property within a few weeks of being notified his offer was accepted. A public sale had disposed of the farm equipment and most of the furniture. Arrangements had been made to join Hobs Adams in Independence in time for the spring departure.

Will looked up to see Ish coming around the side of the house. The big man was sweating in the warm sun. He took off his hat and wiped his brow with a handkerchief.

"You about finished here, Will?" he asked.

"Will be shortly. We'll have time to get to Jefferson City before dark. How about you?"

"Yep. Poor Maggie still fussin' bout this, but she gon' come around. I know it's hard on her, but we both want to move along. Figure we just rest in California for the days the good Lord give us. At least it be warmer there most of the time," said Ish.

"That depends on where we go in California. It can get cool in the mid to north part of the state and up in the mountains," said Will.

Ish, too, had taken Mr. Samuels' offer, despite no small amount of sadness on Maggie's part. She had not wanted to leave her home, but she didn't want to be parted from Kate and Mary Nel. Too, she was growing tired of the hard work in the orchard.

The sale of the farm gave them enough of a nest egg to buy a small home and live in California without the need of much income.

"How you going to handle your own wagon and two of Miz Kate's?" Ish said. "You know Miss Mary going to ride that pretty mare. She don't need to be handling no mule team nohow."

"When we get to Independence, we'll meet up with Hobs. My wagon is waiting there with twenty mules. Hobs knows we're looking for someone to handle Kate's extra wagon and someone to care for the stock. I'm sure he'll find the help we need, and we'll get more later if we need to."

Kate came out into the yard and looked around. Will had noticed she had been quiet today. He knew she would be sad as the departure time neared.

"I think that's everything, Will," she said. "Mary Nel has a small bundle of things, and that's all."

She shaded her eyes as she looked up at him.

"Good. That leaves plenty of room for the supplies we need to pick up in Independence. You were wise to take two wagons, Kate. You and Mary Nel won't be cramped. You'll have ample room to sleep inside at night, and neither wagon will be overloaded."

Mary Nel came out of the house with a small case and handed it up to Will. Like her mother, she was dressed in pants and shirts the two of them had purchased especially for the trail. They both wore sturdy trail boots and leather hats.

Kate had never liked bonnets, and Mary Nel refused to even try one on. Despite the masculine attire, there could be little confusion about their gender.

"Minnie is saddled and ready to go," said Mary Nel. "I think she senses what's happening. I'll ride for a while. I'm not sure how she'd take to being tethered to a moving wagon. We'll work on that a little at a time."

Will placed the case in the wagon that would serve as their home for the long trip and hopped down. Despite all his efforts he still limped slightly. Not enough to slow him down or be noticed, but he knew it was there even if others didn't see it.

He came back to the moment.

"That's a good idea," he said. "She'll feel more comfortable with you on her back. I'm going to tether the bay to a wagon, but he's done that before. I'll put Goldie in Kate's wagon.

"If we want to make Jefferson City before nightfall, we better leave soon. They're holding our rooms, but we want to have time to get settled and get a meal before it's late."

He climbed into the seat of the lead wagon.

"I'll be right behind you," said Ish as he left to get Maggie and his wagon.

Kate turned to look at her home place and stared for a moment. A great part of my life is being left here, she thought. My childhood, my upbringing.

Dick Ward

What would Mom and Pop think about my selling the place and moving on? Pop would fret, but dear Mom would give me her blessing, I'm sure.

But there is a whole new world waiting for me. A new beginning in an exciting place. And much to see on the way. Yes, that is the part of all of this that will keep me going.

She climbed up and took the reins of the wagon. She held her chin up high. There were no tears, only determination on her face. She pulled the brim of her hat down snugly and looked straight ahead.

"Let's go to California," she said for all to hear.

Mary Nel mounted Minnie and turned to look at the house. She was too excited to feel any sadness.

Will clicked the mules, and the wagons rattled off down the lane to the main trail.

The journey to Independence was pleasant, with warm days and gentle breezes. The trailside was alive with spring flowers and plenty of green grass. Showers were mild and cooling, and river crossings were non-eventful. This short leg of their journey provided ample time to get used to the routines of travel by wagon.

Will, Kate, Mary Nel, Ish, and Maggie arrived in the early afternoon just south of Independence at a staging area for wagon trains headed west. Among the scattered wagons, most had campsites already set up.

Several mixed herds of horses, mules, oxen, cows, sheep, and goats grazed some distance away, though some travelers kept the family milk cow staked near their campsite.

The new mules were well trained and made good time. Will hoped the mules waiting for him here were as good as those he had purchased in Jefferson City.

"A nice size train here," said Will. "Looks like some freighters are joining us, too."

"I see a lot of young families," said Kate as she got down from her wagon.

Mary Nel came up beside them, dismounted, and tied Minnie to Kate's wagon.

Finding Mr. Sunday

"Looks just like I thought it would," she said as she surveyed the scene.

"Why don't we pick us a spot and get settled in? Then I'll find Hobs and check in with him. I need to see about my wagon, the stock, and the help we need," said Will.

He and Ish unhitched the teams, staked the animals in a green area near the wagons, and set up an area for a campfire. Will then went off to find Hobs Adams.

After several inquiries, he located Hobs, who was surrounded by a group of travelers. Will stood patiently as he watched Hobs deal with each person in turn. When the number of travelers surrounding Hobs dwindled, Will approached him.

"Hobs," he said. "Good to see you again. Will Sunday."

"Of course, Will. How are you? Good to see you," said Hobs.

The two shook hands warmly. Will could tell the man was in his element, full of energy and enthusiasm.

"I'm well," said Will. "We just arrived a little while ago. I wanted to find out about my wagon and stock and see if you managed to get us the help we need."

"Oh, yes. I've got two good men for you, and they have your wagon and stock. One of the men is a young Mexican fellow by the name of Rio. I know his daddy, and he is a fine young man. He'll be your driver. He's a good cook, too.

"The other is a fellow who's been on the trail a couple of times with me. A little long in the tooth like me, but he's a good stockman, and he'll take good care of your animals."

"I appreciate your help, Hobs."

"Where are your folks?" said Hobs.

Will pointed in the direction of the group. "Over there about three hundred yards. You'll see a pretty palomino tied to one of our wagons, two ladies and an older couple," he said.

"I didn't expect to see this many wagons," said Will. "I thought there would be fewer people going west by wagon now."

"You're right. Nowhere near as many as used to," said Hobs. "But we got some freighters that wanted to join us. We'll be traveling with about sixty or so wagons. That's a nice manageable size.

"In a little while a young fellow who works for me, his name is Peter, is going to be coming around taking roll. He's going to tell everyone where and when we'll assemble for a meeting tomorrow. Our scheduled departure is day after tomorrow."

"Thanks, Hobs," said Will. "I'd like you to stop and meet my friends when you get a chance. You can join us any time you like. For a meal or just plain company."

"That's mighty kind of you, Will. You can count on it," said Hobs with a smile.

Will joined the others a few minutes later and filled them in on his conversation with Hobs.

"Well, it just feels better not to be part of such a large group. Sixty or so wagons is about right for me," said Kate.

Preparation for the evening was a familiar routine by now. As they were getting settled, two men driving a new wagon stopped at their campsite. A young man and an older man got down from the wagon and approached Will. Goldie gave them a welcoming sniff, then curled up under one of the wagons.

"Are you Mr. Sunday?" asked the younger man.

There was only a trace of accent in his voice. He was a compact, wiry young fellow wearing a red shirt tucked into black trousers. His hat hung on his back by a string around his neck, and he had a full head of black hair.

"I am," said Will as he stuck out his hand.

"Sir, I am Rio Reyes. Mr. Adams said you were looking for a driver."

"We are. I'm glad to meet you, Rio," said Will.

"And my name is Hank Willis," said the older man as he stepped beside Rio. "I'm to help with the stock and what all else you be needin'."

He shook Will's hand.

Hank looked to be near fifty. A felt hat covered his head, and gray hair cascaded down behind his ears and well below his collar. His face was tan and weathered, and his eyes matched the steel gray color of the mustache that covered his upper lip and drooped down his chin.

He wore a red plaid shirt, and canvas pants were held in place by suspenders and stuffed into the tops of his trail boots.

"Good to meet you, Hank," said Will.

Finding Mr. Sunday

He turned to Kate and Mary Nel, who were unpacking the kitchen boxes.

"Fellows, this is Mrs. Daniels and her daughter, Mary Nel," said Will.

"Hiddy do, ma'am … and miss," said Hank as he removed his hat.

"Hello," said Rio as he tipped his head in their direction.

"Good to meet you gentlemen," said Kate. "We are sure glad to have your help."

"Rio, you will work mostly with Mrs. Daniels. Hank, you and I will work together most of the time," said Will. "There's another couple traveling with us I want you two to meet."

He took them over to their wagon and introduced them to Ish and Maggie.

"From time to time, I will be asking the two of you to help Ish and Maggie out with a few things."

Will spent some time discussing the additional camp duties each of them would have.

"You both are welcome to put your spread down in our camp at night or anywhere you want. We'll see to your meals," Will said. "I'll meet with you individually to discuss your pay."

He lowered his voice, "I especially want you both to make Mrs. Daniels' trip as easy as possible on her. Hank, before it gets dark, I want to check out the new stock."

"That looks to be exactly what I ordered," said Will as he stepped closer to examine the new wagon.

"Oh, it's a fine 'un. Good dry timber, strong axle, good iron. Ain't a creak in her," said Hank as he scratched his chin and eyed the wagon. "Wait til ya see 'em mules."

As the men talked, a young man approached them with paper and pencil in hand. He was dressed in new trail clothes, was clean cut, and seemed to be on a mission.

"Hello, folks. My name is Peter, and I'm helping Mr. Adams get a handle on who's here and so on," the young man said with a friendly smile.

"Hey, Pete," said Hank, who knew Peter.

"Hello, fellows," said Peter.

He was somewhat taller than average and carried himself well. His brown hair was well combed, and his face clear and youthful. He was likely a little older than Will, but looked younger.

"Hello, Peter. Will Sunday. Hobs told us to expect you," said Will as he shook Peter's hand.

"Good to meet you, Mr. Sunday," said Peter.

Despite his height, he had to look up at Will, as did most people. Peter assumed Will was much older than his actual age.

Kate and Mary Nel walked over to where Will and Peter stood. Peter's eyes widened slightly as he looked at the two ladies.

It wasn't clear whether he was surprised to see two ladies dressed in male attire or if he was smitten with them. Most likely it was a combination of both.

"This is Mrs. Daniels and her daughter, Mary Nel," said Will.

Both ladies smiled and nodded to Peter. "Hello, Peter," said Kate.

"Hi, Peter," said Mary Nel with that disarming smile.

"Ma'am, ma'am," Peter said as he nodded to them in turn. "A pleasure to meet you."

He stood there a moment and seemed to struggle to find his next words. He dropped his pencil and picked it up.

"Uh … I … uh … it's a pleasure to meet you all. I need to write your names here and …"

He turned his head to his paper and began to write, a rosy glow coming into his cheeks.

After scribbling for a minute, he asked, "Is anyone else traveling with you?"

Will told him about Ish and Maggie and pointed to their wagon across the campsite.

"Thank you. I'll talk to them next," said Peter.

"I'm supposed to tell you there's a meeting for everyone tomorrow morning at ten. Mr. Adams is going to go over a few things and talk about organizing a council to decide issues that come up. He'll explain how we are going to choose a captain for the train, too," said Peter.

"It will be on that bluff over there around that big oak," Peter said as he pointed to the site a couple hundred yards away.

Peter stood there a moment, stole another quick peek at Mary Nel, then started to walk away.

"Oh, Mr. Sunday. I almost forgot. Mr. Adams said he was going to stop by tonight to meet Mrs. Daniels and have a word with you," said Peter.

"Good," said Will.

Will could see the young man was still somewhat flustered, and he smiled knowingly.

"Tell him if he comes around six we'll feed him," said Will.

"Uh ... yes ... yes, I will," said Peter as walked toward Ish's wagon.

After Peter left the campsite, Will and Hank went to check the stock. The mules belonging to Kate and Will grazed contentedly on the new spring grass, separated somewhat from the main body of stock.

"That there's a fine bunch o' mules," said Hank. "Them's Boone County mules. Come from them big mammoth jacks and draft horses. Ain't a one less than fifteen hands. You lucky to find 'em."

"I paid a premium for them, too," said Will. "Not a one under six years old and all broke to wagons and riding."

"We gotta give 'em some grain, ya know. Mules need grain along with grass. Not like a horse or ox," said Hank. "We got some, but grain can be had along the way purdy regla' now."

"So I've heard," said Will. "If we take care of this stock, we can sell them in California. Missouri mules are known even in California."

"Don't you worry, Mr. Will. They in good hands," said Hank.

"I think they are, Hank. They truly are," said Will as he patted Hank's shoulder.

Will returned to the campsite, and Hank stayed with the stock to secure them for the night. As Will approached the group of wagons, he saw that Hobs Adams was seated in a circle with Kate, Mary Nel, Ish, and Maggie, already engaged in lively conversation. He and Goldie had become fast friends, and he scratched the dog's head as he talked.

"Hello, Hobs," said Will. "I see you've met my friends."

"That I have," said Hobs. "And a pleasure it is."

"Mr. Adams was just telling us about Peter. His father is a merchant, and Peter is going to California to look at buying goods coming in from overseas at Sacramento and San Francisco," said Kate.

"Now Mrs. Daniels, please call me Hobs," said Hobs.

"I will if you'll call me Kate," she said warmly.

"Agreed," said Hobs.

"Peter seemed like a fine fellow," said Will.

"Oh, he is," said Hobs. "He's worked with his father in the mercantile trade since he was a boy. Got good schooling, too. Smart as a whip. His Pa sets great store by him. His Pa is an old friend of mine. I told him I'd take Peter with me if he'd help me along the way. He's been plenty of help already."

"Hobs, we're going to have some Dutch oven stew here in a few minutes. I hope you'll stay and eat with us. There's plenty. Ish and Maggie are going to join us, and Maggie just baked some fresh bread," said Kate.

"Why, I'd be much obliged, Kate. I have to confess, most of the boys that work for me are better eaters than cooks. Anytime I can set at somebody else's campfire is a blessing for me," he said, laughing.

"How many times have you made this trip, Mr. Adams?" asked Mary Nel.

"Oh, I don't rightly know, miss. Probably six, seven times. A lot more'n most of the guides I'd say."

"You don't get tired of the travel?" asked Kate.

"Only of late. Guess I'm gettin' older. But every trip is different 'cause of the people. Met some mighty fine folks doing this ... and some not so fine.

"The trail seems to change every trip. Not as wild as it used to be. Now we got bridges, ferries, tolls roads even. Stage coaches run regular now. Railroad is coming along. Trading posts everywhere except in the desert and the Sierras. You can buy most anything you need along the way.

"If the railroad comes together like they planning, might not be many more wagon trains. Course you never know if it'll happen. But the railroad oughta be a money maker for somebody. If there's money to be made, it'll happen."

He nodded his head at his own comment.

"Are the Indians a problem, Mr. Adams?" said Ish.

"Now my name's Hobs, Ish," chided Hobs.

"You know, they ain't' been. But I hear some tales of late that some of the tribes are upset. Don't think we will have any problems, so I ain't worried. If I hear any more, and I think there's something to it, I'll take it up with the council," Hobs said.

"I read about the council in the papers you gave Will," said Kate. "And Peter mentioned it, too."

Finding Mr. Sunday

"Yes, that's one of the reasons we're having a get-together tomorrow. I'm going to ask for eight volunteers to represent all the wagons. From the eight, we'll elect a captain who'll sort of be the manager of the council," said Hobs. "By the way, Will. Sure would like to have you on that council."

"Me?" said Will with a surprised look on his face. "I don't know anything about running a wagon train."

"Will, it ain't about running a wagon train as much as it's about common sense and knowing how to deal with people. I got the feeling people would listen to you. I know you got plenty of sense."

"I'm flattered," said Will. "I'll give it some thought."

"I hope you will," said Kate.

She turned to Hobs. "This young man amazes me every day, Hobs ... He can bring a lot to the council."

"You can, Will," said Mary Nel. "I'd feel better knowing you had a say in what went on."

"Thank you ladies for the votes of confidence," Will said.

"Folks, the bread and stew are ready. Hope you all are hungry," said Maggie.

The talking suddenly stopped, and everyone got up and grabbed a plate as Maggie began to dip into the huge Dutch oven.

Early the next morning Will and Ish went to check on the stock as Rio started breakfast. He had chosen to sleep in the camp.

"Morning, Hank," said Will as they approached Hank. He had a small campfire going and was rolling up his ground cloth and blanket.

"Mornin', Boss," said Hank. "Mornin', Ish.

"Fine day. Fine day," said Ish.

"You going to sleep out here every night, Hank?" asked Ish.

"Likely," said Hank. "At least for a while."

He stirred the small fire he had built.

"I want the stock to know my smell. Know I'm the one takin' care of 'em. Be surprised how quick animals come to trust a person that's around them all the time. Specially when it comes to handing out grain," he said with a laugh."I kinda like sleepin' out under the stars, anyhow."

"They look mighty peaceful to me," said Will, looking at the herd of stock.

"Real calm, they are," Hank said. "I got a saddle from your wagon, and I'm gonna saddle up that young gelding and get this herd down to the crick."

"Good," said Will. "He needs to be ridden. He's got some spirit, mind you."

"Oh, the good ones always do," said Hank. "I can handle him."

"I expect we'll have some bread and bacon soon, so come on up to camp as soon as you've watered them," said Will.

"Will do, Boss," said Hank.

The first time Hank called him "Boss," Will was a bit uneasy and not sure how to take it. He paid close attention to Hank as he repeated the salutation a few more times.

He soon realized that Hank was sincere and respectful with the term.

Will and Ish returned to camp to find it bustling with activity. Rio had more or less taken charge of getting things going by starting the coffee and frying big mounds of bacon.

Maggie watched with a smile, secretly happy to see Rio's initiative. However, she told herself, she would withhold judgment until she saw the outcome of his efforts.

Kate and Mary Nel were both up and wide awake, looking fresh in the morning light. There must be some family secret to looking that good so early in the morning, thought Will.

"Good morning, ladies," said Will. "Hank has the stock situation well in hand, and he'll be here for breakfast as soon as he gets the stock to the creek and back."

He kneeled down and poured himself a cup of coffee, sat down in one of the chairs, and took a cautious sip. It was hot and strong, just the way he liked it.

"Ummm, that's good," he said. "Did you make this, too, Rio?"

Rio was removing some bacon from a cast iron griddle that straddled a fire in a slit trench. He looked up with a cheery smile.

"Si, Mr. Will," he said. "You like it, I hope?"

"It's excellent. You are a good cook like Hobs said," he said with a grin.

"Oh, yes, sir. I make fires, I cook, I wash dishes, I drive. I help with anything," he said.

Will could not help but think that his request to make Kate's trail life as easy as possible was being taken seriously by Rio. He must remember to compliment Rio.

Maggie took the top off the Dutch oven and looked in on the biscuits.

"Bout ready, now folks. Looks like Rio has cooked a whole hog over there so let's eat. I'll say a quick blessing."

They all bowed their heads, and Maggie began to pray.

"Lord, bless this food before us. Bless this day you've given us. Bless this world around us. And guide us to live in your light. In Jesus' name we pray. Amen."

At a little before ten everyone walked to the gathering area under the big oak tree. Hobs was standing on the back of an open wagon waiting for the crowd. The sun was warm, and a gentle breeze stirred the leaves of the old oak. Songbirds seemed to have gathered in the oak for a special performance.

There were nearly two hundred people on the train. Some brought their families to the meeting, some came as couples, and some came as a single to represent their families.

"Good morning, folks. I'm Hobs Adams," he said after the last few travelers came straggling up.

It took a moment for the parents to quiet the children and the mumbling to stop.

"I've met most of you already and plan to get around to meet your families as soon as I can. I want to cover a few things this morning as we plan to pull out an hour after sunrise tomorrow."

"Somebody from every family has signed the covenants, and you know the rules and agreements are all common sense. Just something to give us some order. I will say to you now, there ain't any leeway in 'em. If you violate 'em, me and the council will decide what to do. But you are all good people, and I don't reckon we'll have a problem.

"I want to tell everyone the council will help run this train. But you have hired me to guide this train. What that means is, I have final say about how we get there, when we travel, and the route. I've made this trip many times, and my job is to get you all to California safe. I intend to do that.

"After we dismiss, I would like at least eight people to come forward who might be willing to serve on the council. If we have more'n eight, we'll elect eight and choose three alternates. The elected eight will choose a captain to lead the council.

"I want to say something important here. The war is over. Forget your politics. There is no North or South on this train. I won't abide trouble or feuding between parties of any kind for any reason by anyone in the train. If feuding happens, both parties will be forced to leave the train.

"There is a young man who works for me … Peter, step up here, please."

Peter climbed up on the wagon bed and stood beside Hobs.

"This is Peter Forester. Peter here is going to be my right-hand man and will help me by gettin' us off on time and making sure wagons keep up. We have to stay together. There are stockmen keeping hundreds of animals moving behind us, and we have to keep them going. Peter is a good man, and he speaks for me.

"Once we elect the council, we'll meet here around four so you can all meet them. Of course, anyone can come to me anytime if you have questions. Let's all pray for a safe journey and Godspeed."

He stepped down.

The crowd wandered away, and a number of men walked up to Hobs. About half appeared to be farmers or working men. Several were dressed in finer clothing and could have been merchants, businessmen, or tradesmen.

"Let's sit down here a while, men. You fellows all want to be on the council, I guess, so let's get started," said Hobs.

Most men sat down, including Will, but a few remained standing.

"Let's see. We got eleven here. That's good. Now does anyone volunteer to be an alternate? You'd come to all the meetings but not have a vote. If anyone had to drop out of the council you would take their place. First person to volunteer would be number one alternate, then two and three."

There was some discussion among the men, but no one volunteered.

"Are any of you kin to each other?" asked Hobs.

"Yep, me and him's cousins," said one man as he pointed to the man beside him.

"Well, I really don't want kin on the council. Or people from the same place if we can help it. It's okay to be an alternate, but you can't be on the council if your relative is on there," said Hobs.

"Who made those rules?" said one man.

Everyone turned to see who had spoken. He was one of the men still standing. He was dressed in striped black wool pants, a gray shirt, a black leather vest, and shined black boots.

His red face seemed to be in a perpetual scowl. He had dark hair and wore a fine quality wool hat. He wore a .44-caliber Army pistol slung low on his right hip.

As everyone turned to look at him his face broke into what was supposed to be a smile but looked more like a sneer.

"I didn't read that nowhere," he said.

"No. It's something I cover in the election meeting. It just makes sense to make sure the train is represented as a whole and not by one group or one family. Does anyone else here see that as unreasonable?" asked Hobs.

Several men shook their heads and several said "no" aloud.

"It makes perfect sense to me," said Will. "The council should be as diverse as the train itself."

Will addressed his remark to the group, but the stranger took it to be directed to him.

"Di-verse ... Di-verse my ass ... who the hell you think you talkin' to, kid?" the man said to Will with a laugh.

"I'd kind of like to know myself," said Will.

"Name's Pel Ligon. I made this trip before, and you ain't talking to no fool," he said in a nasty tone.

"I think that remains to be seen," said Will.

Most of the group laughed at Will's comment, agitating Ligon. His face turned an even darker red, and he puffed up as he looked around at the group.

"Ligon, nobody else here wants to argue the point. Let's settle down and get down to business," Hobs said firmly.

"I want each man to tell the others about hisself and why you would make a good council member. Anyone can ask questions. Then we'll vote," said Hobs.

"Hobs. Franklin Jones, here. I'll be an alternate if'n it'll make things easier. Just so's I can come to the meetings."

"Thank you, Franklin. That's fine with me if the rest of you have no objections."

No one spoke up.

"Good. And Mr. Mackland, would you or your cousin be an alternate?" said Hobs.

"Yes, suh. I will. Roy will be a better member than me," he said nodding to his cousin.

Soon all the alternates were chosen.

"Let's proceed with the pitches, then," Hobs said.

Each man gave a short talk about his background and why he wanted to be a council member. Few questions were asked by anyone. When Pel Ligon's turn came, everyone seemed particularly interested in what he had to say.

"Well, I ain't interested in being part of no council that just takes Adams' word for everything and goes along. A questioner, that's what I am. And I aim to be one whether on the council or not. So I don't care about no vote," said Ligon.

"Mr. Ligon, we ain't even got started on this trip, and you seem to be mad about something. You know my record like everyone that signed up does, so what's your problem?" said Hobs.

"Humph. My problem is lookin' at this bunch of sheep and believin' they could do anything but nod their heads at anything you say," he said with a sneer.

"I see everyone here as honest, hardworking men who can provide good counsel. If you ain't got any confidence in me and you ain't got any confidence in them, maybe you oughta find another wagon train," said Hobs.

"I just might. I just might do that," said Ligon.

With that remark he turned and walked down the hill toward the wagon camps.

"Huh," said Hobs. "Don't know what set him off."

"Now he's gone we got eight council members and two alternates. Is there anyone here who objects to this group being the council?"

Everyone agreed to that proposal.

"Now, let's see to electing a captain. Anyone want to speak up?"

One man raised his hand.

"Well, Hobs, I've been mayor of a pretty good-sized town in Maryland. Served as a major in the Army during the war. I think I'm qualified and would be honored to give it a try."

Hartwell looked like a military man, tall, clean cut with an erect posture. He was perhaps in his mid-forties, clean shaven, and neat in appearance.

"I know you don't want partisanship, and I assure you I can be objective," he said.

"You know, Mr. Hartwell, I was kinda hopin' you might speak up. But let's see who else might be of a mind to be captain," said Hobs.

No one spoke for a moment, and the men looked at each other. Finally, one man removed his pipe from his mouth and addressed the group.

"We just gettin' to know each other, so all we can do is see how it goes with who all we choose. So I'm for Hartwell 'til I see a reason to change my mind. Seems like he's got experience," said one man.

Everyone nodded.

"All in favor of Mr. Hartwell being captain? If not, now's the time to speak up."

All nodded their approval.

"All right, Mr. Hartwell. You are the captain. Congratulations." said Hobs.

"If there are no other questions or comments, then all of you be at the meeting at four today and introduce yourselves. We'll have our first meeting tonight after supper. I'll have the coffee pot going at my camp, and we'll meet there. It's on the far edge of the group. It'll have a red flag sticking up high on it for tonight. Thank you all. I look forward to working with you," said Hobs.

He stood up as did the others, and the group dispersed, talking among themselves.

Will stayed behind and turned to Hobs.

"What do you know about Ligon?" asked Will.

"Not much. He's traveling with one other fellow. If I remember he's from somewhere down South. New Orleans, I think. Got good stock, good equipment. His partner's a quiet guy, never said much."

"What do you think got him so riled?" said Will.

"Oh, I think he's got a big head and didn't like the boys laughing at him. When I met him he seemed like a bit of a hard case. There always seems to somebody a little mad at the world. Truth is, they're mostly mad at themselves. I wouldn't worry about him, Will." He patted Will's shoulder, and they walked back to camp and went their separate ways.

Will was about a hundred yards from his group when Ligon stepped from around a wagon and directly into his path.

"You got a big mouth, boy. I don't take kindly to you know-it-all types," said Ligon.

Ligon stood there with both thumbs in his belt and his legs spread apart in an attempt to intimidate Will.

Will showed no fear as he came in close to Ligon.

"I'm sorry to hear that, Mr. Ligon. You seem to have a burr under your saddle about something. But if you stay on this train, you better get used to me because I don't intend to go anywhere," said Will firmly.

"Kid, your size don't scare me none. I've put taller timbers than you down, and I ain't afraid to do it again. You run your mouth around me too much, and it just might happen," Ligon said with a smirk.

Will stepped forward to within inches of Ligon and looked him dead in the eye. He was a good four or five inches taller, forcing Ligon to tilt his head back to maintain eye contact.

"Well, I'll remember that, Mr. Ligon. And you have a standing invitation to try to take down this bit of timber any time you want," said Will.

He stood there for a moment looking into Ligon's eyes without blinking. He could tell that Ligon might be having second thoughts about trying to bully him.

With that, he sidestepped Ligon and continued to his camp. Ligon was left standing there looking around and hoping no one saw what just happened.

On the day of departure, the Missouri morning was crisp and clear as spring continued to paint the countryside new green from the treetops to the grassy meadows. The glorious day was forgotten by most of the travelers, however, as the great adventure that would forever change their lives began to unfold.

A flurry of activity rippled throughout the camps. Mules brayed and kicked, oxen bells clanged to a chorus of moos, and little ones ran in circles screaming and laughing while fathers cursed things into order.

Finding Mr. Sunday

The start of the train that should have taken thirty minutes stretched into an hour as new mules and new drivers came to an understanding. Peter rode back and forth exhorting green drivers to hurry and form up for departure while Hobs rode around encouraging the uninitiated.

Rio seemed to be everywhere at once, helping the drivers in Will's group ready their teams and wagons. With his help, Ish, Kate, and Will went forward to begin the journey close to the front of the train.

Hank had brought Minnie to the campsite the night before, and Mary Nel was riding close to the group.

She saw a rider hurrying toward her. As the rider was about to pass, she saw it was Peter intent on another mission.

"Good morning, Peter," Mary Nel yelled to him as he rode past.

Peter quickly turned his horse around and rode back to Mary Nel, pulling the sorrel gelding even with Minnie. He looked at Mary Nel and tipped his hat as a shy smile spread across his face.

"Good morning, Miss Daniels. I … hope you had a pleasant night," he said.

"Indeed, I did, Peter. And you must call me Mary Nel. It's too far to California for any silly formalities."

The early morning sun seemed to focus solely on Mary Nel, putting a sparkle in her eyes and streaks of gold in her hair.

"Why, I'd be honored," he said.

Again, Peter seemed at a loss for words.

"I … I have to get everyone to speed … so … I'll see you later," he said.

"I hope so," said Mary Nel as she flashed her incredible smile.

He turned his horse around, heeled the gelding to a spirited start, and continued toward the rear of the wagon train.

Somehow, through all the ruckus and clatter, he heard a mockingbird singing its heart out.

The first week brought gentle breezes, warm sunshine, and evenings made for sleeping. The trail quickly left Missouri behind and cut through the northeast corner of Kansas. The flat land was broken only by the Blue

Mound as it rose out of nowhere on the Kansas prairie, perhaps an early promise of what was to come in the months ahead.

Alcove Spring, with its twelve-foot waterfall and ring of wildflowers, was like a sparkling jewel in a limestone setting. Even the most eager travelers longed to rest in its tranquility.

The train moved quickly out of Kansas and into the soon-to-be state of Nebraska. A sea of green prairie stretched in all directions, and a constant wind mirrored a voyage at sea, save the water.

Fort Kearny, marking the end of the first long leg of the journey, was a little more than two weeks travel time ahead.

Eventually travelers and animals adjusted to the daily routine. Up at daybreak, round up the teams, have a quick breakfast, move out within an hour. Then, break at noon for all to rest, feed, and water if possible, and back on the trail until late afternoon. The evening hours brought a good meal, rest, some socializing, and an early bedtime.

The prairie seemed endless, as far as one could see, leaving the eye little to do but battle the increasing wind and dust on the well-used trail. The wagons spread out ten to twelve across the front when possible.

A few Indians were here and there, mostly Kaw, looking for handouts and any unwatched property. The travelers were warned to keep close watch on their stock and avoid offering food or anything else to them.

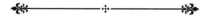

Will, Kate, Mary Nel, Ish, and Maggie sat around the campfire as Rio served up supper. Hank walk into the camp and had his plate filled by Rio.

"We gonna have us some rain soon," said Hank as he sat down on his haunches. "Could be a good'n way them clouds is brewin'."

He nodded to the west. The sinking sun highlighted a line of clouds stretching nearly across the entire western horizon, boiling slowly like a molten mountain.

"Be here 'fore morning," he said.

"We could use a little rain," said Kate as she pushed a loose strand of hair from her eyes.

"Don't get just a little rain from clouds like them, ma'am," said Hank.

Finding Mr. Sunday

"So far it's been easy going," said Mary Nel. "The dust gets everywhere, though. Minnie likes her rubdowns in the evenings as much as I like my baths."

"She has really taken to the trail," said Will. "I was afraid that being such a sophisticated lady, she might have a hard time of it, but she's doing just fine."

"I like to ride with Momma sometimes so I've tethered her to the wagon, and she has adapted well to it," said Mary Nel. "She's such a fine horse, Will. I should thank you every day."

"It's good to handle the wagon sometimes and to ride some. I"m glad to have Luke handling my wagon. I have a hard time being stuck in that seat when I see something interesting along the way," said Will.

Will had asked around for anyone wanting to handle his wagon a few days a week. Luke, who was traveling with his grandson, accepted the offer and enjoyed being occupied.

"I like to go off the trail every so often and see what I can see," Will said.

"I want to go with you sometime," said Mary Nel. "May I?"

"Okay by me, but you better clear that with Kate," he said.

"Oh, it's okay with me as long as she's with you and doesn't go out alone," said Kate.

"Kate, you know you are welcome to ride either of my horses when you want. Hank wouldn't mind taking over for you when he's not pushing the stock," said Will. "Luke would, too."

"Any time, ma'am," said Hank.

"Why, thank you both. I'm going to take you two up on that … soon," said Kate.

"BAM!" The relative quiet of the evening was shattered by a gunshot less than a hundred yards from the campsite. Will jumped up, grabbed his gun belt, and ran toward the sound.

He heard men yelling and cursing as he got closer to the area where the sound had originated.

In the middle of a campsite, two men were facing each other, one holding

Dick Ward

a rifle and the other standing with his hand over his holster as if readying to draw his pistol.

A half dozen men, women, and children had cleared the circle of the campfire and were cowering behind wagons.

"Hold it!" yelled Will. "What's going on here?"

He had just buckled his gun belt in place.

The two men stood staring at each other. One man held a rifle diagonally across his chest with the barrel pointed to the sky. He was the first to speak.

"This polecat threatened to shoot my dog. Was gonna whup me, he said. I'm too old for that bull crap so I got my rifle. He tried to take it from me, and it went off."

The man speaking kept his eyes on the other man as he spoke.

Will walked closer and got a look at the other man whose back was to him as he came into the campsite.

It was Pel Ligon.

"This is none of your concern, kid," he said, staring at the man holding the rifle, his hand still hovering over his holstered pistol.

"I'm making it my concern, Ligon. Whether you like it or not. Get your hands away from that pistol," Will said.

He turned to the man with the rifle.

"Mister, put that rifle down. There are women and children all around here, and you could have easily killed someone. What's your name?"

"Brandt, Jack Brandt," he said. "He grabbed at it, that's why it went off."

"Here, let me have it," said Will as he held out his left hand.

Brandt took his eyes off Ligon and looked at Will for the first time. Will towered over Brandt.

Whether looking for a way out of the situation or merely being cooperative, Brandt handed the rifle to Will and stepped back from Ligon.

"Thank you, Mr. Brandt," said Will. "Try to calm down now."

Will turned to Ligon and stepped closer to him.

"Get your hands away from that pistol, or I'll take it away from you," he said as he faced Ligon.

Ligon looked at him, curled his lips, and spoke through his teeth.

"I'll kill you if you try to take my gun. Nobody takes my pistol from me," he growled.

183

Finding Mr. Sunday

Will could smell the whiskey breath from where he stood.

Hobs Adams rushed into the campsite with Peter following close behind.

In what looked like a single motion, Will lunged forward and hit Ligon with a backhand slap across his face, stooped, and lowered Brandt's rifle to the ground.

Before Ligon knew what was happening, Will straightened up and slammed an upper cut with his right fist hard into Ligon's face.

Ligon was nearly lifted off the ground by the force of the blow and fell hard on his back, his head bouncing off the ground. Will was over him in an instant, removing Ligon's pistol from its holster.

He stood there and began removing the caps from each of the cylinder chambers.

"Enough!" yelled Hobs Adams.

Ligon lay on the ground looking around trying to get his bearings. He lifted himself up on his elbows and shook his head.

"What happened here?" said Hobs.

Brandt spoke up. "This man came into the camp chasing my dog. Said the dog was eating some of his stores. I told him I'd pay him for the stores, but he said he was going to kill the dog. I picked up my rifle, and he grabbed at it and it went off."

"The damn dog was eating my side meat. Shouldn't have no dogs on the train anyhow," said Ligon as he was rubbing his jaw.

"Mr. Brandt, if you can't control your dog, you'll have to get rid of it. Do you understand?" said Adams.

"Yeah. But that ain't no call to kill a dog." Brandt glared at Ligon, who was getting up off the ground.

"This ain't over," said Ligon.

"It better be, Ligon. You stay the hell away from Brandt. Any more trouble from either of you, and you're leaving this wagon train," Hobs said.

"And you," Ligon said, pointing a finger at Will. "You ain't seen the last of me. You'll pay for this, damn you."

"That's enough out of you, Ligon," said Hobs. "You seem to look for trouble. Any more and you're gone."

Hobs was beginning to get angry. "Now get on back to your camp."

Will tossed the disarmed pistol back to Ligon.

Ligon picked up his hat, knocked it against his pant leg, glared at Will, and stalked out of the campsite.

Just then, Hartwell came rushing into the camp. He saw Will and Hobs and walked over to join them.

"Let's take a walk, George," said Hobs to Hartwell. "Come with us a minute, Will."

The three men walked a ways from the camp and stopped to talk, and Hobs told Hartwell what had happened. "Will here handled the situation," Hobs said.

"Good," said Hartwell. "I was a good bit away and wasn't sure where the shot came from. Glad you could get here quickly, Will."

"I don't understand that Ligon," Will said. "He's been drinking. He seems to want trouble. He threatened me the other day. I just let it go, but he definitely has a mean streak. Might even be dangerous."

"Well, I doubt he'd want to tangle with you in a fight, Will, but I'd be careful. He might be the kind to try to get back at you when you least expect it," said Hobs.

"Oh, I'll keep an eye on him, all right," said Will.

"We probably should have a council meeting soon and talk about having a little security committee to address trouble like this. I've had to do that on several trains," said Hobs.

"I agree," said Hartwell.

"Yes," said Will. "I'm all for it."

"I'll be getting back to camp, then," said Will.

He walked back to his campsite. Kate, Mary Nel, and Rio were sitting there waiting for his return.

"What happened?" asked Mary Nel.

Will told them about the quarrel.

"Isn't Ligon the man who got upset at the council?" asked Kate.

"That's him," said Will. "He threatened me later on, too."

"You didn't tell me that," said Kate, sounding a little surprised.

"I didn't need to bother you with it," said Will. "But now, with all that's happened, if you see him around the campsite, let me know."

"Will, please be careful," Kate said in a concerned tone.

Then, with a little laugh, she said, "We don't want to have to nurse you back to health again."

Will got to thinking about that comment. He had not told her about Hurley.

"I guess I should tell you about one of the men who shot me," said Will.

"What do you mean?" said Kate.

Will told Kate about the incident in Independence involving Hurley. Kate and Mary Nel were flabbergasted by the story.

"Will, you could have been killed!" said Mary Nel.

"Ladies, I appreciate your concern for me. But I'm a big boy. I'm not weak any more, and I know how to handle myself," he said sincerely.

"I'm sure you do, Will ... but you know, we kind of count on you being around now...maybe selfishly so," said Kate.

"I know. I'm pleased about that," Will said with a smile. "And you both are in good hands, Kate."

CHAPTER TEN

T he light sleepers were awakened by the sound of the wind as it began to buffet the heavy canvas wagon covers. Everyone else awoke to the sound of thunder and lightning. Acorn-sized raindrops pelted the wagons, and hail stones as big as walnuts slammed into everything on God's Earth.

The wind roared like an angry monster, blowing away anything not tied down. Even the double-layered canvas wagon tops ripped from the support bows. Family milk cows jerked free of their tethers and ran blindly into the dark night. Men, women, children, and animals alike were soaked in seconds, then bruised by the hail that seemed to fall sideways.

Those who had been in such storms expected it to pass in minutes. But, alas, they were fooled by Mother Nature as the beast hung overhead and howled at ear-splitting levels, drowning out the screams of the women and children.

On and on the storm raged, covering the ground with inches of water and hail stones. No one escaped the fury that was unlike any storm they had ever seen.

For nearly an hour there was no let up between the lightning, thunder, rain, hail, and wind. Then the prayers of everyone were finally heard, and the worst of the storm moved on. The rain became a steady downpour rather than a torrent.

Men began to move about, surveying the wreckage, and mothers counted their children and hugged whimpering babies.

Every campsite was torn apart. Cooking pots, utensils, barrels, canvas, clothing, and blankets were strewn everywhere. There was little or no dry wood or fuel to be had. The few lanterns that survived bobbed about, shedding light on the devastated campsites.

"Kate, Mary Nel!" Will yelled.

He had managed to find a lantern and a dry match and stumbled through the ruination.

"Are you there? Answer me," he demanded.

"We're here," answered Kate.

Finding Mr. Sunday

Will held the lantern up higher and saw two shapes moving in the bed of their wagon. The two were struggling to rise, lifting the sodden blankets that covered their bodies. Hail stones filled the wagon bed, making it hard to stand or move around.

"Thank God," said Will as he came closer. "Are you hurt?"

"No, no. We are both fine. Soaked and cold, but we're alive," said Kate.

"Look at this mess," said Mary Nel as she stumbled around in her heavy robe trying to maintain her balance.

"Mary Nel," said Kate. "Can you get to the clothes trunk? Those clothes should be dry."

Mary Nel moved carefully in the dim light to the front of the wagon. She located the trunk and lifted the top, hail and debris sliding off as she raised it.

"They are all dry!" she yelled.

"Can you find the lantern?" asked Will. "Here, take mine and look around."

Kate took the lantern from him and began lifting canvas, covers, and clothing.

"Here it is," she said. "It's not broken."

"Pass it to me and bring my lantern closer. I'll light yours from it," instructed Will.

The two lanterns gave a decent light that revealed even more of the damage. Mercifully, the rain began to taper off to a fine drizzle, and the wind began to die down.

"It should be daylight in an hour. I'm going to check on Ish and Maggie. Have you seen Rio?" Will asked.

"I am here," said a voice from the edge of darkness. "I'm all right."

Will turned the lantern and saw Rio crawling out from under Kate's other wagon. He was wet but unharmed.

"Good. See to Kate and Mary Nel, Rio. I'm going to check on Ish and Maggie," said Will.

He picked his way across the other side of the campsite and went around to the back of Ish's wagon. He held the lantern up and looked inside.

"Hello, Ish and Maggie," Will called. "Are you all right?"

He saw Ish's big face in the lantern light. He was partially covered by a

188

canvas tarp.

"I put a big piece of canvas in here last night, and we covered up with it. Good thing I did. We wet, but we can dry," said Ish.

"I never seen such a storm," said Maggie. "The Lord must of been mad about something."

She was peeking out from the canvas, her nightcap askew.

"Nobody is hurt. That's the important thing," said Will.

"Ish, if you don't need me, I'm going to find Hank and see to the stock."

"You go, Will. We be all right," he said.

Will picked his way through the cluttered campsites to the area where the stock was located before the storm hit. He saw men milling around and heard voices but saw only a few cows and mules. He walked up to the men who were trying to find tracks of the vanished herd.

"Anybody seen Hank Willis?" he asked.

"Over here," said a voice ten or twelve yards away.

Will turned and saw the shape of a man holding a horse and stroking its neck. As he got closer, he saw it was Hank, and he was holding Minnie.

"She came right up to me when the storm started," said Hank as he stroked the animal "Stayed with me the whole time, she did."

Hank was hatless and soaked to the skin like everyone else.

"No tellin' where the stock is. They scattered when the thunder and lightning came. Even the oxen ran. One helluva storm," Hank said. "Been in worse. But this one I'll remember."

"Let's go back to the campsite," said Will. "See what we can do to clean up this mess. Find some coffee. I'll get Ish, and we'll start hunting stock. I bet those bays of mine are fifty miles away."

The sun seemed to rise slowly as it fought its way through the breaking clouds, moving quickly to the northeast. The pink dawn brought with it the full realization of the storm's might.

Dazed families walked among their scattered possessions, picking up the pieces of their lives.

At the campsite, Rio had performed a miracle and gotten a fire going. The smell of coffee brought some sense of normalcy to the tired travelers.

"Minnie!" yelled Mary Nel.

She ran to Hank and took the rope from him. As soon as she heard Mary

Finding Mr. Sunday

Nel's voice the mare nickered, knowing she was going to be all right.

"She rode it out with me," said Hank. "She's smart, that one."

Kate and Mary Nel, now in dry clothes, had been picking up the campsite trying to sort through the debris.

Both layers of canvas on the two wagons were badly torn, but the pieces remained hanging, and it was possible the tops might be restitched. For the most part, food and rations were still usable.

Blankets, clothes, and sleeping pallets were laid out and sorted. Rio was stringing ropes between the wagons and hanging the wet materials to dry.

Ish and Maggie, who seemed to have escaped with the least damage, were busy getting breakfast started.

"No traveling today. No traveling today," a voice called out repeatedly.

Will looked up to see Peter riding through the campsites. He wondered how in the world Peter had found a horse.

Peter stopped at the campsite and dismounted. He tied his horse to a wagon wheel and walked into the center of the campsite.

"Hello, folks," he said. "Is everyone all right here?"

"Yep. A little wet but no one hurt. Have you been around to all the campsites?" said Will.

"Mostly. A few bruises from stuff flying around, but nobody was seriously hurt. Some people lost some supplies, flour barrels, water barrels, and such that were mounted on their wagons. I've made a list of those who need help. Biggest problem is the canvas on the wagons. But most of them can be sewn back together," said Peter. "Mr. Akers, one of the freighters, has two wagon loads of supplies he is willing to sell. He's got some canvas, too. Some of the other freighters are willing to sell some goods, too."

"Hobs is trying to get together a group to help round up the stock. We don't have many horses. I see you have one horse. Do you suppose you can help us?" Peter asked.

"I can," said Mary Nel. "When do we start?"

Then, to Kate, "Is it all right, Momma?"

Kate seemed to give the question some thought, then smiled at Peter.

"I think so. Just stay close to Peter," she said.

"Have you eaten this morning, Peter?" asked Kate.

"Yes, ma'am," he said. "A little hard tack."

"Well, you join us then. We're going to have some bacon and biscuits shortly," she said.

"Mary Nel, we're going to get organized in about thirty minutes. Soon as the sun is up all the way. If you want, I'll come back by here, and you can ride with me to the gathering point," he said.

"Thank you, Peter. We'll be ready to go," she replied.

"Mrs. Daniels, I'll take you up on that bacon biscuit when I come back, if you don't mind," said Peter.

"Of course, Peter," she said as she continued sorting through the mess.

"Peter, Hank, Ish, and I are going to join the group, too. We'll be on foot, though, until we find the stock," said Will.

"Come on up then. We may have an extra horse. But many people will be walking," Peter said.

"We'll be there," said Will.

About forty people were gathered waiting for the stock roundup to begin. All were men except Mary Nel. Hobs was standing on a wagon waiting for the last few men to show up.

"Folks. We got a test of what Mother Nature can do last night. It won't be our last. The prairie storms can be pretty bad sometimes. But there were no serious injuries, and we can be thankful for that.

"We have about twelve horses and mules. We can't make out tracks because of the gully washer. So we're going to fan out somewhat, with most of you going east."

He gestured back down the trail.

"My guess, you'll find them in that clump of trees we passed yesterday afternoon. As soon as someone spots stock or signs of them, get word back here. If you want to fire a rifle, go ahead.

"Now everybody watch out for flooded areas. Somewhere in that flooded area is a creek bed, and you can break a horse's leg easy. Plenty of snakes about, too, so watch your step.

"George Hartwell and me will stay here and oversee things. Other council members are here, too, so yell if you need us."

"Mary Nel, you come with me and stick pretty close," Peter said in a low voice as he leaned toward her.

"I will, Peter," she said.

Finding Mr. Sunday

She had rubbed Minnie down and given her water and grain. The mare seemed eager to be off.

Will, Ish, and Hank, with bridles in their hands, started walking to the east.

Most of the riders headed out, but a few stayed back waiting for stock to be found. It wasn't long before several shots were heard from the east. Two of the riders left to check out the findings. Then a shot was heard from southeast of the camp. The last two riders went in that direction.

Again more shots from the east. It seemed that most of the stock had headed east away from the storm toward the trees, as Hobs had guessed.

An hour or so later, one herd of mixed stock was coming in from the east, then a second herd was spotted coming from the southeast. Animals were brought in throughout the morning, tired and eager to be a part of the herd again.

By noon most of the stock were found. Several animals were found injured or dead, mostly young stock. Will, Hank, and Ish returned riding Will's horses and one of the mules.

Peter and Mary Nel had headed west and after a couple of miles spotted a few cows standing in the lee of a slight rise in the terrain. A calf was lying on its side. Peter jumped from his horse and went to the calf. The nervous mother watched closely.

"Is it alive?" called Mary Nel.

She dismounted and went to the downed calf.

"She's breathing. I don't see a broken leg. My guess she's just tuckered out from the run," he said as he stroked the calf.

"I'll put her up on my horse. We'll see if she gets better," said Peter.

He picked up the animal and laid her small body across his horse in front of the saddle, then mounted his horse.

"Let's go a little more west and see what we can see. I doubt we'll find anymore," he said.

They continued at a slow pace, followed by the mother cow.

"I see some more!" said Mary Nel as she pointed to the northwest.

They made their way to the animals and found four oxen grazing contentedly.

"I don't see any more," said Mary Nel as she scanned the western horizon.

"Let's head on back then," said Peter.

They turned the oxen and headed east until they came back to the cattle they had seen earlier. With the small herd in front and the calf lying across Peter's horse, they headed back to the wagon train.

After getting the herd started, Mary Nel and Peter rode side by side. The eastern sun shined directly in their eyes, dictating that they pull the brims of their hats down low.

"Mary Nel, may I ask you question? Please don't take offense," Peter said.

"Certainly, Peter," she said as she turned to look at him.

"Is Will ... uh ... I mean are you ... or... is Will your fellow?" Peter stammered.

"Will? Oh, no," she said with a smile. "I don't have a ... well, fellow, as you say. He is dear to me, I'll grant you, and to Momma. He was shot by robbers on a trail near our home in Missouri, and we helped nurse him back to health. He has been with us since then.

"He is a fine person. He's very smart, educated, a wonderful man. He is a very caring person, too. Momma and I trust him and have grown to be very fond of him. I think he feels he is our protector, and we kind of like that," she said.

Peter said nothing, and she continued after a pause.

"I think the world of him. But in all honesty, I think Will sees me as his little sister. I'm not sure how I feel about that. All I know is that he's a big part of our lives now, and if he left I would be terribly upset ... as would Momma."

"Why do you ask?" she said, watching closely to see his response.

He lifted his head and looked at her as the sun lit up his face.

"I was just wondering ... you know ... curious," he said with a smile.

Mary Nel could feel her cheeks coloring, but she returned his smile.

By late afternoon, all of the stock had been claimed by their owners, and the herd was calmly grazing just east of the wagon train. The day turned sunny and very warm with a good breeze from the west, perfect drying weather.

The wagon train campsite was a colorful sea of blankets and clothing waving in the wind. Word spread that the departure would be at nine o'clock

Finding Mr. Sunday

the next morning.

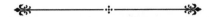

The trail continued northwest toward Fort Kearny with the scenery changing very little. There was a surprising amount of traffic on and near the trail. The occasional adobe house, ranch, or trading post broke the monotony.

To the excitement of the travelers, they often spotted herds of buffalo. Some herds were so large it looked as if the landscape itself was moving.

Travelers headed east often stopped and visited with the train travelers, exchanging goods and tales in equal measure, reminding the travelers that they had not left civilization completely behind.

Will and Kate were riding Will's horses, and Rio, Hank, and Luke handled the wagons. Mary Nel was closer to the front of the wagon train riding with Peter.

"Seems like Peter and Mary Nel are enjoying each other's company," said Will.

"I've noticed," said Kate. "He's a nice young man, and I don't mind as long as they don't venture away from the train. She promised me she wouldn't do that. We're not far from Fort Kearny, and there are all kinds of people around. I'd hate for them to run into the wrong sort."

"We're a few days out yet, but I've noticed the trail is busier," said Will.

"Sometimes I worry how she will handle this," Kate said. "She's led a sheltered life, and all of this is a big change for her. Up until now, her life has been school, books, hard work, and a lot of daydreaming. I don't recall her ever spending time with a boy."

"Well, she's a young woman now," said Will. "And a smart one. She can handle the changes. It takes some doing, though. I know. She still has you, and you're a great influence on her. She'll be fine, and Peter seems like a gentleman."

"I think you are right," Kate said. "But I can't help but remember how I was when I was her age. I was totally unprepared when a boy took an interest in me but intrigued at the same time."

She shared a secret smile.

"You mean you were surprised that a boy showed an interest in you?" Will asked with a teasing smile.

"Of course," she said returning his smile. "I was a little country girl come to the big city."

She paused a minute.

"Oh, there were boys in church who would stop talking and turn all red when I came near them. But they were boys I had grown up with, so I didn't really pay them any mind.

"But when I went to St. Louis with Mother to visit boarding schools, I saw a different world. The city was exciting; the people were so different. And young men were not shy about stopping in the street and doffing their hats when we walked by."

"And why wouldn't they?" said Will. "You swept them off their feet merely by walking by, I'm sure."

"Oh, Will ... don't tease," she said with pink in her cheeks.

"Oh, no, Kate," Will turned to her with a serious tone. "I wasn't teasing. I truly meant it. You do that."

She colored a bit more but did not pursue the comment. They rode in silence for a while.

Then Will spoke up. "Your life will change in a big way, too, you know," he said. "It won't be the quiet life of running an apple orchard in Missouri anymore. You're going to meet a lot of new people. And most of them will be the right kind of people. They'll see right away that you are smart, kind, and compassionate."

He stopped talking, as if trying to frame his next thought carefully.

"Kate, you have this thing about you ... I'm not sure how to describe it, but most of the people who meet you want to become a part of your life."

"You think so, Will?" she asked as she looked him in the eyes.

"I'm sure of it," he said, giving her a special smile. "I did."

That evening as he lay in his wagon, Will thought about his conversation with Kate. He should've come right out and told Kate that she had already become a big part of his life. And that, with all the changes in her life and the people she would meet, he wanted her to continue to be a part of his life.

But, had he said that, he would have had to explain what that meant precisely. And he didn't really know.

Finding Mr. Sunday

He only knew that when he got close to someone, they eventually went away, and he surely did not want Kate to go away.

Fort Kearny could be seen across the flat plain when it was still almost a day's ride away. It wasn't as much a fort as it was a group of low adobe buildings scattered around a plaza flanked by cottonwood trees.

The fort had seen better days and looked somewhat rundown. A few cannons guarded an American flag that waved in the constant wind. A stockade wall was under construction, but it did not surround the buildings and seemed to be a half-hearted effort.

Over the years of westward migration, the fort and surrounding area had become a source for everything travelers needed in the way of repairs and supplies, albeit at high prices.

Most of the travelers just looked at the offerings, but some decided the price was worth the convenience and restocked for the next long leg of the journey.

"I think we should get our canvas replaced while we can. We're going to be in the area a couple of days. We might want to look around and see if we need anything. Fort Laramie, our next stop, is a ways away," said Will.

The group was having the morning meal after having set up camp a couple of miles from the fort the night before.

"I'd like to get some more trail clothes and some good rain protection," said Kate.

"And I would like to have a pair of spare boots," said Mary Nel.

"Well, there is no shortage of sellers," said Will.

"Maggie and Ish, do you two need anything?" asked Kate.

"Only a few food supplies. We good otherwise," said Ish.

"Rio can help you with that if you like. He's going to buy what things we need," said Kate.

"Yes, Mr. Ish," said Rio. "I would be happy to help you."

"Hobs and a few of the council members are going to meet with the Army captain here at the fort to discuss the trail ahead," said Will. "I'll be busy with that for a while."

Will had heard that the stockade wall was being built because the Sioux were making noises. But he didn't want to mention that unless he knew for a fact there was a cause for concern on the trail ahead. He was hopeful the

Army captain would clarify the situation, if there was one to be clarified.

"Then Mary Nel and I will see what we can find," said Kate. "We should all be back by late afternoon."

"Good, I'll see everyone then," said Will.

He strapped on his two Army revolvers and went to his waiting horse. The weight of the two guns had taken some time to get used to, but now he felt undressed without them.

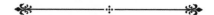

"The Sioux raised a ruckus last year, but that seems to have calmed down," the captain said. "We don't feel anything is imminent. But things could change quickly. The stockade is just a precaution.

"We're asking small trains to join up with other trains from here on out. There is safety in numbers."

Will, Hobs, Hartwell, and several other council members were meeting with the captain at the Army headquarters at Fort Kearny.

Captain Burnett was the epitome of an Army captain. Mid-thirties, perhaps, crisp and clean in appearance, with excellent posture and bearing. He was obviously a man of education and experience who took his job very seriously.

Captain Burnett continued, "Trains with less than thirty wagons are vulnerable, but your train is a good size. I don't think you have much to worry about. You will have the Platte River to your right for quite a while now, and that'll give you some protection from that side. But continue the rotating guard at night.

"Maybe send a couple of good men to scout a few miles ahead of the train. Just to keep an eye out. Make sure your stock is well guarded at night."

"Well, Captain," said Hobs. "We thank you for meeting with us and giving us that information."

"My pleasure, Mr. Adams," said the captain. "It's our job to protect those who are headed west. If I can be of further service, please let me know."

As the men rode toward the train, they saw a rider coming toward them at a fast pace. As he neared the group, they recognized James Burrell, another member of the council. He pulled his horse up just short of the group.

"Hobs, that Ligon feller has taken it upon hisself to get mean drunk, and he's staggering around waving his pistol about in the camp," Burrell said excitedly. "You better calm him down afore he shoots somebody or somebody shoots him."

"Let's go then," said Hobs as he heeled his horse in the side.

The group came into the camp and slowed, looking for Ligon. It wasn't long before they could hear a voice cursing loudly toward the middle of the encampment. They made their way to the source of the sound.

"This here outfit ain't worth a damn. Yellow bellies and liars, all them council members. Why, we ain't never gonna git to California. We ain't even seen the worst of the trail yet and…"

"Ligon!" shouted Hartwell as the group dismounted. "What are you doing drunk? You know that is not tolerated."

At this point Ligon had put his pistol in his belt.

"Damn you, Hartwell," said Ligon as he strained to see through squinting eyes. "I'll drink all I want. Ain't your business."

"It is my business if you're part of this train. I think we've had enough of you and your bad behavior."

Ligon glared at Hartwell as he weaved for balance.

"The hell with all of you. I'm leaving this train anyway. Just wanted people to know what asses you all are … all of you."

He stood there as if fighting a headwind.

"Then get out of here. Right now," said Hobs. "Get your wagon and go."

"I'll go when I want, damn you," said Ligon.

The council members stood watching Ligon as he swayed unsteadily. They knew the man was unpredictable. Ligon turned as if to walk away.

Then he turned back around to face the men and, at the same time, drew his pistol and pointed it at the group.

"Everyone get behind your wagons!" shouted Hobs at the bunch of people who had gathered to watch the disturbance.

"Now! Move!" he shouted loudly.

The bystanders grabbed their little ones and scurried for safety.

"Put that gun down, Ligon," said Will.

He stepped in front of the group of men, facing Ligon head on.

"You. You bastard," said Ligon with hate in his voice. "I oughta kill you."

"Look, we don't want any shooting here. Someone will get hurt," said Will.

As he spoke, Will checked the line of fire should he have to use his pistol. It was clear of people.

"I don't know what's wrong with you. Nobody on this train has done anything to you. Are you just plain crazy?" said Will.

As he spoke Will focused on Ligon's eyes. A little voice in his head told him Ligon was going to do something stupid.

He saw the change in Ligon's eyes just a blink before Ligon moved his gun and pointed it directly at Will.

Ligon's fingers were about to close around the trigger of his pistol when a .44-caliber bullet slammed into his right hand, removing most of his index finger.

Ligon's pistol went flying and hit the ground a couple of feet behind him and to his right. He screamed loudly and grabbed his bleeding hand.

No one had seen Will go for his gun. Either he was too fast, or all eyes had been on Ligon.

Will holstered his .44 and stepped toward Ligon. He handed him a large bandana and watched as Ligon quickly applied it to his bleeding hand.

"Hobs, I'd suggest a couple of men see Ligon to his wagon and then to the fort. There's probably a doctor there. Ligon's partner is around somewhere, and we need to make sure he knows he's not wanted here, either."

"I'll take care of that. Why don't you two men get Ligon to the fort?" Hartwell said to two council members standing nearby.

The onlookers came out from their hiding places not quite believing what they had just witnessed.

"That was some fine shooting, Will," said Hobs. "Don't believe I've ever seen anything like that before."

"I hated to do it, Hobs. The man was drunk. But I could tell he was going to shoot me," said Will.

"Oh, he was gonna shoot you, all right. I could see that. You were just a little bit ahead of him," said Hobs.

Will turned to Hobs and nodded slowly. With a faraway look in his eyes, he spoke the thought that ran through his mind.

Finding Mr. Sunday

"I guess being a little bit ahead is enough ... as long as you don't miss."

Two days later, the wagon train left Fort Kearny and continued on the trail west following the Platte River. The trail was unpredictable, at times flat and easily traveled, and at other times, twisting and narrow, with thick damp sand bogging down the wagons and making passage nearly impossible.

Often the train had to climb the bluff of the river valley to keep going, testing the fiber of the beasts and the patience of the travelers.

Will and Mary Nel were riding side by side, guiding their horses carefully.

"I've never seen such a wide river," said Mary Nel.

"It's charitable to call the Platte a river, at least as we know rivers. It's wide all right, but in many places it's only inches deep. The bottom is nothing more than sandy mud. Almost impossible to cross. If you get water from that river you have to let it set until the sand settles. Even then, you have to be might thirsty to drink it," said Will.

"How come you are not riding with Peter today?" asked Will.

He looked at Mary Nel with a little smile on his face. Despite cheeks that had attained a becoming tan, she colored somewhat before answering.

"I think when he is riding with me he doesn't feel like he is working. And he wants to do a good job for Mr. Adams," she said.

"From what I can see, you seem to enjoy his company," said Will, a little tease in his voice.

"Oh, I do," said Mary Nel. "He is very bright, and he has good manners. Much like you, I should say. But he is a little shy."

She turned toward him and caught his eye.

"Why, Will. You don't mind my riding with him do you?" said Mary Nel, a little tilt to her head.

This time, the teasing was directed at Will.

"Not at all," Will said quickly.

"I think it's good you have someone to talk to. This trip is going to be long and, at times, hard so it's good you have a friend."

"Well, he is a friend. One of the first things he asked me was if you were my fellow," she said with a laugh.

"Just out of curiosity, how did you answer him?" said Will.

Dick Ward

"I told him you weren't my fellow, but you were very dear to me and to Momma. I told him I thought you probably looked upon me more as a little sister than anything," she said.

"Hmmm," said Will as he thought about that.

"Was I right?" she asked. "Do you think of me as a sister?"

There was a long pause.

"Well, it's a bit more complicated than that, I suppose … I mean … in the time that I have known you and your mother, I've grown very fond of the two of you and would do anything for you two. I want to keep the two of you safe. I don't want either of you to have any worries if I can help it.

"If the two of you, all of a sudden, were no longer a part of my life I would hate to face each day."

For a moment, the rattle of the wagons, the squeak of leather, and the sound of hoof beats were the only sounds.

"Beyond that, all I can say is I'm going to take each day as it comes, see what life brings for all of us. And I'd like to be part of your lives, however that comes about."

There was another pause.

"You didn't answer my question, Will," said Mary Nel as she tilted her head again.

"I know," he said.

He kicked his horse in the sides and lunged ahead, leaving her staring at him as he rode off.

Then, an even bigger smile spread across her face.

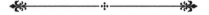

The trail along the river was sometimes narrow, sometimes a few miles wide. Selecting a place for the train to overnight was often a challenge. At times the train stretched the day to find a spot, and at other times, it stopped early when a suitable spot presented itself.

On this particular day, the train had found an ideal spot to overnight in the late afternoon, and word spread that the day's travel would end. This gave the families extra time to prepare the stock for the night, catch up on a few neglected chores and have a little time for socializing before the evening meal.

Several of the men set off to find any fresh game that might come down to the river for water.

Rio had the evening fire going and was chopping ham and bacon to go in the big pot of beans that never seemed to empty. The smell of strong coffee and the bread baking in the Dutch oven enticed each of the travelers to find a comfortable spot around the fire.

"Today was a nice day for traveling," said Kate. "A warm sun without scorching, little dust, and no wind to speak of. I hope it continues this way for a while."

"It would be nice if that happened," said Mary Nel. "But I know we have a long way to go."

"Oh, we ain't seen but a bit of the elephant yet. We'll see a whole lot more when we pass Fort Laramie," said Hank. "More'n we want, I 'spect."

"Elephant? What you mean, elephant? No elephants out here," said Ish.

"Ain't ya'll heard 'bout the elephant?" he said.

He looked around at those in the circle, a mock look of surprise on his face.

"Why, that's what this here trip to California is all about."

Hank took a loud sip of coffee, a little smug smile of secret knowledge creeping onto his face.

The folks looked at each other, silently asking if anyone knew what Hank was talking about.

"I think I might have heard about the elephant from some of the soldiers who fought in the war," said Will. "Seems some of the boys who went to war were all caught up in the glory of it.

But when they went into battle and experienced the fear, the horror, and the awfulness of battle they were said to 'see the elephant.'"

"Yep, very same elephant," said Hank. "Goin' to California seems like a nice, easy adventure at first."

He put down his coffee and pulled out his pipe.

"Then come them storms, the blisterin' sun, the dust, the buffalo stampedes, the mountains, the river crossings, the snow, the fevers, and the deaths. That's when you liable to see the elephant," said Hank.

"The old elephant's anything that gets in your way. Kinda like all the trials, tribulations, and challenges rolled into one big thing … an elephant," he said as he packed and lit his pipe.

"Hank!" said Mary Nel. "You make it seem like it's hopeless to try to do this."

"Oh, no. No, Miss Mary, don't get me wrong. The thing is, the elephant's the challenge…the things that seem to get in our way … to test us, you see."

He waved his pipe as if to emphasize his point.

"Why, some people can't take the elephant. They just quit … or turn around and go back maybe…or just give up when things get tough …"

"But there's the others … the strong ones. Well, they just don't let the elephant get in their way … ever. They just keep going."

"They're the ones taking this country west."

He puffed his pipe into a big cloud of smoke.

The days passed with little change in the scenery or the routine. Traveling by wagon was often numbing but gave Kate plenty of time to think. She thought about what Hank said about the elephant.

She'd seen a few in her time. Losing Ben, Mom, Pop. We've all seen our own elephants, she supposed.

But she had no intention of turning around or giving up.

No, this was a new beginning for her and Mary Nel. Oh, there would be elephants, no doubt. But she wouldn't settle for less than she wanted. It was the Nelson in her.

The biggest elephant in her life now was … what did she want?

A husband? A companion? Someone to ease the loneliness she often felt? Another farm, maybe?

Will had come into her life like a whirlwind and changed everything. Through him she saw all the possibilities in her own life.

Or maybe he had just jostled her into doing what she really wanted to do all along — to change the course of her life and embrace what was to come.

Will. Now there was a man unlike any she had ever met. Strong, smart, ready to take on anything. Mature far beyond his years.

There was a fire deep inside him. She could almost feel the heat when she was near him. Maybe that was why he had become such a huge part of her life so quickly.

Or maybe, it was just the presence of a man in her life that had been missing for too long. She was still a woman after all. With her own kind of fire. It might have been smoldering for a while, but it was there now, warm and alive.

She knew that she needed this time to figure out the rest of her life. And yes, to see the elephants, whatever they might be.

Bring on the elephants.

Mary Nel was riding alone this morning. The day was clear and beautiful. The sandy trail that ran by the Platte was not as dusty as usual. She was far enough ahead not to be bothered by the incessant creaks and rattles from the wagons or the drivers' yells and cracking whips.

She looked back, checking to make sure she didn't get too far ahead. Momma would not like that. But she knew Minnie could turn quickly and close the distance back to the wagons in very short order.

Mocking birds sang, and the striking blue and white magpies watched her every move, flitting away gracefully if she got too close, but too curious to leave entirely.

A nice breeze blew in her face. What a day, she thought. Even Minnie seemed to have a spring in her step. She reached out and patted the mare's neck.

Elephants, indeed, she thought. She hadn't seen any trace of one yet, she thought. But then, they'd not gone five hundred miles. She knew there was an allegorical piece to Hank's story. Aside from the loss of her father, so far in her life she had not let anything get in her way.

Oh, but you are barely fifteen.

Well, she'd have to worry about elephants when and if they came along. She was confident in her ability to cope. And whatever she set her mind to do, she'd do it, by gosh.

She had that Nelson toughness, like Momma. Momma was a determined woman who let very little get in her way despite all that she'd experienced.

There was so much ahead of her. More school? Surely there must be some fine schools in California. If not for educational purposes it would be good to be around other young ladies. Or did she want that?

Maybe. But she knew that she wanted to see more of the world. California, yes, but more than that. The world! Right now she didn't see how that would happen. It surely wouldn't if she just let her dreams die. Wasn't she one of the strong ones who didn't let the elephants deter her?

Maybe I need to marry well, she said with a laugh. That would be easy. But she didn't want to be dependent on anyone else to fulfill her dreams, and she surely didn't want to marry someone for their wealth.

Marriage, there's an interesting thought. She'd not been one to dwell on marrying the man of her dreams like some of her friends or some of the characters in books she read. Marriage was just too distant to think much about.

Why, she'd never been kissed yet. Never thought seriously about boys. But then Peter came into the picture. There was a new kind of feeling when she was around him. She couldn't really describe it. But she liked it.

He made her laugh, especially when she knew she was having an effect on him. He got befuddled easily when he was around her. But she liked being around him.

She had been around Will for a while now. But Will was so different. He seemed much more mature than Peter. Stronger. In charge. Determined.

She had witnessed the real Will emerge over time as he recovered from his injuries. She hadn't had any funny feelings when Will was around.

Or had she? She really had not thought about it much until Peter asked her about Will. She answered his question honestly. But when she and Will talked about her conversation with Peter, she picked up on something.

She was teasing him a little, sure. But she thought she had observed something in Will's reaction...or maybe it was his evasive answer to her question.

She knew that at times, he would look at her in a different way ... when he thought she wouldn't notice. But she had noticed.

Or maybe it was she who felt something that she had not acknowledged before. Was there something else going on? Was some of that new feeling there with Will?

Finding Mr. Sunday

Will was quite a man all right. Yes, she had never seen him as a boy. Even when he lay helpless before her she could sense something powerful in him.

He was smart, big, strong, yet sensitive ... a gentleman ... and he had a confident way about him that drew people to him. Will was an unusual person all right. A woman could do far worse than to end up with Will Sunday.

Will Sunday lay awake despite a long, tiring travel day that brought the wagons over twenty-five miles. It was unusual for him to have difficulty falling asleep. He hated to toss and turn.

He got up, pulled on his boots and picked up his Henry .44-60 rifle and stepped down from the wagon. The campfire was little more than a pile of glowing coals.

The moon, almost full, provided ample light for a walk. He headed toward the stock, as if justifying his wakefulness as something more than being restless.

A slight breeze erased any trace of sleepiness as he strode up the bank of the river valley to a point where the stock grazed peacefully. He spoke in a low calming voice as several of the horses lifted their heads to the night visitor, but only for a moment once they caught his scent.

"Evening, gentlemen," said Will in a quiet voice. "Things seem peaceful tonight."

"Quiet as a saloon on Sunday morning," said a voice he recognized as Hank's. "What brings you up here?"

"Oh, just wanted to get some fresh air. See the night," Will replied.

"You care for some coffee? May have to eat it with a spoon 'stead of drinking it, though," said Hank.

"No, thanks. I think I'm going to that big rock I see up a ways and commune with Mother Nature. Nice night for it."

He resumed his climb up the hill to the rock he saw silhouetted in the moonlight. Yep, he thought, this is a good sitting rock. He took stock of his surroundings, looking up, down, and across the wide river.

A few cottonwoods grew on the small river islands and gave some character to the horizon on the far shore. Sand bars changed the course of the water flow, causing ripples and little water falls.

The flowing water picked up the moonlight and winked, flirting back at the thousands of stars. His head filled with the marshy smell of the river, occasionally catching notes of the green grass and the smell of the livestock below.

What a night, he thought. It all brought to mind the many nights he'd spent with Caleb down by the river. It was not so long ago, but seemed, as did all his youth, like many years ago.

He could hear Caleb talking, his voice always with an edge of excitement or amusement. He could hear his laughter and smiled at the memory. He was always happy around Caleb.

He thought about Hank and the elephant story. Talk about elephants. Yes, he'd seen some. His father was little more than a vision of blue eyes. Burned so deeply in his brain, he'd never forget them. He knew he must have suffered a tremendous loss then.

Losing Caleb was like losing all his youth at once. And getting slammed by the reality that life wasn't always what you wanted it to be. Then Tom. Wonderful, sweet Tom. Who'd always been there for him. He hadn't realized what a void his loss would leave.

And then, this getting shot mess.

Yes, some elephants trampled you right over before you knew it.

And he wasn't the same now. He never would be.

He realized there was a difference in living and making life happen.

He was determined to make life happen.

In the last six months, he had felt himself changing, moving closer to what he wanted to be. Not there yet, but he knew people could see his strength and his confidence. He could feel people respected him as a man now, and not just any man.

And, yes, some elephants lead to sweeter life. Like people who made you stronger because they counted on you, trusted you, and maybe even loved you.

Like Kate. Beautiful, strong Kate. He respected her for her strength, practicality, and determination. But lately, there was something more to it than that.

Finding Mr. Sunday

He wanted to be around her, catch her fragrance, watch her push back that strand of hair from her eyes as she looked at him.

She was older, wiser he knew. And probably would chuckle should she sense any evidence of his growing interest.

Is that what it was … a growing interest?

He had no idea what it was. But it was something sweet, natural, and warming.

He would just have to let it unfold.

And then there was Mary Nel. He had never thought of her as a sister. She was a woman to him from day one.

In the last few months, though, she just blossomed — all woman, full of charm and mystery.

And he thought the world of her. He'd do anything for her.

Yes, he admitted, he was jealous of Peter. Only because it was around him that he saw the evolving Mary Nel. Laughing, talking excitedly, even flirting. It would nice to be a part of that.

Maybe … one day.

Please, dear God. I seem to lose everyone I become close to. Don't let anything happen to these precious people.

He sat there for a few more moments, listening to the night. He inhaled deeply as if to seal his thoughts. Then he picked himself up from the rock and began the walk back to the wagon, passing lazy stock and snoring stockmen.

CHAPTER ELEVEN

The wagon train continued its westerly route with few difficulties. In southwestern Nebraska Territory the train dipped south into Colorado Territory, avoiding Ash Hollow canyon and the necessity of a dangerous and difficult descent.

After turning back north, the wagon train stopped in a little valley near a military fort that was being constructed to protect workers building the Union Pacific Railroad. The area around the fort, soon to be called Sidney Barracks, was fast becoming a gathering point for traders and providers as well as a resting place for travelers headed west.

The wagon train arrived late on a Friday afternoon. Hobs recommended a two-day break in the travel. His suggestion was met with vigorous approval as each wagon set up camp for a well-deserved rest and a chance to catch up on needed repairs.

The small valley was fed by a couple of streams and seemed like an oasis compared with the trail itself. There was something peaceful about the place despite its proximity to the fort and railroad.

As usual, Will, Kate, and Ish formed their own little site with their four wagons. Kate and Mary Nel freshened up from the trail and changed out of their customary trail pants into dresses. Will took a pleasant dip in a nearby stream.

The group sat around the campfire as dinner was being prepared. Maggie had not joined the group.

"We've put around five hundred miles behind us so far," said Will. "I'd say we've made good progress, without any major difficulties."

"I agree, Will. But I'm glad we get a chance to rest a couple of days," said Ish. "Maggie's been feeling poorly last day or two."

"Oh, Ish," said Kate. "I saw she's been a little quiet, but I didn't know she wasn't feeling well."

"You know Maggie, Miz Kate. You won't hear her complain, and she sure don't like to be made over," Ish said. "She just tiring easy, don't seem to want to eat."

"I'll go see to her," said Kate as she stood to go to Maggie's wagon.

Finding Mr. Sunday

"Let's let her rest tonight, Miz Kate, if you don't mind. I think that's all she needs. We'll see how she feels in the morning."

Kate saw the plea in Ish's face. She could see he was concerned, and she didn't insist.

"All right, Ish," she said. "But you let me know if I can help, you hear?"

There was a gentle breeze stirring, and the late afternoon brought a welcomed relief to the air. Kate busied herself giving Rio a hand setting up the camp stove and unpacking utensils. Mary Nel and Will sat near each other, and Ish was busy mending a piece of tack.

"Ish, Hank, and a few of us are going hunting early tomorrow. We might be lucky enough to find us some fresh game. Would you care to join us?" said Will.

"No, Mr. Will. Think I better stick close tomorrow. But thanks," he said.

"Well, some fresh pronghorn broth might be good for Maggie, so you can be sure we'll try hard to find something."

"I 'preciate that, Will," said Ish.

"Will, I'd like to go hunting, too. It shouldn't just be men that go hunting," said Mary Nel.

She looked at him with a slight smile, but Will could tell she was not making a joke.

"I agree with you, Mary Nel. But at this point, you don't know how to shoot a rifle or a pistol. And that's something I want to discuss with you and Kate."

He turned to Kate, who was sorting through a box of dried herbs.

"Kate, what do you think about the two of you learning to shoot? I know it's probably not high on your list of things to do, but I think it would be good if you were comfortable with guns. It might come in handy some day," he said.

He watched Kate's face carefully, expecting to be challenged. Instead, she stopped what she was doing and turned to him with a thoughtful look on her face.

"You know, Will. I've been thinking about that. This trail is very different from the world I'm used to. I can see where it would be prudent for us to at least not be afraid of guns."

She wiped her hands on her apron and seemed to address the group.

"I've seen enough things in the last six months to convince me there is a place for guns ... even if I don't like the idea," she said in a matter-of-fact manner.

Will raised his eyebrows in mild astonishment.

"Well, I have to say I didn't expect to hear that, Kate. Soon as I think I have you figured out, you go and surprise me," he said with a laugh.

"It just makes sense, that's all," she said.

"I think it's a good idea, Momma," said Mary Nel. "Will, when can you teach us?"

"We can start anytime with the basics, how guns work and so on," Will said. "The most important thing to learn first is how to be safe at all times and to respect any gun as a dangerous thing if not handled correctly.

"We'll start firing the two Moore .32-caliber pistols I have. Then we'll move to rifles.

"I'll talk to Hobs and the council and let him know we'll be doing some practice shooting. I think we can get far enough away from camp not to create a problem for the stock or the other travelers. And there might be others who are interested in learning to shoot, too."

Just then, Peter walked into the campsite and took off his hat.

"Evening, folks," said Peter.

Peter looked as if he had just cleaned up from the day's ride.

"Why, hello, Peter," said Kate. "How are you today? I haven't seen much of you."

"Oh, one thing here, one thing there. There is always something to tend to," said Peter.

"Have a seat," said Kate. "We're going to have our evening meal a little late today, but you are welcomed to join us. We are all just unwinding from the day."

"I'd like that very much," said Peter. His face lit up with a smile.

Peter stepped over to Mary Nel, who was seated on the storage box used for the cooking utensils.

"You can share this seat, Peter," she said as she patted the top of the box.

He walked over and sat on the box, being careful not to crowd Mary Nel.

"Will is going to teach Momma and me to shoot. Isn't that exciting?" said Mary Nel.

"It is. I think it's a good thing for you to do. I could use a few pointers myself, Will."

"He'll be a good one to learn from, Peter. I never seen anyone who could shoot like Will," said Ish.

"I'd be glad to help, Peter. I'm going to discuss it with Hobs, and I'll let you know the plan," said Will.

"Mary Nel?" asked Peter softly. "Would you like to take a walk before you eat? I could use a little time out of the saddle, and this is some pretty country."

"I'd like that," she said.

She and Peter stood, and Mary Nel walked over to her mother.

"Momma, Peter and I are going for a walk, if that's all right with you," asked Mary Nel.

"Certainly, I may do the same myself. There's plenty of daylight left since we stopped early. We'll eat when everyone gets back," said Kate.

"I'll sit right here and keep an eye on things," said Ish.

"I'll have the stew ready by the time everyone gets back, ma'am," said Rio.

"Thank you, Rio," said Kate.

She turned to Will.

"Will, would you like to join me?" said Kate.

"I wouldn't miss it for the world," he said.

"There's a pretty stream a little west of here. I could see it from a distance. Let's walk there," Peter said to Mary Nel.

"Let's do," said Mary Nel.

The two of them headed west toward the creek, and Kate and Will headed in a more northerly direction to a little ridge that looked like a nice place to view the valley.

The little valley was a palette of natural beauty. Flowers and shrubbery splashed color in every direction: lead plant, button bush, and elderberry. Yellow, red, and pink roses, black-eyed Susan, shaggy pink coneflowers, pink phlox, and golden plains coreopsis seemed to beckon in the breeze.

"It's so beautiful," said Kate.

Kate had left her trail hat behind. A breeze ruffled her hair, and the late afternoon sun lit her eyes.

"That it is," said Will as they walked side by side.

"It's hard to believe California could be any prettier than this place," said Kate.

"Yep. But this is just a little piece of Nebraska Territory. In California, there must be hundreds of places like this," said Will.

"Probably. I just find comfort in the land wherever I am. You can see it, touch it … let it run through your fingers, smell it, watch it change with the seasons. It's something I can depend on, I guess," she said.

"Do you want to have another orchard when you get to California?" asked Will.

"I'm not sure. But I can't see myself without land. I like the cycle of plant, grow, harvest more than I realized. At one time I was concerned that I would be kind of trapped by the orchard. But now that I know I can do about anything I want, within reason, of course, I miss the land.

"I know I don't want to live in the city. Cities are fine to visit, but I could never feel at home there. Maybe at one time, but not anymore.

"I'm going to get there, Lord willing, and take my time looking around. With what we got for the farm and what my father left me, I'm under no real financial pressure to do anything quickly. It's a good feeling, too," she said.

They strolled leisurely, stopping here and there to look closer at a particular plant or flower. The air was clean and pure, free of the trail dust that plagued them every day. They stopped at a large bed of wild roses and inhaled the soft fragrance.

"What are your plans, Will?" she asked.

"I don't have any specific plans, Kate. Except to keep my eyes and ears open for business opportunities. I've also been thinking about Tom's desire for me to become a lawyer.

"I'm not sure I embraced the idea early on, but it's beginning to have some appeal. I see no reason I can't find some good investment opportunities and study law at the same time."

"You'd make a fine lawyer, Will. Why, you might even be a judge some day. Wouldn't that be grand?" she said, smiling.

"Maybe. I'm afraid what I do may mean living in the city, at least for a while. But that doesn't keep me from having some property in a pretty valley somewhere."

Finding Mr. Sunday

"Of course not. I can't see myself in the city for long," said Kate.

They walked on without talking for a while, enjoying the beauty of the place and the moment.

"Do you think you will marry again?" Will said out of the blue.

Kate colored slightly and looked up at him. There was a long pause.

"Well, Will, I ..."

"I'm sorry, Kate. That was not a proper question. It's none of my business. I don't know what made me ask that," he said.

"Oh, Will," she said, laughing. "Don't be embarrassed. I don't mind the question. I'm just trying to think how I should answer it.

"I've given that some thought. On one hand, the idea of having someone in my life who cares for me is very appealing. On the other, a relationship like that takes time to build, and it isn't easy. There are so many things people should know about each other.

"At least, I feel that way now, having been married before. With Ben, it just seemed the right thing to do at the time. We learned about each other over the years. Fortunately, we liked what we discovered."

She picked a pink rose and held it to her nose.

"I'd probably take quite a while before I committed myself to that kind of relationship, should it happen again. Besides, Mary Nel is so much a part of my life, I'd want her to feel comfortable with anyone I would consider.

"So, to answer your question, it's just another great unknown in my life now, like many other things ... and I kind of like that."

She looked up at him and smiled, pushing that stubborn strand of hair from her eyes.

For some reason, that always disarmed him.

"What about you? Do you see yourself getting married someday?" she asked.

He took a moment or two before he answered.

"I've been so caught up in growing up lately, I haven't given it much thought. I'm not twenty yet. I have no clear-cut plan for my own future, let alone a future with someone else.

"If I do get married my guess is that will be a way off. And I'd be choosy, too," he said. "I'll be honest, Kate, this whole man-woman relationship is all new to me, and I haven't figured it all out yet."

"Well, let me know when you do. It's a riddle as old as time," she said with a laugh.

Mary Nel and Peter walked toward the creek, taking time to enjoy the area. Mary Nel bent to pick a blossom. Her natural beauty was so in keeping with the little valley, she seemed to be a part of it.

"Here, Peter," she said as she put a blossom near his nose. "Isn't the fragrance lovely?"

He wrapped his hand around hers and moved the blossom closer to his nose.

He looked at her as he held the flower and inhaled the fragrance.

Mary Nel smiled at him, lowered her hand, and continued the walk, placing her hand in his.

She could see a little grin creep onto his face.

"How long do you plan to stay in California, Peter?" she asked.

"That depends. I'm going to look at what's coming in on the trade ships. See what we can ship back East and resell at a profit. That should take a few months or more," he said.

"I think my father just wanted me to experience the trip more than anything. He has others who work for him who would have been better for the job. He and Hobs are friends, so I can see how this happened.

"Anyway, I'm glad I came. I would never have met you if I hadn't come on the trip," he said with a smile.

She returned his smile.

"Let's go sit by the creek," she said.

They sat on the soft grass under the young ash trees that bordered the creek.

"Do you know where you are going to settle once you get to California?" he asked.

"The plan now is to stay in Sacramento until we have a chance to look around and see where we want to go. That will take some time. I'm sure Momma will do most of that. We've talked about me continuing my education there, but we have no firm plans," she said.

215

Finding Mr. Sunday

"I will be going to the ports and meeting with the importers along the coast," he said. "So there is a good chance we can keep in touch in California."

"That would be nice, Peter," she said.

"Is there any chance you might stay longer in California?" she asked.

"Possibly. If we're successful in finding opportunities, I might stay and coordinate those activities for my father," he said.

"Do you see yourself always working for your father?" Mary Nel said.

"I'm not sure. I'm an only child, and there are no other family members in the business. He has a very successful business, you know.

"He's around sixty years old. His health is still good. But I don't think he would want me to stay in California indefinitely. I'll probably end up back in Missouri."

She listened to him and watched his facial expressions. She couldn't tell if he was pleased with this eventuality or disappointed. Other than the occasional smile and his perpetual shyness, Peter was not an expressive person.

"I find it very exciting to think about the future," she said. "You never know what will happen. Why, just a year ago if you had told me I would be headed to California now, I would have thought you daft. But here I am."

"Do you think you'll stay in California?" he said.

"Oh, I really can't say, but I hope that's not the last stop for me," she said. "I want to see more of the world, not just California. Everywhere I can go, I want to go. The more I see, the more I want to see."

"You don't want to get married and have a family?" he asked, his voice a little higher pitched.

Ah, she thought, some feeling seeped through with that question, possibly disappointment.

"Someday. But all that is so far in the future. I know most young ladies my age want that to happen as soon as possible. Not me. I'm not one to think that's all a woman has to look forward to," she answered.

They sat quietly for a moment.

"Do you?" she asked. "I mean, is that something you want to do sooner rather than later in your life?"

"Maybe not right now," he said. "But it isn't so far off for me that I

216

shouldn't be thinking about it."

He was chewing on a piece of grass facing her. She looked at his face, now much tanner than when they had met. He wore no hat, and there was a band of lighter skin just below his hairline where the sun hadn't reached.

At that moment, it struck Mary Nel that he looked young, almost boyish. He hardly seemed to be one who could care for a family, even a few years from now. Not a weakling by any means, just immature.

He seemed years younger than Will, but had none of Will's presence. When Will entered a room or walked up to a group, everyone noticed him. Some even stepped back to make way. Peter wasn't that kind of man.

Why was she comparing this young man to Will Sunday, she thought? She had yet to meet anyone quite like Will and probably wouldn't for a long time, if ever. They were just … different … that's all.

"Mary Nel?" said Peter as if calling for her.

"Oh, I'm sorry, Peter," she said, coming back from her reverie. "This place is so peaceful, I was just enjoying it all. I didn't mean to be rude."

"I know how you feel. It's very peaceful. I've been told we have some rough trail ahead of us. Passable, of course, but nothing like this. We should enjoy this while we can."

They sat and admired the scenery for a while. The birds were gathering in the trees for the last serenade of the day, and a gentle breeze whispered in the leaves.

"We both probably have a lot of things to see and do before we settle down. And I like that thought," she said.

He did not look at her but stared off into the distance.

"I suppose you're right," he said, a little disappointed the discussion was coming to an end.

"Well, let's head back now. I don't want Momma worried about us," she said.

Peter got up quickly and helped Mary Nel to her feet. He walked along beside her, thinking what a different young lady she is, unlike any he had met.

But then, he thought, I haven't had much experience with ladies.

Finding Mr. Sunday

Will and Kate were sitting on the little ridge. They could see Mary Nel and Peter off in the distance, sitting beside the stream.

"They seem to be enjoying the day," said Kate.

"It's hard not to," said Will as he lay back looking up at the sky.

"I know some people may not approve of my letting her spend time with Peter. But then, they don't know my daughter," she said.

"Mary Nel knows I trust her. She's a smart one. I'm so lucky to have a daughter like her."

"Well, the acorn doesn't fall far from the tree. And you've done a great job with her, Kate. And by the way, you're not one who is concerned about what other people may think."

She chuckled at that comment.

"Maybe I have had some influence on her, but she has a lot of spirit. I just want to see it channeled in the right direction," said Kate.

"That spirit will make her a survivor in life, Kate. She's not like other girls her age. She's determined, very smart, and pragmatic. I'll bet you she gets what she wants out of life."

"Sounds like you are talking about yourself, Will," she said as she watched his face for a reaction.

He looked at her, holding her eyes with his own.

"Yes, I guess you are right. I've just got to decide what it is I want," he said.

"I certainly understand that," said Kate. "But in time, you will."

"I know what you mean. But I want to have a better handle on it than most people. That's just the way I am, in case you haven't noticed," he said, chuckling.

"Oh, I can see that," she said.

"But having a bit more experience at life than you...since I am older..."

"Not that much ..." he said, laughing a little.

"Then it is the experience, not the years, from which I speak. I think you are moving very fast in your life. Of course, I understand events have sort of made that somewhat necessary. But you need to make sure you enjoy each day.

"I don't need to tell you how much of an advantage you have in life now. But I'll say it just to make my point. You are young, smart, strong, determined, you are financially secure, and already you can hold you own with any other man.

"Look around you, Will. Why, I can't think of a better place than this to remind you to take time to smell the roses in life," she said.

He looked at her for a moment. This woman saw so much in others, he thought. But he wasn't sure she knew how special she herself was.

"Thank you, Kate. I hear what you say and appreciate the advice. And it just so happens, I am doing that very thing right now," he said.

He stood up, put both his hands out for her to help her. She brushed close to him as she stood. He caught her fragrance and found himself inhaling to take in all he could. He squeezed her hands ever so slightly.

"Shall we head back?" she said.

She looked up at him. And, again, brushed that unruly piece of hair from her eyes.

Don't make a fool of yourself, he thought. He exhaled slowly. Not too close, Will.

"I suppose," he said.

They walked side-by-side back to the camp. The silence between them was very loud. And sweet.

Day by day they plodded west. The North Platte River, unlike the South Platte, was a river in the true sense of the word, deep and strong. The trail now ran through flat prairie, unchanging as far as the eye could see, a huge land under a blue canopy sky, broken only by the occasional cloud or distant rock formations. It seemed the earth was carpeted with sage, mile after mile.

The days passed uneventfully, one after the other, marked only by their sameness. Courthouse, Jailhouse Rock and Chimney Rock broke the horizon and stood as natural markers of their progress westward.

One afternoon as the train headed for its next stop at Scotts Bluff, an unexpected halt was called. Word came down that the Hartwell wagon, near the front of the train, had broken a wheel and would need repair.

The travelers dismounted, and many hastened to erect sunshades from

Finding Mr. Sunday

canvas sheets to protect them from the blistering sun.

"Won't be long, folks," said Peter as he rode down the line.

Will, Kate, and Mary Nel, who were riding their mounts that particular day, rode ahead to see if they could assist the Hartwells.

Several spokes had broken on one of the large rear wheels of the Hartwell wagon, and the wheel had partially collapsed. A wagon jack had been placed under the axle, and one of the men was in the process of raising the wagon so that a new wheel could be installed.

Mr. Hartwell bent close to the wheel as the jack lifted the wagon, preparing to remove the wheel as soon as the jack lifted the wheel clear of the ground.

Without warning the jack suddenly collapsed. The full weight of the wagon fell hard on the damaged wheel, breaking the remaining bottom spokes of the wheel and causing it to collapse outward.

The heavy wheel and iron rim slammed into Mr. Hartwell, striking him first in the head, then pinning much of his body underneath the fallen wheel, which now bore much of the weight of the wagon. He was knocked unconscious, and a massive wound opened in his scalp, pouring blood.

People ran to his aid, quickly surrounding the downed man.

"You men! Let's lift the wagon! Hurry. Pull him out from under the wheel!" yelled Will.

A group of men rush to help Will lift up on the wagon. As the weight of the wagon was taken off the wheel, a couple of men pulled Hartwell clear.

The man remained unconscious, his scalp bleeding profusely. Mrs. Hartwell was beside herself as she knelt next to her injured husband.

"George! George! Oh, George. Can you hear me? Please! Someone get me a blanket," she said in near panic.

Several people brought blankets, and others brought cloths and a bucket of water. Mrs. Hartwell applied the cloths to the open wound and held them in place. Another woman put a blanket under Mr. Hartwell's head while yet another covered him as he lay there.

"Let's get him into a wagon," said Will. "Mrs. Hartwell, he would be better off in a wagon."

Will gently helped Mrs. Hartwell up as others kept the cloths in place.

"Yes. Yes, of course. Let's put him in a wagon," she said.

"You can put him in our extra wagon," said Mr. Woolcott.

Several men carefully lifted the unconscious man and carried him to the Woolcott wagon, placing him on a pallet of blankets.

"May I see to him, Mrs. Woolcott? I have a little experience in injuries," said Kate.

"Please, Mrs. Daniels. See what you can do," said Mrs. Hartwell.

Kate and Mrs. Hartwell went into the wagon.

Kate looked at the head injury first, then looked closer at Mr. Hartwell. He was pale and non-responsive. His breathing was shallow and ragged. Kate knew his injury was very serious but remained calm.

"The bleeding from the scalp wound will stop soon. He took quite a blow. The hub of the wheel has caused some bruising in his abdomen. He may have some broken ribs. It's too early to tell if there are any other injuries," said Kate.

She held Mrs. Hartwell's hand.

"The only thing to do now is to keep him warm and wrap his head tightly to stem the bleeding. I wish I could do more, but I'm afraid there is nothing I can do. We'll just have to keep him as comfortable as possible and wait," she said.

"I will, Mrs. Daniels. Will you come check on him later?" said Mrs. Hartwell.

"Of course I will. I'll come see him in a couple of hours. I doubt we will travel any more today. If you need me or if there is any change, our wagon will be very close to this one."

"Thank you, Mrs. Daniels. I appreciate your help," said a teary Mrs. Hartwell.

Several men put a new wheel on the Hartwell wagon. Will, Hobs, and a number of council members were standing in a group a short distance away from the repaired wagon.

"We'll stop here for the day," said Hobs.

In a lower voice he said, "I think George is hurt bad. That wheel hub caught him in the gut. We'll see how he looks in the morning. There's no medical help around 'til we get to Fort Laramie, if then. And that's a few days off yet."

He looked around at the group gathered.

Finding Mr. Sunday

"Fellows, let's have a council meeting tonight. Peter, we'll notify the other council members. We'll meet at my wagon around seven," said Hobs as he gave Peter a nod.

"Yes, sir," said Peter as he headed for his horse.

The travelers began to set up camp for the night. Rio, as usual, scurried around with his typical efficiency and had the camp squared away in no time. Hank was staying in the camp tonight. He and the other stockmen had set up a shared arrangement so none of them had to spend every night with the stock.

Kate had just returned from visiting Maggie and seeing that she was comfortable. Ish was keeping Maggie company in the wagon.

"I'm really worried about Maggie," said Kate to Will and Mary Nel. "She isn't eating. She doesn't want to leave the wagon. Maggie has always been a strong woman, and I've never seen her like this. Something is going on with her."

"Ish said he couldn't get her to take any food. He's really worried too, Momma," said Mary Nel.

"Does she have a fever, Kate?" asked Will.

"No. But her breathing is shallow, her chest has a rattle, and she's coughing. Her ankles are swelled. She says she is too tired to get up and about. She wants Ish by her side as much as possible," said Kate.

"Well, we might be lucky and find a doctor at Fort Laramie. We'll be there in a few days," said Will.

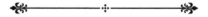

"Hartwell is still unconscious," said Will as he sat down with other members of the council.

"Kate said she is afraid he's hurt inside. His stomach is badly swollen, and he's bleeding from the mouth."

"I saw a man get kicked in the stomach by a mule once. Mule caught him with both hind feet. He was dead by the next day," said one of the council members.

"Well, I don't wanna hasten to no bad end, but Hartwell don't look so good," said Hobs. "Even if he gets better, won't be for some time. That's one of the reasons I asked for this meeting. I'm of a mind we need someone else to be head of the council. If Hartwell gets on his feet, he can come back in as captain.

"I wanna hear what you have to say about that, but before you do, let me tell the other reason I wanted to meet. We are going to have to make some plans — and quick."

The men knew by Hobs' tone that there was a serious discussion about to take place.

"That Army patrol we passed yesterday was out for a reason. The lieutenant told me the Indians were making some noise again. They been attacking ranches, trading posts, even some military supply trains. No wagon trains yet, but it ain't out of the question," he said.

"We're going to have to make sure we are ready in case of trouble. Now I don't want to frighten everyone on this train, but I don't want us to be caught flatfooted if we have trouble."

He scanned the faces of the council members, and their concern was obvious.

"I want an able captain in the meantime. We need to find out how many men can handle a gun, form a militia, even have some drills. And do it so the women folk don't get too upset."

"By the time we get to Fort Laramie, we need to have a plan in place to defend the train. When we leave out of there we need to have plenty of guns and powder. And start training people right away."

"What's got the Indians riled?" said one man.

"Oh, the usual. The Indians claim white men are coming into their land, pushing them out, not honoring treaties, the like. I think they have a point, but they don't need to be killing people. There are other ways to handle it," said Hobs.

"We can't worry 'bout that now, though. The cause for all this is way beyond us," said James Burrell. "We just gotta be prepared to defend ourselves."

"You're right, James," said Will. "Hobs, we need a detailed plan for our defense. We have to get the participation of the whole train without creating panic. I've got an idea."

"Let's hear it," said Hobs.

Finding Mr. Sunday

"You'll recall a few days ago I mentioned that some of my group asked me if I would teach them to shoot, and I asked you about us firing after we stop in the evenings?"

"Yes," said Hobs.

"Well, we could ask the council members to pass the word that I'll be conducting some firearms training and anyone who wants to participate can join me. Then we council members can start to throw out the idea of a militia to some of the members of the train whose opinions we respect.

"If we all start those discussions as a positive thing and something that's for the safety of the train, I don't think we'll see much panic."

"You're on to something, Will. We have some good, level-headed people on this train who would see the value in that sort of thing," said Evan Royce.

"We can progress quickly from the firing training to choosing a militia and in a short time ramp up to attack drills, etc. Even teach the women to fire and load rifles to support the militia," said Will.

"It's all in how we frame the thing, the way I see it," said Will.

"I like that," said Hobs. "We need to get this seed planted and soon. I'd like to leave Fort Laramie knowing how many able-bodied men we have, with plenty of supplies in hand and ready for the training to begin at our first stop.

"Now, let's move to electing a new captain. At the risk of being pushy, I nominate Will to be the new captain and to put all of this together," said Hobs.

To a man, all the council members voiced their approval.

"So be it, then. Will, you are our new captain," said Hobs.

"I'll do the best I can," said Will.

"Evan, you and Walt have been in the Army. Would you two consider helping me with forming and training this militia? " asked Will.

"Sure," said Evan. "There are other Army men on the train that would be glad to help, too.

And Hobs, once I do some figuring, I can tell you what we might need from Fort Laramie in terms of shot, powder, and arms."

"That's good, Evan," he said. "We might even be able to get some Army protection the first week or so out of Laramie. That'll give us time to get this thing going."

"In the meantime, Hobs, I'd like us to double our night guard and day scouts. I'll pick some men I trust and get that going. I also want us to make sure we're all saying the same thing to our folks, so I want to meet every night for a while," said Will.

The meeting continued late into the evening as the discussion around the security of the train continued.

George Hartwell passed away in the night, having never awakened from the accident.

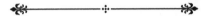

The prairie was now pure sage beds with various rock formations scattered in every direction. The train continued past Scotts Bluff, a marker on the western edge of Nebraska, just short of Wyoming Territory.

Many thought the mountain range on the horizon was their first glimpse of the Rockies. But they soon found out what they were seeing were the Laramie Mountains, soaring ten thousand feet above the plain.

Fort Laramie itself was a mixture of adobe, log, and whitewashed buildings that seemed like a thriving village in the middle of nowhere. As well as being home to a large Army contingent, the fort and surroundings housed an assortment of sutlers, blacksmiths, and other purveyors.

This particular day, the fort was crowded with a much larger number of Indians than usual. Ogallala, Sioux, Cheyenne, and Arapaho were among the tribes represented. Although the Indians were peaceful, great numbers of Indians made the travelers nervous.

The wagon train council decided to camp near the fort for several days to rest, resupply, and prepare for the next leg of the journey to South Pass.

"Thank you for meeting with us, Captain," said Hobs as he shook hands with the officer. This is Mr. Sunday, head of the wagon train council."

"Good to meet you, Captain," said Will as he shook the captain's hand.

"My pleasure," said the captain.

Finding Mr. Sunday

The captain, average in stature, looked up and down at Will's large frame but made no comment. He seemed polite enough, but it was obvious he wanted to get on with the meeting.

"There are a few things we want to talk to you about. There seems to be a lot of goings-on here so we will be as quick as we can," said Hobs, noting the captain's manner.

"I appreciate that, Mr. Hobs," said Capt. Thomas.

The captain continued. "The Indians are here to begin talks with the government. They don't like the fact that we plan to go into the Powder River area. They say we're trespassing on their hunting grounds. Red Cloud and his boys don't like it."

"That's one of the things we want to talk about, Captain. A few days back we met up with an Army patrol that told us some of the Indians were burning ranches and trading posts and attacking supply trains. Is that true?" said Hobs.

The captain hesitated, seeming to take great care in how he worded his response. He leaned forward and gestured with a slight wave of his hand.

"Only to a limited extent. There are always a few young warriors popping up that want to make trouble, especially since last year. But we haven't seen much of that. Here and there, yes, but not anything organized on a grand scale."

The captain shuffled some papers around on the tabletop and avoided Hobs' stare.

Hobs tilted his head and leaned closer to the captain.

"I got the idea from the Army patrol it was more than a few young warriors. But even a few young warriors, as you call them, Captain, could do a lot of damage to our train and stock."

"I understand your concern, Mr. Adams. I think we'll come to some agreement with them in due time," said the captain somewhat dismissively.

Will was taken aback by the captain's cavalier attitude.

"Captain, I understand you can't give us any assurance there won't be trouble, and I don't expect you to. But I do expect you to understand that our men, women, and children are counting on us to keep them safe. If there is any possibility of the train being attacked, or even harassed, we need to be prepared."

The captain turned to look at Will as if he had just entered the room. Will looked him in the eye.

"Many of these men don't own weapons to speak of, maybe a scattergun. We need rifles and ammunition, as well as powder and shot," Will said.

"And we expect to have Army protection for a while as we continue west. Such protection will give us time to train our men. It's my understanding that is why this fort exists," said Will firmly.

The captain was surprised by Will's firm tone. He sat up as if, for the first time, his full attention was on the meeting.

"Is this something within your purview, Captain, or need we see someone else?" said Will, standing in preparation to meet another officer, if necessary.

Captain Thomas looked up at him and immediately stood.

"No. No, Mr. Sunday. I'll take care of this. One of my lieutenants will come out to see you, shortly. You tell him what you need. In the meantime, I'll be looking into an escort for your train."

The captain's attitude had changed quickly. Perhaps he'd had his mind on other things during the meeting. Maybe he felt this was just one more wagon train to take his time from more pressing matters. But he now understood very clearly these men were not your average emigrants.

Hobs stood, walked over to the captain, and extended his hand.

"We look forward to hearing from you, Captain. We'll be here three days before we head to South Pass. Thank you for your help," said Hobs.

"You're welcome, Mr. Adams. Glad to do it," said the captain as he shook Hobs' hand.

The captain, now fully engaged in the matter at hand, turned to Will.

"Mr. Sunday, I have several sergeants with Indian experience who will gladly help train your men. I'll make sure they are in the escort detail."

"Thank you, Captain," said Will. "By the way, do you have a doctor who can look in on a friend of mine who is confined to her wagon?"

"We do, Mr. Sunday. I'll see that he visits your friend as soon as he can."

"Thank you, Captain. And good day to you, sir," said Will.

The men left the captain's office.

"A good meeting, Will," said Hobs as he nudged Will with his elbow and smiled.

Finding Mr. Sunday

"Yep," said Will.

He looked at Hobs, smiled, and gave a wink of the eye.

The next day, a young doctor came out to the wagon train and looked up Will, who took him to see Maggie and Ish. He spent a short time examining Maggie, after which he came out and spoke to Will, Kate, and Ish.

"Folks, I don't know what to tell you. She has no fever, but she is very weak. I'm afraid she may have an illness that could linger for some time. But I'm a surgeon, not a disease specialist," he said.

The look on the young doctor's face was not encouraging.

"You are doing the right things. Keep her warm, try to get her to eat soft foods. I have a tonic that may help her. But she is a very sick lady," he said.

Ish put his head in his hands as the doctor stood to leave.

"Thank you for coming out, Doctor," said Will.

Kate went over to Ish, sat down, and hugged his shoulders.

"We'll continue to pray for her, Ish," she said.

The wagon train departed Fort Laramie well stocked but not overloaded as the travelers had learned their lessons early on about carrying unnecessary weight. The next long leg of the journey would take them twenty to twenty five days of travel through steadily rising terrain that would put an increased strain on man and beast.

A good quantity of Spencer and Henry rifles had been acquired, as well as a supply of .44 revolvers, along with plenty of ammunition. In addition, a detail of twenty-one soldiers would be accompanying the train for the next week.

If there was concern on behalf of the travelers, it was not evident. The rest and resupply had refreshed them, leaving them eager to continue the journey westward. The presence of the soldiers was labeled as a routine courtesy extended by the Army.

Word of the firearms training had spread quickly, and more than twenty people showed up the first evening. Will and the Army veterans from the train were to be assisted by many of the soldiers from Fort Laramie. The presence of more than a few young ladies in the group to be trained may

228

have had something to do with the large number of Army volunteers.

"You are here to learn how to fire a pistol and later on a rifle. I want to say at the outset that we will emphasize safety as much as the mechanics of shooting," Will began.

"In the first group of wagons headed west, one of the first fatalities was a gunshot wound that occurred as a man was picking up his rifle. Ironically, his name was Shotwell. We do not want any fatalities to happen because of careless handling of a firearm."

Will began the session with an overview of both types of pistols, percussion and cartridge. Then the large group was broken into five groups, with a lead trainer and a minimum of two assistants.

No firing was allowed the first night as the training focused on safety, the mechanics of the pistol, loading, and simulated firing.

Kate, Mary Nel, two other ladies, and Peter were in Will's group.

"The cartridge pistols are easier to load. But there aren't many available yet in the larger calibers. These small .32-caliber Moore pistols are great for defensive purposes at close range."

Will went on to demonstrate the mechanics of a revolver, how to load the pistol, and the proper way to grip and fire the small weapons. He did the same thing with his Remington .44-caliber pistols, showing the difference in ammunition, loading, and firing.

"These larger pistols have a good kick to them. I would advise you ladies to hold the pistol in both hands before firing and anticipate the kick. We'll talk more about that tomorrow when we fire," he said.

After a while he allowed the participants to handle the pistols, practice gripping, aiming, and simulating firing. He had each of the ladies handle both types of pistols to become familiar with the weight of the pistols and the feel of the weapons. This continued for an hour or so.

"Peter, I'm going to check on the other groups to make sure everyone is getting similar training. Would you continue the training since you have some experience? I'll be back in a little while," Will said.

Will made his rounds of the other groups, pausing to watch each trainer. Here and there he made a mental note to make a couple of suggestions to the trainers later, but all in all, the training was going smoothly.

When the groups were finished they came together once again.

Finding Mr. Sunday

"I hope everyone learned something tonight. Tomorrow we will begin firing training, continuing our emphasis on safety. I have time for questions now," said Will.

"Mr. Sunday, is there gonna be trouble, you think? I mean from Indians?" asked a participant.

"Well, Mrs. Carney, I wouldn't rule it out, I won't mislead you. It could happen. There is some unrest among the Indians. But that's just one of the reasons you should know how to handle a gun. The West is different from back East. It's just wise to be prepared should the need arise," he said.

"Even when you get to California, there will be times when you are alone on the homestead. Believe me, you will feel better knowing you can handle a gun. I've seen firsthand the trouble that can come to your front door," he answered.

"But we have many able-bodied men on this train and a few women I know can handle guns. By the time we finish this training, we'll be the most secure train that ever made this journey.

"If there are no more questions, we'll call it a night. Same time tomorrow folks. You can bring your own pistol, or we will provide one. Good night," Will said.

Will, Kate, and Mary Nel returned to their campsite to have the evening meal. Rio had prepared plenty of bread, fried ham, a large Dutch oven full of beans, and a huge pot of coffee with a blackberry cobbler.

"Everything is ready, Miz Kate."

"Good, I'm starved," said Mary Nel. She went to a pail of water that hung from a hook on the wagon and washed her hands. The others did the same before filling their bowls and plates and taking seats in the circle.

"Rio, I don't know how we would do without you. You're such a help. I appreciate your handling the wagon, too. I get tired of being in that seat all day."

"My pleasure, Miz Kate. I enjoy helping out. It is good experience for me. One day I want to have my own little business and cook for my guests. A lodging place, too, maybe."

"You'll do a fine job of it, Rio. Do you plan to stay in California?" asked Will.

"For a while. My family is in Missouri, but we're from California. Maybe

I'll stay, but only if my mother and father will join me," he said, talking as he ate.

"I don't think Mr. Adams will make many trips after this. He said the railroad is moving fast, and there is not much use for wagon trains in the future," said Rio.

"He's right, I'd say. But there are still a lot of families that want to leave the East. Especially down South where the war wiped them out financially. They can't afford a boat trip, and they can't wait for the railroad to be finished," said Will.

Just then Ish walked into the circle.

"Hello, Ish. How is Maggie this evening?" said Kate.

"Not good, Miz Kate, not good." Ish shook his head gravely. "I can't get her to eat nothing. No soup, no bread. Just a little water. I was gonna ask you to see if you can get her to take something. She might listen to you."

"I'll see to her right away, Ish. Maybe if I mash the beans in the soup and make it a little thick with bread, she'll eat a bit," said Kate.

"I surely hope so. I'm real worried," said Ish.

Kate finished her meal, prepared a small bowl for Maggie, and went into their wagon.

Maggie lay on a small mattress, among plenty of covers. Her head was propped up, and a small lantern burned by the bed.

"Hello, Maggie," said Kate. "I brought you a little bean soup. I hope you can eat just a little bit for me."

"Oh, Kate, Sweetie. I just ain't hungry, but I'll try a little for you," said Maggie.

Kate sat beside the bed and put a small amount of the food in a spoon. Maggie took it in her mouth and swallowed with some difficulty.

Kate was alarmed at how sick Maggie looked. Her condition had changed dramatically in the last few days. The skin around her eye sockets had darkened considerably. Her eyes were yellowed and seemed unfocused. Her cheeks were beginning to hollow. Her movements were slow and unsure. This was not the Maggie that Kate had known all her life.

"Maggie, darling, you have to eat to keep your strength. You know Ish is worried that you are not eating."

"I know that old bear is worried. I hate to see him so," Maggie said, her

231

eyes tearing. "I'm so tired, Kate. I knew this trip was going to be hard on me, but not this hard. I swear, I don't think the good Lord wants me in California."

Kate knew something far worse than the stress of the trip was at work here. For the first time, she accepted that Maggie was seriously ill and might not recover unless something changed quickly.

She put her hand on Maggie's shoulder.

"Now, now, Maggie. You shouldn't say things like that. You just need to eat a little something at mealtime. I'll fix you something special every day. You just promise me you'll try to eat to make you stronger."

She continued to feed Maggie small bits of the broth. Kate could see Maggie was forcing herself to eat it.

"No more, Kate," said Maggie. "Tomorrow. I'll eat some more tomorrow. For you."

Kate set the bowl down.

"I'll be right back," she said.

She left the wagon and returned with a small pan of warm water, a cloth, and a brush. She gently wiped Maggie down, brushed her hair, and made her as comfortable as possible.

"You get some rest now, Maggie. I'll see you in the morning," said Kate.

Kate came back to the fire, and Ish went to the wagon.

"She is very sick," said Kate. "She doesn't have a fever, but something is wrong. I don't know what."

"Do you think she is going to be all right, Momma?" asked Mary Nel in a whisper.

"I don't know, sweetheart. I just don't know," said a worried Kate.

The number of people wanting training swelled to over thirty. The training continued the next evening and each night thereafter until Sunday. Each member of the group learned to load, fire, and reload both pistols and rifles.

The Army conducted practice sessions for Indian attacks that included circling the wagons, securing the stock, setting up barricades, and putting out water barrels to douse fires. The women who preferred not to shoot learned to load rifles, pistols, and scatterguns.

Those who had participated in the firearms training took stations on the perimeter and were prepared to load weapons for the better shooters or fight shoulder to shoulder, whichever might be needed.

On the following Monday, the soldiers left the wagon train, headed back to Fort Laramie. The wagon train continued its westward trek, eventually crossing to the north side of the Platte. The landscape became more desolate and unwelcoming albeit breathtaking in its natural beauty. The trail wound through ridges and around steep ravines, the rocky trail beds often marked by the tracks of wagon trains gone long before.

Forage was thinning, tending toward succulents, junipers, sparse tough grasses, and the ubiquitous sage. Some of the pools of water they passed were alkali, rendering them undrinkable.

Infrequent streams and creeks provided the only opportunities for fresh water. The travelers plodded, passing Emigrant Gap, eager to reach Willow Springs, the next source of ample, good water.

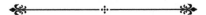

Will was startled to hear gunfire in the predawn morning. He had just finished dressing and was buckling his gun belt. Grabbing his Spencer rifle he rushed from his wagon. The gunfire was coming from the area where the stock had been settled for the night.

"Everybody up. Get the rifles and ammunition ready!" he yelled as he grabbed extra ammunition for his Spencer.

Rio was the first to respond as he began banging a pot with a large spoon.

"Everybody up! Everybody up!" he yelled repeatedly.

The surrounding wagons erupted with people, rifles in hand, any remnant of sleep gone.

"Some of you stay here to protect the wagons. Some of you come with me," Will yelled.

About ten men followed Will in the direction of the gunfire. The firing increased in intensity as the group got closer to the stock herd. They could make out riders charging into the herd trying to separate and cut out certain animals.

"Indians!" shouted Will. "They are trying to get the horses."

About twenty-five warriors were mingled in with the herd, which was quickly scattering in every direction.

A few of the stockmen were lying or kneeling and firing at the Indians. There was little protection for the shooters.

Will and his group were sighted by some of the attackers who wheeled their horses and began to head toward them, firing as they rode.

"Get down. Let them get in closer. Take your time and aim true!" yelled Will.

He kneeled on one knee and put one of the lead attackers in his sight.

"Fire! Let them have it," he yelled above the din.

Several Indians fell immediately. The Spencer rifles were a Godsend. One of the men from the train was hit and fell. The Indians kept coming as if to ride over the men on the ground.

Indians fell, and horses were hit and faltered, some falling to the ground. The repeating rifles took their toll quickly, and soon the few remaining attackers turned back toward the main group.

Will and his men followed, firing, falling low, reloading, and firing again. The Indians attacking the heard started to ride off, some of them with horses in tow.

As soon as the men stopped firing at the Indians, they heard more gunfire in the direction of the wagon train encampment.

"They're attacking the train!" yelled Will. He looked around in desperation and ran to one of the horses from the herd, grabbed the horse by the mane, and headed toward the wagon train. Some of the men turned and headed on foot; others followed Will's example.

As they approached the wagon train, the breaking dawn revealed a full-blown battle taking place as mounted Indians fired repeatedly at the defenders. Some circled the wagons, probing at weak spots. Others ran in, fired, then retreated only to return and fire again.

"Don't fire toward the train!" yelled Will.

As he got close to the train Will realized the only ammunition he had left were the rounds in his rifle. He took stock of the direction of attack, leaned forward on the horse's neck, and headed toward the only opening he could see. His horse slid to an abrupt stop in front of a wagon just as Will jumped and ran to cover.

Several women were loading rifles. Will handed his to one of the women and grabbed a loaded one. He found a spot, kneeled, and began firing steadily. His shots were deadly, felling an Indian each time he fired.

He got up and moved around to another area where the attack was more concentrated. More Indians fell. He moved again, firing steadily, grabbing loaded rifles whenever he ran out of ammunition.

Some of the men from the train lay mortally wounded with arrows or by rifle fire. Others, wounded and bleeding, were being tended to by the women. Several wagons were on fire.

Will made his way around to his wagon and found Kate, Mary Nel, Ish, and Rio, who was loading rifles as fast as he could. Both Kate and Mary Nel were firing steadily from behind quickly set-up barricades of boxes and barrels.

"We're getting them. Give them hell, ladies," he yelled. He took a position between Kate and Mary Nel. He watched in admiration as each of the women aimed carefully, squeezed the trigger slowly, and calmly fired at the attackers.

The defenders proved to be too much for the Indians. The remaining Indians started to peel off out of rifle range, many stopping to pick up wounded brethren. One brave soul, adorned with war paint, started to retreat, then wheeled his horse back in the direction of the train, riding back within rifle range. He waved his rifle in the air and screamed unknown words at the defenders.

Will took careful aim and fired, striking the Indian in the middle of his forehead. To Will's amazement, several of the Indians who had started to retreat wheeled their horses about and rode hard toward their fallen companion. As they neared the fallen Indian, two of them slid off their horses and bent to pick up the man.

Without hesitation, Will shot one, then the other. The third Indian, still mounted, turned his horse to retreat, just as Will fired at him, knocking him from his horse. The three Indians lay in a small group around the Indian they had tried to retrieve.

The firing ceased gradually as the remaining attackers rode out of range, leaving dead Indians in almost every direction.

Will, Kate, and Mary Nel stood in the middle of their camp and looked about. Some water barrels leaked, and several boxes of supplies were hit, but most of their possessions were intact.

"Thank God, we are all right," said Kate.

Only then did Will notice a few tears being shed.

"You two were very brave," he said.

He stepped over and gave each of the women a long and close hug.

Mary Nel sniffed a bit but kept her head high.

"I can't believe this just happened. It's like a bad dream," she said. "I didn't really think we'd be attacked by Indians."

"I knew it was possible, but I didn't think it was likely," said Will.

In all the excitement, no one noticed that Ish had slipped away to check on Maggie. When the attack began, he had taken her from the wagon and placed her behind some crates and bags of grain.

He emerged from behind the barrier holding Maggie in his arms.

"She's all right!" he said. "Just a little shaken, like all of us."

Kate went to her and looked down at her, pushing a strand of gray hair from her face. She leaned over and kissed Maggie on the cheek and was rewarded by a weak smile.

"We a long way from Missouri, ain't we, sweet Kate," whispered Maggie.

"A long way, dear Maggie," said Kate with a loud sigh.

As Ish took Maggie back to the wagon, Kate again surveyed the campsite. She wiped her palms on her pants, lifted them up and stared at them intently as if trying to stop the trembling.

"A long way indeed," she said aloud.

CHAPTER TWELVE

W ill! Kate!" shouted Peter as he approached them. "Hobs was hit, and he is bleeding bad."

"Let me get my basket!" said Kate as she headed toward her wagon.

Mary Nel joined the others as they hurried toward the Adams wagon.

Hobs was propped against a wagon wheel, and a woman was holding a bandage against his chest. He was unresponsive and was struggling to breathe.

"Oh, Hobs," whispered Kate as she knelt beside the man.

She removed the makeshift bandage that had been placed over the wound. There was a hole in the right side of his chest that was still bleeding. She took scissors from her basket and cut away Hobs' shirt. She bent low and looked at the wounded man's back. A gaping hole bled freely.

She knew this was a serious and perhaps mortal wound.

"Can we move him to his wagon?" she asked the group standing around.

Several men carried the still unconscious man to his wagon and placed him on the small mattress that served as a bed. Kate followed the men into the wagon and began cleaning the wound.

She placed thick bandages on his chest and back and wrapped them tightly in place in an effort to stem the bleeding.

Hob's face was pale, and he struggled to breathe. He remained unconscious. She covered the man with a blanket and left the wagon.

"It's bad, isn't it?" whispered Will to the solemn-faced Kate.

She stood washing her hands in a bucket of water and watched the water turn bloody. How many times had she done that very thing, she thought.

"Yes, Will," she said in a low voice. "It's very bad."

Despite her calm and deliberate manner, Will could see the pain in her eyes as she looked up at him.

Several council members were among the group standing around the Adams wagon.

"Folks, I think we should stay put today. Give people time to come to terms with this, care for the wounded," said Will as he addressed the council members.

"Anybody object to that?" he asked.

"No," said one of the men. "I know we got at least two men dead. Maybe more. I don't know how many are wounded."

"Let's see if we can get the council members together right away," said Will.

"I'll round up the others," said one of the men.

Will turned to Peter. "Peter, we need to get extra men on horseback to expand the perimeter guard. I don't think those Indians will be back, but we don't need to be careless."

"Yes," said Peter. "And we need others to start rounding up the scattered stock, too. I'll take care of all that."

Will was glad to see how calm Peter was despite all that had happened.

"Thank you, Peter," said Will.

"Mary Nel and I will make the rounds to see if we can help anyone. We'll get a count on how many are wounded ... and dead," Kate said.

Will touched her shoulder. "Thanks, Kate. Both of you be careful."

Kate and Mary Nel left to begin their rounds as several more council members joined those already assembled.

Will started the meeting. "We need to get word to the Army. There was a troop at Platte River Station, and there's a telegraph there, too. They might be able to send some medical help."

"We might get someone to ride ahead to Willow Springs. Probably find other trains there, too. Maybe a doctor," said one of the men.

"Good. Let's do that," said Will.

"What we gonna do 'bout a guide? Hobs is in bad shape, near as I can tell," said a council member.

"That's a big problem. Hank knows the trail, but I don't think we should count on him taking us the rest of the way to California," said Will.

"We got different ways to go up ahead, and we need someone who knows the best route to get us through," said another.

"I think we need to stay put a day or two, then go on to Willow Springs, see what we might find there," Will said. "Most of the trains stop there for fresh water. We just need a better place to regroup and see what we do next."

For two days the train stayed in place, burying four men and caring for the dozen or so wounded as best they could.

On the morning of the second day Hobs Adams passed away.

A simple wooden cross rose from the pile of rocks that marked his grave.

The wagon train left early the next day, leaving the place that would remain in the memories of many for the rest of their lives.

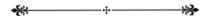

Willow Springs was supposed to be nothing more than a small spring with a fresh running creek. But as the wagon train arrived, the area was crowded with mules, wagons, tents, and campers.

A tie crew, hired to cut railroad ties for construction of the railroad, had converged at the spring as had a large train of Mormons bound for Salt Lake City. Another wagon train, headed toward Fort Hall, had also stopped to water and rest.

From a distance the assemblage resembled a kind of tent city. Campfires burned, and the smell of food mingled with the sound of banjos and fiddles as the tie crews enjoyed the short respite.

Traders and purveyors found their way to the springs, bringing goods of all kinds, including cheap whiskey.

The wagon train continued to the western side of the springs before stopping and setting up camp not far from the Mormon train, which had chosen to distance itself from the revelry of the tie crew.

After setting up camp, Will and a few of the council members went to visit the Mormons. It didn't take very long to find their leader.

"Welcome, gentlemen," said a tall bearded figure in black wool trousers, a white shirt, and suspenders.

"Ewell Brown," said the man as he extended his hand to the men.

"Will Sunday, Mr. Brown," said Will as he shook the man's hand.

The others introduced themselves to Mr. Brown.

"You folks here to water up, I suppose. You have to have a little patience 'cause they're getting the water as it comes in. You kind of have to let it build up a bit. But the creek's steady."

"Good to know. We'll be filling up shortly," said Will.

Finding Mr. Sunday

"Have a seat and sit a spell," said Brown.

They sat and were joined by a couple of other men from the Mormon train.

"You leading the train?" asked Mr. Brown.

"No, we lost our leader, Hobs Adams," replied Will. "We were attacked by the Sioux not too far back. He was wounded and didn't make it. We lost a fine man."

"I'm sorry to hear that. I been talking to some of the travelers from west and east, and there's Indian trouble both ways. I 'spect the only reason we ain't been hit is the size of our train," said Brown.

"You know if there are any doctors around? We got some wounded and sick that need medical attention," asked Will.

"None in our group. But you might want to check the other train. They fixin' to pull out tomorrow so I'd hurry. Understand they're headed to Fort Hall on the due west route," said Brown.

"I assume your train is headed to Utah," said Will.

"Yep. We got a crew meeting us here any day. Then we'll be cuttin' southwest to Fort Bridger. Might be some medical help there. Army has a big detachment of troops there now."

"Thank you, Mr. Brown. We're going to check the other trains. Appreciate your help."

"Sure thing. Ya might want to head out with us. It's a fine group of folks. You'd be welcomed. Doubt any Indians would attack a train that size."

"We'll certainly give that some thought," said Will.

He shook Brown's hand and headed toward the other trains. He found an elderly doctor traveling with his son's family. The kind doctor agreed to see to the wounded.

After spending time with the wounded, he agreed to take a look at Maggie.

"Hello, Doctor," said Kate as she greeted the doctor at Ish's wagon.

"Hello, young lady. Toburg is the name," he said as he held out his hand and tipped his head.

"I'm Kate Daniels, Dr. Toburg. Pleased to meet you."

"Oh, so you the one's been looking after the wounded. You've done a fine job. They're all as good as can be expected," said the doctor with an admiring smile.

"Thank you. I appreciate your looking in on Maggie. She's a dear friend of our family. She is very tired, won't eat, and her color is bad."

"Well, let's have a look," said the old doctor.

He went into Maggie's wagon with Kate and spent a few minutes examining her and talking with her.

"I'm just at the end, Doctor. Too old for this traveling. I just want to go home, that's all," said a weary Maggie.

"Now, now, Miz Maggie. You shouldn't be in no hurry," said the doctor. "You still got miles in you yet. You need to eat and try to get up a little bit, like Mrs. Daniels said."

He covered her frail hand with his own and patted gently.

"Some of this warm sunshine would be just the thing," he said.

"I hear you, Doctor. But the body ain't listening to you," she said, smiling at him.

"Do the best you can, dear. Do the best you can," he said.

He and Kate came out of the wagon and walked a ways away.

"I'm not sure what's going on, Mrs. Daniels. Her heart is mighty weak. I think we got a very sick woman on our hands. There's no way she's going to make it to California unless she gets a break from this traveling. It's just too hard on her," said Dr. Toburg.

"She needs to be some place she can rest. At least for a couple of months. Even then, I don't hold out too much hope for recovery, but that's her best chance."

"I was afraid you'd say that, Doctor," said Kate with a slow shake of her head.

"Now, now. Only the good Lord knows what the future holds. I'm sorry," said the doctor.

"I've got some tonic, back at my wagon. Might give her a little more strength."

"I'll have Rio follow you back and get it," she said. "And thank you again, Doctor."

He left under the glow of one of Kate's smiles, the only payment he was willing to accept.

Finding Mr. Sunday

"Looks like we got three choices," said Will as the council meeting got under way.

He and other council members had spent time talking to the guides of the other trains.

"We can wait here and see if any other trains are coming in that we can join. Or we can join the train headed to Fort Hall. Or we can follow along with the Mormons."

The somber council members looked at each other, then all started talking at once.

"Whoa," said Will. "Let's settle down and take turns."

Marston spoke up. "I don't know about heading out with them Mormons. Don't know what that might be a mistake. Seems like there's trouble everywhere they go. They kind of hard to deal with, from what I heard."

"Yeah. That bothers me, too," said another.

"One thing we need to consider is we've been hit once. The Indians might try it again. We might get some Army help, but I wouldn't count on it," said Will. "Seems to me heading due west to Fort Hall makes better sense than fighting that dry country toward the Salt Lake."

"It's gonna be hot and dry whichever way we go," said one.

"Well, I don't see any sense in waiting on another train," said another.

The men discussed alternatives for a while. No one was absolute in their opinions, but a vote led to joining the train headed for Fort Hall.

"All right. Let's go back. Talk to everyone. If there is any great dissension, let's get back together," said Will.

The men dispersed, and Will headed back to his group to explain the council's decision.

Kate listened intently, watching Ish's reaction.

"Will, can we take a walk after you eat?" said Kate, who then lowered her voice. "The doctor saw Maggie this morning, and I want to share what he said."

"Of course," said Will as he saw the look in Kate's eyes.

After lunch, Kate, Mary Nel, and Will walked around the campsite and

242

found a comfortable place to sit and talk well away from Maggie's wagon.

Kate began, "The doctor doesn't know what is wrong with Maggie. But he said she wouldn't make it to California unless she stopped traveling for a while, a couple of months. Even then, he wasn't sure she would make it."

Will quickly understood the implications of the problem she was addressing.

"If we go all the way with another wagon train, it's going to be more of the same, traveling everyday, day after day. It will surely kill her," Kate said. She paused a moment.

"Is it possible we can get somewhere and stay over and let her rest? That might give her at least some chance of recovering."

No one spoke as the possibility of a long delay set in.

"Will, we know how much you want to get to California. But we owe it to Ish and Maggie to do what we can for them. They are our family," said Mary Nel.

Will looked at the two women. He could feel their sadness at the thought of losing Maggie.

"I know they are, Mary Nel," Will said softly. "And I feel like they are mine, too. If there is any possibility we can get Maggie back to better health, I'm all for doing that. California can wait."

"I knew you would understand," said Kate as she touched his shoulder.

"Let's think about this. Either way we head now it's quite a distance to any layover possibilities. We can't go it alone so we will just have to do the best we can until we get to a suitable stopover," said Will.

Will seemed to be thinking out loud.

"Fort Hall is supposed to be a big trading center, but there is not much between here and there. Fort Bridger is southwest on the way to Salt Lake. But if we went that way we would have an opportunity to see what's there. And if we find nothing, we can go on to Salt Lake. I'm sure we can find a place there through the winter if we want."

"Do you have any worries if we travel with the Mormons?" asked Mary Nel.

"I don't think so," Will said. "I know they are not in high favor with the government. But I kind of liked that fellow Brown. He seemed cordial enough. It's a big train, and I think we should be safe from the Indians.

Finding Mr. Sunday

Besides, Brown may know someone who can find us a place to stay. He said a guide party was coming east to meet them and take them back toward Utah. I'll see if they've arrived and find out if he is still willing to let us go with them."

"Good. That makes me feel so much better," said Kate, a relieved look on her face.

They stood up, and Will, who was between the two ladies, put an arm around each of them.

"Don't worry, we'll get through this and get Maggie the rest she needs," said Will. "I'll go find Brown right away."

As he entered the Mormon camp, he saw that a group of ten or so men had just joined the Mormons.

"Will, this here is John Royston. He led the group up from Salt Lake, and he'll be leading us west," said Brown.

"Mr. Royston," said Will as he extended his hand. "Will Sunday."

Royston was a medium-sized man with dark hair and beard, wearing a flat brim hat, black wool pants, and a gray shirt. He had heavy eyebrows with blue eyes that darted to the object of attention well before he turned his head.

He took Will's hand and shook it firmly but did not smile.

"Brown here said your train might be joining us," said Royston.

"Well, that was a possibility earlier. But they have decided to go with the train headed to Fort Hall. I have a sick woman traveling in my group, and I need to get her to a place we might lay over for a while, maybe even through winter. So it is just my group of four wagons and our stock. I have two men who work with me who will be coming with us. Seven of us all together."

"I'm here to get my brethren to Salt Lake safely," Royston said. "But I guide for a living, and I'd have to charge you to come along with us."

His manner was matter of fact; his face showed no emotion.

Will was a little surprised, and he looked at Brown, who seemed unwilling to challenge Royston.

"I don't think that will be a problem, Mr. Royston," said Will with a smile.

"Then I'll get you to Bridger, then to Salt Lake if you want to go on with us," said Royston.

244

"Fair enough," said Will.

"We don't allow alcohol or gambling, Mr. Sunday. We worship regularly. Everybody pitches in, and we help each other when help is needed," said Royston firmly.

"That all sounds fine to me, Mr. Royston," said Will. "You'll find us good company."

"We leave tomorrow morning at first light," said Royston as he turned to attend to other matters.

Will met with members of the council and told them of his decision. All of the council members, most of whom had grown to admire and respect Will, expressed their disappointment at losing him.

Peter happened to walk up to the group as Will was talking and overheard Will's comments. He walked closer to Will, not quite believing what he had just heard.

"You're going to separate from the train?" he said, his voice a couple octaves higher than usual.

He was visibly upset by the news and, at the same time, annoyed at himself for blurting out the question.

"Yes, Peter. Mary Nel has been trying to find you. I'm sorry you had to find out from me," said a sympathetic Will.

Peter looked at Will and opened his mouth as if to speak, then abruptly turned and hurried away.

"I am sorry you found out that way," said Mary Nel as she sat with Peter some time later. "I couldn't find you."

Peter seemed to be in a daze, not quite believing he and Mary Nel would soon part company.

"We must find ways to keep in touch. I can't let you just drop out of my life," he said with distress in his voice.

He searched her face, looking for some sign of comfort or reassurance.

"Peter, both of us will be in California sooner or later. My mother and I will most likely stay in Sacramento for some time. I wish I could tell you where we'll go from there, but I can't," said a calm Mary Nel.

"Promise me you will send a telegram to my father when you get to California and let him know where you are," he pleaded.

"Peter, I will try. There is so much between here and there. I don't know what our circumstances will be. We may have to stay in Salt Lake for some time. I don't know when we will get to California."

"Then let my father know where you will be in Salt Lake" he said. "Mary Nel, I don't want to lose touch with you. We shouldn't have to if we keep in touch with each other through my father."

There was desperation in his voice.

"Peter, you are a good friend," she said softly. "I would like to keep in touch. I'll try to, but …"

"But what, Mary Nel? " he almost barked.

"Peter," she said as she laid a hand on his arm. "I think you are a sweet person. You're kind and thoughtful, but you are in a hurry to get on with your life, to get married, start a family…"

She could see the hurt begin to well in his eyes as she spoke, but she continued.

"I'm just not ready for those things. But I do want us to stay in touch. Having you as a friend has made the journey very pleasant. I am going to miss you."

She watched his face cloud over as if he was feeling great pain.

"I wish we didn't have to go to Salt Lake," she said, trying to comfort him. "But we must at least try to get Maggie the rest she needs. It might save her life."

"I know, Mary Nel," he said. "I'd go with you and the Mormons, but I promised Father I'd stay with the wagon train. He is counting on me to do that."

"Yes … yes. Your father. I know, Peter. And well you should," she said with weak encouragement.

"I have to go now, Peter. We are leaving at first light. Please come to see us off if you can."

"Yes." He seemed to want to say something more but did not.

"I'll see you then," he said, his voice trailing off.

He watched her walk away. He could feel his chest pounding and hear his own breathing as if he had just awakened from some unpleasant dream.

246

The Mormon train left at dawn the next day. Royston and his men rode up and down the train. Royston's eyes missed little as he noted problem wagons and drivers. It was evident early on that the pace would be brisk, and unnecessary delays would not be looked upon favorably

The four wagons in Will's group were near the head of the train, keeping the pace set by the leaders. At the noon break Will and Kate talked to Ish.

"How is Maggie taking this?" said Kate.

"She just bouncing along," said Ish. "I got her on top of every blanket and quilt I could find." She ain't complaining, but you know her, she wouldn't. I know it's rough on her."

"Well, if it's any comfort, we'll be going uphill for a long stretch before we get to South Pass proper. Then the oxen will set the pace. You can't drive them hard," said Will.

"Our timing is good. We're just into July and coming up on Independence Rock soon. The old travelers say that means we'll beat the bad snows. But we'll most likely be in Salt Lake for the winter anyway."

"I hope we can find a place to stay," said Mary Nel.

"I plan to meet some of the men who came from Salt Lake. See what they may know. Royston may be of help, too, if I can get him to talk to me. He doesn't seem to be the talkative type, but maybe that's just his nature."

Following the evening meal, Will found Royston at the front of the train sitting with some of the others from Salt Lake.

"Evening," said Will to the group as a whole.

Some of the men said hello, and some nodded their heads without speaking.

"We made good time today," said Will.

"Got to make it while we can," said one of the men. "We gonna be climbing soon. Least we got good grass and good water along the Sweetwater River so the animals be fit."

"Hank, my stock man, said the grass was good around here. Not as much stock on the trail as used to be. He's been west before," said Will.

Royston turned to him with his usual flat look.

"The woman and girl traveling with you, they family?"

Will had not expected the question and hesitated slightly.

"Well, they are family to me but not by blood. They are friends I met while I was going through Missouri. I was injured very badly, and Mrs. Daniels and her daughter nursed me back to health. Ish and Maggie are longtime friends of the Daniels family. They farmed together in Missouri."

"So you ain't kin to them, and you ain't married to either of them women?" said Royston.

"No," said Will.

He was annoyed with the implications of Royston's question but held his tongue.

"We're Christians here, Mr. Sunday. We live by God's law," said Royston.

Will felt the heat rise in him but took a breath and tried to calm down.

"Mr. Royston, we, too, are Christians. There is nothing improper going on in our group. I have the utmost respect for Mrs. Daniels and Mary Nel. They are dear to me. You needn't concern yourself with any improprieties."

Will paused and looked directly into Royston's eyes, holding his stare.

"And, that, sir, is all I intend to say to you about the matter," he said firmly.

Royston said nothing but lifted his chin somewhat and turned his eyes away.

Nothing was said for a moment, and the tension drifted away.

"I was hoping you men could help me. As you know, we joined the train because we need to find a place where an older member of our party could have an extended rest and receive medical care."

Most of the men turned their attention to what Will was saying.

"Unless we find some place at Fort Bridger, which is unlikely, it looks like Salt Lake is where we may end up staying for a while," he said.

He scanned the faces of the men and saw he had their attention.

"I was hoping you men might know of a place where we could stay, perhaps through the winter."

No one spoke for a while. Some of the men looked at each other. One man particularly seemed to be looked to more than others. He stepped forward and extended his hand to Will.

"Mr. Sunday, my name is Rheinhardt. I've been in Salt Lake City for many years. I know everything worthy of knowing about the area."

Will could detect a slight accent he believed to be German.

"Mr. Rheinhardt is also a leader in the church," said one of the men.

248

"Pleased to meet you, Mr. Rheinhardt," said Will. As they shook hands, Will was surprised at the softness of Rheinhardt's hand. Slightly older than the others, he was dressed in well-made trail clothes and plain but sturdy boots.

He was a handsome man, perhaps in his mid-forties, who carried himself well. His demeanor was the opposite of Royston's, pleasant and receptive.

"I am sure we can find something for you. We have a good number of doctors and skilled nurses in the area," said Rheinhardt. "We have hotels, boarding houses, and there are even homes available for rent, though not many. Our city is growing fast, and we offer most everything you would need."

"That's good to know, Mr. Rheinhardt," said Will with a smile.

Despite his accent, the man spoke like an educated person and one who took pleasure in speaking with others. His voice was smooth and pleasant.

"I'll be giving your need some thought," said Rheinhardt. "I'll telegraph some people I know when we get to the next station. It's possible we could have something available for you when you arrive in Salt Lake if you choose to continue with us."

"I don't think Fort Bridger will offer us what we need, but we'll see. I assure you, we can pay our way. Maggie is very dear to us. We'd like the most comfortable accommodations you can find," Will said.

"I understand, Mr. Sunday," said Rheinhardt with a slight bow of his head.

"In any regard, sir, I truly appreciate your willingness to help us," said Will.

"My pleasure," said Rheinhardt.

"I'd like to have you visit with us and have a meal while we are traveling, Mr. Rheinhardt. You can meet Maggie and the rest of my friends," said Will.

"I would be very pleased to meet them. I believe we share a few things in common," said Rheinhardt with a slight wink.

"It's settled then," said Will with a big smile. "We'll look forward to seeing you."

"You gentlemen have a pleasant evening," he said to the group.

As he turned to leave he caught the eye of Royston.

Finding Mr. Sunday

"You, too, Mr. Royston," Will said with a slight salute and a smile.

The wagon train continued its westward path as the trail steepened slightly but steadily with each day that passed. The evenings were brisk as the elevation increased, making for good sleeping under the blankets.

Water and grass were plentiful. The beauty of the plains and the vistas of the mountains did not go unnoticed by the travelers as they continued the climb westward.

One afternoon, when the train had stopped earlier than usual to make repairs on several wagons, Rheinhardt made his way to Will's campsite.

Will, Kate, and Mary Nel were taking a few minutes to relax as Rio prepared dinner. Hank sat nearby mending some tack.

"Hello, Mr. Rheinhardt," said Will. "Good to see you."

"And you as well, Will," Rheinhardt said cordially. "I thought I would take you up on meeting your friends."

A quick round of introductions was completed. Rheinhardt seemed especially pleased to meet Kate, which was the reaction of most men.

"Ladies, forgive me for being forward, but I must say you are both lovely. If you are offended by my lack of social grace, I apologize," he said as he bowed his head toward them and upon straightening, flashed a smile that was sure to have won forgiveness many times.

"Not at all, Mr. Rheinhardt," said Kate, beaming. "Please sit and visit."

"I'm to understand you have one with you who is unwell," he said.

"Yes, that's Maggie. She is family to us. She is resting now. Her husband, Ish, will join us soon. I hope you will stay for our evening meal."

"Well, I don't wish to impose, Mrs. Daniels."

"Nonsense. I'm afraid the fare won't be much more than a stew perhaps."

"I assure you, madam, the company will more than make up for any inadequacy in the fare."

"Please call me Kate."

"And would you do me the kindness of calling me Bernard?" he said, smiling.

"Of course," said Kate.

The others observed this exchange while suppressing smiles. Rheinhardt was a charmer for sure but played the role with great sincerity. It was quite obvious he was smitten with Kate.

Rheinhardt seemed to have forgotten for a moment that anyone else was present. Then he turned to Mary Nel.

"Miss Daniels, may I call you Mary."

"Mary Nel, if you please," she said.

"Of course," he said with a warm smile.

"Will, you said you met Kate and Mary Nel as you were traveling through Missouri. May I ask where you are from?"

"I was born in Virginia, but raised in St. Louis since I was four years old," Will said.

"Ahh, St. Louis. I have many friends in St. Louis. I'm sure you can tell I'm from a German family, but I was born in Illinois and went to school at McKendree, not far from St. Louis. And yes, I was once a Methodist," he said, chuckling.

"And you, Kate. Are you from St. Louis?" he inquired.

"No, I was raised in Linn, Missouri, farther west. But I lived for some time in St. Louis. I moved back to Linn after I lost my husband in the war," she said.

"I do apologize. I didn't mean to stir sad memories," said Rheinhardt.

There was silence as Rheinhardt sat with his hands in his lap.

"I know that kind of pain never really leaves you. I lost my Emma less than three years ago," said Rheinhardt softly.

They looked at each other as if to share the shadow of grief that passed over each of them.

"My husband was a fine man and a good father. I treasure the years we had together. But life must go on. Thank you for your concern," she said in a quiet tone.

Rheinhardt quickly changed the conversation. "I think all of you will like Salt Lake City. I have been there since '48. I find great comfort in being with my brethren and watching our community grow," Rheinhardt said.

"I started my time there as a teacher. With the grace of my Maker, I have had good success in business and have enjoyed the embrace of the Church."

He turned to Will. "And you, Will. You are well-educated, I see. Attended university, did you?"

"No," Will said.

He was used to people thinking he was older than he was, and Rheinhardt was no exception.

"I completed public school, but I was also tutored by a retired professor from St. Louis University for over three years. There was some thought that I would study law, but circumstances changed, and I decided to go west. I may study law in California. I haven't decided," said Will.

"You would be good at law. But I sense that you would be good at whatever you choose, Will. You handle yourself well, and you stand up for yourself. People respect that," he said with sincerity.

About that time, Ish came into the circle, having just left his wagon.

"Mr. Rheinhardt," said Will. "This is our friend Ish."

Rheinhardt stood and shook Ish's hand.

"I'm sorry your wife is ill, sir. I had hoped to meet her," he said.

"Thank you, Mr. Rheinhardt. I 'preciate your thoughts. I'm afraid she is resting now, and I don't think she is up for a visit."

"Perhaps another time then," said Rheinhardt. "I hope her condition will improve."

"Thank you, sir," said Ish.

"Hank, I understand you've been west before," said Rheinhardt.

"Been to California, not exactly this way, though," said Hank.

"Well, I think you, too, will find Salt Lake City a fine place. Plenty to do there for a man of your skill with stock. I own a few head myself, cattle mostly," said Rheinhardt.

"How many head ya got?" Hank asked.

"Oh, I never know until I round them up for a drive or a contract. Probably two, three thousand, I suppose." He paused.

"I got a few here and a few there, round them up and sell most of them when I can get a good price. These are not Texas cattle, no tick problems, so I can sell them when I want."

"Got good grass, do ya?" asked Hank.

"We run them in the Wasatch foothills. Not the best, but my boys keep them moving around. I try not to have a big herd in winter," Rheinhardt said.

The smell of baking bread got everyone's attention, and Rio announced that the meal was ready.

Rheinhardt, making sure to sit near Kate, spent most of the time extolling the virtues of life in Salt Lake, as if forgetting their stay would be short term.

After his departure, Mary Nel said, "He seems to be a gentleman."

Several nodded their heads in agreement.

"Oh, yeah," said Hank. "A real thoroughbred, that one."

He exhaled a cloud of tobacco smoke as he removed his pipe.

"Needs watching like one, too," he said as he spit to the side.

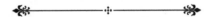

Devil's Gate, Split Rock, and arduous Rocky Ridge marked their passing as they had for thousands of emigrants who had gone before them. Trading posts and ranches dotted the trail as South Pass neared.

South Pass seemed to appear out of nowhere amid rolling hills and low mountains of the Wind River Range.

There was no narrow pass as some expected, but an opening nearly thirty miles wide that gradually rose to nearly eight thousand feet elevation. The emigrants were at the crest before they realized it.

One evening as the train was camped for the night near South Pass, Hank, Rio, and Will sat around the campfire following the evening meal.

"I oughta stay around here and send y'all on to Salt Lake without me," said Hank out of the blue.

He puffed his pipe thoughtfully.

"Why, amigo, would you want to stay here?" inquired Rio.

"Gold, man! You see all these fellows around here traveling with mules and wagons loaded with shovels and supplies? They going to look for gold," he said, gesturing with his pipe.

"Hills s'pose to be full of it, if you ask them. Just here for the taking. Men been scratchin' the hills and pannin' the Sweetwater and local creeks for years now. Some had big luck."

"How much truth is there to that, Hank?" asked Will with a little smile that belied his growing interest.

Finding Mr. Sunday

"Depends on who you talk to," said Hank seriously. "Some big findings in '63 I know of, but the smart fellas don't talk about what they find ... or where."

"I know this, if I was a younger man, I'da been here years ago," he said, underscoring his words with a pull on the pipe. "Indians, though. You gotta watch them Indians. I ain't up to getting no short haircut this late in life. Also, it takes money, men, and equipment to do it right. None of which I got."

Scanning the rolling hills with the many ledges and rock formations that surrounded them, the three settled back to ponder the thought of discovering gold.

It dawned on one of the three that the possibility of looking for gold in these parts could be a reality whenever he chose to make it so.

It wasn't long before the train crossed the Continental Divide and continued its way toward Fort Bridger. There were no more threats from Indians, though the train kept a steady watch for them. The terrain was dry and rough, but water was available, easing the way.

Arriving at Fort Bridger, the travelers found a stockade-type fort occupied with as many traders as there were soldiers. The traders were eager for each wagon train to arrive but disappointed to find the train was mostly Mormons, who tended to buy little and were skilled bargainers for what they did purchase.

After camp was set up for what was to be only a one-night stopover, Will, Kate, and Mary Nel rode around the area. There were living quarters, but most were stark. There were few civilian residents except the traders, many of whom were transient.

"I don't have a good feeling about this fort," said Mary Nel.

The three sat in a small tavern with a simple sign over the door: "Food."

"Nor do I," said Kate.

"I didn't expect it to be what we want, and it isn't," said Will as he sipped a cup of strong coffee.

"It's going to be rough on Maggie, but we'll have to continue on to Salt

Lake. I can't see her staying here, even if it is just for the fall months," said Kate.

"Fortunately, we don't have that far to get to Salt Lake," said Will.

"My guess is Rheinhardt will find us a place. Something tells me he wants to be around for a while, one way or another," Will said, grinning slightly. "Don't you think so Kate?"

She gave him a quick glance, then turned away, a bit of color creeping into her tanned cheeks.

His question went unanswered.

Guarded by the Wasatch and Oquirrh mountain ranges, Salt Lake City was a monument to careful planning and design. The wide streets ran straight and parallel, creating almost identical blocks of well-constructed and maintained buildings.

New construction seemed to be underway in every direction, including the unusual Mormon Tabernacle that would become a hallmark of the city.

The Council House spires soared far above street level as if pointing the way to Heaven itself. The immaculate streets and walkways were crowded, although a common sense of orderliness and calm seemed to prevail as people went about their daily activities.

Will and his fellow travelers were impressed with this urban jewel in the middle of barren land. Despite the inherent anonymity of city living, nods and smiles were common to the newcomers.

"I'm surprised," said Kate. "I didn't think we would find this so far from everything else."

Having arranged for the storage of the wagons and care of the stock, the small party rode in a large carriage down South Street.

"Why, it's a beautiful place. And so clean. I'm sure we can manage here for as long as we need to," she said with a pleased expression on her face.

"It looks like it has everything one could need," said Will as he surveyed the many shops that lined the streets. "We're not far from the hotel Bernard recommended. He plans to meet us there with information on where we might stay for the longer term."

Finding Mr. Sunday

The three-story hotel was built of brick with stone accents, and the quality of the structure rivaled that of similar buildings in the East. Fine woven rugs adorned highly polished wood floors, and elegant upholstered furnishings filled the spacious lobby.

Will secured rooms for the group, and Rheinhardt found a lodge run by Negroes for Maggie and Ish, as black folk were not allowed to stay in white establishments. But Rheinhardt said he had ensured that Maggie's every need would be met.

"How nice to be eating from glass plates," said Mary Nel as they enjoyed a meal in the dining room.

"Imagine," said a smiling Kate. "Eating trail dust one day and having berries and cream the next. This could spoil even the most discerning person."

The two ladies had traded their trail clothes for dresses and gotten the attention of more than a few other diners. Will, too, looked like a gentleman in his brushed suit and collared shirt.

"It's quite a change," he said. "This might do us all some good."

"I saw some shops nearby that we must visit as soon as we can, Mary Nel," Kate said, all but giggling. "We both need to freshen our wardrobes."

"Oh, well," said Mary Nel with feigned resignation. "If we must." She, too, giggled.

"I plan to visit a tailor. I've seen several within walking distance," said Will.

"I don't know if I can sleep tonight. A feather bed? A roof over my head?" said Kate.

"You'll just have to bear, it Momma," she said, laughing.

As they were talking, Rheinhardt walked into the dining room and came over to the table.

"Good day, folks. I hope you will pardon my interrupting your meal," he said.

"By all means, Bernard," said Will. "Please sit down."

"Thank you," he said.

He looked at the two ladies and shook his head slowly from side to side.

"I didn't think you two ladies could look any more beautiful, but I was wrong," he said.

Dick Ward

The two smiled at the compliment.

"Good news. As you know, we sent a wire to my associate before leaving Fort Bridger, and they have secured two places I know you will like.

"One is good-sized house that is almost new, fully equipped with everything you will need. It even has a sun porch.

"There is a stable for your riding stock that has a bunkhouse for your two men. The other is a smaller, but equally suitable cottage that is just two doors away. The properties are located back off the main streets, yet close to everything you will need."

"Wonderful, Bernard," said Kate with that disarming smile. "How good of you to be so diligent."

"Well, there will be a few days' delay as we are making some final arrangements. But I trust you will enjoy the amenities the hotel has to offer."

"Most assuredly," said Kate.

"Will, there is a livery less than a mile away. They have an excellent reputation. You can keep your mules and other stock there. They also have a good supply of carriages available should you need one."

"That will be handy, Bernard," said Will.

"Now day after tomorrow, I would like the three of you to be my guests for a tour of the city and then dinner in my home. I think you will enjoy both immensely," Rheinhardt said. "Ish is welcome also, but my guess is he would rather stay with Maggie."

"I think you are correct," said Kate. "Getting her settled in her room tired her considerably. It is good that she can rest before we move her to the cottage."

"It's settled, then. I will have my carriage here at three on Thursday," said Rheinhardt.

"You have done so much for us, Bernard. I hate for you to go to all that trouble for us," said Kate with a warm smile.

"Nonsense," Rheinhardt responded as he placed his hand on hers. "It is my pleasure, dear Kate. Have a pleasant day and enjoy our fine city."

The house was well-furnished and very comfortable, with a large bedroom downstairs and two large bedrooms upstairs. The kitchen was as inviting as most kitchens, and a large parlor provided plenty of space for visiting. There was even a small but comfortable sewing room with plenty of windows near the rear of the house.

Of course, the stable became home for Minnie and both of Will's bays. The animals adjusted readily to the slower pace and the days spent grazing in a pasture near the house.

Hank attended to the stock, and Rio thoroughly embraced his role as chief cook as he marveled at the well-equipped kitchen.

Will had rented a good carriage from the livery stable, and Hank kept it ready for a ride about town or a journey into the nearby countryside.

Thursday afternoon, Rheinhardt showed up at the hotel. His carriage, a splendid affair painted a glistening black and trimmed in bright yellow, was pulled by two matched horses. There was a separate seat in the front for the driver and a glass-enclosed compartment with bright red overstuffed leather seats for passengers.

"What a fine carriage, Bernard," said Will.

"Thank you, Will. I hope you will find it comfortable," Rheinhardt said. "It was made right here in Salt Lake City."

They toured the city at a leisurely pace and marveled at the quality of the structures. Warehouses, mills, and municipal buildings were built with the same attention to detail as the multi-story mansions.

The wide, clean streets allowed farm wagons and carriages alike to move as each driver saw fit.

Rheinhardt proudly directed the tour.

"It is a wonderful city, Bernard. The markets seem to be bulging with fresh vegetables and produce," said Kate.

"We are very proud of that, Kate. Not so very long ago this area was little more than a desert. But with irrigation and careful stewardship of the land, we have bountiful harvests here," said Rheinhardt, with no little amount of pride in his voice.

He took them for a close look at the monstrous Tabernacle under construction and showed them the landmark Council House. They toured South Street and the others named for the compass points.

It wasn't long before fine mansions began to appear. It was apparent that more than a few residents lived very well.

"Many of these people are merchants and traders. The city has become quite the trade center for points east and west," Rheinhardt said. "Also, many of these gentlemen have benefited from lead and silver mining elsewhere in the state and chose to make their home here."

As the carriage made its way down one of the finer residential streets, Rheinhardt said to his guests, "We are here, good folks. Welcome to my home."

The carriage turned onto a semi-circular drive that led to the front walk of a stately two-story home built of red brick and accented in native stone. Hand-cut stone steps led to a large and welcoming front porch supported by Doric columns.

The porch and wood trim were painted a pleasing green that enhanced the cooling effect in hot weather. A matching wood and beveled glass door with etched sidelights invited visitors to enter the home.

"Why, Bernard, your home is stunning," said Kate as the group stepped into the marble-floored foyer.

"Thank you, Kate. After we relax and have some cool beverages I'll give you a tour," said Rheinhardt, beaming.

The group moved into the parlor and settled in comfortable upholstered furniture that perfectly matched the stained walnut paneling, silk wallpaper, and many fine woven rugs that graced the shiny wood floor. There was a reflection of wealth, no doubt, but it was second to that of comfort and homeyness.

A middle-aged woman wearing a gray dress protected by a long starched white apron came into the room bearing a tray of beverages and treats. She placed the tray on a sideboard and turned to greet the guests.

"Good folks, this is Miriam," said Rheinhardt. "She is a dear friend who happens to be my housekeeper of many years. Miriam, this is Mrs. Daniels, her daughter Mary Nel, and their friend Mr. Sunday."

Miriam, a handsome gray-haired lady, maybe in her mid-forties, stood with her hands interlaced in front and resting on her aproned midsection and nodded politely to each of the guests.

With a big smile she said, "Welcome! Welcome! I'm so happy to have you visit. Please make yourselves at home."

Miriam went about serving refreshments and seeing to everyone's comfort.

"Mr. Rheinhardt tells me you are headed west but have one in your party who is not well," Miriam said with some concern in her voice.

"Yes," said Kate. "Maggie has been a friend of our family for many years. She practically raised me. We are very worried about her. We are hopeful a long rest here will allow her to continue with us."

"Well, Mrs. Daniels, if there is anything I can do, please let me know. I understand Dr. Drayton is looking in on her," said Miriam.

"Yes. He was in this morning and said the same as the other doctors. Rest and time will tell," said Kate.

"We'll certainly pray that she improves," said Miriam. "And do you find Mr. Rheinhardt's houses comfortable? He goes to great length to care for his properties."

Will and Kate exchanged knowing glances, surprised to learn the houses belonged to Rheinhardt.

"Why, yes, Miriam. We already feel at home," replied Will.

Miriam turned to Mary Nel.

"Mary Nel, you are such a lovely young lady. How have you fared on this long journey?"

"I find it very exciting. There have been some frightening times, but all in all, I have enjoyed the trip."

"You will find lots of things to do in the city. There are many young adults here," Miriam said with a smile.

"Yes, ma'am," Mary Nel said. "I look forward to meeting some of them."

Miriam told Mary Nel about some of the activities she might enjoy.

"I'm so looking forward to getting to know you all," she said. "If you folks will please excuse me, I have some things to do before we dine. We will have our meal in a short while."

With a slight bow of her head, she left the room and headed down the hallway toward the back of the house.

Will, Kate, and Mary Nel felt at ease with Rheinhardt, and the conversation flowed naturally. He was a gracious host who seemed to enjoy having guests in his home.

After a while, Miriam summoned the group into the dining room. The large table, made of highly polished walnut, seated twelve people, but Miriam had arranged the seating at one end, and the gathering seemed intimate despite the size of the room.

Dick Ward

A snow-white linen table cloth provided a perfect backdrop for the tasteful china, crystal, and silverware that gleamed in the soft candle light. The setting was a stark contrast to the meals around a smoky campfire that had become the norm in the last few months.

An array of vegetables, beef, lamb, sauces, breads, butter, jams, and side dishes stimulated even the daintiest of appetites and stoked the conversation further.

The group enjoyed a good meal, lively conversation, and an altogether pleasant evening.

"My, my, we've taken up most of your day, Bernard," said Kate just as a mantel clock chimed. "I'm afraid we should go before it is dark."

"My dear Kate, I'm sad to hear that. It has been my pleasure to have all of you in my home. I hope we can do it again soon," Rheinhardt said. "I very much enjoy visitors who have so much to offer in the way of conversation. Miriam, would you ask James to bring the carriage around?"

"We very much enjoyed the meal. You are going to spoil us for the rest of the trip," said Will.

"And I hope I may have that privilege on numerous occasions, Will," said Rheinhardt. "Too, I hope you all don't mind if I come around to check on your welfare from time to time."

"Not at all," said Kate politely.

With the farewells completed, Rheinhardt accompanied them to the carriage, and the party headed back to their temporary home.

Rheinhardt came into the house to find a waiting Miriam standing in the foyer.

He reached for her hand and gave a slight squeeze and nodded knowingly. She returned his smile and turned to attend to other matters.

Upon returning to the house, Kate suggested a cup of tea. Even Will, who drank coffee most of the time, accepted the offer. Kate went about putting on the water and setting out the cups.

"We're going to make a tea drinker of you yet," Kate said with a smile.

"I don't know, Momma," Mary Nel said as she gave Will a teasing smile. "It has to be very strong for him to enjoy it."

"Bernard seems to have done well," said Will. "Apparently he is not one to talk much about his own success."

Finding Mr. Sunday

"I agree," said Kate. "There is a little mystery there, I think."

"I'm new at all this, but I believe there is more to Mr. Rheinhardt than meets the eye," said Mary Nel.

"He is very nice, respectful, proper and all, but I don't know ..."

"You have very good intuition, my dear daughter," said Kate.

"I think he likes you, Kate," said Will.

"Why, of course, he does," said Kate. "It's just my charming way." She laughed.

"Will is right, Momma. I can tell. I think you're going to see a lot of Mr. Rheinhardt."

"You don't think he is devious or anything like that, do you, Will?" asked Kate.

"I don't know enough about the man to give an opinion," answered Will. "But I would be a little wary. My guess is he is a man of great influence... beyond the church, I mean. I also think Mr. Rheinhardt is one who is used to getting things to turn out his way."

Kate stirred her tea and stared at it thoughtfully.

"Well, I don't intend to worry about Bernard's intentions."

She lifted her chin up as she set her spoon down and stared off in the distance.

"My main concern now is to see that Maggie gets better and we get on to California. That's the next big step for me."

"You do know, Kate, it will be at least late spring before we can leave for California. That's if we can get on to another train," Will said as he leaned forward and looked at her.

"Of course, I'm sure we can hire our own guides and head out earlier. But the Utes are restless now, and traveling in a small group is no more advisable than it was on the first leg. About any way you look at it, there is ample time for us to find out more about Mr. Rheinhardt."

"I may know all I care to know already," said Kate with a little smile that volunteered nothing.

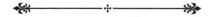

The warm summer waned, and the mornings brought a chill to the air. Maggie showed little improvement and continued to rest, leaving the bedroom on rare occasions and only when helped by Ish.

Kate spent much time in her company but had ample time to explore the city with Mary Nel.

Rheinhardt stopped by often. He invited the group to his home again and was, as usual, the perfect host. There was no lessening of his attention to Kate.

In fact, the two of them often walked in his garden and around the neighborhood admiring the fine homes and grounds.

Will was restless. The routine of breakfast followed by the newspaper soon became boring. He found himself taking the bay farther into the mountains each day, exploring and observing and returning to the local tavern to blend with some of the non-Mormon residents.

Winter came to the area like an angry monster. Long-time residents were ready and dug in for a brutal few months of wind, snow, and bitter cold. There was little to do but let nature run its course.

Will was seated at his usual table at the tavern one day in late January talking with Pierce Randley, one of his newfound friends.

Pierce was a man in his forties who presented himself well and was a good conversationalist. He had recently sold a grain company and was trying to decide on his next venture. The subject of gold prospecting came up.

"You know, when we went through South Pass a while back, gold in the Sweetwater area seemed to be on everybody's mind," said Will.

"Why, it's no wonder." said Pierce. "There's gold up there all right. All around the Sweetwater and South Pass. I know fellows right here in Salt Lake that have been up there. Said they could see gold right in the streams." He winked at Will.

"I doubt that's the case," Will said, laughing, "or every man around would have headed there."

"Oh, I know that," Pierce said as he scratched his neatly trimmed beard. "But there's gold there, and that's a fact. Soldiers from Fort Bridger have been going up there to find it every since a detail chasing some Indians found some while camped by a stream."

He nodded his head knowingly. "If you can keep the Indians off your back and have the right equipment, a patient man can find gold."

"This is not a tale is it? I read the bits in the newspaper about it, but you can't believe all you read," said Will.

"Well, I met a man who's been up there. An Englishman. Seems to know a lot about mining. Came here by way of California. I think he's keen to get to mining up there and knows more than he is willing to talk about," said Pierce.

"He told me you could do placer mining and find some. But panning a creek is slow, and everybody's trying that when the season lets them."

Pierce leaned over the table and lowered his voice. "He said if a man was to invest in the right equipment and methods you could get the stuff out of ore. Lots of it."

"Why isn't he doing it, then?" asked Will in a low voice.

Pierce looked around the room to see who might hear him. Everyone within earshot was talking themselves.

"He doesn't have the capital to get the equipment. That's how come I know about it. He asked me if I was interested in investing in the equipment and splitting the profit. But he needs more than I care to risk."

"Do you trust this man?" asked Will with a tilt of his head.

"I don't know him well enough to say. Seems on the up and up. Carries himself well. Quiet sort. Fairly young, maybe late twenties. Well spoken. Stays in a good hotel. Dresses well. Clean. I don't know much more than that. We have a drink now and then."

"What kind of money was he looking for, if you don't mind me asking?" said Will.

"Thousands. Thousands. Said something about building a mill of some kind," said Pierce.

Will got a gleam in his eyes and looked off in the distance.

As winter set in, Will was at his wits' end. He read every newspaper he could get. He even delved into Blackstone's tome. Every newspaper story about gold and silver mining got his attention.

Doing nothing wore on him. His thoughts about gold prospecting wouldn't leave him alone.

Mary Nel, Kate, and the others seemed to take it all in stride, content to sew, read, and visit the many shops when they could get out. Maggie seemed to be holding her own, with no improvement, yet no further decline.

Will met Pierce one day at his usual table in the tavern. He had not talked much about the Englishman in their last few meetings.

"Pierce, is that Englishman still around? The one you told me about a few weeks ago?" asked Will.

"That he is. Saw him just yesterday," said Pierce.

"How would you feel about introducing me to him? I'd kind of like to hear more about what he has on his mind."

"Wouldn't mind it a bit. You two would get along fine, I think. Have a lot in common," said Pierce. "As I said though, he is looking for big money. But I'll see what he has to say."

A few days later as Will headed to his table, he saw Pierce sitting with another fellow. The man was dressed in a well-cut gray suit, white shirt, and a thick knotted tie. As Will approached the table the young man stood and extended his hand.

"Chester Fields," he said with a polite smile on his face.

"Will Sunday. Glad to meet you, Mr. Fields."

"Call me Chester, please," he said in an accent that hinted of Scotland.

Fields was as Pierce had described. Well groomed and with a trim, neat appearance. His brown hair was parted in the middle and carefully brushed.

He was about average size, medium complexion with brown eyes. He, too, had a tendency to look directly into one's eyes as he spoke, something Will always appreciated.

"For some reason, Mr. Sunday, I had expected someone a bit older."

"Call me Will. I'm not sure age is important to our discussion, Chester. I'm hopeful our discussion might allay any concerns you might have about my age ... or abilities," said Will.

His smile softened the delivery, but the message was not lost on Fields.

"Pierce tells me you are on a layover here and eventually will resume your trip to California."

"That's right. I'm not sure how long I'll be here, but it doesn't look like we will be leaving anytime soon. I understand you are from England by way of California," said Will.

"Scotland, actually. I've been in America for a little over a year," said Fields.

Finding Mr. Sunday

"What brought you here, if I may ask?" said Will.

"I guess you might say I am here looking for opportunities. I'm an engineer by training. I've been around mining all my life. I missed the California gold experience, of course, but I've learned a lot about it. I came to this part of the country to explore what it has to offer," he said.

"Despite the late tragedy, I believe the country will be back on its feet soon and that progress will continue."

Fields wiped his mouth with a napkin.

"In Europe, things tend to move slower. But we have experience in some things that could benefit the right people. Mining, for example." Fields sat back in his chair and crossed his legs at the knees.

"I came here to leverage that experience, under the proper circumstances and with the right parties."

"Have you been in the gold mining business before, Chester?"

"No, not really. But I know the process. I know the equipment and material you need to do it the right way, how to set it up and build the necessary facility. I have enough knowledge of geology to look in the right places. I'm not talking about placer mining here. I'm talking about gold mining on a much larger scale," he said.

He paused a second, waiting for a response, but no one else spoke. He realized his enthusiasm might have come across the wrong way.

"I know that sounds boastful, Will. If so, I apologize. But the only thing I have to offer is my expertise … and my integrity, which to me is of equal if not greater importance."

"I appreciate your saying that. You don't know me, and I don't know you, Chester. But expertise and integrity can go a long way. Especially the latter. That alone means more to me than any other trait.

"I was raised in St. Louis by a friend of my father's family. Tom was a kind, gentle man who taught me the value of integrity, as well as many other things that have served me well so far.

"I share this because I believe integrity has to be at the heart of any relationship. That's the only way trust can evolve between two parties."

Having said that, Will, too, sat back in his chair.

"I couldn't agree more," said Chester in a serious tone.

"Then there is the issue of capital. Let's not forget that," said Will.

"I assume you must have means, Will, or you wouldn't have wanted to hear more about my endeavor."

"Let's order some food and discuss that, if you'd be my guest," said Will.

"Of course," Fields replied.

The three ordered their meals. Pierce spoke little but listened intently, his interest in the matter now going somewhat beyond the intermediary role he had played.

Conversation was more social than business as the gentleman shared another drink while waiting for their meals. The initial awkwardness of getting to know each other was fading.

"You were kind enough to tell me some of your background, Will. At risk of boring you, I'll share some of mine," said Chester.

"I was raised in Scotland, Glasgow to be exact. My father was a coal mine owner in the communities north of the city. I was going to mines with him when I was very young.

"He wanted me to be in the family business, and I was for a while after university."

He sipped his drink and seemed to be lost in memory.

"He was very upset when I told him I wanted to go to America. Hurt, I guess you might say. But I didn't want to spend my life in his shoes," Chester said.

"Don't get me wrong. He has done very well in his lifetime, and some deem me out of my mind not to follow along. But I wanted to seek my own opportunities, and the more I learned about America the more I wanted to come here.

"I suppose if I were to go back, I might persuade him to provide the capital I need, but that is the last thing I want to do. It is contrary to the whole notion of my being here on my own."

Will nodded to Fields and spoke.

"I understand. I know what you mean by wanting to make it on your own. I've been very fortunate in a number of regards, but to me, my self worth can't be measured by what has been given to me, only by what I create on my own.

"It could be that I have to prove something to myself, or I'm just driven by some innate need for accomplishment, whatever the endeavor," Will mused.

Finding Mr. Sunday

Will sensed that Chester was very much like him in this way. There is a lot about this fellow that I like, he thought.

"So tell me Chester. What is it that you are wanting to do?"

"I think the area of South Pass, they are calling it the Sweetwater now, even though that is a river more than an area, has great potential for gold mining. I've heard the stories, even as far away as California.

"Of course, it is hard to separate fact from fiction. So I went to see for myself. I've seen enough to make me believe there is gold there. But it is not just in the Sweetwater or the streams around there, it's in the hills. In rock ledges and quartz formations."

A waiter brought out their food and set it before them. Fields paused and waited for everyone to be served.

"I rode around the area and walked over a lot of land. I believe there is gold ore there. But you won't get at the gold with a pick axe and shovel."

He picked at his meal.

"It needs to be mined, by the tons. If you start processing great amounts of the ore, you will soon find out if gold is there. But that requires a big upfront investment in equipment and manpower, all without any assurance of success."

He took several bites and chewed reflectively.

"One could lose every penny expended up front and walk away empty handed. On the other hand, if you process enough ore, you might get lucky. And if you had the right equipment in place, you would not necessarily need to find gold on your own, you could process ore for others for a percentage.

"Ideally you would want to do both. That is, prospect for your own ore and provide an independent milling service to others. You could mill for others for a flat fee per ton or by the hour or for a percentage of the gold rendered, whichever is higher. With the right equipment, you could run almost twenty-four hours a day."

"You mean as long as somebody was finding gold, you could share in the proceeds if there was gold to be found. As long as you milled it for them," said Will.

"Exactly. And with the kind of equipment I'm thinking about, you could scale up as demand dictated."

"Tell me about the equipment and the process."

"I've looked at everything that is available. There are the arrastra mills that have been around for centuries — basically stones connected by rope and spun in a wooden tub by a water wheel.

"You can build one of those if you got good water. But I'm thinking about a stamp mill. It is a huge machine, run by a steam engine. It takes the raw ore, crushes it, mixes it with mercury to form a kind of sludge, or amalgam. You run the mix out on copper plates covered with mercury. It separates the gold from everything else. That is a simplified explanation, of course.

"You can do tons in an hour. And the machinery can readily be expanded by adding more sections. You start with five or ten components and expand in fives, to ten, fifteen, and so on."

"And where can you get these machines?" asked Will.

"Several places. For our purposes, California. San Francisco to be exact. They are shipped unassembled. We can get it here using California wagons. They can carry six tons of freight each. We'd need a wood source and a water source for the steam engine. But there is plenty of that."

The discussion went on and on. Will asked question after question, and Fields had credible answers for each one. Many of the details were carefully illustrated and written on papers that Fields extracted from a leather binder. It was obvious the man had given this potential endeavor a great amount of thought and planning.

Fields' enthusiasm for the project was palpable, and his knowledge of the issues proved to be almost endless. Too, Fields was duly impressed with Will's quick grasp of even the most technical issues as they were explained.

The men sat long after the meal was completed, their sense of time lost in the moment.

"Bottom line, how much do we need to get this to South Pass and up and running?" asked Will.

Fields extracted another sheet of paper from his stack and moved closer to the edge of the table, sharing the list of items and costs with Will.

"I have gone over this again and again. I don't want anyone interested in this to have any surprises down the road. I'm sure we can get it started for $12,000 in capital for the first set of stamps, the steam engine, and the necessary housing.

"Of course, if we expand the size and capacity, there would be more expenses down the road. But that would only be the case as success dictates."

Pierce sat back in his chair and turned to gauge the reaction on Will's face. This was getting very interesting to him. Fields, who looked as if he was holding his breath, stared at Will.

Will continued with more questions. It was obvious to both men that Will was an unusually bright young man. The issue of age was not on anyone's mind by this point.

"I want to think about this, obviously. There are some personal considerations I need to resolve. You have presented an intriguing proposal, Chester, and I thank you for all the work you have done," said Will.

Chester was crestfallen. He was afraid all his hard work and diligence had come to nothing.

"I know that is a lot of money, Will, I ..."_

Will lifted his hand off the table as if to mitigate Chester's concern, then interrupted Chester.

"The money is not an issue, Chester. If I decide to do this, I can have it in your hands in a few days," said Will.

Both men opened their eyes, whether in shock or disbelief was uncertain.

"Let's meet here again on Thursday, same time. That will give me several days to mull this over and fully consider the personal side of all this. I can't make any promise other than that we'll meet again," Will said.

With that remark, he stood and shook hands with Fields. As he did so, he looked Fields directly in the eye and gave him a quick wink and a big smile.

He walked out of the room leaving the other two men staring at his back until he went through the door, both somewhat astounded by this young man.

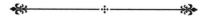

Will was fascinated with the prospect of finding gold. But he realized the dangers of jumping into such a costly venture where success lay largely in the hands of others.

He felt good about Fields, but he knew he would have to be there, hands on, involved in every detail of the project to protect his investment. Even then, success was not a given. It was, after all, a venture, not a sure thing.

As he wrestled with the idea, he finally came to the conclusion that the most he could lose was his investment. An expensive lesson, no doubt. But the very challenge it represented excited him. It was fuel for him, something that he needed right now.

Will, Kate, and Maggie sat at the table after breakfast the next day.

"Kate and Mary Nel, I want to discuss something with the two of you," said Will.

His announcement drew their attention immediately. Both Kate and Mary Nel sat still, anticipating what they knew must be something very important.

Will's expression softened. There was a warmth in his eyes as he looked from one to the other.

"You know what a big part of my life you two have become. We have come a long way together, and I want us to see this trip through, and we will," he assured them.

"Something has developed that might alter our timing somewhat, and I want to lay it out and get your reaction."

Kate and Mary Nel exchanged quick and somewhat worried glances, anticipating news they did not want to hear. Will picked up on this and was quick to ease their obvious worry.

"Now both of you settle down. There is no bad news in this."

He reached over, gave a gentle squeeze on the arms to both of them. His reassurance had an effect, and the two women seemed to simultaneously exhale in relief.

"I don't think we are going anywhere for the next few months, even longer maybe," he said.

"I think you all are doing well. The accommodations are good, shops are near, and, of course, you have Rheinhardt watching out for you."

He smiled a little at his comment.

"You may recall that when we came through South Pass, there was a lot of talk about the possibility of gold being there. There were prospectors all around."

He took a breath.

"That kind of piqued my interest then, but I put it in the back of my mind. I have followed the articles about the Sweetwater area and South Pass in

Finding Mr. Sunday

The Deseret News and The Union Vedette. But several days ago, I was having a drink with Pierce Randley. I have mentioned him to you but have not had the opportunity to introduce him to the two of you.

"The topic of gold mining came into the conversation, and he told me about a fellow who was looking for an investor in a gold-mining project. I met with this fellow. I like him. I think he knows what he is talking about."

Will studied their faces as he spoke.

"He has already been up there looking at the area. I think this is a good venture for me, but I have a few things I want to look into before I decide invest.

"But investing would just be part of it. I would want to be on site, at least for a few months, to keep an eye on things and learn as much as I can. If we have any success, it may require my being there even longer."

Again, the women exchanged glances. He gave them a summary of the project and the proposed venture. They could see the excitement pour out as he explained the opportunity.

"I wouldn't even consider such a thing if I didn't think you two were perfectly safe here," he said, looking them both in the eye.

"I can make the decision about the investment on my own. That is not a concern. But I want to know how the two of you feel about this. It might mean a longer delay in heading on to California. I just can't tell you how long.

"I know I'm being a little selfish here, but I am having a hard time just being here doing nothing."

There was a long moment of silence.

"Well, Will," began Kate after a moment. "I can tell you are miserable here. We all know you are not one to sit around all day, and this has been hard on you. I was half expecting to hear something like this."

Mary Nel said, "I don't know how you have stood it this long, Will."

"Please understand, my goal is still to get to California as soon as situations permit, but this may be a once in a lifetime opportunity," Will said.

"Going ahead without you is out of the question, for a lot of reasons. And right now things are so uncertain. Maggie is about the same, and she certainly is in no condition to travel," said Kate.

Mary Nel spoke without any uncertainty.

"Will, I think you should do it. If nothing else, for the fun and adventure of it. My only wish is that I could go with you. I know a mining community is no place for a lady."

"You are right about that. But I appreciate your support, Mary Nel. I think you know exactly how I feel."

He gave her one of his special smiles.

"Kate? You know how much I value your opinion," he said.

She looked into his eyes and something transpired between them that was almost palpable.

"I ... I think it would do you good. Will, we don't want to stand in the way of anything you want to do. You are smart. You can take care of yourself. We'll miss you terribly, though."

"Go. Go and throw in all that vigor I see smoldering all the time. Why, goodness gracious, you might even find gold," she said, laughing.

"I might," he said. "And if I do, I promise to bring some back to the two of you."

He laughed, but the words stayed with him.

"Good. You know I will keep in touch and provide you with an address where you can telegraph me. I can be back in a matter of days if I'm needed here," said Will.

"It's not the best time to head to high altitudes, but we have a lot to do before we leave. And the sooner we get started, the better."

CHAPTER THIRTEEN

W ill, Pierce Randley, and Chester Fields sat at the same table on Thursday. Chester's face was taut with anticipation as he awaited Will's words. They ordered a round of drinks and engaged in some preliminary casual conversation. The drinks came, and the casual conversation stopped momentarily.

"Chester, here are my thoughts. All of this will be put in a written agreement drafted by a lawyer after we settle the details," said Will. "I'll provide the working capital you have requested."

He could hear Chester's audible intake of breath.

"You and I, Chester, would be fifty/fifty partners in all profits. You will be responsible for keeping an accounting record of all expenses, income, and so on. When it becomes necessary we'll hire professional bookkeepers.

"I will have oversight and final say on every aspect of the operation — every aspect, whatever the nature.

"You may allow Pierce to participate in equity or profits to whatever extent you deem appropriate, but that's between the two of you, and any such participation would come out of your half.

"You and I will draw no salaries, but living expenses will be provided for, which are later to be repaid by those receiving such, if there is a profit to do so.

"Those are my stipulations. If you want to add things, let's discuss them. I can have the funds here day after tomorrow." Will paused.

Fields was about to explode. He stood up and grabbed Will's hand, a huge smile splitting his face.

"Will, that's exactly what I was thinking. You go ahead with the legal agreement. Nothing you said is a problem with me, and I trust you to add anything else you feel appropriate."

He pumped Will's hand.

After a while the meeting ended. On his way out the door, Will was stopped by Randley.

"I need to tell you, Will, I think I got left out of this deal," said Randley.

"Left out? What do you mean?" said Will.

Finding Mr. Sunday

"Well, if it hadn't been for me, this whole thing never would have happened," he said.

Will could see Randley was clearly upset.

"What is it you want?" asked Will.

"I want five percent out of your share and five percent out of Chester's," said Randley.

Will was surprised at the request.

"You place a pretty high value on circumstance, Pierce," said Will.

"Like I say, I set it all up," said Randley.

Will did not hesitate.

"I'm not about to agree to that. Like I said, if you want to make a deal with Chester, go ahead. Or put up some capital, and we'll talk," said Will firmly.

"I don't think you're treating me fair," said an angry Randley.

"That, Pierce, is your problem," said a defiant Will.

Randley stared at him but said nothing. Will saw no reason to say more.

"Good day, Randley," he said as he put on his hat and walked away.

Randley stared hard as Will walked out.

Within a few days the agreement was signed, and the initial elements of the project were reviewed, machinery and equipment were ordered. The only thing that held them up was the weather.

South Pass was an area of rolling hills and valleys with rock formations scattered in almost every direction. But this time of year the heavy drifting snow, driven by the gusts from the Wind River mountains, filled the small valleys and hid the frozen creeks, disguising the rolling terrain while capping the rock ridges with ice.

Some called it snow, but the stinging swirl of whiteness felt like tiny razors as it slashed exposed skin. Wrapped, gloved, and muffled, the men walked over the piece of ground, yelling to each other to make a point, stepping first in one direction, then another.

They had carefully chosen the site of the stamp mill and the enclosure that would house the other moving parts of the mill.

The topography would allow easy carting of ore to the upper level of the mill, and the chute for the ore would be aided by gravity as it traveled into the mouth of the stamp mill for crushing and mixing. Rough trails and paths nearby would simplify access from most directions.

A work shed was being built, and a huge outside bonfire was kept burning for the workers. Work was slow in the unending cold, but steady enough for the structure to gradually take shape. Everything had to be freighted in, mostly from the west, and the weather was merciless for all things living.

"The rest of the lumber will start coming in by next week, provided the passes aren't blocked. With the weather like it is, we'll probably be two months finishing the mill structure, at least to the point that we can get the machinery in place. Then we'll have to complete the structure," said Chester.

He laid out a series of drawings on the crude worktable as Randley threw several logs on the fire in the hastily built fireplace. The fire gave little more than the impression of warmth.

Randley seemed put out, sulking most of the time. He took part in most of the meetings but said little.

Will did not know whether Randley had made his case to Chester, nor did he concern himself with the issue.

"That will put us into late March or early April," Chester said as he wrapped his hands around a steaming cup of black coffee. "Maybe later if the machinery is delayed. But there won't be much serious prospecting until maybe the middle of May."

"Any word yet on the mill and engine?" asked Will as he poured some coffee.

"No, not yet. I expect to hear both the two engineers and the machinery have left any day now. These are experienced fellows, and they should have us up and running within a few weeks after they get here."

"That will give us some time to do some prospecting," Will said. "I've already got a line on a couple of claims that might be up for sale. I'll want you check them out as soon as we can."

"Good. I want to show you those places I told you about as soon as we can get a few days of clear weather," said Chester.

"All right. But for now, let's head back to the hut where it's warmer. I can't feel my feet. Maybe Charlie's got some stew on," said Will as he downed the cup of coffee.

Most of the prospectors had shut down for the winter, choosing to head elsewhere for more permanent shelter. But some brave souls stayed on in the ramshackle community, now aptly named South Pass City, living in heavy tents or hastily built cabins, venturing out only rarely to pick at the frozen diggings. The few bars and stew shacks saw steady traffic.

Will and the two other men had found living space in a partially underground building that was heated by a scarce metal box stove. There were bunk beds against one wall, a few handbuilt pieces of furniture, and stacks of buffalo skins for blankets and for use as robes in the bitter cold. The men were as comfortable as possible under the circumstances.

Will had retained the services of an older man who went by the name of "just" Charlie to keep the fire and the ever-present pot of stew or beans going. If he was not in the hut at any given time, he usually showed up shortly with red eyes and a smile on his face.

"Hello, fellers," Charlie said as they came into the hut. The oil lamps provided a greasy glow, and the red fire box seemed to huff and puff as the pot of water steamed on top.

"Just cut up some venison and added it to them beans. Be just the thing in a little while," said Charlie.

His cracked leather hat sat at a jaunty angle on the back of his head, in place during all waking hours. A scruffy gray beard covered most of his face and ran head-on into the thick mat of gray hair that peaked out from his now pink longjohns.

His face, or the part that could be seen, was an age-lined brown that had not benefited from a wash in recent memory. When he laughed, he had a habit of thrusting his tongue out between what was left of his front teeth.

"I think you been in the whiskey mill," said Randley as he watched Charlie stand and weave a bit.

"Mebbe ... Man's gotta live, ain't he? Might as well enjoy every minute. No telling when somebody'll blow out your lamp," cackled Charlie.

"You have any luck finding us more firewood today, Charlie?" asked Will.

"Yes, sir, Mr. Will. But it's gonna cost a pretty penny," said Charlie in a flash of sobriety.

"Good dry wood. Man'll be here first thing tomorrow with a load. Wants ten dollars for it, damn his hide."

Charlie widened his eyes in disbelief.

"I say we take his wood, then shoot him, drag him down the hill. He'll stay there froze 'til we can bury him in the spring," he cackled again.

"Go easy on him, Charlie. Just make sure he's willing to keep us supplied. You can start picking up scraps from the mill, too. That'll help some," said Will as he held his hands above the fire box.

The men were worlds away from the comforts of Salt Lake. The cold journey to South Pass had been just the start of the misery that was in store. But the anticipation of what lay ahead more than offset the lack of creature comforts.

Chester was consumed by the project and took their conditions in stride. Will had prepared himself mentally for the hardships and seemed to be unaffected by the difficulty of just staying warm and fed. Randley groused when he could, but most of it fell on deaf ears.

They took a turn in the juice tent most days in the evening. Will, who had never been much of a drinker of the hard stuff, tried the so-called "rye" whiskey the first few days after arrival.

One evening, Chester, who was more experienced in such matters, cornered the bartender and engaged him in a serious private discussion. After a few minutes of intense whispering, Chester returned with a bottle of real Scotch whisky and a rare clean squatty glass.

"Now fellows, you are about to try one of the finest malt whiskies ever produced," said Chester as he placed the bottle on the table.

"Where in the world did you find that?" asked Pierce, his jaw agape.

"Quite simply, it was magic. I gave the bartender a new San Francisco twenty-dollar gold piece, and this is what he turned it into. Amazing, don't you think?" Chester said, smiling.

"I accepted it only on one condition, that future transformations would require less tender for the same effect. He quite agreed," said a happy Chester.

Chester picked up the glass, reached in his pocket, found a miraculously clean handkerchief, and proceeded to polish the small glass. He placed the shiny glass on the table in front of him.

Finding Mr. Sunday

He carefully pealed the seal from the top and gently twisted the cork top from the bottle. He put it to his nose and sniffed.

"Hmmm … no mold, a delicious aroma. This could be even better than I thought," he said as he closed his eyes and inhaled the aroma.

He poured an inch or so of the golden liquid into the clean glass. He gently swirled the liquid and again placed it under his nose and inhaled deeply, after which he took a good sip of the whisky.

"Ahhhh, yes, gentlemen. Truly the water of life," he said after he rolled the whisky in his mouth and swallowed.

He lifted both hands in the air as if to halt any proceedings.

"Wait, gentlemen. Don't move."

He got up, went over to the bar, and returned with two more glasses.

He poured a measure into each glass.

"Now, taste the glory of it," he said as he closed his eyes in reverence.

"You don't have to ask me twice," said Pierce as he reached for the glass in front of him.

He downed the whisky in one gulp and placed the glass noisily on the table.

"Oh no, Randley. You must savor this," said Chester.

Will reached for the glass. He raised it slowly to his nose and sniffed lightly.

"It is definitely whisky," he said.

"Now take a tiny sip. Let it roll around on your tongue. Taste the melons, the berries, the sweetness of the toasted barley, all bathed in honey," said Chester.

Will did as he was instructed.

The liquid felt warm on his tongue, a strange taste indeed, not altogether unpleasant but not quite berries and honey. He swallowed slowly and felt the warmth go down his throat. There, was that a hint of sweet … honey? … not quite, but good. His body responded to the warmth as the whisky settled in his gut.

"Well?" asked Chester.

"Interesting. I'm not sure my palate is as well trained as yours, but it wasn't bad," said Will with a sheepish smile. "I think I could get used to that … with a little practice."

"Then, by God, we'll just have to see to it that you do. I promise you there will come a day when rye or corn whiskey will be a thing of the past for you," said a grinning Chester as he poured a bit more into Will's cup.

The three of them sat for a couple of hours. The cold was forgotten, and all the uncertainty ahead of them evolved into a promise to themselves of good fortune and success. And the fine Scotch christened the voyage.

The weather began to clear somewhat, and the time between snows lengthened. The creeks and streams started to thaw and rise as the snow melt began. The mill was on target, and telegrams heralded the slow approach of the men and machines from California.

One day in late April the men and machinery arrived. Four large freight wagons, each pulled by twelve mules, wound to the top of the last hill and pulled up to the nearly finished mill building.

Most of structure was finished except for one side of the building through which the machinery would be taken in and installed. The engineers rested one day before beginning the task of unloading and assembling the stamp mill pieces and the steam engine parts.

The stamp mill was a ten-unit mill run by a steam engine that alternately lifted eight-hundred-pound columns of steel and dropped them onto ore that came down a chute and fed into the stamps. The crushed ore was mixed with mercury on copper-topped tables that separated gold from the mix.

Will and Chester were everywhere at once, asking questions, referring to drawings, making on-the-spot decisions. But every effort was made not to impede the progress of the engineers. They were hired to do the job and were given great latitude to do it.

The men worked carefully but steadily, infected by the excitement and enthusiasm of the owners. Will found them highly capable and likable, and a cooperative spirit developed quickly.

Huge stacks of firewood for the engine boilers were beginning to grow as the bad weather abated. A larger, more suitable building was built to provide sturdy, warm housing and working space for Will, his crew, and the engineers.

Finding Mr. Sunday

Lumber, lumber, lumber. It was being used as fast as they could acquire it. The advancing spring was a boon.

Another larger building was built to provide a facility for the mill workers. Sleeping quarters and a full kitchen were incorporated, providing the best living arrangements to be had in all of Sweetwater and the surrounding towns of Lewiston and Atlantic City. A steady job and regular meals drew a steady stream of workers.

They prepared for around-the-clock operation of the mill, and incorporated expansion areas into the design should another stamp mill be warranted.

As soon as the weather allowed, they dug additional wells to increase the supply of usable water. The mill and its surroundings became a monument to the ever-present fever of optimism inherent in a capitalist venture.

Expenses were high, but Will was careful with every penny. He never lost sight of the speculative nature of the venture and stayed within his allocated commitment, if for nothing else than to cap his possible losses.

"I looked at many places during my first visit here before the snows. In the last few weeks I've had some time to look at even more sites," said Chester. "I think we should start our own digs in this area."

He waved his hand in a semicircle.

The two men were on horseback overlooking the undulating hills surrounding South Pass City. They could feel an unfamiliar but welcome warmth from the spring sun as they surveyed the terrain around them.

"These greenstone and light granite shelves you see over there are where we are likely to find gold-producing ore, quartz with gold veins. We can dig pits straight down to check the quality of the ore," said Chester.

"We can get started with that reasonably quick. We don't need much to file a claim in this mining district. If you are in agreement, I'd like to start right away."

"I don't see why we can't. The engineers have everything under control at the mill," said Will. "Word's getting around, and we're already getting business."

Will removed his hat so he could feel the sun on his face.

"If you think this is the place to start, go ahead. Get the crews started. Let's file as soon as you can. Tomorrow, I'd like you to look at one of those claims I'm thinking about buying."

He paused as the both of them escaped momentarily in their own thoughts.

"I've got a good feeling about this, Chester."

Will put his hat snuggly on his head.

"This thing may be bigger than either of us had hoped for."

Kate was surprised at the void she felt from Will's absence. As the weeks turned into months, she still found herself half expecting to see him in his reading chair as she passed through the parlor.

Something was missing in the house when he was not there, something beyond his physical absence.

When he was near, or she knew he would return soon, she felt a sense of inner comfort. She could not define it beyond that, but the lack of it when he was not around was more than a mere distraction.

Oh, there was plenty to do when Will was away. She enjoyed looking after Maggie who, sadly, showed little improvement. Usually, Ish was by her bedside so Kate wasn't needed every minute.

Weather permitting, she and Mary Nel enjoyed carriage outings and frequent horseback rides into the countryside, despite the occasional raised eyebrows from some of the local ladies seeing unaccompanied women.

And then there was Bernard. Oh, yes, Bernard. He was the perfect gentleman, charming, kind, gracious, and always seeing to their wellbeing. But she was sure there was much more to his constant presence in her life than simply their comfort.

She was not ready for that, she thought. Even if she were, she was quite sure Bernard was not the one she wanted in her life for the duration. In fact, there was something about Bernard that made her wary.

He seldom talked about himself. And for the life of her, the only comment she could get from others when she subtly brought him up in conversation was that Mr. Rheinhardt was "well regarded." No other discussion ensued. In fact, most often the subject was quickly changed.

She heard a knock at the door one day as subtle signs of spring were visible. Probably Bernard making his "check" to see if everything was all right.

He was careful not to couch his visits as anything but business, as was proper. But his increasing familiarity did little to hide his real intentions.

She reached for the door and pulled it open wide enough to peek outside before fully opening it.

"Will! Will!" she all but screamed.

She jerked the door wide open, and he stepped inside. Without waiting for him to remove his coat she encircled the big man with both arms, hugging him close. He returned the hug and squeezed her tight.

"Oh, I'm sorry, Will. I should at least let you get in the house," she said, laughing as her face colored a deep pink.

"It's good to see you, Kate," he said as he released her and held her by the shoulders at arms length. "You are the best sight I've seen in months." His big grin lit the room.

"You must be bone tired. Can I fix you some coffee? Oh, I have some fresh pastry just delivered this morning. Would you like some?" she said without a pause for answers.

"I'm sorry I seem so befuddled. I just didn't expect to see you. I thought it was...well, I'm so happy you are home," she said as she seemed to catch her breath.

She helped him remove his coat and hung it on the hall tree.

"I decided to surprise you and Mary Nel. Is she here?" he asked.

"No, she and several other young ladies have a reading group. They all read a book, then meet to discuss it and have tea and so on. She enjoys the company. I expect her in an hour or so. She'll fall over when she sees you. She has really missed you. We all have."

"And Ish and Maggie...how is Maggie?" he asked, a worried expression on his face.

"I wish I could say she's better, but she's taken a recent turn for the worse. She coughs most of her waking hours, her chest rattles, and she can no longer stand. She's skin and bones. She just won't eat."

Kate shook her head back and forth. "I don't think she has long, Will. Even Ish has said the same thing. It's breaking his heart."

"I'm sorry to hear that, Kate. I'll go see them shortly," he said.

"Let's go in the kitchen. I want to hear all about the mining venture," she said.

She encircled his arm in hers and escorted him into the kitchen.

"I sure have missed this spot," said Will. "I thought at one point months ago that if I had to sit at this table one more day reading the paper I'd go stir crazy. But how nice those days were."

He laughed.

"It was mighty cold and snowy up there. It's just now getting decent. We finally have good quarters, and we have our own kitchen and cook now. The mill is up and running. Not day and night yet, but the amount of ore we're processing is increasing daily. As the weather improves so does our business," he said excitedly.

"I've purchased several claims. Chester and I are partners in some others. We've got some good yielding ore, but nothing I'd call a strike. Chester is everything I thought he was...and more. He knows his business. He's the hardest working fellow I ever met and as honest as the days are long."

She poured him a cup of steaming coffee, herself some tea, then sat across from him at the table.

"I've got a good feeling about this, Kate. Somebody must be looking out for me because everything is coming together. So smoothly, in fact, I felt I could take a few weeks off before I go back. I think the mill itself is going to make us some good money and...."

He stopped talking as he heard the front door open and close.

He turned and saw Mary Nel rushing into the kitchen.

"Will! Will!" shouted Mary Nel.

He stood up, and she rushed to him. He bent down, hugged her tightly in both arms, and picked her up off the floor. She was laughing and trying to talk at the same time.

"I thought I heard your voice as soon as I stepped in the door. It's so good to see you. I've missed you!" Mary Nel said between breaths. Her eyes filled with tears as she stepped back to look at him.

"And I have missed you. Both of you. Terribly," he said, smiling that smile.

"Now, you must sit down and tell me everything you've been doing," he said as he let her go.

"Oh, no, what I have been doing can't compare to what you have been doing," she said. "Besides, I've been doing the same thing as when you were here, except maybe the reading group."

"Did you strike gold?" she said as she widened her eyes in anticipation.

"Well, not really. But our mill is up and running. Business is picking up, and we make money whether or not there's gold in what we process. If there is gold we get a share," he said.

"We have claims in Willow Creek, Spring Gulch, and Rock Creek. Chester has been all over the area and well beyond the range of the current diggings. If there is gold to be found, we'll find it," said Will.

His confidence was evident.

"It must be hard living up there with no towns or the like," said Kate.

"It's what you would expect. Some little communities are coming up. Mostly hastily built cabins. Everything is very expensive. Goods come in from Cheyenne mostly. Nothing but men scrambling to find gold. Some going broke, some making a living.

"We've gone to the trouble of getting decent quarters built, so it's much better than it was when we first arrived. We have no trouble finding help."

"How much longer do you plan to do this?" asked Mary Nel.

Will put his arms on the table and was playing with a spoon, thinking out loud.

"I'm not sure. But the real mining time is just beginning. That's one of the things I wanted to discuss. I know you two had not counted on something like this, and I know at some point, I might be the reason for further delay in heading to California."

He looked up at the two.

Kate looked to Mary Nel, then turned to Will.

"Will, we can't go anywhere now. You know how uncertain things are here. In the meantime we're comfortable, safe, and warm. Spring is almost here. We'll be able to get out more soon," she said.

"I think you should do what you need to do to see this thing through. California won't go anywhere. Do you agree, Mary Nel?"

286

"I do. Of course, I want to continue our trip. But we are surely not suffering any hardships here. I'm excited for you, Will, and I'm sure you will have success."

Will sat there, quiet for a moment. The excitement so evident earlier began to fade as it was replaced by a look of gratitude and tenderness.

"I don't know what I did to deserve such great friends. But I thank the Lord every day that I have you two in my world."

"Hello, dear Maggie," said Will as he entered the small bedroom.

She opened her eyes, seemed to have difficulty focusing, then recognized her visitor.

"Mr. Will," she said hoarsely.

He sat in the chair beside the bed as Ish stood beside him.

"Hasn't been the same without you, Will. Missed you poppin' in every day," she said. She labored to speak, breathing hard.

"I have missed our visits, too. But I see you are being well cared for," he said.

"This old man won't leave me alone," she said as she looked up at Ish.

"And I know you wouldn't have it any other way," Will said, laughing.

He saw she was little more than a wisp of her former self, her skin a chalky dark gray, her eyes yellow and rimmed in red. Her chest moved up and down at short intervals as she struggled for breath.

"You back now?" she said.

"For a while. I'm heading back in a couple of weeks or so," said Will.

"I'm sorry, Will. I did not mean to … I'm sorry I can't travel yet," she said.

"Maggie, Maggie. Don't you be fretting about anything. You just think about getting better. That's the important thing now," he said as he patted her hand.

She closed her eyes, and he could see she was slipping back to sleep.

He walked out of the room with Ish.

They communicated without saying a word. Each knew there was little time left for the dear lady.

Finding Mr. Sunday

"Ish, you stay with her. If you need anything, anything at all, you let me know," he said as he shook Ish's hand.

"All we need now, Will, is the hand of the Master, just the hand from above," Ish said with tears in his eyes.

For the next couple of weeks, Will renewed his routine — breakfast, coffee, papers. He hadn't realized how much he needed a break. Something seemed very right with his world now that Kate and Mary Nel were near.

Seeing them again after such a long absence, even though it was only two months, only reinforced how important these two were to him and to his happiness.

There was no question that, somehow, they must remain in his life. He would do everything possible to ensure that happened.

"Kate, have you seen much of Rheinhardt?" he asked one day after breakfast.

"Well, he seems to find a reason to drop by at least a couple times a week," she said.

"Does that bother you?" he asked.

"No, but I'm being careful to not let him get the wrong idea. I hope allowing him to visit unchaperoned doesn't mislead him," she said. "I have no interest in anything but a friendly relationship. Not now, certainly not with him. Being on my own for a while wasn't entirely unpleasant. I had plenty of time to think about Kate. Not crops or the farm or anything else. Just about me.

"I am determined that this is an opportunity for me to take time to know myself, decide in my own time frame what I want to do, and I want no hindrance to that," she said.

She looked across at him and said, "Sorry for the long-winded answer."

"Not at all. I'm glad to hear that is your thinking. I've told you before, you are a special person, and I'm hopeful you're beginning to realize that with all the introspection," he said.

"Thank you, Will. You always seem to know how to lift me up," she said.

"Kate, be honest with me. Am I a hindrance to your plans?" he asked with a serious tone.

"Oh, no, Will. You're the reason I have the luxury to make plans. Your coming into my life seemed to be the opening of a door. I would be very upset if you were not a part of my life."

She reached for his hand.

"But don't ever think you are a hindrance to me or my dreams. You most likely are a part of them."

With that she got up and poured him some more coffee.

"I must go to the bakery today," she said as she removed her apron and went to get her coat.

He sat there sipping his coffee after she left. He didn't know quite how to react to her words, nor for that matter, what she was trying to say. "Part of her dreams?" Now that was interesting. Was this a turning point in their relationship or was she simply saying don't go anywhere?

He mulled it all over. Again he decided he would just take it day by day and see what happens.

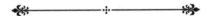

The return trip to South Pass mines was much easier. No new snow, and the trails and roads were clear. He came into the mill area to find the population had swelled, and there was a constant flow of men, mules, and equipment going in all directions.

Freight wagons were arriving daily with food, whiskey, and supplies of every kind. Hunters were everywhere with fresh elk, deer, and buffalo. Spirits were high as the weather improved daily.

"Will! Good to see you," said Chester as Will entered the new work building. "And just in time for the good news. One of our smaller claims is producing some fine ore. We're getting a good yield. No veins yet. But good yield.

"We are now running long days. Some miners are finding some high-grade stuff and even the occasional vein. Presently, we'll have to go to night shifts." Chester grinned.

"We're going to make this pay off. I'm sure of it, even if we just run the mill."

"That is good news, Chester," said Will.

"We haven't even started on the claims you bought, and several of our sites haven't been touched yet," Chester said.

Finding Mr. Sunday

"Randley is getting pretty hard to deal with. Seems he feels cheated. I told him I'd think about what would be fair. From my share, of course."

"That is between the two of you," said Will.

Will changed the subject. "Let's go for a walk around the mill, and you can update me on everything. Tonight over a meal you can give me the numbers."

Will and Chester spent the next few hours looking at their operation. Chester had refined the crushing process to get a finer crush and had replaced the screens on the mill to reduce the chance of losing gold.

The always particular Chester had everything running smoothly. The machinery and buildings were in excellent condition. They were running the best operation around, and others were impressed with the way their business was being managed.

The weather continued to improve, and the mill began processing day and night. Mining shafts were being dug all over the hills, and the ore was pouring in to the mill. They expanded the workforce to meet demand.

One day in early June, Chester came rushing into the office as Will was going over some paperwork.

"Will! We've done it. We hit a vein on the claim just above Willow Creek! It's a good one. I don't know how deep it goes yet, but it's big. This one alone may carry us over the top. We'll surely cover your investment now."

Will stood up and came around the desk and grabbed his jubilant partner.

"I knew it was only a matter of time," he said as he grasped the man by the shoulders. "Congratulations, partner!"

After some celebratory laughter, they gathered their wits.

The trip back to the pits overlooking Willow Creek seemed longer than ever before, but they arrived in an hour or so. Slim was waiting for them as they tied their horses and climbed to the pits on the ledge. Randley was watching with interest.

The men had started digging a pit along a strip of white stone that ran along a ridge high off the valley floor. They were less than twenty feet down in a pit about eight feet wide.

"The quartz is almost pure white, and much of it is laced with gold. I'm not a miner, but it looks like a lot of gold to me. I think you've hit it big," said Slim with a big grin.

"Let's go see," said Will.

"Just what I thought," said Chester as he examined what had been brought up in his absence. "What I saw earlier was just the beginning. This could be one of the biggest strikes in the area so far."

At first the ore had started looking very promising, showing some color. Then as the men continued to dig, the gold was visible in the ore. As they kept digging they could see the beginning of spider veins of gold, which later converged into one large vein, ever widening with the depth of the dig.

"We've got tons of high grade ore here. And the vein is pure. It's just a matter of how wide and how deep it goes," said Chester.

The excitement of the discovery was still echoing as the men withdrew to discuss the additional plans needed to safeguard as well as extract the treasure.

Will turned to Chester. "We've got some men on site I trust. Slim, Rowe, Andrews. Others I don't know at all, and we're going to need more. I suggest we start talking bonus money to those three based on the take, get them vested in the job even more."

"Good idea," said Chester.

"We're going to need to run night and day to get this stuff out as quick as we can. So count on around-the-clock operations. Put Randley on at night. Maybe we can get some work out of him," Will said.

The weeks that followed went by in a blur. The stamp mill ran nonstop. Customer ore still had to be processed, despite the fact that the Willow Creek overlook claim, now officially known as Tom's Lode, was producing high-grade ore and some almost pure gold.

Ore was stored in secure locations watched by armed guards and processed as fast as possible.

The constant use of the stamp mill took a toll on the machinery, and they had to replace belts and cam parts. They ordered extra parts to ensure against an extended breakdown. Men were working long hours, and sleep became a precious commodity.

Word of the strike spread quickly, and, as expected, the stories were greatly exaggerated. News spread far beyond the Sweetwater area, and within weeks the population of miners swelled, straining supplies of food and materials that were already limited.

Finding Mr. Sunday

Will sent some of his trusted men to Salt Lake and all the way to Cheyenne to obtain whatever they could, buying his own stock of mules and wagons to freight the goods to his operation. He even telegraphed Rheinhardt to enlist his help in securing supplies.

He was in constant touch with Kate, telling her as much as he could in letters and telegrams about the success they were having.

And the success was considerable, despite the fact that the vein and much of the high yield ore was depleted within a couple of months.

Will and Chester had made a good profit on the one strike, and profit from the mill added to the coffers. Randley said little.

"It is almost unbelievable, Chester," said Will as he went over the latest tallies. "I think you will go back to Scotland a fairly well-to-do man. And we still have some of our claims to be worked."

Near the end of the summer the activity at the operation slowed to a normal pace. Will and Chester turned their attention to some of the other claims with pits being dug in several locations at once.

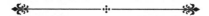

"I know Will is beside himself," said Mary Nel. "Imagine. A gold strike." Kate and Mary Nel read the latest letter from Will as they sat at the kitchen table having tea.

"To tell you the truth, Mary Nel, I originally thought this was just something Will needed to do to use up all that energy he was wasting while here. I was happy to go along with it because I know Will can't sit still very long. But I never expected this."

She went on.

"It's strange, though. Will did. He said he had a feeling about it. He is such an unusual person. It's hard to believe he's the same young man I first saw lying on a table near death."

"Oh, but life has been very interesting since then," said Mary Nel, laughing. "And I have a feeling as long as we know Will Sunday, it will continue to be."

There was a knock, and Kate went to the front door to find Rheinhardt waiting.

"Dear Kate, forgive me for stopping by without notice, but I wanted to see if everything was all right and to tell you I have heard from Will."

He said this as if this was the first time he had stopped by without notice, even thought it was his usual habit to do so.

"Come in, Bernard," said Kate. "We were just talking about Will." She showed him to a seat in the parlor.

"Hello, Bernard," said Mary Nel. "I hope you are well."

"Quite well, thank you, Miss Mary," said Bernard with a tip of his head.

"Momma, I'm going to finish my reading," said Mary Nel.

"Good to see you, Bernard," said Mary Nel as she looked over his head and gave her mother a teasing smile.

"I hope things are to your satisfaction, dear," said Rheinhardt.

"They are fine, as usual, Bernard," she replied.

"Good. Good," he said.

"You have heard from Will?" asked Kate.

"I have. He has asked my help in obtaining materials and supplies that he apparently is needing immediately. He is sending some of his men to get them. He didn't say why he needed them so quickly. Apparently, supplies are short up there," said Rheinhardt.

"It is very possible. When he was here some time ago, he said things were hard to get," said Kate.

"I'm just surprised," said Rheinhardt as if expecting Kate to shed some light on the issue. "You know, at the urgency of it all."

He lifted his chin as if he were looking over spectacles.

"You never know with Will. Patience is not his strong suit. You'd be better served by asking him," Kate said coyly.

"Would you like some tea or coffee, Bernard?"

"Yes. That would be most enjoyable" he replied.

Kate excused herself for a few minutes and returned with a tray containing a pot of tea and cups.

She poured Bernard a cup of tea, then one for herself and settled in her chair.

"Kate, while we have some time together, I'd like to have a frank conversation with you," he said in a serious, almost secretive tone.

"Of course, Bernard," she said.

Finding Mr. Sunday

"Well, I ... I must say that I have enjoyed getting to know you, Kate." He seemed to hesitate.

"And I you, Bernard," she said with a slight smile.

"I don't want to seem presumptuous, dear Kate. Far be it from me. But, I ... I have become quite fond of you ... in many ways ... you see." He stammered, then seemed to gain his composure.

"I must ask, are you still set on going to California? I mean, do you like it here?"

Kate cleared her throat softly and placed her cup of tea on the saucer beside her.

After some delay she spoke.

"I do like it here, Bernard. And I owe our comfort to you. You have been most kind and considerate. But you must remember, we are here because of circumstances beyond our control."

"But would you consider staying here permanently if things were different? I mean if you were here under different ... ah ... circumstances, should I say?"

Kate could see that Bernard was uncomfortable with what he was about to say.

"Why, Bernard, I'm not sure what you are asking me," she said.

She watched him sit upright, become a bit emboldened.

"Why, would you consider matrimony... marriage, to me?" he asked, again his chin rising.

He shifted in his chair seeming to find it suddenly uncomfortable.

"I am quite aware of what matrimony is, Bernard," she said trying to not to smile at his unease.

She picked up her tea and took a sip, wishing there were other distractions at hand.

"Bernard, this is quite a surprise. I had no idea that was anywhere in your thoughts," she said.

"Oh, you must have, Kate. How in the world can any man not be smitten with you? You are smart, you are beautiful, you are determined. Kate you must know the effect you have on men," he said, almost pleading.

"I'm flattered, Bernard. I think you are a fine, sweet man. But, no. No. I'm not ready for that. Not with you or anyone else right now."

She watched as he seemed to deflate before her eyes.

"I have things I want to do. Things I never thought I'd be able to do. And I want to be able to do them."

"But you can still do those things, Kate. You can do whatever you want to do, with me, believe me. I am well off, Kate. I can give you anything you desire," he said, leaning forward to the edge of his chair and clasping his hands in hope. "I won't restrain you, I promise."

"I'm sorry, Bernard. It is out of the question," she said firmly, not wanting to hurt him but trying to make no mistake of her position.

"Maybe if you wait a while. Think it over, Kate. I don't need an answer right now," he said.

"There is nothing to think over, Bernard. I'm not being coy. It is not something I'm willing to consider, and I hope you will accept that, and we can remain friends."

This time she was quite firm.

He seemed to accept her answer, and he sat back in his chair feeling the sting of rejection.

"All right. All right. I'm sorry if I upset you, Kate. Of course, I want to remain your friend."

He stood up abruptly, red in the face, retrieved his hat and walked quickly to the door.

"Good day, Kate," he said as he walked out of the door.

His departure had happened so quickly, Kate was stunned. She sat staring at the closed door.

If she was not mistaken, she thought, he was actually angry. Well, he is most likely a man used to getting whatever he wants.

But she could not imagine any circumstances under which she would consider marriage to Bernard. There was simply nothing there. He was a nice man, but there was something underlying his veneer. Some inner voice warned her about him, a feeling she seldom experienced about anyone.

And the fact that he was angry underscored her feelings.

It was nearing the end of August. Will had just received a telegram. Poor

Finding Mr. Sunday

Maggie had died in her sleep.

Will had been informed in telegrams of her turn for the worse and had already been preparing for the trip prior to receiving the news.

"I am sorry we have to go," he said. "But I must be there for Ish and Kate."

"Don't worry about anything here, Will. Everything is going well, and I expect it to stay that way. We'll keep the mill going and work those claims," said Chester.

"I'm not worried, Chester. Everything is in the best hands possible," he said as he shook Chester's hand.

"I should make good time in weather like this. I don't think I'll find it necessary to camp out. There are places to stay all along the trail now. Some rough, but shelter and food, all the same," Will said.

Will, on his trusted big bay, headed for the well-worn trail to the Great Salt Lake City.

As he rode into the yard, Hank came out to greet him and took his horse. He was the same old Hank, a little heavier around the middle because of the good meals and light workload.

"Hello, Boss. Good to see ya," said Hank as he shook Will's hand.

"Hey, cowboy," said Will as he grabbed Hank's hand. "You still fussin'?"

"I am, but ain't nobody paying no mind any more," Hank said, laughing.

As he entered the house Ish, Kate, and Mary Nel were in the kitchen, sitting around a table laden with all kinds of food. Both Kate and Mary Nel jumped up and ran to Will as he entered the room. They were both rewarded with big hugs. Will stepped over to Ish.

"I'm so sorry, Ish. But you know that good woman is looking down and smiling at you now," he said as he held Ish's big hand in his.

"Thank you, Will. She wanted to go to the Lord, and I know she's by his side," Ish said.

They sat for a while, catching up and nibbling.

"You must be weary," said Kate. "The service will be tomorrow. In the meantime, go get some rest."

The funeral was held in a small church with only a few attending. Bernard Rheinhardt and Miriam were the only outsiders. Ish was calm, accepting of Maggie's passing, knowing she was finally at peace. Following the service the small group of people, absent Miriam, returned to Kate's temporary home.

Rheinhardt sat with Kate, Mary Nel, and Will having tea and cake. There was an unusual quiet about the house as the finality of Maggie's death closed in around each of them.

"I suppose this means you will soon continue on your journey to California," said Rheinhardt.

He addressed his question to Kate and Will, but his eyes surveyed all of them.

"I'm glad you asked that question, Bernard," said Will.

He placed his cup of coffee on the saucer in front of him and looked at Kate before continuing.

"Are you in need of your property or will it be available should we choose to stay longer?" Will asked.

"I have no need of the houses for a while. You are welcomed here as long as you would like to stay. I had just assumed you would continue your journey."

"We will. But I have talked it over with Kate, Mary Nel, and Ish. I have reasons to delay our departure for as yet an undetermined amount of time. Kate and Mary Nel are being very patient with me," Will said.

"It seems that my little venture in Sweetwater has evolved into something bigger than I had expected. I'll need a little while longer to wind things up there."

"So I have heard, Will. Word of your success has spread far and wide. Please accept my congratulations. Perhaps I should have taken Mr. Fields up on his proposal earlier on," said Rheinhardt.

"Oh," said Will with some surprise. "I wasn't aware that Chester had approached you."

Reinhardt sat forward and repositioned himself in his chair.

"He didn't directly. But he talked to some of those in the community with whom I am well acquainted and they asked me for my advice. I have a little experience in silver and lead mining, you see," said Rheinhardt.

"I wasn't aware of that," said Will. "Perhaps I should have talked with you and gotten your opinion before I jumped into this."

Will gave him a slight smile.

Finding Mr. Sunday

"It seems your own intuition served you well," said Rheinhardt.

Will got up and poured himself some more coffee.

"Just out of curiosity, is there a particular reason you decided not to entertain Chester's proposal?" said Will. "Something, perhaps, I should know about?"

"No," said Rheinhardt. "Fields insisted with everyone he talked to that he be a fifty-fifty partner, despite the fact that he would provide none of the capital. He insisted that his expertise in mining was his capital.

"I, as well as most of the men he approached, already had expertise in mining. So no one wanted to take all the risk financially and only share in fifty percent of the profits," said Rheinhardt.

"What he proposed was exactly the kind of thing I was looking for," said Will. "My concern was doing business with someone I didn't know. That proved to be a non-issue. Fields is a fine man and a good partner."

"You were lucky this time, Will, if you will allow me to say so. I guess you figured you would only lose so much and were willing to gamble that much. You knew your maximum exposure, but what intrigued you was that your profit potential was unlimited if you were lucky."

"That's about the way it happened, Bernard," said Will over his cup.

"Well, you must be, well, let me say, you must have been well capitalized to risk what was no small amount on such a venture," said Rheinhardt in a bit of a teasing manner.

Will looked directly at the man as he set the cup of coffee down.

"Well, Bernard, whatever the circumstances were before I invested in this venture, I am, to use your term, quite well capitalized now," he said, smiling broadly.

Despite the elevation, the South Pass area was hot and windy with thunderstorms forming in the hills nearly every afternoon. Will arrived to find the mill running at capacity with tons of ore backed up to be processed.

"Will!" shouted Chester as Will rode up to the front of the work shed and dismounted.

Charlie came and took his horse as Will slapped dust from his trail clothes.

"Don't remember it being this hot when I left," said Will as he shook Chester's hand.

"We've had a spell of this for the last week. It'll tire you out in a minute," said Chester.

"I see the mill is running full speed," said Will.

"It is. We had a lull there just as you left, but we're backed up now. And we're getting good color from one of our claims over on the ledge near Strawberry Creek. Good color. Not pure but very high content. I'm going to start running some of it tonight. It is good you'll be here.

"Another thing, Randley left two days ago. Said he'd had enough."

"Well, we can do without him," said Will dismissively. "Let's go inside and catch up. I want to go over the numbers."

The men spent several hours reviewing the business results. Money was coming in steadily from the mill, and Tom's Lode, while relatively short in duration, had indeed been a rich one.

Much of their profit was in pure gold, more than Will had expected. They had secured a strong safe to hold the gold between trips to Salt Lake to the relative safety of the local banks there.

The afternoon turned to early evening, and Chester and Will were still talking. Chester went to the safe to prepare another run to the Salt Lake banks.

"Will!" Chester shouted. "There is gold missing from the safe!"

"What?" said Will.

"When did you open it last?" Will asked.

"A few days ago. You and I are the only ones who know the combination," said Chester.

"How much is missing?" asked Will.

Chester picked up his ledger book and scanned the numbers.

"About $10,000, near as I can tell."

"Randley!" said Will. "Is there any way he could have gotten the combination?"

"Well, he has seen me open it, I guess," said Chester.

"Damn!" said Will. "I should have sent him on his way before I left. How dumb of me. He was mad, and I should have known he'd do something. But

Finding Mr. Sunday

I didn't think for a minute he'd steal from us."

"I'm sorry, Will. I should have been more careful, but I never thought he'd stoop to this."

"I should go after him. He probably headed for Cheyenne, or maybe even farther east. He's got a good head start. The timing couldn't be worse." Will said. "We need to talk later, Chester."

Will left the office and headed to his quarters.

How stupid of me, he thought. You let someone take advantage of you. Again. When are you going to realize the world is not the cozy one you grew up in? You can't trust everyone. This time your naive way cost you a lot of money. When are you going to learn?"

He decided he couldn't go after Randley. It would only delay his return to Salt Lake and eventual departure to California.

He'd know better next time, he thought.

"Chester, it looks like you and I have to have a serious talk about some things," said Will as they met later in the evening.

Chester reached in the drawer and pulled out a bottle of good Scotch and a couple of glasses.

"I'm ready, Will. But I think I'm a little dry. Let's wet our tongues a bit, shall we?" he said, laughing as he poured two good drinks.

"Here's to us," said Will as he took a sip and rolled the good Scotch in his mouth.

"As good as always," he said as he swirled the glass.

"Chester, this has been a great venture. I think we both have done much better than we expected. But I have a decision to make."

He took another sip and sat forward, putting the glass on his desktop.

"I promised Kate and Mary Nel we'd go on to California as soon as we could. They've supported me in what I'm doing, and they've been very patient. But I'm holding up their lives."

He looked directly at his friend and partner as he spoke.

"I want you and I to agree on a timetable. You don't need me now. We don't owe anybody anything. We've got gold and money in the bank, and we've done very well in a short amount of time. Call it luck, call it your science, call it whatever, but those are the facts."

Will stood up and went over to the always ready coffee pot and poured himself a cup and sat down.

"I've found coffee is good before and after Scotch," he said as he took a sip of the strong brew.

"What kind of time frame are you thinking, Will?" asked Chester.

"I'd like to be ready to settle up in a few weeks or so. It'll start getting cold soon after that, and things will settle down for the winter. I want to leave before then. We'll get a final accounting done. You buy my share of the assets then, and we split the profit like we agreed. How do you feel about that?"

"What about the claims we haven't started?" asked Chester.

"They're yours," said Will.

"Well, Will. It's sooner than I thought, but I knew you'd want to leave before I was ready. What you are proposing is fine with me. It'll be more than fair. You never know what's in those other claims," Chester said.

Chester sighed loudly.

"I hate to see you go, partner," said Chester. "We've had one great ride together. Who knows? Maybe it won't be our last."

He held Will's eyes for a moment.

"I'd be your partner anytime, Chester. You're a real gentleman. True to your word."

He walked over and shook Chester's hand, then turned to go to his quarters.

Four weeks later, Will departed for his last trip home from South Pass. Chester had purchased Will's share of the assets. In addition, Will had profits of more than $72,000 dollars in gold and cash waiting for him in Salt Lake City.

CHAPTER FOURTEEN

We can sell our stock and equipment and take the stage lines," said Will as they all sat around the kitchen table.

"Of course, we can hire folks to guide us all the way. Then we can travel at our own pace. With Hank and Rio to help us, it would be much the same as it was getting to Salt Lake."

"What about the Sierras, won't they be hard to get over?" asked Mary Nel.

"Not as bad as they used to be. We can avoid some of the higher elevations. The mail and freight stages have cut good roads. There are stations all along the way. Of course, they cater to the stage coaches mostly. The only problem with the Sierras would be snow," said Will.

"I reckon we could get ahead of most of the snow if we leave early. It ain't like it used to be. There are places all along most of the trails now 'cept the dead of winter," added Hank.

"You think our stock would make the trip, Hank?" asked Will.

"Why surely. We carry along some grain for the mules. Them mules are stronger than most. They all a little lazy now, but we can get 'em up to snuff quick," Hank said.

"Kate, Mary Nel, you two ready to hit the trail again? We've been spoiled with all the comforts we've had here," Will said, smiling.

"I'm ready!" said Mary Nel. "As long as we have plenty of supplies and equipment, I say we hire the help we need, get extra wagons if we need them, and head to California."

As usual, Mary Nel was ready to go toward the next adventure.

"Kate?" said Will. "You've been quiet."

She sat for a moment looking off into the future.

"I hate the thought of leaving Maggie here. But we set out with a purpose in mind. If she were alive she'd scoff at any thought of further delay. And yes, I want to get on our way."

"Then we'll all pitch in and get ready as soon as possible. Hank, you see to our stock needs and the wagons. I know about a half dozen men who'd gladly see us through the trip. I've already been making inquiries."

Finding Mr. Sunday

"Good!" said Kate.

"Are you sure Kate? You aren't worried about leaving any friends behind?" He gave her a teasing smile.

"Not in the least, Will," she said firmly. "Not in the least."

The next two weeks were busy with preparations for the trip. A party of six hired men, including two experienced guides, would accompany them all the way to Sacramento. Each man was carefully selected from the surprisingly large number who had expressed an interest in the job. Some of them, if fact, planned on staying in California. None were Mormons.

When news spread that a group was traveling to California, five other families asked to join the train. Will, after consulting with the others, agreed to allow the families to join the train as long as it was understood that he would act as the wagon train leader. There would be no governing council.

After some negotiations, the Army agreed to have an eight-man patrol accompany the train as far as the South Fork of the Humboldt River in case the Utes or others saw them as easy prey.

Altogether, there were ten wagons, more than eighty mules, assorted live stock, and a party of nearly forty travelers, counting the Army patrol.

They were a small train, indeed, well-armed and well-supplied, but not overburdened. Such a small train would be able to move quickly despite the inhospitable geography that lay ahead.

On the first day of the trip, Will rode his big bay at the head of the train. Branson, one of the guides, rode alongside him. Branson was regarded as a man of solid character, honest, tough, and trustworthy. He had made the trip from Salt Lake to Sacramento many times.

"Salt Lake is a fine place, but I'm glad to be putting it behind me," said Will. "There just seemed to be some kind of tension in the air all the time. I'm not sure how to describe it other than that."

"You're right. I believe it's because the place was set up to be a Mormon sanctuary, and the Mormons see everybody else as in the way," said Branson.

"I got that feeling. What brought you there?" asked Will.

"The freight business. Started an operation there a few years ago. Did all right. I'm like you, I just want to see what California has to offer," said

Branson.

"You have to know some of the inside boys there to make it in Salt Lake," said Branson.

"You mean in the church?" asked Will.

"Yep. They like to take care of their own, and that's understandable. They're a pretty close bunch," he said.

"Did you know a fellow by the name of Rheinhardt?" Will said.

"Oh, yes. If you hang around Salt Lake long you know about Rheinhardt. He's high up in the organization, I know that. Made a bunch of money in silver mining."

"Did you have a business relationship with him?" asked Will.

"For a while. He was fair. Cut and dried. Pretty high minded, if you ask me. Seemed to be a smart fellow, though," said Branson.

"I guess if you got all those wives you have to be pretty smart to manage them. A man can hardly manage one," Branson said, chuckling.

Will was taken aback by the comment.

"Wives? You mean Rheinhardt is a polygamist?" said a startled Will.

"Course he is. All those way up in the Mormon church are. They won't tell you that, but they are."

"But you know for a fact, he is?" asked Will.

"Afore I get myself in trouble, let me say I didn't go to any of his weddings. But I know he has one wife that lives in town with him, Miriam."

"Miriam is his wife?" Will said.

"Yep. Maybe the main one, if there is such a thing. He's got a ranch about ten miles up in the hills, and three ladies and a few kids live there with him. Now, he does have a couple of houses on the property. I guess they could have been boarders there, but I doubt it," Branson said.

"I don't believe it," said Will.

Branson was surprised at Will's reaction.

"You seem a little rattled by that," said Branson. "It's no secret to most people."

"Just surprised. That's all," said Will.

Finding Mr. Sunday

The wagon train traveled without incident to the Humboldt, where the Army turned around and headed back to Salt Lake City. The long delay in Salt Lake City seemed to strengthen the resolve of both Kate and Mary Nel. They thrived in the usually fresh air, despite the challenges of traveling by wagon train.

The train continued along the Humboldt all the way to the Truckee River, averaging a good eighteen miles per day with few delays and no serious issues.

The weather cooperated, and all trails were passable, a fairly unusual occurrence for the fall. By the middle of October, the train had cleared the Sierras and was on the final leg toward Sacramento.

The city of Sacramento lay like a sparkling jewel in the crown of the nation near the confluence of the American and Sacramento rivers that flowed not far from the Pacific Ocean.

Its beginnings could be traced to a small fort built by one courageous and enterprising man, John Sutter. But it was the economic necessities of supply and demand resulting from gold fever in the late 1840s that drove the rapid development of the city.

Surviving fires, floods, and epidemics, Sacramento had transformed itself from a tent city frontier town to a thriving state capital that had gained an international reputation as an enlightened city.

An influx of wealthy Southerners and Europeans made its mark on the city. There was a social strata not unlike the larger cities in Europe where elegant parties and balls were more the norm than the exception.

By 1867, a great many buildings were in place, many of them built of brick, precisely aligned, and laid out along streets that had been carefully planned.

There were foundries, breweries, lumber mills, flour mills, opera houses, libraries, churches, banks, hotels, and every kind of merchant, supported by thousands of acres of fertile farmland that produced cattle, sheep horses, mules, and an abundant supply of vegetables, fruits, and grain.

The Sacramento Valley Rail Road, California's first, moved tons of goods daily. A solid infrastructure of public utilities, including water, gas, fire protection, and sewerage disposal, was in place along with modern hospitals and a large public education system.

Dick Ward

Through the foresight of a well-intentioned city government and the strong will of the merchants, the city streets and adjacent buildings on the waterfront were being raised eight to ten feet to ward off the frequent floodwaters. Though the ambitious endeavor seemed to defy common sense, such was the scene that greeted visitors.

Will and his party came to the eastern edge of the city on a cool afternoon in the late fall. With the permission of a local farmer, the wagon train camped in a large, freshly harvested wheat field, perhaps for the last time.

"At first light, I'll go into town and find a livery that will take our mules and a warehouse where we can store our goods until we can decide our next steps," said Will.

"Kate, you and Mary Nel should come with me so we can find acceptable lodging. I think I'm ready to be spoiled by civilization again."

"Ah, yes. I'm ready for warm meals served on a fancy table and clean sheets on a feather bed," said Mary Nel.

"All that sounds wonderful," said Kate, looking toward the city. "It's time for us to celebrate. We just completed a trip more than halfway across this country. We are actually here! It's hard to believe it."

Rio, as if on a tight schedule, assembled the stove and started cooking. The journey might be near its end, but Rio still took his job seriously.

"Take your time, Rio," said Kate. "I'll settle for a nice cup of tea as soon as I can freshen up a bit. How about you, Mary Nel?"

"Yes, that would be nice," Mary Nel replied.

"I'll throw together some coffee," said Will. "We'll take our time tonight and enjoy the fact that we made it here."

"I think we're near 'bout the last to be doin' this," said Hank as he came in from settling the herd. "I saw the railroad going out to the east headed straight up the Sierras. Pretty soon, it won't make no sense to come like we did. You just hop on the train."

"Mr. Lincoln's dream of a transcontinental railroad is coming true sooner than expected, I think," said Will. "I hear there are thousands of Chinese building east and thousands of Irishmen building west, laying track at the rate of several miles a day."

"I sure wish my Maggie could see this," said a pensive Ish.

Finding Mr. Sunday

Kate walked over and hugged him.

"I know, Ish. I miss her, too," she said.

They relaxed as Rio fixed the meal. There were occasional periods of prolonged silence as each person contemplated life in this new land. They finished the meal before sundown.

"Kate, you and Mary Nel care to take a walk? It's a little cool, but I feel like I need to stretch a bit," said Will.

"Thanks, Will, but I want to get some of my clothes ready to go into the city. I can hardly wait to see it," said Mary Nel.

"I'm ready," said Kate as she donned a warm shawl.

The two walked westward as if wanting to get a head start going into the city. The hills provided a splendid view as the lights from the town signaled the start of the evening.

"It's a beautiful sight," said Kate as she walked cross-armed holding the shawl around her.

"It is," he said. "Seems like we're at the end and the beginning at the same time."

"I found my self getting emotional about what is behind me, the closer we got to the end. I mean, there are so many things I would have liked to have seen turn out differently. But you can't change the past," Kate mused.

"Then I started to put the past away and think about the future, and I am excited about what's ahead. More so than I have ever been, I'm afraid to say."

"You shouldn't be afraid to admit that, Kate. That's what keeps us going sometimes, the future and all the possibilities it brings," he said. "Which brings up something I want to talk to you about.

"You know finding gold in the Sweetwater mines at South Pass was a stroke of luck, one of those you have only once in a lifetime. Aided by Chester's expertise, of course."

"Well, it couldn't happen to a nicer person, Will," she said with a smile.

"Kate, you have done so much for me, I'm going to share that luck with you and Mary Nel," he said.

"What do you mean?" she said, slowing her pace as she turned to him.

"I set aside $20,000 of that gold for you and Mary Nel. I told you I would."

"What ..."

"Now wait ... wait just a minute," he said holding up his hand. "Let me finish."

"Will, you can't ..."

"I'm not finished, dear lady," he said with a devilish smile.

"Also, I intend to make sure Ish has what he needs to be comfortable, too. And if Mary Nel wants to attend school and travel like she has dreamed about, I'll make sure she can."

By this time they had stopped walking and were standing face to face. They looked into each other's eyes.

"Can I speak now?" Kate asked.

"Oh, yes. I'm sorry," he said.

"Will, you are such a kind, generous person. But I can't let you do that. You don't owe me anything. If anything, I owe you for ... for so many things. I can't tell you what an impact you have had on my life."

She reached for his hand and held it in both of hers.

"You don't realize it, Will, I know, but you lifted me up as much, if not more, than I lifted you up, at a time in my life when I really needed it. It was like I was walled in.

"I couldn't see anything changing in my life. Watching you come around and finding out the kind of person you were, well, it opened my life, tore down that wall. The whole experience renewed me, Will."

"That means a lot to me, Kate, that you would say that. and I'm glad things turned out the way they did, for both of us."

He squeezed her hand, then let go gently.

"And Kate, I'm not trying to repay a debt with this. I'm simply taking care of those who mean something to me. And you and Mary Nel mean so much to me.

"Kate, promise me you will take the money. Buy land, a house, use it for a business, use it to live on, use it for whatever you want, but take it."

He put a hand on each of her shoulders and looked at her.

"Look at it this way, Kate, it will give you options."

"Besides," he said, and out came that powerful smile. "The money has already been deposited in an account for you in a bank here in Sacramento."

He pulled her to him and hugged her softly.

Finding Mr. Sunday

He closed his eyes briefly as he held her, feeling her warmth and taking in her womanly freshness.

"We'd best get back to camp," he said as he let go of her and turned around.

Sacramento reminded Will of St. Louis in many ways. The waterfront, the mix of people headed in every direction. But the air was clean, washed by a steady breeze from the west, pleasant, despite the industry spread throughout the city.

Will took the ladies to one of the better hotels and saw to their comfort before joining Hank at a livery a couple of miles away.

They decided to sell all of the stock but their personal riding horses and a couple of their best horses for a carriage. The big bay and Minnie were boarded at a local livery that had good pasture land adjacent to it.

Hank had already begun negotiating the sale of the stock at a livery. The Missouri mules were much admired by the Californians.

By the time Will joined him, a very good price for the stock had been negotiated, and Will approved the sale immediately. He then went about finding lodging for Hank, Rio, and Ish.

He found rooms for the three men in what looked to be a clean, well-run boarding house not far from the hotel where Kate and Mary Nel were lodged. That would do until he found something more permanent.

He then paid a visit to the bank to which he had forwarded his proceeds from the mining venture. The manager, Mr. Brooks, greeted him warmly.

"Please take a chair, Mr. Sunday. I'm delighted to make your acquaintance," said Brooks.

He was a clean-cut man perhaps in his late thirties. He wore a tailored gray suit of tightly woven wool, a brilliant white starched shirt with a high collar and a black and silver silk tie. His black shoes shined like patent leather.

"We appreciate your business, sir. I know you have just arrived, and there must be many things I can do to help you," said Brooks.

His smile and his offer seemed genuine.

"Do you intend to make your home in Sacramento, Mr. Sunday?" said Brooks.

"For the foreseeable future, yes," replied Will. "We arrived a day or so ago, and I am just getting my bearings. I'm impressed with what I see of Sacramento."

"We welcome you here. Sacramento has its charm, no doubt. And aside from some construction that is a bother right now, you'll find the city a pleasant place with everything you need here or fairly close by."

"I could use your help in locating suitable accommodations for me and my friends. Right now we are in The Orleans. But I need a longer-term place for myself and a home in a good neighborhood for Mrs. Daniels and her daughter, Mary Nel. Of course she would have to see and approve it. Mrs. Daniels is also a depositor at your bank."

"Of course," said Brooks as he began writing on a paper.

"As to the house I need, it would be helpful if there were several bedrooms and an office until I find something more suitable. Could you refer me to someone who could help me with that?"

"Yes, by all means," said Brooks. "I know just the person who could help you."

"I'm sure you must know of a good tailor and a good boot maker. I've been living in trail clothes for too long," said Will.

"I know just the man, sir," Brooks said, beaming.

"Also, if you know of an attorney who knows his way around the business community, I'd like to meet him. I'm looking for someone with impeccable credentials and some standing in the community. I don't want a politician. He needs to be tough when tough things need to be done, but his integrity should never be in question."

Brooks looked at him a minute, perhaps surprised at the young man's self-assuredness.

"Also, here is the name of my attorney in St. Louis. He handles my assets there, and you will, from time to time, be asked to deal with him on money transfers and other matters."

Brooks seemed to straighten in his chair at this young man who seemed to know his way around. Will was clearly not some young fellow who just happened to get lucky in the mining business.

Finding Mr. Sunday

"Mr. Sunday, if you would do me the honor, perhaps we could dine together around noon tomorrow. We can talk more, and I will have these things on paper for your convenience."

Brooks realized that this young man represented tremendous business potential.

"Good. I'd like to include Mrs. Daniels and her daughter, Mary Nel. I think it would be a good idea for you to meet both of them, for a number of reasons."

"Excellent. I was hoping I might be able to meet her soon. There is a good restaurant at this address, The River House."

Brooks wrote out the address and handed it to Will.

"If you and your friends can join me around noon, say, we can go over the information I'll have for you."

Will shook Brook's hand and was ushered to the door of the office.

"Tomorrow, then," said Will.

Will took himself on a brief tour of the city. He walked on a strange pavement made of wood, gravel, and tar that adjoined streets paved with cobblestones. Single-story structures blended in with grand multi-story brick buildings, many with ornate stone fronts. A covered walkway that fronted most of the shops was an invitation to stroll leisurely while perusing the glass display windows.

He hired a carriage so he could view the massive California capitol that was gradually rising prominently in the city skyline. The grand building had been under construction since 1861. California granite on the first floor provided a strong foundation to the brick comprising the upper floors. It was said the final structure would soar to more than 200 feet and be topped with a crown of gold.

The carriage dropped him off at the shop recommended by Brooks where he was measured by a meticulous tailor who was careful to check his measurements a number of times. He ordered several suits made of the finest cloth as well as a good selection of custom shirts, ties, and accessories.

From there, he went to the boot maker and ordered several pairs of boots and shoes.

He returned to the hotel to find that Kate and Mary Nel had also spent much of the day shopping.

"I have never seen so many shops. And the fashions are very different here," said Mary Nel. "There is a strong European influence in the designs and colors. It will take me weeks to select all the things I need."

"That's the fun part of it all," said Kate.

The two women had wasted little time in exploring the area around the hotel. They, too, were impressed with what they had seen of Sacramento, especially the diversity of the population.

"It is interesting to hear the different languages being spoken and the heavily accented English. If I didn't know better, I would think we were in Europe," said Kate.

"I noticed that, too," said Will. "I am also surprised at the many different American accents. People are here from many of the states and territories, especially from the South," said Will.

"Did your meeting with the banker go well?" asked Kate.

"It did," said Will. "We are to have a meal together tomorrow, and he's going to refer me to a lawyer and someone who can find us more permanent accommodations. Also to talk about the community.

"I took the liberty of asking that you and Mary Nel be included. It might be beneficial if you were to come along to meet him and hear what he has to say. I'm sure he would like to meet you. After all, you are a depositor in his bank."

Kate looked a little surprised but, nevertheless, pleased.

"Oh, I am sure you have business you want to discuss with him, and I wouldn't want to interfere," she said with a polite smile.

Will looked at her and spoke softly but firmly.

"Now Kate. You would not be an interference. Furthermore, you're welcome to be a party to any business I would discuss, with him or anyone else, both of you."

He turned to Mary Nel.

"Mary Nel, I hope you will come."

"Oh, yes. I'd like that. I want to hear what he has to say about the area," she said.

Her enthusiasm seemed to waver a moment.

"I'd like to have time before the meeting to send a telegram to Peter's father. I promised Peter I would."

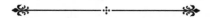

The River House was just off Front Street, only a short distance from the banks of the Sacramento River. The restaurant was on the first floor of a three-story building that housed an elegant hotel.

The entry to the restaurant was just off the grand lobby. Stained carved walnut doors with leaded bevel cut glass greeted the diners, as did a maitre d' wearing a fine fitted long tail jacket over a starched white shirt, a black silk tie, white gloves, and gray striped trousers.

"Mr. Sunday, I presume," said the gentleman.

"Yes," said Will.

"Good day to you, sir," he said with a slight bow of his head. "And to you ladies."

He turned to Kate and Mary Nel with a similar bow.

"Allow me to welcome you to the River House," he beamed with evident pride in the establishment.

"May I show you to Mr. Brooks' table? This way, if you please," he said.

He led the three to a table in the corner that was somewhat offset from the main dining area.

Brooks rose from his chair to greet them and shook hands with Will. He turned to Kate and bowed slightly, taking the tips of her fingers in his.

"You must be Mrs. Daniels," he said. "What a pleasure to meet you, madam."

"Hello, Mr. Brooks," said Kate.

That enchanting smile seemed to light up the room, he thought.

"And this is my daughter, Mary Nel."

"Hello," said Mary Nel.

Another incredible smile.

"Please have a seat," said Brooks.

There was a brief scramble as both men moved to aid the ladies in seating.

"I'm pleased that you ladies could join us. I think you will find the food here is exceptional, as is the service," said Brooks.

Brooks was impeccably groomed and looked every bit the successful banker. He had sparkling brown eyes and a very precisely trimmed mustache. His brown hair was parted near the middle, and his tanned complexion bespoke of one who enjoyed the outdoors despite his inside occupation.

Like everyone else, Brooks was struck by the natural beauty of the two women before him. But he seemed relaxed, comfortable, and confident in their presence, unlike many others.

Kate was a bit startled when she met Brooks. He reminded her of her husband, confident, gracious, and not lacking in charm.

"Ladies, if you will permit me to say, I find it hard to believe the two of you have so recently endured the challenge and rigors of cross-country travel by wagon train."

"Thank you, Mr. Brooks. It was quite the adventure. But we are no stranger to challenges and certainly not to hard work," Kate said with a warm smile. "But we are quick to appreciate what civilization has to offer. I fear we could easily be spoiled by life in Sacramento."

"And well you should. You will find Sacramento has everything to offer. While we like to pretend we are not, we've all become a bit spoiled, and, frankly, we enjoy it," he said.

His handsome smile was not lost on the two ladies.

"Ladies, with your concurrence, I suggest we have something to drink, perhaps, while Mr. Sunday and I attend to some matters of business. Then we'll order our meal, and I'll tell you anything you want to know about our beautiful area."

"Please proceed, Mr. Brooks," said Kate.

The ladies ordered tea, while the gentlemen ordered coffee.

"Mr. Sunday, here are the names of two gentlemen who can help with the matters you discussed with me. I have notified them that you wish to meet with them. If you concur, I'll see that they contact you at your hotel to arrange meetings at your convenience."

"Fine," said Will. "And please call me Will."

"My pleasure. My first name is David, which I much prefer," said Brooks.

"Mr. Kettleman is the first person on the list. He is a highly regarded individual who has been here since the late forties. He's honest, reliable, and

Finding Mr. Sunday

quite successful because of it.

"Buying land or a home here can be a challenge and very trying, especially land. It is extremely important to have the right adviser. But I'll allow him to tell you about that. You will enjoy meeting him, and you have my assurance he will act with your best interest in mind.

"He'll contact you in a few days, if you wish me to proceed."

"Does he speculate in land, or is he essentially a broker?" asked Will.

"I'm sure he holds property he'd like to sell at some point. But he has made his reputation selling as well as finding property for others. I've yet to hear of anyone who says he was misled or treated unfairly by Mr. Kettleman."

"Is Mr. Kettleman a friend of yours, David?" asked Will.

"No. We have a business relationship. But I respect him, and I believe he feels the same about me," said Brooks.

"I'm relying purely on your judgment here, David," said Will firmly.

"And I appreciate that. You won't be disappointed, Will," said Brooks.

"Have him contact me, then," said Will. "Tell me about Barbour, the lawyer."

Will took a sip of coffee and set his cup down to listen to Brooks.

"He has been here since the mid-fifties. He's from Virginia. A William & Mary law graduate. He clerked for two high-profile judges in Virginia. He came here with some good references, and I personally checked into him," said Brooks.

"How did you meet him?" said Will.

"He was representing a corporation with whom we had a large lending relationship. He was impressive. He's bright, energetic, and has a reputation as a highly competent lawyer in litigation, real estate, and the practice of general law. He is the senior partner in his firm.

"He has the respect of all of the judges and lawyers I know, both here and in San Francisco. He is highly sought after. He is very particular in accepting new clients."

"And he is willing to represent me without meeting me?" asked Will, a little skeptical.

"He wants to meet you. Whether or not he will represent you is up to him."

316

"Is he a friend of yours?" said Will.

"No. He is my lawyer. That's why he agreed to see you," Brooks said, giving him a slight smile.

"Have him contact me. We'll see how it goes," said Will. "Now, let's order our meal and get better acquainted."

"Excellent suggestion, Will," he said.

Brooks liked this fellow. He could tell this young man was not going to stand still in life.

They ordered their meal. Brooks was a regular patron and made recommendations accordingly. The conversation turned somewhat more personal as they awaited their meal.

"Mrs. Daniels, I understand you're from Missouri. Do you plan to settle in the area?" asked Brooks.

"That depends. I intend to take some time to determine that. I was raised on an apple farm and continued to operate it after my parents died. There was a time when I didn't look forward to the prospect of running an orchard for the rest of my life, but I confess I miss it already."

"Well, you will be pleased to know this is an excellent area for almost any agricultural venture. Especially wheat. But fruits are quickly becoming a large part of the agricultural effort — grapes, peaches, apples, pears. They are even attempting to grow oranges here, which are mostly grown down in the southern part of the Central Valley," said Brooks.

"I've read something about that. I understand wheat is the biggest crop because of the hardiness of the particular type grown here," said Kate.

"That's true. There are some very large wheat operations here and many successful smaller growers. There is an excellent export market for it. Of course, like all agriculture, you are at the mercy of Mother Nature.

"You will be pleased to know that Mr. Kettleman knows the agricultural community perhaps better than anyone I know. He's just the person to talk to about what is growing and where it grows."

"Then I will look forward to meeting him," said Kate.

"Miss Daniels, do you have plans here in California?"

Mary Nel politely wiped her mouth with the napkin, giving her time before answering.

"My mother and I have talked about me continuing my formal education

317

in one way or another. That would give me an opportunity to decide what I might do beyond that," said Mary Nel.

"We have some fine institutions here, both private and public. My wife went to a particularly fine school after she finished public school. I'll get you some information about it if you would like," Brooks said.

"I would like that. Perhaps I could talk with her about it," said Mary Nel.

Brooks paused for a moment and cleared his throat softly.

"My dear, I so wish that was possible. I lost my wife nearly three years ago to illness," he said.

Mary Nel covered her mouth in mild embarrassment.

"I am so sorry ... I ..." said Mary Nel.

"Thank you, dear. It's not necessary to apologize. It is one of those harsh realities one has to come to terms with. I'm still working on that," he said kindly.

There was a long moment of silence.

"I don't usually share that with people I've just met. You folks just seem so easy to get to know."

He smiled and said in a gentle voice, "Now, now, let's not let it put a damper on the occasion. All right?"

He turned to Will as if to dismiss the matter.

"Will, do you have any immediate plans?" Brooks asked in a cheerier tone.

"I'm kind of like Kate. I'm in no hurry to do anything until I've taken plenty of time to look at the opportunities. I want to buy some land. Maybe look around for some good business opportunities. My mentor had thoughts of my becoming a lawyer. I might do that," said Will.

"Well, law is a noble pursuit. You'd make a good lawyer, I'd say. Here in California, you are allowed to read for the law and apprentice to become a lawyer. I'm sure Barbour would be delighted to talk with you about that," said Brooks.

"Do you live here in the city, David?" said Will.

"I do have a home here. Not far from my office. But I have a ranch in the country. South of the city down in the San Joaquin valley. A beautiful part of the state you might consider viewing.

I raise race horses — harness racing horses. I spend as much time there as

I can. One of these days I'd like to do nothing but that."

"That's wonderful ... racing horses!" piped an excited Mary Nel. "I love horses, as well. But I don't know much about raising them."

"I'm learning every day myself, Miss Daniels," Brooks said. "It's strange how a hobby has turned into such a passion."

"Please call me Mary Nel."

"Thank you, and please call me David."

"I'm sure you have some beautiful animals," said Mary Nel.

"Well, I promise an invitation to all of you will be forthcoming down the road. It would be a good way to see some of the valley, too," said Brooks with a broad smile.

"It would be a pleasure," said Kate. "And that would give us some time to make more permanent living arrangements. We'd be delighted to visit."

"You can count on it," Brooks said.

The meal continued as did the good conversation. Brooks, as it turned out, was not the formal banker one might assume him to be, but a warm, friendly sort who was indeed good company.

Will, Kate, and Mary Nel were pleased with the meeting and the new friendship.

Later Kate reflected on the meeting with Brooks. He was an impressive person, knowledgable and self-assured. There seemed to be a softer side of him that emerged as they got to know him. Perhaps it was the loss of his wife that made him so down to earth.

She sensed some kind of connection between the two of them. She couldn't put her finger on why, but she liked the man she had seen. She found herself hoping they would meet again.

Now that is a new feeling, she reflected.

"Buying land in the valley is easily done as there is plenty for sale," Kettleman explained a few minutes into the meeting. "And therein lies the problem. Speculators have bought up large tracts, many with uncertain titles, much of it laying as beautiful as a painting one day and flooded the next."

Finding Mr. Sunday

They were meeting in Kettleman's office a few days after their lunch with Brooks. They sat at the end of a large polished walnut table. The opposite end of the table was burdened with stacks of papers and rolled drawings.

Kettleman adjusted his glasses as he spoke. He was small in stature, impeccable in his dress and mannerisms, more like a professor than a land salesman.

His salt and pepper beard was trimmed neatly, and he had a habit of looking over his eyeglasses, which often gave the false impression of snootiness.

"People come here from all over, find a beautiful piece of land, and year after year get flooded out. Or the rains hold off for several seasons, and the drought breaks them. Sometimes they buy land that was once part of a Mexican land grant and end up battling in court for proper title.

"I can't do anything about the weather, but I can make sure the land you buy is out of the flood areas, has good title, and is worth the price you will have to pay."

"I haven't quite decided what I want to do yet or if this is where I want to settle," Kate said. "I miss my apple orchard in Missouri, but I don't know about the potential for apples in this area. I'm hopeful you might help educate me somewhat on the agricultural possibilities."

Like most men, he gave her his undivided attention, seeming to hang on every word.

"I understand, however, that you make your living selling, and your time is quite valuable," she said with a polite smile.

"I assure you, dear madam, I have already made my living, as you say. And I further assure you, my time is yours."

His eyes lit up with a surprising level of charm as he smiled and gave a gentle tilt of his head in her direction.

Will sat there with a little smile. He was familiar with the effect Kate had on men, but it always amused him.

"Peaches, pears, apples, even oranges can do quite well around here. Especially in the San Joaquin Valley. South of Sacramento, north of Stockton. Good sandy, loamy soil. I know of several parcels that would be perfect for either of those."

You could see his eyes brighten as he spoke. He stood up and grabbed a

320

map from the other end of the table.

"Here. In this area," he said. He placed the map on the table in front of them, pointed to a spot, and moved his finger around in a small circle.

"Here is the city, and here is the valley I'm talking about," he said. "With the canals and inland channels, you can get your produce to San Francisco through Stockton. And the railroad will soon go south from Sacramento all the way down to Stockton.

This area would be just what you need."

Kate nodded as she looked closely at the map.

"I've heard of that area," she said.

"I'm looking for land that can be used for both crops and pasture land," Will said. "Something on which I could raise a few cattle, maybe horses. Four or five hundred acres, maybe more. And I'm willing to pay up for the right property."

That was perhaps the only comment that could distract Kettleman at the moment. He turned to Will and looked at him as if he had suddenly appeared in their presence.

"Of course. Of course, Mr. Sunday," said Kettleman almost too quickly. "That area would serve your purposes as well. Beautiful land. Beautiful land."

They spent the better part of two hours talking with Kettleman. Brooks had been correct in his assessment of Kettleman. He knew the area for hundreds of miles in either direction. He also knew small and large landowners to whom he could refer Will and Kate.

Will and Kate left the meeting with a list of names and a promise from Kettleman to get back to them soon with some specific recommendations.

Kate and Mary Nel moved into a small but well-appointed rental home a mile or so from the riverfront. It was a pleasant little home with two bedrooms, a good kitchen, a parlor, and a room devoted to sewing, reading, and games. There were plenty of shops nearby for all the necessities.

Will found a larger home not far away that accommodated the men. They were somewhat closer to the business district where Will began spending much of his time.

Rio assumed the duties of chief cook and housekeeper, keeping the home clean and comfortable.

Finding Mr. Sunday

Will kept his eye out constantly for business opportunities. Each day he scanned the Sacramento Bee and the Sacramento Union getting a feel for the community.

Roger Barbour's law office was in the heart of the business district on the second floor of one of the more impressive stone-front buildings. There were nine lawyers in the practice overseen by Barbour, their names etched on a brass plaque beside the entry to the suite.

If office decor and furnishings were any indication, Barbour's firm was enormously successful.

They sat on finely upholstered furniture in a seating area beside Barbour's huge walnut desk. Bookshelves and cabinets of stained walnut, fine woven rugs, and crystal lighting seemed to reflect strength and power.

"It's good to meet you, Will," said Barbour.

His voice was deep and resonant, just the timbre one would need in a courtroom. He was dressed in a tailored black suit trimmed in gray, a white starched shirt and a colorful silk cravat. Not a large man, but powerfully built and trim.

Barbour was probably in his early fifties with a neatly trimmed beard, perfect salt and pepper hair, and excellent posture. His presence seemed to project competence and confidence.

"Brooks spoke highly of you," he said as they settled in the plush furniture.

"I enjoyed meeting him. He seems to be a good man. Honest and straightforward," said Will.

Will had donned one of his new suits and tailored shirts. He had been to the barber and was immaculately groomed. He looked like a successful businessman, relaxed, confident, and self assured, his usual strong presence magnified by the surroundings.

"I've dealt with Brooks for some time. You can count on what he says. He knows his business," said Barbour.

"Will, by the way, I abhor formalities, except in the courtroom, so I hope you don't mind if I call you Will," said Barbour. "I go by Roger, if it's all the same to you."

"Of course," said Will.

The two spent thirty minutes or so sharing backgrounds and getting acquainted. It was apparent that a mutual respect was building, despite the difference in their ages and backgrounds.

"Tell me, Will. What can I do for you from a legal perspective?" asked Barbour.

"Well, an attorney in St. Louis manages my accounts. I'll give you his name so that you can contact him. I will be asking you to assume the legal work he does for me," said Will.

"Most of the real estate I inherited has been liquidated, so my assets are mostly cash. It will be deposited with Brooks. But I want a will drawn up. Beyond that, I want someone who can represent my interests in business transactions, reviewing contracts, and so on."

"More importantly I want someone who can introduce me to the right people here in Sacramento. I'm looking for business opportunities, investments, that sort of thing. I'm sure you know many of the people I should meet."

Barbour looked at Will for a moment before speaking.

"I look forward to representing you, Will, in all legal matters and needs. I'm kind of particular about the clients I take on, but you come with David's endorsement."

Barbour's countenance seemed to firm for a moment.

"But I'm very careful who I choose to introduce to other people. It's a matter of maintaining my own credibility, you see. I really don't know you. But I hope to get to know you. Once I have done so, we'll see where that might lead us."

Barbour was far from being unpleasant as he spoke, but there was no lack of seriousness in his tone.

Will looked at the man, somewhat annoyed that his integrity was questioned. But then he realized he was putting Barbour in a difficult situation by expecting his endorsement right away.

"I understand. I'm unknown to you. But that will change as we go forward," said Will with a little smile.

"Good," said Barbour. "I appreciate that."

Finding Mr. Sunday

"There is one other thing I'd like to talk to you about," said Will.

"My mentor felt I was well suited to become a lawyer. After I completed public schooling in St. Louis, I was tutored by a retired professor, mostly in literature and the classics. But I had started readings in law, albeit briefly. What advice do you have for someone who might be thinking about a career in law?"

"We need good lawyers. In the brief period I've known you, you seem to be articulate, astute, and assertive. You'd probably make a good lawyer," said Barbour.

"Let me give this some thought. In a few weeks, let's sit down and talk some more about that possibility."

Will knew that Barbour would contact Evers, his attorney in St. Louis. Good, he thought. That will be a good start for Barbour getting to know him better.

"By the way, Roger. Do you know a man by the name of Kettleman, a land agent here in Sacramento?"

"Oh, yes. Everybody knows Martin," Barbour said, chuckling.

"Is he one to be trusted?" asked Will.

"Generally speaking, there are a lot of pitfalls in land dealings hereabouts and some fellows you want to avoid. But Martin Kettleman is one of the few men in the business I respect. He'll serve you well," said Barbour.

After a few more minutes of conversation the two men set a date for their next meeting, and Will departed.

Later, Will was having lunch with Kate and Mary Nel at a local restaurant.

"What did you think of Barbour?" asked Kate.

"He seems to be the kind of lawyer I'm looking for. Competent, successful. He's cautious, too. Mindful of his reputation and the good practice he has built. I liked him. I could learn a great deal from him," said Will.

"Good," said Kate. "Have you heard from Mr. Kettleman yet?

"No. Not yet," said Will. "But I have a note that a package is being held for me at the front desk. That's probably what it is."

"I've found a school I like, Will," said Mary Nel. "Well, it's not really a school, but it's a place where young ladies learn about topics that are beyond the public school offering."

"You mean, like a finishing school?" Will asked.

"Yes, but Mrs. Chandler, who is the owner, dislikes the term "finishing" as she thinks completing her program is more the 'beginning' of a successful young lady's adulthood," said Mary Nel, smiling.

"Well, it's going to take a special place to improve upon you. You could probably teach them a thing or two," said Will.

"Oh, Will," said Mary Nel.

"No, I mean that," said Will. "Few people would think you are your age. I haven't seen much 'girl' in you. You have always seemed to be a lady to me."

"Why, thank you, Will," Mary Nel said with a tip of her head and a shade of pink. "I'll take that as a compliment."

"And I agree," said Kate. "But this program helps prepare a young lady for entering into society, and it covers a wealth of subjects that are very practical. Besides, I'm sure she will get to know some very nice people here in Sacramento."

"I'm very happy for you, Mary Nel. Is the school far from your house?" said Will.

"No, about fifteen minutes by carriage," she said. "And they actually pick me up and bring me home every day except Wednesday and Thursday. Those two days they want you to stay in the living quarters overnight just so you have the opportunity to be with other participants."

"That's a good idea," said Will.

"Have you heard anything from Peter? I was wondering if his father received the message," said Will.

"No. Nothing. I can only assume he did," said Mary Nel.

By her expression she did not seem overly concerned one way or another.

"I did what I promised him I would do," she said with a shake of her head.

Upon returning home, Kate found a message from Mr. Kettleman. He requested a meeting with both Will and Kate and provided several dates. As it turned out, Will had received a similar message and showed up later in the afternoon at Kate's house. They decided upon a date and responded to Kettleman.

Finding Mr. Sunday

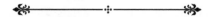

"I think I have something that each of you will like. All the properties are in the San Joaquin Valley, and it just so happens that in most cases, the properties adjoin. And in a couple of cases, the parcels are large enough that they can be divided between the two of you however you see fit," said Kettleman.

They sat at the table in Kettleman's office. As usual, he was armed with rolled drawings and maps.

"All of these properties are excellent for growing anything you want, and each has plenty of cleared land for pasture. Some have older buildings in place, but most are unimproved. All of them have good water, and they drain well," said Kettleman.

"And I have gone to great lengths to look at the title histories. They are good. If you buy any of these parcels, the ownership will not be in doubt, I can assure you.

"The parcels are all south of Sacramento, across the Mokelumne River and just east enough to pick up a bit of contour. Good land for orchards," said Kettleman.

The four of them spent well more than two hours reviewing the maps and drawings.

"If there is a parcel you want to eliminate from the selection based on what you see here, let's do that. Otherwise, I suggest we spend the several days it would take us to see them in a series of trips."

"I think that is a good idea," said Will. "Offhand, I'd say I want to see them all. What about you two?" he said to Kate.

"I agree, Will. All of these parcels look very appealing, and I see no reason we have to rush unless Mr. Kettleman says otherwise," said Kate.

They made plans for the trips. They decided that Hank and Ish should be with them, especially as it related to selecting property for stock.

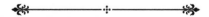

The early morning air, though not cold, had a bit of crispness as the small caravan made its way south toward the valley. There was plenty of water, and the land was mostly flat as they crossed the Mokelumne River and continued south and slightly east.

The valley floor had its own kind of beauty — lush in some places but with stretches of land that had dried considerably in the hot summer. Tule marsh grass, blackberry, primrose, cattail, concha and lots of salt grass could be seen, depending on the moisture or lack of it on the valley floor.

"Parts of the valley get water from the rivers flowing north, and the mountains provide runoff water in the early spring. When we get to the parcels, pay close attention to the soil. You'll see it's rich, loamy soil. There are also canals, creeks, and runoff lakes that are sources of water," said Kettleman.

They traveled most of the day, arriving at a small settlement in mid-afternoon. They found a tavern that had several rooms and sleeping quarters for others in the livery. After paying in advance for the rooms, they continued another two hours to the first parcel.

It consisted of more than five hundred acres of rich land with four or five bold creeks, several small lakes, and stands of cottonwoods, willows, and valley oaks. They spent more than two hours seeing as much of it as they could before heading back to the tavern.

"This is a good parcel. It has everything you will find in the valley. The trees help keep the moisture in the soil, especially in the winter when the tule fog rolls in," said Kettleman. "And there are plenty of open spaces for planting."

"I like this very much," said Will as he scanned the area.

"It has a good feel," said Kate.

"Plenty of range," said Hank.

They headed back to the settlement, had a light meal, and retired for the evening. The next morning they headed out again, more to the southeast this time. The spent the day looking at two more parcels, each having the same characteristics as the first parcel but increasing in contour as they neared the foothills.

The next day they began the trip back with lots of discussion about the merits of the parcels.

Kettleman had done his job well. All the land they had seen so far was just what they were looking for, making the decision all the more difficult.

One more parcel to see and they would have seen all of his recommendations. The last parcel was farther south and closer to the foothills, and it was the largest of all the parcels. Seeing that parcel would require another two or three-day trip, which they scheduled for the following week.

The next week the group spent a full day looking at the largest parcel yet, but because of its size they were not able to see it all. They sat around the dinner table discussing the land they had just seen.

"I like the last parcel we saw," said Kate. "It has some contour and is not absolutely flat. There are plenty of trees, water, and vegetation. Lots of open space, too. It almost felt like home."

"I liked it, too," said Will. "It is well over twelve hundred acres. That's a lot of land where I come from. But I really did not see many wasted acres. Of course, there is much we didn't see. I don't think it would be a bad investment."

"What you didn't see is just as good as what you saw, good, rich land," said Kettleman.

"Do you have any idea how many acres you might want, Kate?" said Will.

"Oh, I don't think I would want more than a couple hundred, regardless of which parcel we choose."

"Well, we don't have to have contiguous land. If you want a different parcel than the one I choose, I'm sure we can find that," said Will.

"No. I'll take great comfort in knowing who my neighbor is," she said, smiling.

"Good," Will said, returning the smile. "Then I think the last piece would suite both our needs."

The two agreed on the larger parcel, with Kate having first choice and Will taking the remaining thousand acres.

Their attention then turned to a discussion of the many things that needed to be done to turn their dreams into reality.

A couple of weeks later Will received a message from Barbour requesting a meeting. The meeting took place at one of the more exclusive business clubs in Sacramento.

The dining area was as good, if not better, than the finer restaurants, with a level of service unmatched by any other establishment, public or private.

"I'm glad we could get together. I hope you've been spending some time getting to know Sacramento," said Barbour.

"Some," said Will. "I've been keeping busy one way or another. In fact, you'll be receiving some purchase agreements on some land Mrs. Daniels and I are buying. I'd like you to look them over and make sure they're in order."

"Of course," said Barbour. "I'd be happy to do that."

The conversation continued along more of a social vein while they had their meal. Afterward, Barbour changed the course of the conversation.

"I have had ample correspondence with Evers in St. Louis and have done as you asked. In that regard, I have some papers for you to sign. He had good things to say about you, by the way," said Barbour.

"I'm glad to hear that," said Will. "He's a good man and worked with my mentor a long time."

"Will, I also want to discuss something else while we have some time together," said Barbour. "I've given your question about a career in law some serious consideration."

He paused and looked at Will, wiping his mouth with his napkin.

"I appreciate that, Roger," said Will.

Barbour waited a moment while the table was cleared.

"I think you would be a good lawyer. You're smart, a good thinker. And I like your self-confidence. I don't see many young men who carry themselves the way you do. How would you like to apprentice with my practice?" said Barbour.

He continued without waiting for an answer.

"We specialize in several areas of practice, civil, criminal, corporate. You'd be exposed to it all. When you're ready and have progressed the way I think you will, I believe I could convince one of the best judges in California to offer you a clerkship."

He paused to watch Will's reaction for a moment, then proceeded.

He could see the interest in Will's eyes.

"We'll develop a study plan for you, involve you in the fundamentals, research, writs, hearings, trials. We have an extensive law library so you would probably have every tutorial and reference you'd need," he said.

Finding Mr. Sunday

Will sat there, not quite believing all that he was hearing. There was a long pause.

"I'm very flattered that you would make me such a generous offer, Roger," said Will.

"Well, the generous offer means a lot of work on your part. Nothing that you can't do. My concern is that it will take a lot of your time, and you seem eager to explore other business opportunities," said Barbour.

"Give me an idea of that," said Will. "How long should it take and what would be the commitment to do it correctly?"

"Probably three or four days per week. For how long depends on how fast you progress. Probably two years, maybe less."

"It's very appealing," said Will. "I don't think I could find a better opportunity if law is what I want to study."

Will sat back in his chair and thought a while.

"If I accepted your generous offer, would there be any restrictions on what I do outside of the practice? From an investment and business perspective?" said Will.

"Not at all. Your personal life is your own, provided, of course, you are not involved in anything that would be criminal or a breach of our practice ethics policies. And we'll share those, but they are no more than what you would expect of any reputable law practice," said Barbour.

"I don't want you to think me ungrateful, but I want to think about this for a while. If I do make a commitment, I want you to feel comfortable in knowing that it would be a solid one — one that I'll follow through on without any misgivings, hesitations or delay," said Will.

"Of course. The offer is there and will stand as long as you like. I think you'd be a real asset to the legal profession," said Barbour.

The conversation turned to other matters, and the meeting ended shortly thereafter.

Will began his apprenticeship one week later.

Will steeped himself in the study of law at the same time laying out his ranch and home and helping Kate with her place. With Hank's valuable help, he began the development of a herd of special breeding stock.

The months passed quickly.

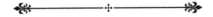

Roger Barbour sat behind his great, polished desk. He and Will were having a cup of coffee.

"I've not seen the likes of you, Will," said Barbour with a shake of his head.

"What do you mean, Roger?"

Will was attired in one of his tailored suits, starched shirt, and silk tie, already looking like a successful attorney.

"Well, you come in here, you burn the midnight oil for nearly a year now. You've read every law book in our library, some several times, I know.

"When we give you an assist case, you prepare it better than some of my senior fellows. Your case plans are excellent, your written arguments are concise, and your research is always impeccable."

Barbour set his coffee cup down, put his elbows on the desk, and laced his hands together.

Will smiled at Barbour's comments.

"You have completed our study plan faster than anyone ever has," Barbour said.

"Thank you for the compliments. I truly enjoy the study of law. I like the challenge. I like that it forces you to question everything and take nothing for granted. I appreciate considerably the latitude you've given me to go at my own pace. Where do we go from here, Roger?"

"That is what I wanted to discuss. This week, we're having lunch with Judge Weathers. He is a friend as well as a colleague. I've talked with him about you on a number of occasions. I think I have convinced him that you would make a good clerk for him. And, of course, he wants to meet you. Over lunch, at first."

"From what I have seen and heard, Judge Weathers is one of the best judges in the state. Gets to hear every type of case. That would be a very good opportunity," said Will, excitement in his voice.

"He is one of the best, if not the best, in California. My guess, he's headed for a chief justice chair. That is, if he doesn't become the next state attorney general. We'll continue to involve you in cases here as time permits while

331

you clerk for Judge Weathers, as long as there is no conflict of interest, of course," said Barbour.

"Well, Roger. I can't thank you enough for working on my behalf. I'll make sure I don't disappoint you."

"I'm not worried about that. You'll be the best he's ever had if he takes you on. I'm sure of it," said Barbour.

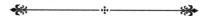

Judge Weathers didn't look like a judge. Of course he was dressed in a fine suit, albeit a little behind the current fashion. He had a head of salt and pepper hair that was naturally curly, with a mind of its own. He had given up any hope of controlling it years ago and let it go its own way, a little long for the times. This gave him a bit of a shaggy appearance. But one look at the man's demeanor and his hair was quickly forgotten.

He had heavy eyebrows and hooded, dark piercing eyes that seemed to strip away a person's deepest secrets with one look. He did not often glance at a person offhandedly. He turned his head completely in the person's direction, making him feel as if he were alone with the man, regardless of how many people were near.

The middle-aged man wore no facial hair, unusual for the time. His skin was pale and lined, with a visible, almost feminine softness. He seldom smiled. He spoke with well chosen and precise words, the tone in his voice leaving no doubt of his authority.

The usual get-to-know you conversation broke the ice. Apparently, Barbour had more than adequately briefed Weathers on Will Sunday. They talked for some time of St. Louis, Will's earlier tutelage, and the trip west.

The judge was an avid reader himself, especially of the very classics Will had studied.

The tone turned a bit more serious as the conversation progressed.

"Mr. Barbour has spoken highly of you, Mr. Sunday. You seem to have taken well to the study of law and progressed very quickly," said Judge Weathers.

"Yes, sir. I am enjoying the experience. I'm certain, however, one never completes the study of the law as the very practice of it provides an ongoing learning opportunity."

"Quite so. The practice of law is much like practicing medicine but without benefit of any scientific certainty. There is never a sure outcome. It is not always true that one argument can be applied to a case that resembles another, though we lawyers like to hang our hats on precedent. An argument is, after all, an argument. The delivery can drastically affect the outcome."

The good judge put both hands on the table and leaned slightly toward Will. His eyes seemed to bore into Will as if they alone were transmitting the judge's message. Will felt spellbound by the voice and the stare.

"How an individual presents himself is almost a sure indication of how he will present his cases. Jurors like to see presence, self-confidence, and credibility in a lawyer. And believe it or not, likability. Few lawyers have it all. Sadly, most miss the mark entirely."

He paused a long moment before continuing, looking much like he was pondering a verdict on a case.

"You seem to have it all, Mr. Sunday. I can count on one hand the lawyers I've seen in my career that have what you have. It will be interesting to see you in action one of these days."

"Thank you, Your Honor," said Will.

"Save that for the courtroom, Mr. Sunday. It's Judge Weathers," said Weathers. "Do you intend to start your own practice when you become a lawyer?"

"That depends, sir. I'm interested in other business opportunities also. Being a lawyer can serve me in many ways. Mr. Barbour and I have had some discussion around that question. My guess is I will practice with his group for a while, then go my own way."

"I sense you are an independent sort. I would advise you, however, to stay with Mr. Barbour's firm as long as you can. His firm is one of the best in California."

"I appreciate the advice, sir," said Will.

"I must warn you, Mr. Sunday, there is an inherent peril in being the kind of lawyer I think you will become. Lawyers tend to become politicians. From what I see in you, you might very well be asked to consider that one day. You are just beginning, but that time will come, I can almost assure you."

Finding Mr. Sunday

The meal was served, and the conversation shifted to other topics. At the end of the meal Judge Weathers looked at Will.

"I apologize for not being able to visit longer. But I have court soon," said Weathers.

The judge stood and shook Will's hand.

"Monday morning, Mr. Sunday. I like to get an early start on the day," said the judge.

With that the judge turned and left the room.

CHAPTER FIFTEEN

B oth Will and Kate finished construction of their houses, barns, fences, corrals, and the assorted structures needed to support their properties. The fine homes were built of California redwood by the best builders they could employ.

The once empty land evolved into prosperous homesteads alive with activity. Orchards were planted, and the trees were maturing. Stock roamed the pastureland, and barns were filled with hay and fodder. Many hands worked both properties under the guidance of Kate and Hank.

Kate had fallen in love with her farm. She awoke each day excited about the day ahead. Mary Nel had finished her education and was learning all she could about the horse-breeding business, her newest interest.

Rio, Ish, and Hank moved into the completed bunkhouse on Will's place, lending a hand at whatever was needed at both homesteads. Rio served mainly as the cook and housekeeper for Kate. With Hank's management, the herd of special breeding cattle was flourishing.

Ish built a small house not far from Kate's home, but during the day could be found helping Kate with one chore or another. The little group somehow found time to spend evenings together catching up on what was happening on the properties and in each of their lives.

"You are spending most of your time with Mr. Barbour and Judge Weathers," said Mary Nel as they all sat around the large dining room in Kate's new home. "Are you enjoying all of this?"

"I am, Mary Nel," said Will. "For some reason there is a torrent of activity at the firm. I'm getting involved in as much of it as I can, but most of my time is spent clerking for Judge Weathers.

"I know it might be hard for someone who is not involved in it to believe, but the study of law is fascinating. It certainly is not a boring profession by any means."

"Do you find it challenging?" asked Kate.

"Yes, somewhat. But learning seems to come naturally to me. I didn't think I would enjoy it as much as I do."

"Are there any parts of it you don't like?" asked Mary Nel.

Finding Mr. Sunday

"I find the judicial process cumbersome and slow. But I guess if anything should be deliberate, the legal process should be. It just takes getting used to, that's all."

"That's all good, Will. You're gonna make a fine lawyer," said Hank. "But I do need you this Friday. I'd like you to look at these two bulls I'm ponderin'. Both real high-end stock like you asked, the best I can find.

"But I still want you to see 'em before I pull the trigger. There ain't no better 'lessen we go to the breeders in Mexico, and they ain't cheap, I can tell you that."

"Ordinarily, Will, I'd do this without you, but these bulls will be the foundation of our next herd," said Hank.

"I'll be here for that. I'm planning to take next Monday off, too, so I can ride the eastern part of the parcel. Haven't spent any time much on the far side yet," said Will.

"I hope you can meet Mr. Moss, too," said Kate. "Mr. Moss owns the big orchard operation just south of us, and he has already been very helpful. He's going to help me with the next part of the orchard. He raises seedlings as well as grafting stock, so we can get our trees going both ways. He knows the varieties that do best here in the valley. I plan to have about twenty more acres planted in peaches and pears within the next several months."

Will could see the sparkle in her eyes as she told him of her plans.

"You've missed all of this, haven't you, Kate?" said Will.

"I have, I confess," she said, laughing. "It's good to get back to the land. This valley is full of people like me who live for the land and what it can produce. I've met just about every family for miles around. And they're are all so welcoming and helpful."

"I know what you mean, Kate. Maggie would have loved seeing this place and watching it take shape the way it has," said Ish.

"Well, Ish, I can assure you she is here in spirit. I sometimes expect her to come through that door any minute," Kate said as she touched Ish's hand.

"That she is, Kate. That she is," said Ish softly.

"I'm headed over to see some of David Brooks' new racing stock tomorrow," said Will. "It's a nice coincidence that his ranch is so close. I think he's going to be very helpful as we get our horse stock started.

"He has a fine operation going. I couldn't help but be impressed. One of the best selections of breed stock I've seen. And not just racing stock. I think we can work a deal with him on a couple of his best. After all, that's the business he's in. It's hard to picture him as a banker when I see him on his ranch. Would you and Mary Nel like to ride over with me, Kate?"

"Why, yes. We'd like that. He has been kind enough to check on us several times, and we have been remiss in thanking him. I want to take some fresh bread I just baked, and maybe a pie," she said.

There seemed to be an extra sparkle in her eye as she spoke.

"Why, he is the finest horse I have ever seen, David!" said Mary Nel.

Will, Kate, and Mary Nel were at the Brooks ranch. He had taken them out to one of his several barns. Brooks held the horse by the bridle and stroked his massive shoulders.

The ebony horse glistened in the sun. He was not huge, perhaps fifteen and a half hands. His head was finely shaped, as if chiseled from stone, his neck medium-sized and graceful. His hindquarters rippled with muscle, and his legs were set back on his frame, giving the illusion of motion even as he stood.

"I just got him last week," said Brooks. "One of his distant ancestors was the great Hamiltonian, one of the best trotters in the world. I've had my eyes on him since he was a colt. Watched him train, watched him run his first race. If I'm right, he has more potential as a harness champion than any animal I've ever seen."

"Look at his muscles ripple, Momma," said a wide-eyed Mary Nel.

She reached out and gently stroked the horse, who turned and looked approvingly at her.

"You are becoming a good judge of horses, Mary Nel," said Kate. "I am certainly no expert, but this is an exceptional horse, David."

"He is a Standardbred, of course. His conformation is impeccable," said Brooks. "I expect he'll do very well. But if he doesn't, his stud services will more than pay for him over time.

"Mary Nel, Minnie is a fine mare and a well-bred horse, a Missouri fox trotter, I believe. So you have an appreciation for good horses. Have you ever considered breeding trotters?"

"No, but you have piqued my interest. May I ask what a horse like this would cost?" said Mary Nel.

"He was around three thousand," said Brooks. "But you needn't start with a horse like this. There are plenty of fine mares and stallions that can be found much cheaper.

"If you and Kate would like, you both could be my guest at the breeders show in San Francisco a few weeks from now. I'll show you what I mean. In the meantime, I have some good literature on the breed and the breeding business if you care to read it," said David.

"I would. Momma, would you like to go to the show?" she said.

"I certainly would. And I think you could learn a lot from David."

"And I'd be happy to help all I can," he said with a sincere smile. "But I warn you, you will fall in love with the business."

He showed them another mare that belonged to another breeder. She, too, was an excellent specimen.

"Here is a beautiful mare. Excellent conformation. This breeder bought her a few days after she was born. He knew what to look for and ended up paying less than a thousand dollars for her just based on her looks. She's worth several times that now," said Brooks.

"So you see, it's all in knowing what to look for in an animal. And you seem to be a natural around horses, Mary Nel."

A few weeks later Kate and Mary Nel accompanied Brooks to the horse breeders show in San Francisco. They saw hundreds of beautiful animals.

After two days of looking and talking to breeders, Mary Nel and Kate bought a colt and a filly from two breeders, spending a reasonable amount, counting more on potential than lineage. The pair was a good start for Mary Nel's venture.

"Mary Nel has two really good animals, Kate. Bill Harris has a keen eye and has produced some fine champions over the years. He has a well-regarded operation. He has a standing policy of buying back any animal he sells if the owner is unhappy," said Brooks.

Later, Kate and David were dining in one of David's favorite restaurants near the hotel. Mary Nel had decided to have a light dinner and rest after such a productive but tiring day.

Dick Ward

They were discussing one of the horses Mary Nel had purchased.

"I don't know Marshall as well, but I've seen a few of his stock, and they all have been quality horses," he said.

"She is so excited, David. And you were very helpful," said Kate.

"I'm glad I could be of help, Kate. She is quite the young lady," he said. "And almost as pretty as her mother."

He gave her a smile as he picked up his glass of wine.

"Why, I'll take that as a compliment, although I believe she is far prettier than her mother."

She gave him one of her trademark knockout smiles.

"I am so proud of her. She had a hard time after losing her father. But she came out of it. She is smart, practical, and, from what I have observed, nobody's fool," said Kate with no small amount of pride in her voice.

"You know the old saying about the acorn. And without a doubt she is a prime example," he said.

Neither of them spoke as they continued to enjoy the excellent meal of fresh-caught fish, steamed green vegetables, and potatoes.

"Your farm looks like a calendar painting, Kate. So well built and laid out. Even the new orchards are perfectly planned," said Brooks.

"Thank you, David. I've envisioned the place for years, I think. Even before I left the farm as a young lady I had planned how I might one day lay out my own place. It was only a dream then, which I forgot about once I got married and moved to the city. But it all came back to me when I started planning this place."

"Did you find it hard putting it all together?" he said.

"No, I had a great deal of help from Will and the local people. It was much easier than I imagined it would be."

She wiped her mouth and sipped her wine. She tilted her head a certain way, and the soft light on the table reflected in her eyes. She was radiant and lovely.

Brooks gazed at her and was lost in her for a moment. He forgot what he was about to say and had to take a deep breath to gain his composure.

He put the napkin to his mouth and gave a short cough.

"Are you all right, David?" she asked, concern in her voice.

"Oh, I'm sorry. Yes, I'm fine. Just a little catch in my throat. Maybe I ate a

Finding Mr. Sunday

little fast," he said from behind the napkin.

That sat silently for a moment. He had always known she was a special woman, but tonight...tonight for some reason, she overwhelmed him.

"Kate, may I ask you a personal question? I don't mean to be rude and apologize if I'm being so ..."

"Why, yes, David. You certainly may ask. But I don't guarantee you an answer," she said, smiling.

She was making an effort to lighten the situation as she could see his slight discomfort.

"That's fair enough," he said, returning her smile.

She tilted her head again and played with an earring. The slight gesture almost caused him to lose his composure once again. What a lovely woman, he thought.

"Kate, I know you and Will are close. I was just wondering. If you and he are...or, I mean... is he your companion ... or are ..."

He was having a hard time getting his question out.

"I believe you are asking me if Will and I are romantically involved," she said, smiling, again trying not to add to the awkwardness of the moment.

"Yes, thank you," he said with relief.

"Let me say first that it is very hard for me to describe how Will fits into my life. He has become an important part of it in the last three or four years. He is my rock in many ways," she said.

She thought, choosing her words carefully, then returned her gaze to Brooks.

"He is extremely intelligent, tough, hard at times, but compassionate and sensitive. I trust him more than any man I have known except my husband. He is mature well beyond his years.

"I've never met anyone quite like him. It is my guess there are very few men like Will Sunday. He is very protective of me and Mary Nel. We've been through many things together.

"I am very close to him, and I want him to be a part of my life ... always. But we do not have a romantic relationship. I don't know that we will, or what, in fact, I would do should it move in that direction."

She held the napkin in her hand and began playing with it.

"I hope you are not angry with me for asking," he said.

340

"Not at all, David," she said with a smile. "I'm sure many people who know us wonder the same thing. I've answered awkwardly perhaps, but honestly."

"And I appreciate it, Kate."

He took a deep breath and smiled a big smile — whether it was from relief that he had the answer he wanted or that the moment was over was hard to tell.

"I must insist that you try the egg soufflé. It is delicious," he said.

"Oh, then I simply must," she said, laughing aloud as she looked at his face.

Kate felt a gentle warmth spread over her, and she knew it wasn't the wine.

Judge Weathers certainly did like to get an early start. But most days, Will was there when the judge arrived in the morning. Will liked that the judge expected much of him, loading him with case research, drafting trial memoranda, and outlining and briefing the judge on the legal issues of cases.

In a short period of time, the judge had Will drafting opinions. And the judge always challenged the opinions Will wrote, testing the soundness of his findings.

But Will was gratified that most of his opinions evolved into the very judgments rendered by Weathers at the bench. To Will's dismay, however, the good judge very seldom commented on Will's progress and development.

It had been nearly a year now that Will had served as a clerk for Judge Weathers. They had just completed a long and difficult case that had gone on for weeks. They were ending the week with a discussion of the complexity of the case in the judge's chambers.

"Will, your work on this case was remarkable," said the judge. "You were thorough, and your opinion draft was excellent."

"Thank you, Your Honor," said Will, surprised at the rare praise.

The judge reached into a desk drawer, pulled out a bottle of whiskey and

Finding Mr. Sunday

two glasses.

"In fact, Will, it is time we celebrate," said the judge as he poured whiskey into both glasses.

"I remember our first meeting. I told you what I thought made a good lawyer. Do you recall?" he asked.

"I do, Judge."

"I told you very few lawyers had it all, did I not?" said the judge.

"Yes, sir."

The judge leaned forward and stared at Will with those piercing eyes.

"Well, Will, I propose a toast. For it is my worthy and learned opinion, borne of many years of both practice in the courtroom and sitting at the bench, that you are, indeed, one of those rare men who have it all as a lawyer."

The good judge held his glass out to Will. They touched glasses, and the judge drank down the whiskey, as did Will.

"Thank you, sir," said Will. "I am honored by your comments."

"So today, we end your clerkship," said Judge Weathers.

"Today?" said a startled Will, who almost choked on his drink.

"Today, sir," said the judge, with a rare smile. "You are henceforth a lawyer, and will, most likely, be one of the best out there."

The judge stood and held out his hand. They shook hands.

"It has been a pleasure, Mr. Will Sunday," said the judge.

A somewhat rattled Will shook the judge's hand vigorously.

"Go forth, young man. I expect we will meet again soon."

CHAPTER SIXTEEN

Kate had prepared a very special meal with the help of Rio. The table was laden with ham, poultry, fish, beef, and vegetables prepared in various ways, and a sideboard nearly sagged under the weight of puddings, pies, and cakes.

Will, Mary Nel, Ish, Hank, David Brooks, Roger Barbour, and assorted neighbors were attending.

"We have much to celebrate," said Kate as they finished the blessing.

"Will is now a lawyer, my orchards are planted and growing, Mary Nel has started her horse breeding business, and we have found so many wonderful new friends.

"It may be a while before we can do this again since Will is going to open a law office in San Francisco."

"Now, now, Kate," Will said in a teasing manner. "I can get here pretty quickly."

"Yes, I know," she said, sighing. "But it's not like having you a short ride away."

"We're going to miss you terribly, Will," said Mary Nel, who made no effort to hide her feelings.

"San Francisco just seems to be the place for me to start my own practice," he said.

"Well, Will, I think you've made a good decision. San Francisco is becoming a world-class city. You should have no trouble establishing a law practice," said Roger Barbour.

"The city seems to draw me there," said Will. "It looks full of intriguing places to explore. I didn't think I would ever miss being in the city, but I do."

"Well, you can enjoy both the country and the city now," said Hank. "With the boys we hired on, we can take care of the ranch. You'll have a herd ain't like nobody else's soon, a coupla hundred of the finest breeding stock there is."

"I don't think I could leave the place in better hands," said Will, smiling.

A few days later, Mary Nel and Kate were standing just inside the big redwood barn that housed the start of Mary Nel's horse-breeding venture. They could see a lone horseman making his way to the ranch house.

As he got closer they could see that the rider was attired in fine clothes. His polished boots reflected the sunlight.

The two women came out of the barn, as did Hank, unhooking the leather loop that secured his pistol in the holster. Both women shielded the mid-morning sun from their eyes as the rider came toward them.

Mary Nel audibly inhaled as she recognized the rider a second or two before Kate.

"Peter! Peter!" Mary Nel almost screamed.

She picked up her skirt and hurried toward the man as he dismounted.

The rider dropped the reins and stepped toward Mary Nel. He stopped short and took both of her hands in his and gazed at her face for a moment.

"Mary Nel. Dear, dear Mary Nel," he said as he raised both her hands and kissed them.

"I can't believe it's you," said a breathless Mary Nel as she stepped up and gave him a hug.

"It's me all right. It seems like it has been forever since I saw you. I was afraid you would have forgotten what I look like," he said.

She looked closely at him. He had changed. His hair was a little longer, and his side whiskers grew down his jaw line. His suit of clothes was of a European cut, fine green wool trimmed with tan silk, with a multi-colored tie around a starched collar.

"You haven't changed all that much," she said with a warm smile.

"And you ... I didn't think it possible, but you are more beautiful than ever," he said, gazing at her.

"Hello, Peter," said Kate as she stepped forward.

"My dear Mrs. Daniels," he said as he turned toward her.

He took one of her hands in his and bowed his head toward her.

She stepped forward and gave him a hug.

"You needn't be so formal, Peter," she said, smiling. "It is good to see you. And you look like a prosperous gentleman."

"And you, madam, by the grace of God, are the same as I remember," he smiled.

Kate could see a subtle change in Peter's face. Gone was the boyish look of years ago. The trail tan was replaced by a pale, nearly stern demeanor, with more roundness and a slight pinkness to his cheeks. He had gained weight, and the leanness had evolved into a slightly enlarged waist.

"Come. Let's go inside. We have much catching up to do," said Kate.

They sat in the parlor as Rio served tea. Peter seemed to be beaming as he kept his gaze steadily on Mary Nel. Kate was a little amused at his total fascination with Mary Nel.

"How did you find us?" said Mary Nel.

"My father got your telegram quite a long time ago. At the time, I was traveling in Europe, and it was four or five months before I returned home. I began to try to locate you through an acquaintance in San Francisco, but before I could make much progress, my father passed away."

"Oh, Peter, I'm so sorry," said Mary Nel.

"It was a tremendous shock. He was so involved in every aspect of his businesses. He never really trusted anyone to run things."

Peter paused to sip his tea, but his eyes did not leave Mary Nel for even a second.

"It consumed me for more than two years just trying to get a handle on the situation. He not only had his merchant business, but he had delved quite heavily into the import business. I had to make a number of trips abroad. There were creditors to deal with, as well as customers who had never dealt with anyone but Father."

He placed his teacup and saucer on the table beside him. He wrinkled his face.

"It was very difficult filling his shoes. I was the only one people turned to for decisions. I worked ten to fifteen hours a day trying to keep up with everything. I still don't know how he had managed all of it himself."

"Didn't he have a staff after all theses years?" said Kate.

"He did," replied Peter. "But he never gave them any authority. He told them everything he wanted done, when to do it, and how to do it.

"Even his professional advisors, accountants, lawyers, and so on did as he instructed them," he said. "I had to put any personal aspects of my life on hold. I had some health issues as a result of being overworked and carrying the burden."

"Are you all right, now?" said Kate.

Finding Mr. Sunday

"I think so," he said. "I've got good people in place now. I sold the retail part of the business, which was a big relief. In the meantime, I've greatly expanded the import side of the business through hard work and much travel.

"As soon as I had free time, I resumed my search for you. I hired a firm to find you and through that group tracked down the land purchases Kate and Will had made. As soon as I felt my staff was ready to handle everything, I came west."

"In fact, I will be conducting some business in San Francisco while I'm here," he said. "We're working on an import relationship that will be a big part of our business as we go forward."

He tilted his head and looked again toward Mary Nel.

"I will be here on the West Coast at least two months, possibly longer," he said and turned to Kate. "I am hopeful I may be welcomed here to visit and renew my dear friendship with your family."

"You are welcomed to visit, Peter. Also, Will is in San Francisco now. He is a lawyer just beginning his own practice. He'll be delighted to see you. I'll give you his address before you leave," said Kate.

"A lawyer? I'm impressed," said Peter.

They sat for a couple of hours catching up with each other. Peter was surprised to hear about the horse-breeding business that Mary Nel had started.

"It is a bit unusual for a lady to be pursuing that type of business," he said.

Mary Nel said nothing but glanced at him, with a questioning look, her face reddening a bit.

There was a moment of silence.

"Maybe," said Kate. "But we have close friends who advise her. She has made some good decisions, and we are off to a good start."

"Well, I'm afraid I must be taking my leave. Mary Nel, would you do me the honor of walking with me to my horse?" Peter said.

He turned to Kate.

"My dear Mrs. Daniels. So good to see you again. I hope I may have the pleasure again soon."

"It is good to see you, Peter," she said with a smile. "Here is Will's address. He'd like to see you, I'm sure."

Kate watched the two go to the front door.

That was Peter, she thought, but not the Peter she had known years ago. There was something about this Peter that disturbed her.

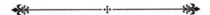

"Peter seems so different. Like a prosperous gentleman of the world," said Mary Nel. "Don't you think so, Momma?"

Kate knew her daughter well and could see that Peter had made quite an impression on Mary Nel.

"I do, dear. He is certainly not the shy young fellow of years ago. I think the years of responsibility have changed him. He seems to be very sure of himself. And obviously very successful in his business," said Kate as she busied herself making tea.

"And he has been to England and France and so many fascinating places. How exciting it would be to travel as he has and see the world," said Mary Nel with a wistful look on her face.

"Yes. He seems to have worked very hard to get where he is now. He has had to make many hard decisions since he took over his father's business. When you are forced to do that you succeed or fail by your own hand. That alone tends to mature a person quickly," she said.

Kate wasn't sure Mary Nel was hearing her.

"You know, Mother, my friend Charlotte at Mrs. Chandler's school has been to Europe. She told me all about it, and it sounds so exciting. I've dreamed of going there. I can't wait until Peter's next visit. He promised to tell me all about his travels," Mary Nel said.

"Just remember, dear. He is a changed person. Give yourself plenty of time to get to know him again."

She watched her daughter's face, but her advice seem lost to a Mary Nel envisioning the life Peter must be living.

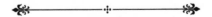

David Brooks was coming to see a new colt Mary Nel was considering

347

and had been invited to stay for the evening meal.

"He's a fine-looking animal, Mary Nel," said Brooks as he ran his hands over the animal's sleek coat. "The more I see of Marshall's stock the more impressed I am."

"This colt is out of a sire and mare from Mexico," said Mary Nel. "I will admit, I bought him on faith from Mr. Marshall, but you can see why I did by just looking at him. Your opinion makes me feel I wasn't too impulsive."

"No, I don't think so," said Brooks with a reassuring smile. "At the price you paid, I'd say you made quite a deal for yourself. I doubt you will regret it, Mary Nel."

"Thank you, David. Now I know Mother has made some fresh cookies for you, so please go and visit. I have a few things to do before I come in."

"Mmmm. Cookies. You got my attention," he said with a laugh and turned to go to the house.

"And David, thank you so much for all your advice and help," she said, beaming.

"You are welcome, Mary Nel. But I've got a feeling you may not need much in the near future."

Brooks went into the house and began talking to Kate.

"He is a fine animal. Good bones, excellent shape. A fine example of the Standardbred," said Brooks to Kate. "That young lady has a true breeder's eye."

"I'm beginning to think so. Though she truly values your opinion and appreciates your advice," said Kate.

"If my nose isn't deceiving me, I think there are fresh cookies about," said David.

"Your nose is working fine. I have some in the kitchen. Let's go sit down and have some. But let's not spoil our dinner. I have a nice roast in the oven, and Rio has been very busy making some of his famous dishes."

"I can't wait. But I have to confess. Mary Nel told me about the cookies," he said.

She returned his smile, and as usual she almost took his breath. She was wearing a narrow-waisted dress gathered at the back. A pretty silk scarf encircled her fine neck and served as a small collar. Her shining hair was neatly arranged, held in place by tortoise shell combs. Two ruby earrings dangled from her ears.

Brooks had never seen a more natural, unassuming beauty in all of his life.

Kate had looked forward to David's visit. She had put off wearing this particular dress until his visit. She smiled to herself as she saw his reaction.

They sat across from one another at the kitchen table. Rio was in and out putting the finishing touches on the evening meal.

"Hello, Mr. Brooks," he said cheerfully. "We are pleased to have you with us. I have prepared some dishes especially for you."

"Thank you, Rio. Whatever you have prepared, I know I will enjoy it," said Brooks.

"I'll be back in about an hour to finish the meal, Miz Kate," said Rio.

"Thank you, Rio," Kate said as Rio left the kitchen.

"Kate, I'm glad I had an excuse to come visit today," said Brooks.

"Why, David, do you really think you need an excuse to visit? You are welcome any time. But you know, a woman likes to be prepared so it's good to know a little ahead of time."

She looked at him with a teasing tilt of her head.

"Of course. And, if you will permit me, I must say how beautiful you look. I mean, you always look beautiful, but today you look, uh, I'm not doing this very well ..." he said, struggling.

She laughed politely at his expense, not to be cruel but because she thought his bumbling was charming.

"Well, so much for my attempt at a compliment," he said, feigning hurt.

"Oh, David, I accept your compliment. Thank you for being so sweet."

She reached across the table and touched his hand.

He took her hand in both of his and looked in her eyes.

"Kate, I must tell you. I think of you all the time. I know I'm being forward here. And I make no apology for it."

He leaned forward as if to shorten the distance between them.

"I would like to call on you. Not as a friend or a neighbor, but as a suitor, one with serious and long-term intentions."

She put her other hand together with his two and squeezed gently.

"I'm not blind, David. I've noticed, and I am flattered that you would feel that way. I have to admit, I have grown very fond of you."

Finding Mr. Sunday

"And?"

"It has been a long time since I have had a companion or a romantic interest. I have thought about us, I confess."

She paused, not for dramatic effect but to select her words carefully.

"You are a fine man. A gentleman. And quite handsome, I might add. You are everything a woman could ask for … but I have to think about sharing my life with someone else. It's not easy. I've grown accustomed to my independence. I don't want to rush into anything. Not quite yet. When I'm ready I want to be sure it is forever."

She watched his face fall in disappointment.

"David, I'm not saying no … not at all … All I'm asking is for you to be patient with me."

He exhaled deeply and continued to hold her hand.

"I will, my dear lady. I'm not going anywhere. I'll wait as long as I have to. I want you to be happy more than anything, with whatever comes."

She smiled and held his gaze.

"Now, madam, I must have a cookie."

They both burst out laughing a she reached for the plate of cookies.

Kate knew at that moment that she was about to take a big step in her life. She did not want to rush things, but she was finding great comfort in this man's presence…not to mention a rush of some long-quiet feelings.

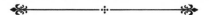

The streets of San Francisco seemed never to rest. Sidewalks, when not being built or rebuilt, were crowded with people moving as if all were late for the next appointment or meeting. Will observed the activity from the window in his second-story office.

He had hung out his shingle, and despite some misgivings placed a small business card listing in the morning newspaper to run several times a week. It simply gave his name, Attorney at Law, and his address.

He made a habit of going to the sumptuous free lunches provided by many of the local clubs and saloons and introducing himself to as many people as possible.

As yet, he had no clients. He spent the time organizing his office and furnishing the three additional offices that were part of his suite. He was pleased with the design of his offices, upfitted in fine walnut paneling, oriental carpets, and handmade shelving for his library. He might not be prosperous at this point, but his surroundings certainly gave that impression.

As he sat pondering the day, he heard someone open the entry door to the offices and walk across the marble foyer to the reception desk, which still awaited a receptionist.

He came out of his office to see a gentleman dressed in a dark morning jacket over a gray suit, obviously tailored, with a starched white shirt and a perfectly tied bow tie. As the young man turned in his direction, Will sensed a familiarity.

It took only a second for the name to come to him.

"Peter. Peter Forester," said Will as he extended his hand.

"Hello, Will. I hope Mrs. Daniels told you I was in San Francisco."

"She did. I didn't expect to see you so soon. But it is good to see you. Please come into my office and have a seat."

The two of them sat in the fine upholstered chairs in the seating area in the front of Will's desk.

"You have a beautiful office here, Will. It is much different from the back of a horse, I should say," said Peter with a little laugh.

"Quite. It took a while for me to feel as comfortable in an office as I do on horseback. Fortunately, I am in a position to appreciate both venues," Will said, laughing.

They spent some time catching up on the last four years. Peter explained his presence in San Francisco. Will listened with interest as Peter explained the import business.

"Our company does business in several countries in Europe, and we are just now establishing business with several firms in the Orient. Silk, teas, ivory, porcelain. High-quality merchandise that we then sell to the best merchants in major cities — New York, Philadelphia, Baltimore, and so on. I have sales people in most states on the East Coast. We can hardly keep up with the demand."

"You must be very proud of the business you have built," said Will.

"Yes. Of course, it has not been without sacrifice," Peter said.

"I know you have just started your practice, but you should look into the

351

legal side of international trade, Will. My legal representative here stays very busy in that area of practice. Were it not for the fact that I am very comfortable with him, I would ask you to represent our company here."

"Thank you, Peter. I might just look into that as a specialty for my firm. I have been interested in that business with the Customs House being nearby. It would be a good fit for me."

The conversation continued for the next half hour.

They were about to adjourn when Will asked about Peter's local living arrangements.

"I am leasing a very nice place about a half mile from here. I'm thinking, however, that I just might buy some property in the San Joaquin area. I liked the lay of the land when I visited Mrs. Daniels and Mary Nel."

Will was a little surprised at the statement.

"Well, it is a special area, indeed," he said.

"Besides, I think it might be wise for me to be closer to Mary Nel. I have a feeling it would be to my advantage to do so," said Peter with a strange smile.

For some reason the comment bothered Will. Something rose up inside of him, and he didn't know exactly what it was or why it happened.

After a short while, Peter prepared to leave.

"Well, best of luck. Let me walk you out," said a still stinging Will.

Will commenced a special effort to become a student of the import business, and in doing so met a number of gentlemen in the business. It wasn't long before he brought on a receptionist, then a partner who specialized in that area.

Additionally, his practice developed specialties in real estate and general corporate matters. Will continued to keep a hand in criminal and civil law, the areas that he found most interesting.

He spent most of his time, however, developing new clients.

He joined several prominent men's clubs, mingling with judges, other lawyers, publishers, and many of the community leaders. It wasn't long before he found himself surrounded by San Francisco's elite both in the legal community and the business arena.

Will somehow found time to visit his ranch and his friends in the valley at least once a month. Most of the time he stayed only a few days but managed to stay a week or so every couple of months.

Shortly after bringing on his first partner, Will sat at the table having coffee with Kate.

"Will, I have something of a personal nature I want to discuss with you," said Kate.

"You know I'll be happy to listen, Kate," he said.

"It has to do with David ... and me ... but also you."

She held his gaze.

"I needn't tell you that you are a dear person in my life. I owe you so much. You are a part of my family. I trust you. And I'd never do anything to hurt you."

"I know you wouldn't, Kate." Will placed his coffee cup on the saucer and gave her his full attention.

She continued. "I have grown to love you. I don't know how to put all this together so it makes sense, but I love you in a very special way. There were times when I thought it might be another kind of love, but that hasn't happened. But I think you have a deep affection for me. I can feel it. I know it is there."

"I do, Kate," he said solemnly. "I'd do anything for you."

He knew these words were difficult for her. Words from the heart don't always come easily.

"I am in love with David, and he is in love with me. I wanted you to be the first to know how I feel. Over the last year of being around him, I like his gentleness, his intelligence, his sense of humor. He is very much like Ben ... but different, too. I didn't think I was ready for that kind of relationship, but he has helped me find a part of me that was set aside some time ago."

She paused, trying to be sensitive to Will's reaction.

"I haven't even told Mary Nel this, though I suspect it would be no surprise to her. She, too, is very fond of David. They seem to be kindred spirits.

"David has asked me to marry him, and I intend to say yes."

Finding Mr. Sunday

She watched his face. His expression changed. What was it? Surprise? Bewilderment? Was he upset? She had not seen that face before.

Neither of them said anything for a while.

"Kate, yes, I do love you. But I could never tell you that. I didn't know how ... Maybe I was afraid you would reject me, and I'd lose what we had, and I didn't want to take a chance on that.

"What you are telling me makes me angry at myself for ignoring there was something there, for not letting you know."

Now she could see the emotion on his face. It was hurt. Pain.

"Oh, Will," she said as tears came. "I have hurt you, and that is the last thing I wanted to happen."

He inhaled deeply. Looked away from her. Fighting tears himself at the loss of her. He turned back to her.

"No, no, Kate. You did nothing to me except be my best friend. Any pain is my own fault."

There was a long pause. Kate used a small linen handkerchief to wipe away her tears.

"Kate. Dear, dear Kate," he said softly as he reached for and held her hand.

"All I want is for you to be happy. David is a fine man. I think the two of you will be very happy together. You have made the right decision. He is the perfect man for you."

With that he got up and walked around the table, stood behind her and put his hands on her shoulders. She turned in her chair and looked in his eyes.

He bent down and lightly kissed her on the cheek.

"Besides," he said to her. "You will always have me."

He gave her shoulders a gentle squeeze and walked out into the fresh air.

Peter Forester sat in the parlor beside Mary Nel. He had visited Mary Nel and Kate several times during his extended visit in the spring. Now it was late summer, and he was back in California for a few more months. He had been corresponding with her in the intervening months.

"Dear Mary Nel, you must know how I have missed you the last few

354

months. I am miserable without you," he said, sighing deeply with a pouty look on his face.

His cheeks seemed to have reddened even more, and his weight gain around the middle was unabated.

"Now Peter, we both know you have been consumed by your work as you have just told me so. And where would I have been all this time? And don't forget, I have my business to run," said Mary Nel.

"Mary Nel, put an end to this foolishness and marry me. I'll give you anything you want. We can live here in the valley if you feel you must, and in St. Louis. You can travel with me and see the world."

"I know, Peter. I'm not sure that is what I want just yet. Besides, we have just finished with a wedding in this household."

"And aren't your mother and Mr. Brooks happy? Don't you see we could be the same way?"

The tone of his voice was only slightly shy of a whine.

"Why, Peter, we've actually not had a lot of time together since you first came to California. I can't make a life time decision in that short amount of time," she said firmly.

"But we have known each other for years. What would you have me do to win your hand, Mary Nel?"

"Time, Peter. Just give me more time to get to know you better," she said.

He looked perturbed.

"Peter, you must respect my wishes on this," she said.

Will busied himself with his growing practice. There was a painful feeling of loss over Kate's marriage to David. The only solace he allowed himself was that she seemed beside herself with joy over her husband and her marriage. He could see it every time he had visited since the wedding. Brooks, knowing nothing of Will's pain, was still a great friend and sometime advisor.

Will reflected on his feelings. Analyzed them. Tried to rationalize them. But it was the biggest disappointment in his life. And it was nobody's fault but his own. It deeply wounded his pride and caused him to take a hard look at his life.

Why, when his life seemed so charmed and successful, had he not been able to develop and foster a relationship with someone whom he obviously felt so deeply about? What was he afraid of, he asked himself. He knew that for some reason he, even now, avoided getting involved with women he met every day.

And he was surrounded with lovely ladies, women of society, many of whom overtly sought his attention. Successful associates and clients went out of their way to introduce him to single females, even their daughters.

So successful and lucky, he thought. But why was he afraid of the kind of love that came so easily to others?

And now, he saw that Peter had spent much of his last few trips west making frequent visits to Mary Nel, almost begging her to marry him on each visit.

She was a striking woman now. The embodiment of self-confidence. She had good business sense. Will could not picture her being married to someone like Peter.

But, over time, she might change her mind. He had deep feelings for Mary Nel. But were they those kinds of feelings?

Mrs. Wolfe, his assistant and receptionist, knocked lightly and entered his office, interrupting his reverie.

"Mr. Sunday," she said. "Miss Farrell, your mid-morning appointment, is here now. Shall I show her in?"

"Thank you, Mrs. Wolfe. I will come out to meet her," he said.

He walked out to find a young lady he estimated to be about twenty-five to thirty seated in the foyer. She wore a small hat that sat upon red hair arranged perfectly atop her head. Her dress was of a new design, pulled tightly at the waist and gathered in a fall at her back and covering at least one petticoat. The cut was tailored to her shapely figure.

"Miss Farrell, Will Sunday," he said with a slight bow.

Without hesitation she extended a gloved hand that he accepted quickly and gave him a firm handshake.

She was an attractive woman, he thought. Flawless complexion with only a trace of makeup and beautiful green eyes.

Her full lips curled into a dazzling smile that could make a man forget all but her presence.

"Hello, Mr. Sunday, I am pleased to meet you," she said.

"Please come into my office, madam," he said.

"Thank you," she said as he stepped aside and allowed her to go before him.

He noticed she was holding a coat that matched the rest of her attire. He reached for her coat.

"Mrs. Wolfe will hang that up for you," said Will.

She handed him her coat and smoothed the hang of her dress.

He sensed a change in her demeanor. Not unpleasant, but pure business nevertheless.

"Mr. Sunday, you were referred to me by Mr. Lancet. He is a frequent guest in one of my employer's clubs. He said you were an honest man with a reputable and growing practice who knew how to get things done."

Will recalled the name and remembered Lancet was a client his firm had assisted in a real estate dispute. The case was settled without trial in his client's favor.

"Yes. Mr. Lancet. A fine gentleman," said Will.

He caught himself admiring the young lady and chastised himself mentally.

"My employer owns a number of restaurants, clubs, and entertainment businesses here in San Francisco. The man who does our corporate legal work died suddenly last month. Mr. Merlin Rhodes. Did you by any chance know him?"

"No, Miss Farrell, I did not. But that isn't unusual. There are many lawyers in San Francisco," he said.

"I'm sure. He worked many years for Mr. Broome. He had planned to retire soon. I worked with him on all legal matters. And will do the same for our new attorney," she said.

There was a toughness about this lady he didn't often see in one so young. She probably knew how to handle herself, he thought. He didn't relish the thought of being on her wrong side.

She extracted some papers from a leather case.

"Here is a list of Mr. Broome's holdings. You will see that I am the appointed corporate secretary for all of them. Here also is a power of attorney that spells out my authority in all matters related to those corporations.

"Should we proceed with an arrangement, I will provide the charters for the various corporations and pertinent files from the legal work Mr. Rhodes performed."

"You certainly came prepared, Miss Farrell," he said.

"Well, I'm certain you would not allow me to discuss my employer's business without proper authority. Further, I am assuming you will want to look into these corporations to assure their validity."

"You are correct, Miss Farrell."

He liked the way this lady conducted business.

She packed up her leather case, rearranged her position, and flashed that smile.

"Now, Mr. Sunday, tell me about yourself and your practice."

Her tone softened somewhat.

They spent nearly an hour discussing his background, that of his associate attorneys, the experience and expertise of the firm. She asked many questions. He was impressed with her knowledge of the practice and process of law.

"May I answer any other questions, Miss Farrell?" he asked.

"No. You've been quite thorough, Mr. Sunday," she said. "I noticed you did not mention the name of any of your clients, and that means a great deal."

"No, I do not divulge the names of my clients nor do I discuss their business with anyone. Discretion is of the utmost importance here in my firm. That is a principle that we hold sacred here, Miss Farrell," he assured her.

"Excellent. There is one more thing, Mr. Sunday. If I do decide to hire you and you, of course, are satisfied with your due diligence on our firm, there are some ground rules in how we communicate."

"All right, let's hear them," he said, smiling.

He watched as the woman seemed to become even more serious.

"Mr. Broome relies on me for the legal work. When I speak to you on matters, I am speaking for him."

She delivered this with a deliberateness that surprised him.

"Further, all correspondence between our firms must be sealed and hand-delivered to me only, not to Mr. Broome's receptionist."

Her look and demeanor underscored her words.

"I understand," he said. "As you prefer."

He had not had this come up before, but the power of attorney was clearly written. She could manage the relationship anyway she desired.

She prepared to leave.

"Thank you for your time, Mr. Sunday. I will send a message to you regarding our next appointment. Will about two weeks give you enough time?"

She seemed to soften her tone and her posture.

"I believe so. If there is any delay beyond that, and I don't foresee one, I'll be in touch," he said.

"Then I'll bid you good day, sir."

She stood, and he escorted her to the foyer, retrieved her coat, and said goodbye. What a woman, he thought.

Will used a local investigative firm that had gained his loyalty for their competence and discretion. In a week or so he received a comprehensive report on Broome's establishments.

The corporations owned by Broome varied from high-end men's clubs and restaurants to saloons. Several of his properties were in the better parts of the city, but some bordered on the rough areas and were only slightly better than most gin mills.

One of his clubs was quite exclusive, and membership was private and restricted to the very upper end of the social scale. Information on the businesses was limited, but there were no records of illegality for any of the enterprises. Mr. Broome's establishments seemed to be well-managed based on the reports given to him.

Will visited several of the restaurants and saloons himself. Each one was full of customers, and business was brisk at every location. The drinks were well poured in every case, even those in less desirable areas.

In total, Mr. Broome's businesses appealed to a variety of customers in the bustling city. Will speculated that Broome must be grossing thousands of dollars each day. With the quality of management Will had observed, the profits were no doubt enormous.

Finding Mr. Sunday

He sent word to Miss Farrell that he was ready for the next meeting wherein they concluded their arrangement and he assumed duties as their legal counsel.

Will had made a practice of meeting with the same group of men each day and having his daily drink or two of fine Scotch. It occurred to him that such a pattern limited his exposure to the many establishments in the city. Thus, he started going to other places several days a week.

He was in one of the finer restaurants dining alone one evening a couple of months later when he felt a light tap on his shoulder.

He turned to find Miss Farrell standing by his side.

"Miss Farrell, what a surprise," he said as he stood, napkin in hand.

"Hello, Mr. Sunday. I hope you don't mind my interrupting. This is one of my favorite restaurants."

"Have you dined yet?" he asked. "I am just studying the offerings. I've not been here before."

"No, I have not. I have a regular table here on Wednesday nights," she said.

"Would you care to join me? I'd be honored to have your company," he said.

"Just a minute. I'll be back," she said with a smile.

He watched as she spoke to the man who seemed to be keeping his eye on everything. He was surprised that she was joining him.

"You must live nearby since you dine here regularly," he said as he helped her with her chair.

"No, not really. I'm out most evenings. I have my routine. My driver takes me to the restaurant I have chosen. I dine. Then I make my rounds to our businesses. Different places each night. It keeps the managers on their toes."

"I'm sure it does," he said. "But some of Mr. Broome's establishments are for men only. How do you manage that?"

"Oh, I have a separate entrance. I don't make a fuss. Most of the members know who I am and what I do. They enjoy seeing me for the most part. I am very discreet, you see."

"Ah. And do you dine in your own establishments?" he asked.

"Yes. There are a couple that I defer to one of my assistants," she said.

This evening, she was again the picture of fashion and elegance. Everything perfect, not a hair out of place. The men who were not regulars seemed to find reasons to look frequently in her direction as did a few of their female companions.

"How long have you worked for Mr. Broome?" he asked.

He sensed that she did not like the question.

"Let's just say a very long time and leave it at that," she said. "May I call you Will?"

"Of course," he said.

"Will, I don't like discussing business in a non-business setting. I'm not trying to be rude. It's just that if I am not careful, I find myself working all the time, and I can't do that. I have to make an effort to separate myself from what I do, at least part of the time."

She then gave him her best smile.

"I understand, Miss Farrell. I'll keep that in mind from here on out," he said, recovering somewhat.

"And my name is Bonnie. And yes, my father was Scotch Irish, if you haven't already guessed."

She seemed to relax at that point, almost taking on a new persona.

"Will, I'm in the habit of having a drink before my dinner....and wine with dinner. I know you might find that unlady-like, but it helps me wind down. Do you mind?" she asked.

"Not at all," he said.

"And, to surprise you even further, I prefer Scotch. I learned to drink it at an early age."

She laughed pleasantly as she shared her secret.

"Well now," said Will. "You are speaking my language. That is also my preferred drink.".

He summoned the waiter and asked her, "Do you have a preferred brand?"

"Surprise me," she said, laughing.

He ordered one of his favorites.

"I think you will like this. I once saw a man give a twenty-dollar gold piece for a bottle of it. It was well worth it, as I recall," he said.

Her eyes sparkled under the gas lights, and the light reflected off her fiery red hair. He was lost in her for a moment.

"Somebody really got your friend on that. Twenty dollars is a lot of money for a bottle of Scotch," she said. "Even one of the best."

"Well, it was way up in the cold Wyoming mountains. My business partner was a Scot, and he knew his whisky. I have appreciated it since that very night."

"What were you doing in the mountains of Wyoming? That is, if you don't mind my asking."

"Not at all. We were mining for gold in the Rockies, the Sweetwater area, and running a stamp mill to extract gold from ore."

"You, a gold miner? I find that hard to believe."

She held his gaze as she talked, her hands neatly folded on the table in front of her.

"Well, I was really an investor and manager of the project more than anything. My partner was the miner. He knew his business. He had studied mining in Scotland before he came over."

"Did you have any success?" she asked politely.

"I did. It was a very good investment for me. I sold him my half after less than six months so I could continue on to California."

"I had left friends and traveling companions in Salt Lake. One of them was ill, and we had wintered there hoping she would recover. Unfortunately she did not," he said.

"When did you come to California?" she asked.

"A little over four years ago. We settled in the San Joaquin Valley."

"That's farm country. Do you have a farm or ranch there?" she said.

"Both actually. One of my friends owns an orchard. I own a cattle-breeding operation and raise some horses."

"My, Will, you are a man of many surprises. A gold miner, a lawyer, and now a cattleman. Is there anything else that you do?" she said, laughing.

He liked the sound of her laugh. No pretending there.

"Oh, I'm a man of many talents," he said with a laugh.

This lady was getting his full attention. He didn't want to rush the meal. Not tonight. Not with her.

They finished their drinks, ordered a bottle of wine, and were soon served excellent fare.

The conversation was becoming easier and more casual. Miss Farrell seemed to have relaxed considerably. He liked this woman's honesty and directness.

"Tell me about yourself," he said.

She set down her wine glass and gave him a guarded look.

"There isn't much to tell," she said. "I've been in California all my life. My mother died when I was eleven, and I was raised by my father. If you could call it that.

"His only success in life was as a drunk. I left home when I was sixteen. I've been on my own since then."

It seemed a shadow crossed over her face as she spoke. It was clear that she did not want to talk about her past.

He changed the subject quickly.

"San Francisco is a beautiful city. I imagine you have seen about all of it," he said.

"No, I haven't. I work almost every day. I try to have some free time on Sundays."

He felt the Scotch and the wine. He couldn't help but think she must have felt the whisky, but she showed no sign of it. The conversation, lively and interesting to both of them, went way past the meal.

"Bonnie, I must ask you a question."

He picked up his napkin and wiped his mouth. "We don't know much about each other, and I don't want to be presumptuous, so forgive me if I am."

He watched her closely, knowing he was about to cross some line, but disregarded his conscience.

"You are a client of mine. I don't make a habit of socializing with clients, I can assure you. But you ... or rather ... I find you to be very interesting ... intriguing even."

He stopped there.

"Oh, my, Mr. Sunday, that was a bold thing to say," she said with no small amount of coyness.

"But I'm not really your client, Will. Mr. Broome is."

Finding Mr. Sunday

She looked him in the eye and let her gaze linger for a long moment.

"That is a fine line, I must say. One I don't wish to debate, however," he said with a devilish grin.

"I enjoy your company, Will. I must say that I find you ... well ... intriguing, also."

She gave him a teasing smile, then got a bit more serious.

"Will, you must have surmised by now that I do what I want to do. I had to in order to survive. I don't care very much for what other people think is proper or improper," she said firmly.

"But — and this is a must — if we are to get to know each other. We must agree never to bring business into it, ever, yours or mine."

He saw she was preparing to leave. He was concerned that he might have offended her.

"I hope you don't think me rude," he said.

"No. No," she said. "I'm afraid I must go. You stay seated. I will be escorted to my carriage. They watch out for me here."

The manager was rushing over to her. Will stood anyway, and she walked over to his side of the table, grasped his hand, and whispered in his ear.

He felt like he was being touched by fire. Her warm breath sent a heat wave through his body.

She stood on her toes and whispered in his ear.

"Yes ... intriguing is a good word, Mr. Will Sunday," she whispered.

He could smell her fragrance as she turned away to leave. She took the other gentleman's arm and left the dining room.

He sat there, a little stunned, thinking. I just spent two hours with this lady, and all I want now is to see her again.

He had to sit there for a while to calm himself.

A few days later Will was on his way to his home in the valley. He had almost canceled the trip in hopes of seeing Bonnie, but he had not heard from her. She was still on his mind.

Nevertheless, his friends were expecting him. Mary Nel had also sent word that she wanted to talk with him on a personal matter. He wasn't about to ignore that.

Mary Nel, he thought. He had not thought as much about her since he had dinner with Bonnie, but she was always in the back of his mind. He had to admit to himself that he was jealous of Peter.

Bonnie had awakened something in him that was almost purely physical. He found himself picturing Mary Nel. She was a beautiful woman, but he had not thought of her in that way. Or had he?

When he arrived, Mary Nel and Kate greeted him warmly. They were in high spirits, and the hugs were special and loving. Brooks was still in the city but was planning to join them in the evening.

"The orchard is loaded with fruit, Kate. I see you are working your magic just like you always have," he said.

"It's the soil here, Will. It's rich. The trees thrive in it. I've never seen such pretty fruit. We will be harvesting and shipping peaches very soon, then the pears will be ready," said Kate.

Will looked closely at her. She was glowing with happiness.

He turned to Mary Nel.

"Mary Nel, I'm going to ride the eastern part of the ranch tomorrow. Would you like to go with me?"

"Yes," she said. "I'd like that."

"Good. Now I'd like to see your new stock," he said.

They spent the rest of the day catching up and sharing news.

"My practice is doing well," said Will. "I'm considering another partner."

"Peter's business is doing well, also. In fact he is planning a trip to New York and then on to Europe in the coming months."

"I've really been delving into the import area and international trade. It is a fascinating area. He is in the right business at the right time," said Will.

Brooks arrived shortly, and they all sat down for one of Rio's feasts.

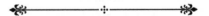

Mary Nel, on her beloved Minnie, rode beside Will as they headed to the pastures of the ranch. Will was pleased to see the fencing in good repair, creeks flowing clear of debris, and his herd of prized stock grazing peacefully. His land was something to be proud of, he thought. He was renewed by the fresh air and peaceful countryside.

"Will, can we stop and sit under those trees for a while?" asked Mary Nel.

"Sure, good idea," he said.

Finding Mr. Sunday

They dismounted and seated themselves beneath one of the large trees on a slow moving creek. The horses began to graze contentedly nearby.

There was a gentle breeze, cooling to the face. One had to fight the temptation to lean against a tree, shut out the daylight, and nap to the soothing sound of the creek.

"Will, you know I appreciate that you are always willing to take time for me and listen when I need to talk. I don't know if I have ever told you that," Mary Nel said.

He looked at the once pretty girl who had grown into a lovely woman. Her hair was tied behind her head with a ribbon. Her face was radiant with the glow of youth, unmarred by her many hours outside.

Unlike most women of the time, she refused to wear a dress or skirt when she rode, sitting astride her horse like a man. The riding pants and blouse she wore, however, did little to conceal her graceful womanly figure.

"You have, but it is always nice to hear," he said, smiling.

She was leaning against the tree trunk. He was sitting beside her, leaning back on his hands, a little forward of her so he could see her face.

"It's about Peter," she said.

She looked down at her hands resting in her lap, pausing a moment.

All at once it occurred to him that she might be getting ready to tell him she was to be married to Peter. He felt a wave of deep concern bordering on illness.

"Peter has asked me to marry him ... a number of times," she said with a nervous laugh.

"Yes, I know, and he seems to be in a big hurry," said Will.

"I tell him each time he asks that I need to get to know him better. This has been going on now for more than a year," she said. "Peter has changed in many ways. He is much more sure of himself. And I believe he is accustomed to getting what he wants. There is an edge to him, too."

"He was most likely forced into that. You can't do what he has done with a business if you don't assert yourself. The business world has its own set of rules for survival. You learn that quickly. And the cost of letting your guard down can be ruinous," said Will.

"Mother said something very similar to that," said Mary Nel.

She paused a moment.

"I think I'm pretty smart, Will. But when it comes to relationships, with men, I mean, I know nothing. My head may be telling me one thing and my heart another. It's complicated," she said as she toyed with the grass in front of her.

"Tell me more about that," he said gently, knowing that she needed to talk.

"Well, the practical part of me says I'm just not ready. I've not really had the opportunity to be around many men. I feel like I shouldn't rush into anything with anyone," she said.

"Then, when he comes to visit, I like the attention he pays to me. He tells me I'm beautiful. That he misses me. That he can't stand not being with me.

"All those things most girls want to hear from a man, I suppose, and I sometimes think, yes, I'll go with him wherever, you know, I feel like it would be the right thing to do."

She looked off in the distance.

"Do you love him, Mary Nel?" asked Will.

She said nothing for a while. He waited patiently because he knew it was a hard question. To him it was the crux of the matter, not a simple question. If she really loved him she would have blurted it out.

"I don't know what that feels like. I have some feelings for him. He cares for me."

She knew she had not fully answered the question.

"I've not been in love in the romantic sense, Mary Nel. And I certainly can't tell you anything from experience."

He paused.

"But if everything I see and hear is right, you certainly know when you are in love. I will say this. I think you can do better than Peter. I mean, he does not seem to be a man with much excitement about him, no fire — unlike you, Mary Nel," he said.

"Well, I'm afraid there is no fire there ..."

She colored a bit.

"Then taking your time right now is the best thing I could advise. You don't need to hurry. Don't let yourself be pressured. Please."

They sat there for a moment, the only sound being the murmur of the creek and the breeze whispering in the leaves of the trees.

Finding Mr. Sunday

"Will, can I ask you a personal question?"

"You can ask me anything, Mary Nel," he said sincerely.

"Well, you're handsome, you are kind, gentle, considerate, intelligent, successful, all those things a woman would want. You must encounter many eligible ladies every day."

There was a prolonged pause.

"Why haven't you fallen in love?" she asked, gazing steadily into his eyes.

The question startled him. It was as if she had pried open his head and discovered the dilemma in his life that had recently smacked him hard in the face and left his emotions ringing like a huge brass bell.

He waited a while to answer, then sat upright, adjusted the position of his gun belt, and rested his elbows on his knees.

"I don't know, Mary Nel. I just don't know."

He was somewhat embarrassed to say the words.

He could feel heat in his face and a burn in his cheeks. She had hit a nerve. Not just a nerve but the nerve. How could she know?

He looked her in the eye, comfortable with the connection.

"I ... uh ... I feel good about every other part of my life, but I seem to avoid that kind of relationship. Not consciously, I don't think, but the fact is, I have. I don't know why. I wish I knew."

He shook his head slowly back and forth. She could see the question had affected him deeply.

"There is something holding me back. I can't explain it because I don't know what it is. I just have this avoidance, maybe it is fear, of falling in love with someone, then losing them."

"People take that chance every day, Will. When, and if I fall in love, I'm not going to think about that. I'm going to love that person every day we do have together, regardless of what happens down the road."

He saw something in her eyes. Something so strong he almost yelled out, tell me Mary Nel, tell me, please.

The energy of the moment waned as they sat there in silence.

"I truly hope I will fall in love one day."

"Oh, Will," she picked up his hand. "You, of all people, deserve to be in love if anybody does."

"So do you, Mary Nel," he squeezed her hand. "So do you."

She turned her head away and avoided his gaze as her cheeks reddened. He saw her wipe away a tear.

"We should go now," she said as she rose.

They spent much of the rest of the day riding the property.

The return ride was quiet. Not much was said. The silence was not awkward, however. Something had transpired between them, and they embraced it.

That evening, Mary Nel had difficulty falling asleep. What had happened today between herself and Will? She wasn't sure.

In her heart she had wanted Will to say, "No, Mary Nel, please don't marry him." Had he done so, she would have ended it with Peter. But he didn't.

It hurt deeply.

She had no right to expect anything from Will. But she had been looking for even the slightest hint that there could be more to their relationship. Was it there? She wasn't sure.

But she knew Peter was not for her.

CHAPTER SEVENTEEN

Will put the finishing touches on his bow tie, smoothed the front of his shirt, and put on his jacket. He tucked the small Colt Cloverleaf revolver in its own special pocket of his tailored jacket and looked at himself in the mirror. No bulge, and he looked like the prosperous businessman that he was.

Bonnie would be waiting for him at the restaurant as she had on this day for a couple of months. At least once a week the two would meet for drinks and dinner at one of their favorite restaurants.

She never allowed him to escort her, preferring instead to be driven to the restaurant by her driver and picked up by him after the meal. Will assumed that she went on to visit one of Broome's places.

Beyond what she shared during their first meeting, she talked little of herself or how she occupied her time. Will learned to respect her privacy and never asked anything of a personal nature. And never discussed business, his or hers.

She was an unusual woman in many ways. She had no pretense, was outspoken and not shy about expressing herself. Most of the ladies hereabouts would consider her brash, but he liked her straightforward manner. Here, he thought, was a lady who could make her own way. She didn't need anyone else's help.

She had admitted she did whatever she wanted to do. Now he could see that she most likely got whatever she wanted, also.

When he arrived at the restaurant, he was surprised to see she wasn't at her usual table. When the manager spotted him, he came up to Will.

"Good evening, Mr. Sunday. I have a message for you, sir."

With a polite nod, he handed Will an envelope and walked away.

The envelope had a wax seal, the letter F showing in the wax. He opened the envelope and read her perfect cursive writing.

> *Dear Will, I prefer to dine in my room tonight. I have ordered dinner and wine for both of us. It will be served at our usual dining time. I am in Suite 201. Bonnie.*

The note surprised him and sent a warm rush through his body. Now this could be interesting, he thought.

It was a moment before she answered his knock. She was her stunning self, dressed perfectly in a white long-sleeved dress, green lace around the collar and cuffs. The dress was tightly gathered around her slender waist. An emerald hung on a gold chain around her neck.

"Hello, Will," she said.

The room was softly lit, the gas lights were turned low, and the curtains were closed. She stepped close to him as he shut the door, put her hands on his shoulders, leaned close to him, and kissed him softly on the cheek. She had never done that before.

"I have one of our favorite bottles of Scotch and two excellent French wines. I hope you don't mind dining in my room tonight. I'm having a rare and leisurely evening off tonight," she said.

"Of course not," he said. "I'm surprised to see you relaxing. I was beginning to think you never did."

"Very seldom. I'm not the relaxing kind. I've tried the leisurely things like reading, games, even sewing, believe it or not. I'm bored within minutes. None of that is for me. It's just the way I am."

He really didn't know this lady at all, he thought. To get to know another person, you had to share many things. At least get beyond surface matters. They had done little of that. So why was he attracted to this lady who was so different from all the others he had met?

"Dinner should be here soon. We have time for a drink before it comes," she said as she turned to the table and began to pour two drinks into cut crystal glasses.

She moved to the sitting area of the suite, choosing to sit on the large, upholstered camelback sofa. The piece of furniture easily sat three of four people, but Will chose to sit in a stuffed companion chair.

"No. You must come here and sit with me," she said as she patted a place beside her. "You aren't afraid of me, are you?"

"No, I was just being polite," he said.

"I think we can dispense with formalities tonight, Will," she said looking him in the eye. "We've had enough evenings of that."

She placed her drink on the table in front of them, then took his, doing the same.

She reached for him and slowly pulled his head down to her level. He wasn't prepared for that, but as soon as he realized what was happening, something else took over.

He felt the heat of her body as her scent enveloped him. Her lips were full, soft, and moist. This was new to him, but he did not hesitate to return the kiss, slowly and gently enjoying the sensation.

He was immediately transported to a heady place where the world was just her. Lost in her fragrance, her taste, and even the warm touch of her hand on his neck.

She gently broke the kiss and sat back, looking at him teasingly, herself moved by the intimacy.

"If that was improper, sir, I make no apology," she said, her green eyes sparkling in the light.

"And you needn't," he heard himself say from some place far away.

He leaned in slowly and kissed her again, pressing softly but firmer this time to take in all she had to offer. She seemed hungry for the contact, and he could feel an urgency in her.

He felt like he was floating, his closed eyes enhancing the sensations, the taste of her lips and the feel of her body next to him.

A voice, then a knock on the door shattered the moment.

"Room service."

He pulled away from her slowly and reluctantly. Nourishment was not on his mind now.

"Don't lose that thought," she said with a look that made him want to tell the waiter to go away.

The waiter brought the food in and arranged it on a small table by the window, lighting two candles.

"Miss Farrell, the chef asked me to tell you that he took the liberty of adding your favorite apricot cake to your meals. He hopes you don't mind," said the gentleman.

"Frank, you tell Morris I will be forever in his debt," she said, laughing.

"Yes, ma'am. You two have a wonderful meal and enjoy the evening," he said as he turned to leave.

"Frank," said Will as he stepped closer to the waiter and handed him a three-dollar gold piece as he whispered. "Thank you. We'll put the tray in the hallway."

"Yes, sir," said Frank with a little bow as he discreetly pocketed the coin.

They sat down to the meal, eating slowly, enjoying local shrimp bisque, fresh oysters in butter sauce, field salad, filet mignon with mushroom sauce, wild rice, and fresh rolls with plum jelly and an excellent French Bordeaux.

They capped the meal with the delicate apricot cake topped with fresh whipped cream and a cup of black coffee.

They sat back, satiated.

"I've got an idea," said Bonnie as she took the last sip of her coffee. "Let's take a stroll down the avenue. It's a beautiful night, and I need to get some fresh air."

"Let's do that," Will said.

Whatever was to come, he thought, needn't be rushed.

They put on their coats and went down to the lobby and out through the massive front doors.

The evening was cool but pleasant as they strolled down the boardwalk. Several carriages passed them by, but there were only a few other couples enjoying the outside air. A policeman stood on the corner, keeping an eye on things.

"It is not as crowded as usual," said Bonnie. "There must be a play in the theater down the block."

"Do you enjoy the theater?" Will asked.

"I do occasionally. But I seldom take time out for it. We might like to take in a play soon. Would you like to do that?" she said.

He was surprised at the offer, but then this entire evening seemed to be full of surprises.

"Why, dear lady, I'd be delighted. You just tell me when we might have another night like this," he said.

They heard a commotion a ways down the block. A well-dressed gentleman seemed to be having a disagreement with a lady. He was loud and obnoxious, using foul language. The young lady was having none of it, giving it back as it was given to her.

As they got closer they could see the gentleman was obviously intoxicated and unsteady on his feet as he ranted. The event quickly got the attention of the policeman, who rushed toward the couple just as the gentleman struck out at the young lady.

It was a glancing blow, and the young lady responded by striking the man with her folded umbrella, knocking him off balance and landing him on the sidewalk.

They were close enough that Will quickly turned Bonnie around and headed back the way they had come to avoid the fracas. But not before Will realized he knew the man now struggling to stand.

It was Peter Forester. And upon closer examination, he saw the young lady was a professional, or at least she dressed the part. Will turned before he could be recognized.

"I've seen that man before," said Bonnie.

"Do you know him?" asked Will with some alarm.

"No, but I have seen him about. He seems always be in the company of ... that type of lady ... never the same one. He dines in fine places, I can tell you that.

"But he seems to be unable to hold his whiskey since most of the time I see him he is intoxicated."

Will then recalled that Peter's apartment was within a few blocks of where they were standing.

"Well, then, let's cross the street and head away from this unpleasantness," he said.

They did so and enjoyed an otherwise pleasant walk before returning to the hotel.

They returned to the hotel room, refreshed and renewed by the walk.

"I think I'd like some more wine. Would you mind opening that other bottle of Bordeaux?" she asked.

He opened the wine as she readied two fresh wine goblets. When the wine was poured, she held up her glass in a toast.

"To intrigue," she said as she clinked her glass with his.

She returned to the sofa, leading him by the hand. He needed little encouragement to follow.

"Where were we?" she said as she pulled him in close.

"Just about here," he said as he leaned forward and kissed her softly.

He was immediately taken away by all that he sensed. There was no hesitation, no deliberation, yet no hurried fumbling, either.

Finding Mr. Sunday

He felt her body press into his, broke the kiss only to place his lips softly on her neck, then her neckline.

He was guided by pure instinct with no small amount of passion, something that had eluded him up until now.

She placed her hands on the back of his head and gently pulled him to her, offering all of herself to him. The heat enveloped the two of them, overtaking all else and urging them on.

After a while, she stood, pulled at him with a gentle but steady urgency, and led him to her bedside. They became lost in each other, blocking out all else, blending as one, long into the night.

A few weeks later, Will sat with several of his friends. They were enjoying an evening out at his favorite club. It was crowded with well-dressed men engaged in lively conversations and laughter.

"You know, every club and restaurant I go into these days is crowded," said Ralston Chambers, a private investor by trade. "Somebody must be making a whole lot of money. I've a mind to put together a group and build our own restaurant, hotel, and club."

"You're talking big money there, Chambers. Big money. Millions. Especially with some of those palatial establishments I've seen going up around here. Why, the land itself would be in the hundreds of thousands," said George Latham, a real estate developer.

"Well, George, I'm not saying it has to be silk curtains and polished walnut. There are opportunities for good solid operations that don't involve the likes of you," Chambers said, laughing heartily.

"Those places are cash on the barrel head. Beer is cheap when you can buy a glass of beer for a penny and sell it for five cents. If you have a good clean place, a hearty free lunch spread, and a good pour of whiskey, you can make a lot of money."

"I don't think you are far off, Ralston. I have some knowledge of that business, though limited, I'll grant you. But I seldom see a place that's not full of people. Not everybody belongs to a club," said Will.

"Why, you're out and about often. What do you see?" said Morris Preston, an editor of one of the local papers.

"I think Ralston is right," said Will. "Good saloons are the most popular places — free food, cheaper beer and whiskey.

"The more you put into an establishment, the more people you have to attract. A hotel needs travelers, a restaurant needs diners, and a bar needs drinkers. Seems to me you need to narrow down who you want your customers to be if you want to keep your investment at a reasonable level."

He sipped his drink.

The other three men leaned forward. What he was saying had gotten their attention.

"You're saying having a hotel complicates things?" said Chambers.

"It just means a higher investment and a more expensive location, and that's fine if you have the stomach … and investment for it. Me? Just give me a good saloon that serves good food and drinks at a fair price that's in the neighborhood," said Will.

"That makes good sense. Sort of put your toe in the water and see what happens," said Chambers.

"Yep. I've seen those places just as crowded as the finer establishments. And as you say, Ralston, somebody is making money," said Will.

"And we can probably lease the land if we look around enough. Maybe south of Market. A good mix, but plenty of people in the area," said Latham.

"What do you think it will take?" asked Preston.

"Depends on the location, equipment, staff. Many factors," said Chambers. "If you fellows are serious about this, I have friends who have some experience in the business. Let me talk to them."

Will thought of Bonnie. But never would he discuss such a thing as this with her. Never business was their rule. And besides, she was a pleasant escape from business, law, and any other serious endeavor.

Peter and Mary Nel were sitting in the parlor of Kate's house. He had arrived earlier that afternoon, and they had spent the time catching up.

"I've so missed you," he said to her. "And here I am about to leave for

England in a couple of months. I'll have to be without you for another few months."

He was almost pouting.

"Peter, I think it might be a good thing that you are going away for a while. I have much to think about, and this will give me some more time," she said, looking at him.

"I must tell you, Mary Nel. I'm getting impatient. I know I shouldn't, but I can't help it."

He spoke a bit firmly, then caught himself.

His look softened.

"But you are right, this will give you more time," he said with a look of defeat.

"But you must promise me, dear Mary Nel."

The look changed to one of expectation.

"I simply must have an answer when I get back from my trip." His raised his chin firmly, and his face took on the look of a demanding child. "I don't think that is an unreasonable expectation."

She stared at him for a moment, the look on her face one he had not seen before. He was alarmed that he might have gone too far.

He continued, less assertive.

"Even if we must have a long engagement, I must know where I stand," he said.

He took both her hands in his, softening the moment.

"I don't want to lose you, Mary Nel."

"You will know when you return, Peter."

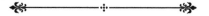

Bonnie and Will descended the wide steps of the hotel and walked into the grand lobby. Bonnie had sent her driver away for the evening, and Will had arranged for a carriage to take them to a restaurant a mile or so away.

"There is a bit of a cold wind tonight. I told the driver we would need a blanket or two even though the carriage is enclosed," said Will.

"That was very thoughtful of you, Will," she said as she walked beside him.

Bonnie was careful to avoid any displays of affection when they were in public. At the right time their passion was unbridled, but she was careful not to confuse that with any other emotion.

Often he would find himself looking at her as she lay beside him, admiring her beauty and marveling at his good fortune that this lady desired him.

On one such occasion, some time ago, she had opened her eyes, and he had smiled down at her.

"You are beautiful," he said to her.

She stared at him a long moment, then reached up and touched his cheek gently.

"You must never fall in love with me, Will ... I'm not the kind of woman you think I am."

She then turned away, leaving him staring at the back of her head.

He was stunned momentarily. The comment just added to the mystique of this lady.

Since that time, Will knew to expect nothing more from the relationship than what it was on the surface.

All he knew was that she was an unusual woman with an unwavering independence who lived life on her own terms. He accepted that and respected her for living to her own standards.

When they arrived at the restaurant, they ordered wine, which Bonnie enjoyed without hesitation. She paid no attention to the occasional looks of surprise and whispers from other diners, who were not accustomed to seeing a lady drink in public.

"Excellent," he said as he set his wine glass down after an appreciative sip.

"I agree. We'll have to remember this one," she said.

He was about to say something and felt as if he was the object of someone's attention. He turned to his right and looked squarely into the red face of Peter Forester, who was seated a few tables away.

Will moved his gaze to the young lady with Peter, who glanced in Will's direction then turned away dismissively.

Neither Will nor Peter acknowledged the other. In a few minutes, Peter and his companion left the restaurant, much to the dismay of his guest.

Finding Mr. Sunday

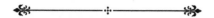

"We have other investors who want to join us in this," said Ralston Chambers. "If we each put in the $30,000 we discussed, we'll have more than $200,000. If we can lease the land, we can build us a nice place for that. Nothing palatial by any means but well upfitted and furnished."

He placed a large envelope on the table.

The group was meeting at the club and having drinks and dinner.

"Here is a rundown of how we would invest the capital."

Ralston discussed the other investors, and the other three men were satisfied as to their character and financial standings.

"I have been directed to three locations just off Market. We're getting together some dates to look at the sites."

"You've put a lot of work into this, Ralston," said Will as he scanned some of the sheets. "I'll go over these in detail tomorrow."

"I had a lot of good help. Winton, one of the investors, knows this business in and out. He's made a lot of money at it. I'll have a list of dates to see the sites delivered to everyone's office in a few days," said Chambers.

Thirty thousand dollars was a lot of money to Will. But he believed the investment would pay off handsomely.

A few weeks later, Will visited Kate and Mary Nel. The harvest was over, and a cold wind reprimanded those who did not dress warmly.

The three of them sat around the kitchen table catching up on all that had happened since the last visit. David was in Sacramento.

Will was always happy when he was with the two of them.

The two ladies sat across from him, both looking fresh and wholesome. Kate was happier than Will had ever seen her.

"Marriage agrees with you, Kate," Will said, smiling.

"It does, Will. David is a fine man, and we get along well. The harvest is over, and it was much more than I thought our young trees would produce. I have few worries, so I'm fortunate to have a good life."

"Mary Nel, I heard you did very well with your latest trade."

"I did. One of my long shots turned out to be a fine horse. I thought he might be, and I sold him for an excellent profit, but I retained stud rights for three years," she said, trying not to sound boastful.

"I have two more that I'm selling and one more that I'm buying. She's a proven mare, and I think she will turn out some beautiful horses."

Will noted that she brightened up at the discussion of her breeding business, but otherwise seemed distant and unengaged. He was close enough to her that he could sense she was bothered by something.

Will had struggled with his knowledge of Peter's activities in San Francisco. He wasn't sure how to tell Mary Nel, but he was certain she needed to know. How to do it and when was another matter altogether.

"Have you heard from Peter since he left for Europe?" asked Will.

"No, but that's not unusual. I seldom hear from him when he's traveling. I'm sure he's busy when he's on these trips, and I don't expect to hear from him."

Mary Nel looked as if she had more to say, and no one spoke for a moment.

"I have shared this with Mother, Will, and I've been waiting to tell you."

She twisted a napkin in front of her and looked down a moment before continuing.

"Peter has said that he wants a decision from me as to whether or not I'm going to marry him when he returns from Europe."

She looked up at Will, watching carefully for his reaction.

Will caught himself before he blurted out his initial thought. His face turned red as he sat there.

He took a deep breath.

"Mary Nel, is this something you want to discuss with me or have you made up your mind?"

"Yes. I very much want to talk with you about it. Mother and I have talked about it, and she, of course, just wants me to be happy."

Mary Nel leaned over and kissed her mother on the cheek.

"I know it's my decision to make. But I really want to hear what you have to say," she said.

Will looked closely at this beautiful girl and could feel her anxiety. She deserved his honest opinion. Besides, he wasn't ready to see this girl he felt so close to make a big mistake.

He had thought of Mary Nel every day and was trying to sort out his feelings for her. He knew that was self-serving, but he didn't want to risk losing her because of his indecision.

"All right, Mary Nel. But you may not like what I have to say, and if I hurt you, I'm sorry," he said gently.

"No, Will. Don't worry about hurting my feelings. I want your opinion," she said firmly.

"Well, he is pressuring you unreasonably," he said. "And if he was the right one, I don't think you would be questioning it. You have a good head on your shoulders. I think your feelings of uncertainty should tell you something. Peter is a changed person. Successful, wealthy by all indications. Those things make a life with him seem attractive.

"But, at risk of hurting you, I have to say I think you are more enchanted with the kind of life Peter represents for you than you are with Peter himself. And it should be the other way around."

He could see her eyes starting to water and fully expected to see a tear any moment.

"You are too good for him, Mary Nel. In every way."

He could feel himself becoming very disturbed, even angry, at the thought of Mary Nel being with Peter. He struggled to calm himself.

"I've seen another Peter, and he isn't the kind of man you think he is, I can assure you."

"What do you mean?" Mary Nel said guardedly.

"I have seen him in the city... in compromising situations."

Will tried to be as gentle as possible.

"He is often in the company of a prostitute. He drinks heavily and loses his temper when he gets intoxicated."

Mary Nel put her hand over her mouth and opened her eyes widely.

"Peter? Drunk? With a prostitute?" she said in disbelief.

"I ... I can't imagine that," she said, her face colored.

"I know. I planned to tell you this, but I wanted it to be the right time and place. I guess this is it. I'm sorry if I seem insensitive. I know this hurts you."

Kate said, "Will, I am not doubting your word, but are you sure?"

"I am, Kate. He has also been seen in these same situations by an acquaintance of mine."

He reached out and took Mary Nel's hand.

"I am so sorry to have been the one to tell you, Mary Nel," he said compassionately. "But you needed to know the truth. Better now than down the road."

The tears came. No one spoke until Mary Nel calmed herself.

"You did the right thing, Will. And I believe you. I do recall now there were times when I thought I smelled whiskey on his breath," she said as she wiped her eyes.

"Whiskey itself is not the problem. You both know I enjoy a drink. But when it's overused and you allow whiskey to dictate your behavior, that is a problem."

He held both of her hands in his. "Mary Nel he has been deceiving you. His behavior is certainly not like a man who has committed himself to one woman. Don't marry this man. Please don't. It would be a big mistake. You can do so much better."

The three of them sat in silence. The only sound was the ticking of the mantle clock.

Mary Nel seemed to recover somewhat.

"Thank you, Will."

She pushed a strand of hair back from her face.

With that, she got up, smoothed the front of her dress, then slid her chair under the table.

"If you two would excuse me," she said.

She left the kitchen and went down the hall to her room.

Will looked at Kate, shaking his head.

"I hurt her, Kate. I hope she will forgive me," said Will.

"Will, you did the right thing," said Kate.

"I think too much of her to see her used by him, and that's what a marriage to him would mean," he said.

He exhaled heavily and put his coffee cup down.

"I've got a new business investment, and my practice is doing extraordinarily well. But I'm going to be here more often, Kate," he said with resolve. "And I'm going to spend more time with her."

"I think she would like that, Will," said Kate.

Finding Mr. Sunday

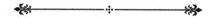

The investors in the saloon decided on a site at a busy corner south of Market Street.

"My only concern is that there are already two saloons within a few hundred yards of the place," said Chambers. "But Winton says that's good because all we have to do is serve a good drink and better food than either of them, and we'll do well."

"I think he's right," said Preston. "The size of the neighborhood can well support another place. There are hundreds of homes around there on the back streets."

"I'm for it," said Will.

Construction on their saloon began almost immediately.

Several weeks later, Will and Bonnie were seated in a restaurant having drinks. He had not seen her in more than a month. Mary Nel had been so much on his mind that he had seldom thought of Bonnie, nor had he heard from her.

He had gone to the valley each week, staying several days each visit and spending much of the time with Mary Nel. She always renewed his spirits. He marveled at the woman he saw emerging from the girl he had always appreciated. He was at the point where he missed her badly while he was in the city.

"I've missed seeing you, Will," said Bonnie.

They were seated in one of their favorite restaurants, enjoying drinks.

"Thanks for saying that," Will said with a smile. "But there are some things back in the valley that need my attention, so I have been trying to get there more often. Things tend to slow down in the office after court day and the week comes to a close, so I've been leaving on Thursdays and some Wednesdays if I can."

"Are things not running smoothly back at the ranch?" she asked.

He was surprised at the question as she never inquired about his businesses.

"Well, we're expanding the herd and adding some new barns. Trying to get ready to start building in the spring."

"I see," she said. "I know you enjoy getting away from the city."

He noticed that she seemed preoccupied and distant, though she was never one to be demonstrative. He had ceased trying to understand or to define their relationship.

It remained free of emotional entanglement, and they both seemed satisfied with that unspoken reality. But he could feel the earlier excitement waning.

He heard her speaking through his reverie.

"I, on the other hand, could not see myself enjoying the countryside. I saw too much of that when I was younger. I like the city life," she said.

"I need both worlds," he said as he sipped his drink.

He watched as she held her drink in front of her, running her fingers down the sides. He saw her face color lightly.

"Will, I'm kind of glad we had this break for a while," she said.

"Oh?" he tilted his head with interest.

He knew she was about to say something that was coming from a place she seldom shared.

She looked up at him, and her green eyes held his gaze.

"Will, you are a good man. You are honest, kind, and considerate. A real gentleman. I've not met many men like you in my lifetime."

"Thank you, Bonnie. But that sounds like a prelude to something else. Am I right?" he asked.

"Did I forget smart?" She gave him a wan smile.

"What we have had has been mostly a pleasant distraction for both of us. I don't believe either of us was looking for more than that."

She paused a moment.

"But I think it's time for it to be over and for both of us to move on with our lives," she said.

"Bonnie ..."

"Please hear me out, Will," she said calmly but firmly. "You deserve more. More than I am capable of giving to you, or any other man for that matter, but especially you. You need to be free to find whatever ... or whoever ... is out there for you. You've done nothing wrong, and being with you was what I needed for a while, for a lot of reasons.

"You know me well enough to understand that I do things my own way.

Finding Mr. Sunday

And that is the way it's going to be. I'm taking some time off, going away for a while. And when we see each other again it will be only as business associates. Just business, Will, that's all."

"Bonnie, I want to talk ..."

"No, Will. Please, don't make a big deal out of this."

He sat there dumbfounded as she stood to leave. He looked to see the manager coming for her.

"Good night, Will. I will let you know when I need your legal services," she said.

He tried to get her attention as she turned to walk away, but she would not look at him again.

He did not see the tears in her eyes when they came.

He had felt it was going to end, but not this abruptly.

In the meantime, a meeting of some significance was taking place in another part of the city.

"Who are these people building near my place on Market?" William Broome asked Jamison, his right-hand man. One of my sources told me it was a saloon."

They were sitting in Broome's office, which was grandly furnished with oak paneling and fine woven carpets.

Broome was dressed in a tailored black suit and a white shirt with a small tie of silk. Even seated one could see he was a tall man bent by time. His gray beard was neatly trimmed, complementing his blue eyes.

If one looked closely, small vertical scars were visible on the upper part of each cheek, then disappeared into his full beard. He was immaculately groomed.

"I don't rightly know yet, boss. It's a group of investors," Jamison said. "I know one of them is Winton. He's had some saloon dealings here in town before. He oughta know better than to try to cut into your business."

"Well, keep close tabs on their progress ... for now," Broome said.

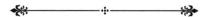

Will sat at his desk going over a writ for an upcoming trial. His mind was not on it. He was thinking about Bonnie's abrupt announcement.

Dick Ward

There was nothing emotional between them, so why did he feel uneasy about the whole thing?

Maybe it was rejection he was feeling ... an odd but somehow not altogether unfamiliar feeling from somewhere deep inside.

Maybe it was just his pride that was hurting.

It's strange, he thought, you can never tell what's going on in another person's head. He saw himself as fairly intuitive, but this caught him off guard.

Bonnie had said he needed to be free to find whatever or whoever he was looking for in life. But then, he had never felt encumbered by their relationship.

Or maybe he had unknowingly.

Because, from somewhere, he felt as if a burden had been lifted.

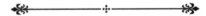

It was early afternoon in the valley. There was a hint of warm weather on the way, but the peaceful calm of winter still lay over the terrain.

Kate heard a carriage approaching. She looked out of the window and was startled to see Peter Forester coming into the yard.

He wasn't supposed to be here, she thought, not yet. There must have been a change of plans. She rushed to tell Mary Nel.

"Mary Nel, Peter is here!" she said with some concern.

"What! He is not supposed to be here for a couple of months yet," she cried in anguish.

She grabbed her mother's hand.

"Momma, please stay close by. I don't know what to expect when I tell him what I have to say."

"I'll be near, sweetheart. Don't worry," she said.

Mary Nel answered the door.

She stood staring at Peter and wondering what she had found attractive about this man she saw in front of her.

"Hello, Peter," she said. "This is certainly a surprise."

"I know, dear. I know," he said. "But I couldn't go without you."

"Without me?" said Mary Nel.

Finding Mr. Sunday

"I'm exhausted," said a winded Peter. "May I come in and sit down?"

"Yes," she said as she closed the door.

"I didn't want to leave you behind. I kept putting off the trip. Besides, business is slowing down, and I really do not need to be buying more inventory now."

Now she knew the real reason for the cancellation of the trip.

He sat heavily in a chair.

"Have you given my proposal due consideration?" he blurted out without any preliminaries.

She was startled at his abruptness.

"Yes, Peter, I have," she said.

She took a deep breath of courage.

"Peter, I am not going to marry you. I know that is not the answer you wanted to hear."

"WHAT! You are not going to marry me! After all this time! After all my proposals!"

The man was nearly apoplectic. The pitch of his voice rose an octave or two, and his face turned scarlet as he struggled for breath.

"Peter, I have never once misled you about the idea of my marrying you. Nor have I ever said I was in love with you. I'm sorry if you believed otherwise," she said calmly and firmly.

"Why? Why won't you marry me? I can give you everything," he said, his eyes wide with disbelief.

"You don't understand, Peter. I don't want everything."

His deep disappointment turned quickly to anger and then to rage. It was as if he had been struck by lightning. The look on his face was pure hatred.

His lips curled in a nasty snarl. He slammed his fist on the table and stood up in a threatening manner.

"You! You refuse me!" he said, his breath coming in spasms.

"Why you are, you are nothing but a dirt farmer's daughter…just a pretty face. Nothing more!"

He stepped toward her, and she sprang back out of his reach.

"How dare you refuse me! I can have a pretty face any time I want. To hell with you. I don't need you!"

"I have heard about your pretty faces," she yelled back at him, no longer backing away.

He raised his eyebrows and locked his jaws, seeming ready to explode physically.

"Now get out of my home. I never want to see you again. Ever!" she yelled.

He stood there boiling and furious.

"Sunday! Will Sunday. So that's it. He's been spreading lies, hasn't he!"

"Get out of here!" she yelled. "Now."

She pointed to the door.

He looked as if he might strike her.

Ish and Kate stepped into the parlor. Ish had a scattergun in his hand. He stepped up and pulled Mary Nel close to him, then leveled the gun on Peter.

There was an audible click as he cocked the hammer.

"You heard her," he said.

"Get out! Don't you ever come back here!" Kate screamed.

"I'll get him for this. I'll ruin him. You haven't heard the last from me!" Peter yelled.

He turned abruptly and kicked a small table on his way to the door, sending it tumbling across the floor.

Ish followed Peter to the door and watched him jerk it open and slam it as he left. He watched as Peter mounted the carriage and slashed the horse with his whip.

Mary Nel broke down crying, and Kate took her into her arms.

"It's over, sweetheart. Now you see the kind of man he is."

She held her sobbing daughter tightly in her arms and kissed her wet cheeks.

The next day Will received a long message and left immediately for the valley. He was seething at the thought of Peter's behavior.

"Where is she?" he said quickly when he arrived at the farm.

"She and Hank went over to David's place. I expect her in an hour or so," said Kate.

"How is she?" he asked, deep concern on his face.

"She was terribly upset at first. She has never been treated that way. I think she'll feel better now that you're here. I'll let her tell you the full story. I just hope going over it won't upset her again."

Finding Mr. Sunday

"I won't press her, Kate. I'll just let her tell me what she wants to," he said.

"One thing you should know, Will. Peter figured you had told her about his behavior, and he said he would get you. Be careful, Will, please," she pleaded.

"Thanks, Kate. I will. And don't you worry."

It wasn't long before Mary Nel and Hank came into the yard. Will stepped out on the porch, and she ran toward him.

"Will, Will, I'm so glad you're here," she said as she hugged him tightly, and he did the same.

They went into the parlor and sat down.

"Will, Peter was here," blurted Mary Nel.

"I thought he was in Europe," said Will.

"He didn't go. He said he could not go and leave me," she said.

"Did you tell him your decision?" Will asked.

"I did."

She teared up.

"Oh, Will. You should have seen him. He went mad. He said terrible things to me. Things I never imagined anyone would say to me."

They were sitting on the sofa. He reached for her hand.

"He was more than furious. He told me I was nothing more than a pretty face. He said he could have pretty faces anytime," she said, wiping her tears.

"I was angry. I told him I knew about his pretty faces. He then blamed you and said he would get you."

She wiped her face with a handkerchief.

"It's all right. It's all right. I'm here now. You don't have to worry," he said, consoling her.

"But he could hurt you," she said, sniffing.

"No, no, he won't. Don't worry about me, Mary Nel. I can take care of myself," he said.

He said nothing, allowing her to calm herself.

"I would die if anything happened to you because of me," she said.

"Nothing is going to happen to me," he said as he squeezed her hand. "The important thing is that it's all over now. I know you, Mary Nel. I know how strong you are. And I know you are not going to let this bother you any longer. It's done. I'm going to make sure he doesn't see you again. I'm going to take some time off and be close by for a couple of weeks."

She seemed to feel better as he talked.

Will looked at this lovely woman and found it hard to believe anyone could treat her as Peter had. He had seen her mettle, and he had seen her gentleness. He knew that if the Lord created special people just to make the world a better place, she was one of them.

Over the years he had felt nothing but admiration for her and an undying appreciation for the privilege of being her friend. And now, he knew his feelings were well beyond appreciation. He would do anything for her.

Anger welled up in him like a blow on the head. He wanted to go after Peter. To beat him within an inch of his life. To make him hurt.

He closed his eyes and took a deep breath until the storm passed.

You are better than that, Will, he told himself. He was learning to control his anger and felt better for it.

He turned to Mary Nel, pulled her to him, and kissed her lightly on the cheek.

"Everything is going to be all right, Mary Nel."

She smiled at him and put her head on his shoulder.

There was something very right about that.

Will spent time going over his ranch operations with Hank during his stay at Kate's house. The cattle-breeding operation was beginning to show signs of success.

The calves being produced were of excellent quality, far superior to any that were on the market. The few young bulls that he had sold gained the attention of other cattlemen, prompting frequent visits by curious breeders.

Mary Nel built new buildings to support her growing business, using profits she had earned buying and selling horses. She sold a half dozen of her colts and was fast building a reputation as an excellent breeder of racing stock.

On the afternoon of the day he was preparing to return to the city, a carriage could be heard approaching Kate's house. Will went to check on the visitor and was startled.

"It's Peter Forester," said Will with concern in his voice.

"Oh, no, Will," said an alarmed Mary Nel. "I don't want to see him."

"I'll handle this. Ish, will you see the ladies to the back of the house?" Will said.

Will opened the door to see Peter dismounting from the carriage. He saw immediately that he was unsteady on his feet.

"You might as well climb back up there, Forester," said Will. "Nobody here wants to see you. And that includes me."

He could see that Peter was red in the face and obviously drunk.

"Get out of my way, you bastard," Forester said, slurring his words. "I'm not here to see you. Where is Mary Nel?"

"That's none of your concern," Will said. "I'm telling you to get back in the carriage and leave. And do not come back. Do you hear me?"

Forester did not respond immediately. He stood maybe ten yards away, swaying visibly.

All of a sudden he produced a pistol and pointed it in the general direction of Will.

Will was unarmed.

"You ... you ... you caused this to happen ...You told lies," said Forester as he continued to sway.

"Peter, you better come to your senses. You don't want to do this. Put away the pistol, and we'll talk," said Will.

Forester walked a few yards closer, the pistol still pointed at Will.

Will could see the man was out of control. Not only drunk but furious. He knew an angry, armed drunk was one of the most dangerous people to confront.

Will held his arms up in the air. He wore no coat, just a vest over a buttoned shirt.

"I have no weapon, Peter," said Will. "I am not going to harm you. Just put the gun down."

Inside the house, Mary Nel had become understandably distraught.

"I need to go out there and talk to him," she said in tears.

"No. No, you can't Mary Nel," said Kate as she went over and put her arms around her daughter both to comfort and restrain her.

Kate prodded Mary Nel to the far back bedroom of the house.

"Please, stay back here, ladies," Ish said firmly.

He then went to the front door to watch the situation in the yard from a closer vantage point.

BAM! Forester fired the pistol, and the bullet slammed into a porch column near Will, burying itself in the thick redwood.

"I don't care if you are not armed, " said Forester, as he lurched closer.

Forester leveled the pistol and fired once more.

This time the bullet came within inches of Will's head, sending splinters in the air. Will ducked down behind the porch rails, which offered little protection.

Forester moved faster now, still unsteady, but able to aim the pistol point blank at Will.

BOOM!

Forester's entire body jerked backward, and he collapsed within a few yards of the porch, blood pouring from his body.

Will turned to his left and saw Ish standing in the doorway holding a smoking scattergun.

"Will, you all right?" said Ish.

"Yes," said a shaken Will.

"I'm sorry I had to do that. I was 'fraid if I had just wounded him, he'd still be able to get another shot off," said a solemn Ish.

"You did the right thing, Ish," Will said as he touched him on the shoulder.

"I've got to see to Mary Nel," said Will as he hurried into the house.

He found a crying and trembling Mary Nel and encircled her with his arms.

"It's over ... It's all over now," he said as hugged her and then Kate.

"Will! Oh, Will! I heard shots. I knew you didn't have your pistol," she stammered.

"You don't have to worry anymore," he said.

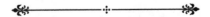

The saloon was completed several months later. While not grand, it was well-appointed with a long bar seating more than twenty-five people, a mirrored bar back stocked full of whiskey and spirits and barrel after barrel of local beer. There were plenty of tables and chairs for additional seating and a wall of tables usually laden with good food to lure the customers.

Drinks and beer were fairly priced, and business was brisk from day one. The saloon quickly became a favorite of the neighborhood crowds, drawing night factory workers early in the morning and day workers from the early evening until closing time shortly after midnight.

Security wasn't ignored as several men were on duty at all times, sometimes doubling as waiters and bar keeps. Those customers who had too much to drink were politely asked to leave, and those who felt the need to argue were quickly removed from the premises.

Will and the investors knew it would take time to get their investment back, but they were delighted with the early success of the business.

Will left most of the running of the business to Winton and his fellow investors. He was careful, however, to review the books regularly and monitor cash flow and expenses. The saloon, as he had expected, provided a steady and reliable flow for the coffers.

The thriving law practice and saloon kept him busy when he was in the city. He still enjoyed his own caseload, especially the court hearings and trials.

"You're as good as I thought you would be," said Roger Barbour as they were sharing a meal one day. "I have my fellows bring all their work to me when I hear we are going up against you and your firm." He laughed.

"Well, your fellows put some lumps on our heads early on. But that's all right. It only made us better lawyers," said Will, smiling.

Barbour and his wife were often guests at either David's or Kate's ranch. Will was often able to join them. Roger now had an interest in ranching and often rode with Will as he surveyed his holdings.

"I see Mary Nel seems to have weathered that bad incident with Forester, and I understand her breeding business is doing well," said Roger.

"Yes, that's been almost a year now. It was a terrible thing for everyone, but there seem to be no lasting scars. She is thriving. I spend quite a bit of time with her when I'm in the valley."

"Now there's a catch for some lucky man," said Roger.

He then caught himself.

"I'm sorry, Will, I meant no disrespect," he said apologetically.

"That is all right, Roger," said Will with a chuckle. "That is simply the truth of the matter. I think Mary Nel is enjoying the discovery of Mary Nel these days. She doesn't want to rush into anything just yet. But she is very busy. She goes to the harness races regularly, and, of course, horse shows and sales. She attends all the social events that are a part of that and enjoys being with others.

"She certainly is not being reclusive. She is quite happy, from all I can tell. And I think I know her better than anyone, except Kate.

"This breeding business has been her salvation. She is getting a solid reputation with that community. Not only is she good at it, she has developed a passion for it. On top of that, she is, after all, Mary Nel. Who in the world could not like her?

"You may have heard that she, along with Kate, David, and Hank, are planning a buying trip into Mexico in a couple of weeks. I'm unable to go, but Hank is looking at stock for me."

"I'd like to know how that turns out," Roger said. "I may ask you to help me get something started in the near future. I've already got my eye on some property not far from David's place."

"It would be good to have you in the valley, Roger," said Will.

"We'll see how it goes," said Roger.

That night Will lay in bed wide awake. Roger's comments about Mary Nel had been echoing in his head all day. Indeed, he thought, Mary Nel would be quite a catch for someone.

But why had Roger's words made such an impression on him? They were like a revelation to him. And why would that be? Was it because he had taken Mary Nel for granted all this time, ignoring the truth about how he felt about her? Or had he thrown up that emotional wall that plagued him, avoiding the possibility of something more than the great affection he had for her?

It's time you open yourself up, he thought. Go to this woman. She is the one.

And cherish each precious day you have with her.

Finding Mr. Sunday

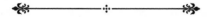

He always looked forward to going home to the valley, but he could not get there fast enough this trip.

When he arrived, Kate was meeting with some of her crew. She excused herself when she saw him come in the door and gave him a warm hug.

"It's good to see you, Will. I'll be free in a little while, and we can visit," she said.

"Good to see you, Kate. Take your time though," he said. "Is Mary Nel here?"

"Yes, she is in the small barn," said Kate.

He walked the short distance and saw Mary Nel at the far end of the barn in front of one of the stalls, her back to him. She did not turn at the sound of his footsteps. A fine-looking mare nickered a welcome as he got closer.

"She's a beauty," he said.

Mary Nel turned to him, a surprised look on her face.

"Will!" she said, a big smile on her face. "I thought you were Hank. He went to get a bridle for me."

As she turned toward him, a long tress of hair tied by a ribbon at the back of her head flipped around and rested on her shoulders. She looked different to him, or maybe he was looking at her in a different way.

He stepped toward her, opening his arms to receive his usual hug. She hugged him tightly. He felt her warmth, put his cheek on top of her head, taking in her freshness.

He then felt something strange and good. It felt right, her strong clasp and her body next to his.

After a moment, he released his hold on her, stepping back so he could look into her eyes. Something was different.

This girl was so confident, glowing with life, eager to find what was around the next corner.

No, he corrected himself, this was no girl. She was a woman in every sense of the word, beautiful, alluring, and alive with an unmistakable sensuality he had not acknowledged before.

"Will? Are you all right? You seemed so far away for a moment."

"Uh … no, not at all … never been closer," he said awkwardly.

Just then they heard Hank come into the barn, a bridle in his hand.

"Hey, boss," he said cheerily. "Good to see you."

The man stuck out his calloused hand and accepted Will's with a firm grip and spirited pump.

"Did you see that fine little lady here?" asked Hank.

In his nearly dazed state, Will thought for a second Hank was referring to Mary Nel.

Hank stepped to the stall, and the mare nuzzled the man's hat, knocking it askew.

"I did. She's a fine one. Looks like she likes you, too," Will said.

"Well, now, I bet a dollar it's that grain bucket I carry that she finds so charming."

"Now, Hank. I might just take you up on that bet," said a laughing Mary Nel.

"You goin' over to your place today? If you are I'd like to ride with you," said Hank.

"In a couple of hours, we'll do that," said Will.

"I'll be ready," said Hank.

He walked out of the barn to attend to other matters.

"You want to sit and visit a while?" said Will to Mary Nel.

"I'd like that," she said with a smile.

Without thinking about it she grabbed Will by the hand, and they headed to the house.

"I see you found her," Kate said as the two entered.

"Will, would you excuse me for a moment?" asked Mary Nel.

"She seems in great spirits," said Will.

"She is, but she is in even better spirits when you come home," said Kate.

"Coming here keeps me going, Kate," he said. "And she is no small part of it."

Mary Nel returned, having freshened up and changed into a pretty dress.

They sat down at the table, with Mary Nel beside Will.

"How is San Francisco, Will?" Mary Nel said.

"About the same. The saloon is booming. I'm as busy as I ever have been at the firm. But, you know, the city can be pretty lonely sometimes, despite all the people."

"Well, you are in for a treat. If we buy horses in Mexico, Hank and I will be in the city for a couple of days picking them up from the wharf. I'm hoping I will be entertained by a handsome friend while I'm there," she said, laughing and nudging his shoulder.

"You can count on it," Will said.

The three of them visited until it was time for Will to head to his ranch. But something different was in the air. And Kate could sense it, too.

CHAPTER EIGHTEEN

After returning to the city, Will spent the better part of the first day sorting out what needed to be done. A runner came into the office with a note from Chambers, who said he needed to see Will right away.

When he arrived at Chambers' office, he and two other men were in the conference room waiting.

"Glad you're here. Thought you might want to be in on this," said Chambers. "This is Lewis Smith. He's one of our guards at the saloon."

He pointed to Smith, and Will shook the man's hand.

"This other fellow, who has yet to tell us his name, along with an accomplice, was caught breaking into the saloon early this morning before daylight," Chambers said.

"His accomplice was shot by Smith and is being taken care of, then he is being turned in to the police. The other guy did manage to wound Forman, but not badly. He, too, is being treated.

"They had a can of coal oil. Looks like they were about to set fire to the place. I thought you would like to be here and talk to this fellow before we take him to the police."

"Thank you, Ralston," said Will.

Will looked closely at the fellow. He was young, maybe eighteen or so. He was rough looking, probably took the job for a few dollars from whoever was behind this. The young man sat staring at the table top, refusing to look at anyone.

Will stared at the young man.

"I happen to be a lawyer. Every day I see young people like you going to prison for doing dumb things. But the judges don't care if you are young with poor judgment ... or if you have been misled by someone else. You still go to jail."

The fellow still refused to look up.

"You are looking at breaking and entering, possibly attempted arson and maybe accessory to attempted murder. You could go to jail for a long time. They won't put you in jail with just the nice guys. You'll be in there with murderers, thieves, people who would strangle their mothers for a dollar."

"Judges don't like people who do harm to businesses, especially," said Chambers. "Crime on business is not good for the growth of the city."

"What's your first name?" asked Will.

The man ignored the question.

"I can make this easy on you or very hard. But if you don't talk to me, I have no choice but to turn you over to the police," said Will.

He looked up for the first time. "Clem."

"All right, Clem," said Will. "I know my partners want you in jail, but if you cooperate with me, I may be able to persuade them to go easy on you. What do you think, Ralston?"

"I'd just as soon see him off the street for a few years," he said to Will, a silent exchange taking place between them.

"I kind of agree with you. Maybe he would learn a big lesson there," said Will.

"Let me remind you of something, Clem. We have your partner. He's going to the police. But we're the only ones who know about you except your partner.

"Why, we could let you go and inform the authorities you just ran out the door when we were not paying attention."

The young man looked at Will with a glimmer of hope in his eyes.

"You tell us who hired you and all you know about him, and that might just happen," said Will.

"Looks like you don't have too much to lose by cooperating, son," said Chambers.

There was a long pause. The young man sat there nervously playing with his fingers on the table top.

"It's your call," said Will

"Pernell … his first name is Shot. We do stuff for him from time to time. At the Cat's Eye," said Clem.

"You mean the saloon down the street?" said Will.

Clem nodded his head.

"Do you know who his boss is? Who he works for?" asked Will.

"I ain't sure. But a guy named Jamison hangs around the Cat's Eye all the time, and they talk. He says 'sir' to him, so he's somebody," said Clem.

"Do you think Jamison owns the Cat's Eye?" said Will.

"He might," said Clem. "I don't rightly know."

"Okay, Clem," said Will. "Where are you from?"

"Up near the Oregon line," said Clem.

"Ralston, let's step outside a minute," said Will.

"Mr. Smith, would you keep an eye on Clem here?" asked Will.

"Yes, sir," said Smith.

In the hallway, Will and Ralston spoke quietly.

"You think we need this kid anymore?" asked Will.

"No, I think he told us all he knows."

"I do, too. What do you say we cut him loose?" said Will.

"Fine with me. Scare the hell out him with a warning, though," said Chambers.

They went back in the room.

"Okay, Clem. We are going to let you go. Now here is the situation. If we even see you again, you will be in trouble. And you need to get of town because someone else may be looking for you soon. You hear me?" said Will.

"Yes, sir," said Clem, jumping up.

Will opened the door for him, and the young man almost bolted down the hallway.

"Wait," called out Will.

He then reached into his pocket and pulled out some bills.

"Here. Here's $200 dollars. Do what I said and leave town," said Will.

The young man's face became a huge smile as he took the money.

"Yes, sir."

And he turned and ran out of the building.

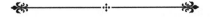

"You ever hear of a guy named Jamison?" said Will.

He was in his office talking to Liam Whit, a private investigator who often did work for his firm.

"Jamison. Jamison," said Whit as he looked afar and rubbed his chin. "I know a couple, at least."

Finding Mr. Sunday

"This fellow is connected to the saloon, restaurant, and club business," said Will.

"Yeah. Yeah, I do now that you say that," said Whit. "Works for some big guy here in town who owns a lot of saloons and clubs. Runs his security. He's a tough guy. Had a few run-ins with the law, but nobody's been able to get anything on him yet."

Whit was a former San Francisco policeman who kept in contact with some of his friends still working at the department.

"Shootings!" said Whit out of the blue as his memory jolted him. "Shootings."

"Yeah, I remember now. He's been involved in a few shootings here in town. Always able to prove the other guy drew on him. But I think most of his witnesses were his buddies.

"He's got a reputation as being handy with a pistol. I know of at least two men he's killed. No telling how many he has wounded. Always got off, like I said."

"Know where I can find him?" asked Will.

"Well, I can give you an idea, but, Mr. Sunday, he's not somebody you ought to be messing around with, I can tell you that," said Whit.

"It's all right, Liam. I just want to ask him a few questions," said Will.

"Is it something I can do for you?" asked Whit.

"No, I need to handle this. I want to meet him face to face," said Will.

"I have to warn you. You won't likely find him alone. Seems to have somebody hanging with him most of the time." said Whit.

"Don't worry. I'm not looking for trouble. Just want to talk with him," said Will.

"Here. Let me write some things down for you," said Whit.

He scribbled on a sheet of paper for a moment.

"Here's a list of places he goes to right often," said Whit. "I don't know when he goes where, but these are some of places where he hangs out."

The names looked familiar to Will. They were all Broome-owned establishments.

"Thanks, Liam," said Will. "I appreciate your help."

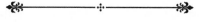

"That new place is really cutting into our business down near South Market, Mr. Broome," said Jamison.

Jamison and Broome were having one of their sitdowns in Broome's office.

"Yeah, I've noticed. I want you to get our guys on that. Find out all you can about who all those investors are. Do it carefully, though. I don't want anyone to know we're looking into the place," said Broome.

"I don't like people opening places near mine. Five years ago that wouldn't have happened. Things are different now. We may have to do something about that. See if you can get an idea of how much business they're doing. Maybe put one of our boys behind the bar somehow."

Jamison smiled to himself.

"I'm on it, boss."

Will started working the list, going one by one. He didn't know what Jamison looked like so he asked the bartenders. Most of them just shook their heads "no" and turned away.

On the third night he went into the Cat's Eye on a hunch. He walked up to the bar and ordered a Scotch.

"Thanks," he said as he was served the drink.

He decided to try something new.

He tipped the bartender with a $5 gold piece.

"Well, thank you, sir," the bartender said with a grateful smile.

"Sure," said Will. "By the way, is Jamison here tonight?"

The bartender's expression changed immediately.

"Don't worry. I do work for Mr. Broome," said Will. "But I haven't met Jamison yet, so I don't know what he looks like."

"Oh," the bartender said, relaxing a bit. "That's him in the corner table up front. He's the one in the brown suit."

Will could see two other men sitting at the table. All three had drinks in front of them. Apparently Jamison said something funny, as the other two started laughing.

Jamison looked up as he saw Will approaching.

"Mr. Jamison," said Will. "Sorry to interrupt you, but I was wondering if I might have a private word with you."

Jamison's expression turned sour, and he inhaled as though irritated at the interruption.

"Who are you and what do you want?" said an annoyed Jamison.

"My name is Will Sunday, and I want to talk to you about what I think is a little misunderstanding."

Will watched the expression change on Jamison's face. The annoyance turned to concern, then what could only be described as cockiness.

"What misunderstanding?"

"Wouldn't it be best if we talked alone?" asked Will.

Jamison looked the big man up and down. He could not tell whether or not Will was armed.

Jamison looked at the other two guys and gave them a curt nod. Both got up but moved just a few tables away, facing Jamison's table.

"Have a seat, Mr. Will Sunday," said Jamison, his attitude patronizing now.

Will sat down with his back to the two other men. He took a sip of his drink.

"You have a friend named Shot Pernell. I believe he may work for you," said Will.

Jamison looked off in the distance, then back at Will.

"Maybe."

He was being cagey.

"What if he does?"

"Well, we have reason to believe Mr. Pernell hired two fellows to burn down that new saloon not too far from here, the one just off Market."

Why in the hell had he done that, thought Jamison. I told him to hold off for now. Broome will kill me. What a mess up. I'll shoot that bastard.

Calm down, he said to himself.

Jamison pulled a cigar from his vest pocket, clipped off the tip, and rolled the cigar in his mouth to wet the wrapper leaf. He took his time lighting the cigar, glancing occasionally at Will.

He blew a big cloud of smoke from the cigar, looked at Will, and smiled.

"That's quite an accusation, Mr. Sunday. What makes you think I would want Pernell to do that if, in fact, he did work for me?"

"I'm really not sure, Mr. Jamison. That's what I'm here to find out."

Will took another sip of his drink and set the glass down, rolling it in his fingertips. He leaned in close to Jamison, holding him in a stare.

"It just might be that's the way you do business, Jamison. But I don't think Mr. Broome would approve, or maybe I'm wrong. You being his strong arm and all, he might have just told you to give us a hard time.

"If that is the case, I'm surprised. He has plenty of other places. That little old establishment shouldn't be a threat to him."

At the mentioned of Broome's name, Jamison seemed to jump into an upright position, and the cockiness disappeared quickly.

"What do you know about Broome?" came a terse question from Jamison.

"Oh, I know a little about him. Doesn't like meeting with people. Kind of lets everybody else do his work. People like you. I know because I do a little work for him, but he doesn't know it."

"You do what?" demanded Jamison.

"Oh, a little legal work here and there," said Will.

"Then you better be damned careful what you accuse me of," said Jamison.

An angry look painted Jamison's face. He leaned forward as if to threaten Will with his body.

"You look here, you don't have proof of anything. I don't know what you do for Mr. Broome, but I'm telling you to drop this. Now. It could be pretty dangerous if you go messing where you have no business," said Jamison.

"When people try to burn down my investment, it becomes my business," said Will.

"So, you got a piece of that place, huh?" said Jamison.

Jamison stood up, pushed his chair back, and came around to Will's side of the table.

He leaned over, his face within inches of Will's. Will could smell the cigar and whiskey on his breath.

"You listen here you, son of a bitch," Jamison growled with clenched fists. "You don't know what you are getting into, coming around here trying to push me around."

Will turned around enough to look at the two men. They were standing now and watching everything.

"I see, Mr. Jamison," he said softly as he stood slowly and turned to Jamison, who had straightened up.

Finding Mr. Sunday

Like a rattler striking, Will's right hand struck out and grabbed Jamison by the throat. His huge hand nearly encircled the smaller man's neck, and his crushing grip shut down Jamison's breathing.

At the same time he whirled to his left facing the two men who had leapt toward Jamison's table, putting Jamison between him and the other men.

The .41-caliber Colt Cloverleaf was in Will's left hand, leveled at the two men.

"Stop right there, boys," said Will, cocking the pistol.

Jamison, instead of hitting at Will who was holding him at arm's length, was trying with all of his might to pull Will's hand from around his neck. The man was struggling to get his breath and was already turning dark red in the face.

"Don't move an inch, or I'll shoot you both," Will said to Jamison's boys.

The two men looked at Will with their mouths open. They knew by the look on Will's face that there was no question he would shoot them.

"Go back to your chairs," said Will. "Sit down!"

The men backed up as told but didn't sit.

Will fired a shot that slammed into the floor between the two men, about an inch away from their feet.

"Sit!" he yelled.

Their butts slammed into the chairs.

Will turned his attention to Jamison. He shoved him backwards with great force toward the table where the two other men sat. Jamison stumbled on a chair, collapsing it, then landed hard on the wood floor. Will was over him almost before he landed, pulling Jamison's Smith & Wesson from its holster.

He held both pistols on the three men.

"Jamison," he said. "Don't ever threaten me again. And if anything, the least little thing, happens to my business, I'm coming to look for you. Not your boys, you, and we'll settle this thing."

Jamison rolled into a half sitting position, holding his throat and wheezing loudly.

All this happened in a matter of seconds. The noise in the saloon had stopped, and everyone was staring at the commotion. Will scanned the crowd, looked over at the bartender. Nobody had a weapon visible.

He kept his eye on Jamison and his men as he backed up to the wall and worked his way out the door, throwing Jamison's pistol across the street.

Only when he stepped outside did he feel any effects from the encounter, a slight quickening of breath. He went back to his house. He wondered if he had done the right thing.

It could be that Broome knew nothing about what Jamison was up to. Could be he was giving the orders. He would just have to see how things played out.

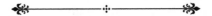

A couple of weeks later, Mary Nel and Hank arrived in the late afternoon at Will's home in the city.

They had spent most of the day inspecting the horses that Mary Nel, David, and Hank had purchased in Mexico and had shipped by boat to San Francisco.

"Hello, hello," said a delighted Will. He shook Hank's hand and gave Mary Nel a hug. She returned it with a hearty squeeze, then reached up and kissed Will on the cheek.

"Got some mighty good horse flesh for you, boss. Spent a bunch of your money on 'em, too," Hank said, laughing.

"Well, Hank. You are yet to disappoint me with any of your purchases — mule, cow, or horse," said Will.

"Nope," Hank said. "You'll like these for sure."

"And how about you, Mary Nel. Did you find anything?" he asked.

"Oh, yes!" she said enthusiastically. David introduced me to a breeder who had the perfect stallion I'd been looking for. My girls are going to love him." She giggled.

"The breeder drove a hard bargain, but he hadn't been up against me. I got the beauty at a very reasonable price."

"It had to be your charm, no doubt," Will said with a laugh.

"No doubt," she said with a cute expression.

"I hope you two are up for a great evening. I've got just the place for us to dine. One of the finest restaurants in San Francisco," Will said.

"Oh, I'm starved," said Mary Nel. "Hank eats like a bird, so we've yet to

Finding Mr. Sunday

have a good meal."

"Naw, I don't," said Hank. "I just save up 'til I can keep the feed bag on for a while. And I eyed a steak place coming here that I'm going to hit tonight. You two can have your fancy restaurant."

"Come on, then. Let's get you two settled in your rooms. I've got a carriage coming in a little over an hour, Mary Nel. Will that give you enough time?"

"I'll be ready," she said.

Hank left for the steak house. Will, dressed in one of his fine suits, silk shirts, tie, and sparkling shined boots, waited in his parlor for Mary Nel to come downstairs.

He heard her coming and got up to greet her as she came down the last few steps. He stopped in his tracks and caught his breath when he saw her.

Her hair was arranged perfectly as if she had been to the hairdresser. She was wearing a dazzling dress of light blue satin trimmed with dark blue piping tailored perfectly to her tiny waist. Her eyes sparkled in the gaslight, and she glowed with a natural beauty that would shame any royalty.

He reached for her hand, bowed deeply, and kissed the tips of her fingers in a dramatic gesture.

"Good evening, dear princess," he said with a teasing smile.

"You are a vision of loveliness unlike any this gentleman has ever beheld. How privileged I am to be in your presence."

She giggled at his comment, and he, too, burst out laughing.

Then he stepped closer to her and became quite serious.

"Truly, Mary Nel, you are breathtaking. I'm going to have a hard time taking my eyes off of you tonight."

She gazed steadily at him, and her cheeks colored slightly.

"Well, dear sir, I'm glad you approve," she said coyly.

He helped her with an outer wrap, and they headed out to the waiting carriage.

The dinner was everything promised, served in grand style by the most meticulous waiter. They shared a bottle of fine French champagne, although Mary Nel was somewhat reluctant at first. After a few sips, she no longer concerned herself with what others might think.

She turned the head of every man in the place and a number of women.

They looked like the perfect young couple, animated, laughing, and totally absorbed in each other.

In all their years of knowing each other, never had they seemed so open, in touch, and enamored of each other.

Two hours flew by before the couple realized the meal was over, and the evening was coming to an end.

Will, with Mary Nel on his arm, never felt so proud to be with anyone as he did escorting the lovely lady to the carriage.

When they arrived at his house, they took a stroll along the streets, talking and laughing like they were just getting to know each other.

"Will," said Mary Nel, as she stepped into the house and he helped her remove her wrap. "I have to say you lived up to your promise of showing me a great night. I cannot remember a more enjoyable evening or better company."

She looked up at him as she spoke, a sparkle in her eyes and a smile on her face.

He stepped close to her and put his arms around her. Their gaze met, and something magical happened between them.

He bent to her, kissing her full on the lips in a way she had never experienced. Softly and gently at first. Then deeply and lovingly. Her lips were warm and sweet.

She was tentative at first, then she pressed herself to him and responded to him, leaving nothing unanswered.

He stepped back a bit.

"Mary Nel, I'm not very good at this. I have never felt like this with anyone before. I..."

"Like what, Will?" she said, studying his eyes.

"I love you, Mary Nel. I love you. For the life of me, I can't understand why I never realized it before. I have never felt this overwhelmed, to be near you, to be with you, to touch you."

"Oh, Will," she said, tears filling her eyes as she held him.

"I love you!" she cried. "I have always loved you. Before we even spoke, I knew I would love you."

They held each other tightly, rocking in each other's arms. She let go of him, wiping her eyes.

Finding Mr. Sunday

"I'm sorry, Will. It's just, I have waited so long to hear those words. I've dreamed of it, over and over, and now it's true. It has really happened."

He put both hands on her shoulders and looked at her.

"I'm the one who should be crying, for all the time I have let pass by not realizing I was in love with you." He laughed.

He kissed her again. Her kiss was like no other.

And he knew. He knew this was right.

Mary Nel and Hank left the next morning. He had held her tightly and whispered a promise.

Jamison and Broome met in his office the next day.

"There are seven investors in that saloon, Mr. Broome. You know Winton. Ralston Chambers and two other fellows. I can't find out who they are 'cause Chambers is handling their money. George Latham, you know. Morris Preston is part of the group. Then there is a lawyer by the name of Sunday.

"In fact, this guy Sunday gave me a hard time the other night. But he ain't heard the last of me."

"What did you say his name was?" asked Broome slowly and deliberately as his eyes widened.

"Sunday, Will Sunday. He's a local attorney with a successful practice. Owns a ranch out in the San Joaquin Valley. He came here from Sacramento," said Jamison.

"Then he is from California?" said Broome with a hint of relief.

"No, sir. He's from Missouri, St. Louis, I've been told.

Broome stared at Jamison as if hypnotized.

Jamison watched as Broome's face seemed to drain and turn ashen. Broome leaned back in his chair, sank deep into the upholstery, slumping and worsening his already bad posture.

"You all right, sir?" said Jamison.

For a long moment, his question hung in the air. Then Broome looked up at him.

"You say he gave you a hard time?" said Broome.

Dick Ward

"Yeah, the guards at that saloon caught some of our boys putting a scare into them. That was before you told me not to do anything. This fellow Sunday somehow got onto me.

"Damn it, Jamison," said Broome.

"Sir, it's about what we've always done when somebody cuts into your areas," said Jamison.

Broome seemed to ignore the statement.

"What does this Sunday look like?" said Broome.

"He's a big guy, sandy hair, decent-looking, well-dressed."

"Leave him alone, Jamison. Leave all of them alone. Do you hear me?"

"Yes, sir," said Jamison.

When he left, he rushed out, trying to locate one of his boys so he could put a stop to something that was already in the works.

That night, Will was preparing for a trip to the valley in the morning. He wanted to be with Mary Nel. He needed to see her. The thought made him smile.

After he packed, he headed a short distance around the corner to one of his favorite neighborhood dining spots. He rounded the corner, and a gunshot shattered his thoughts.

At the same time a bullet whizzed within inches of his head and exploded into the plaster pillar on the corner of the building. His cheek burned as tiny particles of the plaster hit him.

He dropped back behind the pillar and pulled his pistol. He could hear someone running on the boardwalk across the street. He went running toward the sound. Under the dim glow of a gas light he saw a coattail disappear down an alley.

When he got to the alley he couldn't see or hear anything. There were no windows in the sides of the buildings to provide even the slightest bit of light in the alley.

He knew if he went down the alley he would be a perfect target, backlit by the gas lamps on the street behind him.

Will was angry. Jamison or one of his men! That bastard didn't waste any

411

time getting revenge. He would take care of that.

The next morning he got up before dawn. He sent a telegram to Mary Nel saying he would be arriving in the late afternoon instead of the morning.

Will decided he would deal with Broome himself. He didn't care about Broome's business any longer. He might even find Jamison there.

Will entered the marble lobby of the building, walked across the thickly carpeted reception area, and climbed the oak stairway to the second floor.

He looked up and down the hallway and spotted a massive oak door with intricate carvings. The door was marked private.

He pushed open the door, surprised to find it unlocked, and walked into a reception area. An older lady was sitting behind the desk.

She stood up quickly and said, "Sir, this is a private office, not part of the hotel."

"I know," he said. "Where's Broome?"

"Mr. Broome only sees people by appointment," she said defiantly. "Who are you and what do you want?"

Will looked to his right and saw another massive oak door. Without hesitation he walked over to the door and reached for the door knob.

"Stop, you can't go in there," she yelled as she rushed toward him.

Will, ignoring her, pushed hard on the door and let go of the knob, slamming the heavy door against the wall as he walked into the office.

"Oh, Mr. Broome, I'm sorry I couldn't stop him, he just ..."

"Shut the door and leave us alone, Lillian."

"But sir," she insisted.

"Get out!" Broome shouted.

She closed the door quickly.

Broome sat calmly behind a huge desk. He was pointing a nickel-plated pistol directly at Will. His hands were steady. Will walked slowly to the front of the desk.

"Who are you and why are you busting into my office like this? I should shoot you," said Broome.

Will was angry but tried to control his emotions.

"I wanted to meet the man who tries to run me out of my business by attempting to burn it down, then has his henchmen shoot at me. I wanted to find out what kind of man would endanger the lives of others just to keep away a little competition," said Will.

All of a sudden the old man looked as if he had been slapped. His gaze never left Will. He looked Will up and down. He held the pistol in place like he had frozen.

Then he lowered the gun slowly. The clunk of the gun on the desk was the only sound.

Will watched as the man's eyes watered. The man put his elbows on his desk and seemed to wipe his eyes and smooth out his face at the same time.

Will saw the scars on the man's cheekbones. He saw the man had no index finger on his right hand.

Will was puzzled at the man's sudden change in demeanor.

"My name is Will Sunday. I'm an investor in a saloon here in the city. The one you have been trying to ruin," Will said. "Jamison or one of his boys also tried to kill me last night."

Broome looked up at him quickly.

"I … I didn't tell him to do that. I told him to leave you alone. Not to touch you or your business, " Broome said quietly.

"You were trying to ruin my business," said Will.

"Yes. I did some of those things. I thought you were just another one trying to cut into my part of town. I didn't know or care who you were. When I found out who you were I stopped everything."

"So you know I do your legal work, then?" Will said.

"You do what?" asked a surprised Broome.

"Your corporate legal work. Bonnie hired me. I thought that was what you meant when you said you found out who I was," said Will.

"No. I had no idea you did that. Bonnie handles all of that," he said quietly.

"Then what did you mean?" said a puzzled Will.

The man looked away from Will. Then he turned back and held a stare. As he looked at Will, his china blue eyes filled with tears that ran down into his beard. The man started to tremble as he struggled to speak.

"Because …" The old man could hardly speak.

Tears flooded his eyes. "Because I knew who you were."

Will stepped close to the desk, put his hands on the edge and looked down at the crying man, wondering what in the world could have brought the man to his emotional knees, right before his eyes.

His eyes, Will thought. His eyes. There was something about the man's eyes.

"You were born in Virginia in 1847, in Petersburg," Broome said, his voice faltering as he pulled out a kerchief and dabbed his eyes.

"Your mother died when you were very young. You went to St. Louis with your father in 1852. You were kicked by a mule and badly injured. You were left there in the care of Tom Peyton while your father went on to California."

The man sniffed.

"How do you know all this?" Will asked incredulously.

The man looked down and sobbed gently. Then he looked up at Will.

"Because you are my son."

The man wept openly, unable to control himself.

Will's knees weakened. He became dizzy. He reached blindly behind him, pulled a chair up, and sank into it, feeling like he was going to be sick.

This can't be, he thought. This is not happening. This is a dream, he thought.

He looked at the man again. What he saw and what he remembered took his breath away.

Now he knew. The eyes. He could never forget those eyes.

He had known one person with eyes like that.

His father.

Will sat unbelieving, looking at the man. He was unable to speak. Something welled up inside him. He bent over and put his head in his hands. He could feel his body begin to shake.

After a moment, he looked up at Broome.

"You ... you left me ... and you never came back ... I cried almost every night for you, wondering where you were."

He felt the tears come. The anger. He couldn't see clearly. He was shaking. His breath came in spasms. He lost control of his breathing.

He wiped his eyes with the back of his hands.

But he couldn't gain control.

"Every wish I made ... at every birthday ... was to see you ... to have you come back. And you never did."

414

Dick Ward

He stood up just to walk around, to move, to prove he was alive and awake.

The man sat at his desk, crying, awash in guilt and remorse. Sick at the sight of his son's agony. He had never been man enough to imagine what this would be like.

"I could only console myself by believing something had happened to you … and you were not able to come get me … I thought you were dead," Will said.

Broome got up from behind his desk and walked toward his son. He put both hands out as if pleading to be understood.

Will recoiled.

"Get away from me," he yelled.

"You … you were alive all this time," stammered Will.

Will looked at the man whose once tall frame and proud stature had long ago left him. His face was frail and worn. He looked far older than his years.

"And you never came for me! You never tried to get in touch! You just left me there!" yelled Will. "And now look what you are. Why? Why?"

"It's … It's a long, long story … I can't … I'm sorry … I'm sorry," pleaded the man.

Will saw the pain on the old man's face. But he had no sympathy. It was nothing like the pain he had felt all these years.

"I'm sure you are … I'm sure you are," Will muttered through gritted teeth.

Will stood erect, looked once more at the stricken man.

"So am I. Damn you. So am I."

He turned and strode angrily out, slamming the door.

He headed to his ranch. He had to leave the city. Nothing had prepared him for what he had just experienced. Not in a million years. In all the dreams he'd had about meeting his father again, nothing was even remotely like that.

He was completely drained. He stared into the distance, a thousand questions on his mind. None of the possible answers gave him any consolation.

The business investment meant nothing to him anymore. He would sell out his shares as soon as he got back. He knew his partners would buy them. He doubted there would be any more trouble from Jamison or Broome.

Broome? Where did that name come from? Was he ashamed of Sunday? Wasn't his own name good enough? Just another one of the thousand questions that might never be answered.

He had no desire to see the man again. He had abandoned him. There could not be any love there on his father's behalf.

The trip was agonizing. As he got close to the ranch he realized he had to get hold of himself. No one could see him like this. He needed to talk to someone. This was too much to handle alone.

Mary Nel. Sweet Mary Nel. At the thought of her, he quickened his pace.

He arrived very late in the night and went quietly to the room set aside for him. He slept little that night. He had nightmare after nightmare of being alone in the middle of nowhere. Abandoned by all of humanity.

By morning the drama of the day before felt unreal. Will focused on the most important thing in his life — Mary Nel.

Before breakfast, he found her and asked her to sit with him on the sofa. She saw the serious look on his face, and her eyes widened.

"Oh, Will, are you sorry for what's happened between us?" she said, trembling.

"No, no, Mary Nel, my heart is yours," Will said. He reached for her hands and paused. Not for drama but because he found it difficult to speak at that moment.

"I saw my father yesterday morning," he said.

The look on Mary Nel's face reflected the same incredulous reaction Will had experienced.

"What? Your father? How could that be?" said Mary Nel.

He could feel the emotion rising in him.

"I can't get over it," said Will. "All these years of thinking I'd never see him, and through a very unlikely series of events, I find him. He is sitting before me, alive and talking to me."

He had to get control, he told himself. He took a deep breath and went on.

416

Dick Ward

He spent some time going over the circumstances that led up to meeting Broome. Mary Nel sat listening to every word.

After he finished, she sat in stunned silence.

"Why is his name Broome? What happened to him all these years?" asked Mary Nel.

"I don't know. I was so overwhelmed. I was angry. I was hurt. I had to get out of there," Will said.

He felt the anger rise up in him again.

"I didn't want to be in the same room with him. I said some things I shouldn't have, and I left. I still find it hard to believe."

Mary Nel didn't speak as she absorbed the strange story. She looked at Will, and they almost spoke at the same time. "We have to talk to Momma," Mary Nel said. "Yes, Mary Nel, we have so much to tell her," Will said.

They went into the kitchen, laughing and almost crying at the same time.

Kate looked up with surprise. "What is it? What's going on?"

"Two big things have happened to me, Kate," Will said.

First, he told her about his father.

"Will, you can't leave it like that. You have to go back and talk to him. There has to be an explanation. You have to give him the opportunity to tell you what happened," said Kate, her face softening as she spoke.

"Momma is right, Will," said Mary Nel. "You must. You won't have any peace until you do. It will be painful. But it's something you must do, Will."

No one spoke for a moment.

"Will, you had to have loved him at one time, didn't you?" said Mary Nel.

He sat there thinking about her question. He remembered little about his father. But he remembered moments of being hugged and the comfort he felt in his father's arms. He remembered his father leaving and how much he missed him. And the pain when he didn't return.

"Yes. I'm sure I did. When my mother died, he refused to leave me alone. I remember that. He was always there to comfort me. He loved me. He must have," said a sad Will.

"Then for that reason, Will, if for no other, you must hear him out," said Mary Nel.

Will looked at the two women. These two were the most important people in his life. He loved, trusted, and respected them for many reasons, not the least being their common sense.

He knew that his deep emotions and the pain of meeting his father had clouded his judgment.

"Thank you for hearing me out. You two are making good sense, something that has eluded me on this whole thing," he said.

"Momma, there's something else," said Mary Nel. "We have good news."

Her face was radiant with happiness as she clasped her hands in front of her.

There was a pause, and the three of them exchanged glances.

"Well, darling. Are you going to tell me or am I going to tell you?" Kate said with a knowing smile.

"Will and I are in love Momma, truly in love, like I have always dreamed about," she bubbled.

Will reached for Mary Nel's hand.

"It's true, Kate. It just took me a while to realize it," he said.

Mary Nel saw the look on her mother's face.

"Wait … you knew?" Mary Nel said.

"I guessed. Mothers can sense these things," said a laughing Kate. "Besides, there was an attraction between you two since the day you met."

"You are right, Momma. I've always loved him," she said, beaming as she pulled Will to her side. "But you never seemed to think of me that way, did you?"

Without waiting for an answer, she continued.

"I tried over and over to get you to say even the tiniest thing that might give me some hope you were interested in me," she said, giggling. "And now you have. It is like a wonderful dream, and I don't want to wake up." She kissed him warmly on the cheek. "I'm so happy, Will."

Will hugged her close and whispered in her ear, but not so quietly that Kate couldn't hear.

"I love you," he said.

Kate came around the table and hugged them both.

"I'm so happy. I love both of you," she said with tears in her eyes. "David will be home tomorrow. It will be nice to confirm with him what we both suspected."

Will took a deep breath as he climbed the stairs to the second floor of Broome's building. He had stayed nearly a week at the ranch, spending most of his time with Mary Nel. The time together was precious to both of them.

He opened the heavy oak door. Lillian was at her desk. She looked up, alarmed as she recognized Will.

"I'm not here to make trouble. I just want to talk to Mr. Broome," he said, holding up both hands.

She looked at him skeptically, very annoyed at his return.

"Would you ask him if I could see him, please?" said Will calmly.

She got up and went into Broome's office and closed the door. In a moment she came out.

"He will see you now," she said.

Will walked to the door and opened it slowly. Broome was standing by the window peering out.

He turned to face his son.

The man looked drained. There was little color in his face. But there were no tears in his eyes this time.

"We need to talk," said Will.

"Let's sit over there," said Broome as he pointed to a group of chairs around a low table.

Broome settled into one of the chairs, and Will sat opposite him.

He gazed at his father, unsure of where to begin. In all his dreams this was supposed to be a sweeter moment than this.

"I was unfair to you. I was angry. Hurt. I couldn't believe what I was hearing," Will said slowly.

As he talked, he saw remnants of his father's face from many years ago. The eyes, of course. His ears and the shape of his mouth. His face was still lean, but there were age lines around the corners of his eyes and on his forehead. His large hands were wrinkled by time, and dark spots mingled with the veins on top of his hands.

"I came to say I am sorry. I didn't give you the courtesy of hearing what you had to say. I owe you that."

Finding Mr. Sunday

"You owe me nothing," said Broome. "I am the one who should be apologizing."

Will could see the man's eyes beginning to water.

"For all the pain I have caused you. You. The only person left on earth that I loved. I abandoned you. Left you for others to raise. It was heartless. Cruel."

A tear seeped from one eye, and Broome pulled a handkerchief from his pocket and dabbed his eyes.

"I have no right to ask anything of you, Will."

Will was moved as the man called him by name. Yes, he could remember his father's voice calling his name.

"But please, please let me tell you my story. It may not stop the pain, but maybe you will understand."

"Go on," said Will.

"I left St. Louis in the spring of 1852 and headed to Independence. I missed the wagon train I was going to join. I was eager to get to California so I could get settled and come get you. But there were no other wagon trains ready to depart for a couple of weeks.

"Other folks came in late, and a few just showed up looking for a train. So about twenty other families got together and decided to strike out. We had a young guide who had made the trip before.

"Looking back, the trip didn't seem that hard. We didn't lose any people. Time has erased all the hard things, the weather, the river crossings, the lack of water at times. But we made good progress. We were all young, eager, wanting to get there.

"Some of the people planned to go to on to Oregon. I listened to them talk about that part of the country. All along I had thought I'd go to California. But Oregon began to sound like a better place, so I decided to go there."

The man seemed to relax as he told the story. Sometimes he would look far away, but his eyes always returned to Will.

"We were going to take the southern route to Oregon, avoid the Dalles and the bad crossing on the more northern route. In September of 1852 we were in the northern part of California headed to Oregon. We were in Modoc country up in the lakes region. Travelers coming south had told us the Modoc tribe was making trouble.

Dick Ward

"We had a meeting and decided to go on. We were too close to our destination to worry about a few Indians.

"One morning we were traveling on a narrow part of the trail. There were high hills and ridges on one side of the trail and a lake shore on the other. The Indians hit us there from three directions, coming down the ridges, from the trail ahead of us and the trail behind us.

"We had no place to go. We had no room or even the time to circle the wagons."

His father's hands began to shake ever so slightly.

"It was a slaughter. Women, children, animals. Everyone. The wagons burned. The wounded were trampled.

"I was under a wagon like most of the others. After a while I couldn't hear any more of my friends firing their guns. They were all dead or unable. I only had a few shots and little powder. I figured it was my time."

Broome paused to pour himself a glass of water from the pitcher on the table and drank most of it.

"I crawled out from under the wagon and tried to run up one of the ridges. A young warrior on this big pony saw me and started to run me down. I stopped, turned around, and shot him dead."

Broome looked down at his trembling hands and clasped them together.

"That was my last shot. A half dozen of them fell on me and were about to kill me. Then another Indian rode up and stopped them. Turned out he was the chief. They tied me up. Looted the train and then took me up in the hills to their village.

"When we got there, they took off all my clothes and tied me to a post. The women and old men came around, laughing, throwing rocks at me. Then the women started using these reeds, like cane stalks. They were sharpened on one end, and they started sticking them into me, all over, laughing and dancing all around. Not enough to kill me but enough for me to bleed each time they stuck me.

"They took turns beating me, whipping me, poking me. I was bleeding all over. I passed out. And they threw water on me and started all over again.

"After a couple of hours, the chief made them stop. But they kept me tied there, naked, all night. Some of the boys would run up every once in a while and throw manure on me and run away laughing."

421

Finding Mr. Sunday

He dabbed his eyes again and took more water.

"Would you like to stop for a while?" said Will.

He could see the storytelling was taking a terrible toll on the man. It made him uncomfortable to watch, but Will was transfixed by the story.

"No. No," said the man. "I've never told this to anybody ... ever ..."

The blue eyes had turned red around the rims, but he was determined to keep going.

"The next day and into the next night, I was tied up to the post. One of the old squaws gave me some water. I was sure I was going to die.

"On the morning of the third day they had some kind of ceremony. The women came after me again. This time they had heavy sticks, not reeds. They beat me again. Not hard enough to break any bones, just again and again. I passed out several times.

"Then they dumped water on me, and women scrubbed my naked body with some bundles of sticks, like crude brushes, that cut into my skin. They covered me with some kind of oil, cut me down, and dragged me to another post and tied me tightly. I thought they were going to burn me alive."

The man stopped, put his head in his hands for a moment, drew a ragged breath, then continued.

"They all gathered around, and the chief came up leading a pony. I remembered later, it was the pony the young brave was riding when I shot him.

"The chief started talking to me, gesturing to the pony. Then he let the pony go, and it ran off a ways. He came up to me with a knife in his hand and grabbed me by the hair. I thought he was going to scalp me or kill me. But he didn't. He put three deep cuts into each of my cheeks."

Broome held his fingers to his cheeks touching the scars. At the top of each cheek, three scar lines were visible, going from under the ear slanting toward his chin.

"Then they untied my hands, and several of the braves held out my right hand."

Broome paused for a moment.

"And the chief cut off my index finger."

He held up his right hand up. There was a ragged scar where his finger had been.

Dick Ward

"A warrior staunched the bleeding with a burning stick. They hobbled me and put me in a tent with nothing to wear but a loin cloth. At night they tied me down so I couldn't escape.

"They made me a slave. I gathered wood, cleaned up dung, cleaned up old people who were sick. I was fair game for anyone to punch, whip, or beat, as long as I wasn't crippled.

"The young boys would shoot me with blunt arrows. I was given scraps for food, leftover stews sometimes.

"After three or four months, they got tired of torturing and beating me. But I was still hobbled all the time.

"Sometimes white men raided the village. The Indians would fight, then move somewhere else. They would raid mining camps, taking prisoners sometimes. And they would make me watch them torture their captives until they died.

"As I learned their language I came to realize the brave I had killed was the chief's son. He cut off my finger because I used it to kill his son. I guess the chief wanted my punishment to last as long as possible.

"This went on and on, day after day, month after month. I wanted to die. I was less than human. I was skin and bones. I got sick at one point, and a fever almost killed me, but somehow I lived through it.

"They left me alone after a while as long as I did as I was told. But they still tied me at night. To this day, I wake up at night, thinking I'm tied up.

"One day, they were packing up to move. I later learned about two years had passed. They stripped me naked and told me to run.

"I had no idea where I was. I ran for days. I had no food, but I managed to find water. I saw smoke one day and finally stumbled into a mining town by the name of Yreka. A miner there took me to a saloon, found some old clothes for me, and fed me.

"The owner of the saloon let me take a bath and paid for a haircut. I kept my beard. I soaked for hours trying to get the stink out.

"The fellow who owned the saloon had a cot in the back, and he let me sleep there and fed me. In return, I cleaned up, swept the floors, and did odd jobs for him. I never told anyone who I was. I didn't talk unless I had to.

"That's when I found whiskey. I crawled in a bottle and stayed. Drinking helped me forget. It helped me sleep. I tried many times to drink until it

423

Finding Mr. Sunday

killed me, but I never succeeded.

"I worked cleaning tables and so on. The fellows would leave me a few coins every day. Enough to buy food ... and whiskey, always whiskey.

"That's where I got the nickname Broome, from the guys who came to the saloon who always saw me sweeping the place up."

The old man looked up.

"For the entire two years of captivity and slavery, I thought of you ... every day ... and at the saloon ... every day ...

"I pictured your face, how you must have changed, how you must have grown. I wanted to see you. But I couldn't go out into the world. I couldn't leave where I was. I couldn't leave the bottle.

"Whenever I told myself I was going to come for you, I asked myself why you would want a drunk for a father.

"No home, no farm. I had nothing to offer you. I finally came to the conclusion I could not be a fit father for you, but I dreamed about you, about your mother. When I was drunk I cried myself to sleep. I felt worthless ... used up ... dead."

The tears had come again.

Will could hardly bear seeing the man's pain.

"I only lived to get drunk. I fell in bed every night when I could no longer walk. I'd wake up late in the night, screaming with nightmares. I'd just go to my bottle and drink more until I fell asleep again.

"But I worked every day. I was never too drunk to work until long after we closed for the night. Eventually, the owner started to let me carry drinks to the tables. Then I started tending bar when we were busy.

"I got tips, coins mostly, sometimes little nuggets of gold or silver ore. I got a jar and started saving my money. I had few expenses. But always, always there was the whiskey at night and whenever I needed it.

"I kept myself clean all the time. I couldn't bear the thought that I still smelled. I bought some decent clothes. I worked all the time, waiting on tables, tending bar, cooking, serving, cleaning. And the whiskey every night.

"The owner had five or six girls who worked the place. Taking care of the miners. They were in rooms upstairs. He got a cut of whatever they made.

"If someone got rough with one of the girls on the floor, I'd go over and settle them down. I kept a billy club handy.

"The girls started counting on me to keep order. I got along with all of them.

"If they had a rough customer who wanted to go upstairs, they would signal me, and I'd follow them up and stand by the door. I had a key. If a girl needed me in the room because some guy was mistreating her, I'd go in and take care of the situation.

"We had less and less trouble as time went on. We were packed every night because the miners knew there wouldn't be much trouble there.

"It wasn't long before each of the girls would slip me a dollar or two most nights. I started to stay sober longer into the night. The owner started paying me a little more because I did everything, including keeping the peace.

"I started to talk to the customers some. Miners are lonely people. My jars began to fill up, and I had to convert my coins to paper every night so I could put more money in the jars.

"I stayed there for almost four years. Working. Drinking.

"One Sunday, I was in my room. I had been drinking since midnight. I had hidden all the jars in the wall behind my bed. I counted all the money. I had over $5,000 in cash and two jars of tiny gold nuggets. I got to thinking about my own place.

"Gold and silver mines were popping up everywhere. Mining towns were coming up all around the mines. I heard about a town going up about fifty miles away. Someone in the saloon was complaining they didn't have a saloon up there yet.

"I told the owner about my plans, and he was fine with it. But when the girls heard I was going to open a place up in the hills, all of them wanted to go with me.

"That upset him. By now he had about ten girls. We sat down and decided to split the girls, and he gave bonuses to the ones who were willing to stay.

"I left with four of the girls, started a place of my own. The mine had a big strike, and the town grew almost overnight. Then another strike not far away. Within a short while I had three places going, working about twenty girls. I took care of them, too. People learned quickly hurting one of my girls was not the thing to do.

"I hired good cooks and bartenders, served good food and good whiskey.

Finding Mr. Sunday

I worked every day and every night keeping an eye on everything. I was still drinking every night. But just enough to keep the edge off. I just couldn't sleep for the nightmares if I didn't drink.

"All this time, I thought about you. But I was deeper and deeper into the kind of life that I didn't want you to be a part of, and I couldn't bear the thought of bringing you into it.

"My businesses grew, but there was nobody I could trust.

"One day this little red-headed gal came in wanting a job, you know, working upstairs. She told me she was eighteen, but I knew she was lying. I talked to her a long time. She was different from any of the girls I had hired. Smart. Gutsy. Not afraid to speak her mind.

"I hired her, but I wouldn't let her work upstairs. She became my assistant. Within a year or so she was taking care of so many details I became dependent on her.

"I eventually gave her twenty-five percent ownership in all my places. To this day Bonnie is still with me, and quite well off, I must say.

"I was drinking still. I wanted see you. I wanted to know how you were doing, but I had no confidence in myself as a father.

"I hired an investigative firm to check on you and see what your life was like. I kept them in my employ for years, getting reports.

"I knew your life was good. I knew Tom was taking care of you. I knew you went to church and that you were a good boy."

The tears came again.

"I couldn't take you away from that, Will. I had no fit life to offer you. I was too deep into the wrong kind of life for a son."

He dabbed at his eyes again, took a ragged breath, and paused.

Will himself was now feeling some of the emotion he was seeing in his father. He sat listening, trying to withhold any judgment, trying to understand why his father had done what he had.

"I followed the mining towns. When a mine closed, I left and went on to the next. When the war came I opened places near the forts. Before I knew it, I had plenty of money.

"One night years ago, I went to pour myself a drink. I looked into the glass, set it down, and I have never touched a drop since then.

"I made some trips to San Francisco and decided I was going to stop traveling and open places here. I opened saloons. I opened high-end clubs with restaurants. Private clubs. I followed the same formula, good drinks, good food, fair prices, and hired good people.

"I never went back to my real name. I stopped checking on you the last year of the war when I knew you wouldn't be going."

"How did you know I wouldn't be going?" asked Will.

"Because I paid the authorities in St. Louis to leave you alone," said Broome. "All I had to do was get to the right people. Besides, I knew Tom would keep you out at all costs. He knew nothing about this."

Broome stood up, walked over to the window, and looked out for a minute. He came back and sat down again.

Will sat there astounded that his father had been so close to him all these years but so far away.

"Now you know it all, and anything else you want to know, you can ask and I'll tell you," he said.

"You are rich, successful. Why did you worry about my place when you have all you have?" asked Will.

"I don't know how much you know about San Francisco. But in my type of business, it's cutthroat. I was burned out at least twice when I tried to move close to an established business. It's the way it is here. Not now so much as it was, but you still have to protect your interests," he said.

"That is why I pay people like Jamison. I have to be tough to protect my businesses and my people."

"And you never knew that I was hired to do your legal work?" asked Will.

"No. I didn't know that. Bonnie handles all of that and has since we came here. We never discussed who she hired for anything. She managed that, the leases, the property, even the money. I have never had reason to question her loyalty or honesty.

"Everyone works for her, except Jamison. I don't interfere with her or her life. She is her own person. She does what she wants to do."

There was a long pause. Will could not believe how his world had come full circle and he was sitting here looking at a stranger who was no doubt his father.

The man leaned forward in his chair.

"Will, I don't know if we will ever see each other again, and I'm sure my opinion of you means very little to you after what you have heard. But I'm proud of you. You seem like the kind of son any man would want. You were raised right. I couldn't have done that for you."

Will stared at him, saying nothing. No words would come to him.

Will stood up, straightened his clothes, and looked at his father. He didn't know what he should do.

His father stood up, too. He looked like a tired old man, worn out by his experiences and drained by relating it all to his only flesh and blood. He looked powerless and crippled by the bonds of guilt he had experienced much of his life.

"Will we see each other again?" asked Broome.

"I don't know, sir. I don't know," said Will.

He gathered himself and walked calmly out of the office.

After working several days, Will returned to the valley, but not before making the rounds of the finest jewelry merchants in San Francisco.

When he came into the yard, Mary Nel was coming out the front door of Kate's house.

He looked at her. Never had he seen such a lovely woman. And this beautiful woman was his best friend and soon to be his wife.

He felt a calm and a happiness he had never felt before.

They ran to each other, and he picked her up in his arms and held her tightly.

"It's so good to see you, darling," he said, grinning from ear to ear.

She kissed him full and sweetly on the lips.

"Does that tell you anything?" she said.

He laughed, and they walked arm in arm into the house.

Kate came from the kitchen into the parlor and gave Will a warm hug.

"Mary Nel, come sit here for a minute," he said.

She sat in the stuffed chair before him.

Will dropped to his knees, took her hands and said, "Mary Nelson Daniels, will you marry me?"

The room was split by a loud scream. Mary Nel leaned over and kissed him deliriously, again and again.

Between kisses she yelled "YES! YES! I'll marry you, Will Sunday!"

He reached into his pocket, took out a small box, and extracted one of the finest rings money could buy.

Another scream as Will slipped it on her finger.

She held it up and stared at it open-mouthed.

"Momma! Oh, Momma! Look!" she said, holding out her hand to her mother.

"It's beautiful, sweetheart!" said Kate.

"When? When?" said Mary Nel.

"As soon as you are ready. The sooner the better so we can leave."

"Leave?" she said excitedly.

"Yes. We're going to take the train east. Go to St. Louis, Philadelphia, New York, Boston, and anywhere else you want to go. Then we are going to spend at least three months touring Europe."

Another scream.

"Oh, Will, I love you so much!" she said.

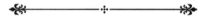

Will spent two weeks preparing for a long sabbatical from his office. He had sold his interest in the saloon and was eager to be married and off on his honeymoon.

Preparations were hastily being made at Kate's house for a big ceremony, after which the couple would retire to Will's ranch for the night, then leave the next day to board a ship in San Francisco.

He was about to leave when Mrs. Wolfe knocked softly on his door.

"Will, Miss Farrell is here to see you. She said she apologized for not having an appointment."

Will was surprised. Even the mention of her name seemed like something from the distant past.

He went out to greet her.

"Miss Farrell, it's good to see you. Please come in and sit down," he said.

They went in, and he closed the door.

He wasn't sure what to say. He waited for her to say something, but she didn't.

Finding Mr. Sunday

"Your trip wasn't as long as I expected," he said.

She sat there looking at him with a smile, seeming to ignore his statement.

"I see you broke the rules, Mr. Sunday," she said softly with a slight smile.

"Yes ... yes, I did Miss Farrell. And if you want to fire me I under ..."

"I have no intentions of firing you. I don't think your father would like that," she said.

"You know, then," he said.

"Yes. He told me all about it. I couldn't believe it," she said, shaking her head.

"Will, I just needed to tell you something. I hope you will keep this in mind as you go forward. Your father does not know I am here and knows nothing about what I am going to say."

Then her demeanor changed. Serious. Sincere.

"William is a good man, Will."

"He is a tough man, but a good man. Since I was sixteen he has taken care of me. He saved me from a life of ruin. He has never once been inappropriate and has shown me only the greatest respect for all these years. And yes, I love him. But not in the way you think."

He now saw a tenderness he had not seen in her before.

"I'll always love him for what he did ... and continues to do for me. But it is his strength I love. I don't know much about his past. But I do know he has been a haunted man for many years. I have seen him battle something day after day. Most men would have given in and given up. But not your father.

"Finding you is the best thing that has happened to him. You should see him now. There is life. There is hope. There is a spark in him I've never seen.

"I know you were hurt. But you are a strong person, Will. I can see it in you. Just like him. But please, please ... find it in your heart to forgive him."

Bonnie never dropped her guard, but he could see this was coming from her heart.

She was pleading with him.

He sat there, staring at her, then looking away. He took a deep breath.

"Thank you, Bonnie ... It ... it's going to take some time."

"I understand, Will," she said.

She stood up preparing to leave.

"Bonnie," he said, "there is something I want you to know. I am deeply in love with someone I have known for a long time. I'm just now preparing to leave. We are getting married next week."

Bonnie looked at him for a long moment. He searched but saw nothing in her gaze. It was business Bonnie.

But then she softened her look and smiled.

She stepped over to his side and kissed him softly on the cheek.

"She is a lucky woman, Will."

With that she walked quickly to the door and let herself out.

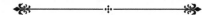

Preparations for the wedding were well underway. Will and Mary Nel could hardly leave each other's sight.

In a lull in the activity Will asked Mary Nel to sit with him for a moment.

"I've been thinking about my father. Over the last few weeks I've been to trying to sort out my feelings. I don't know if I can ever fully forget what my father did, but I'm prepared to forgive him."

"Oh, Will, I'm so glad to hear you say that. I knew you were troubled by it, and I don't want it to weigh on you forever."

"Would you consider going to San Francisco with me to meet him? I want him to know you. After all, he will be the grandfather to our children," said Will.

"Will, I would like very much to do that," she said, beaming.

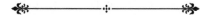

Hand in hand, they both climbed the stairs to Broome's office. Will opened the door to find Lillian sitting at her desk.

"Good morning, Lillian," said Will. "Mr. Broome is expecting me."

"Yes, he is, Mr. Sunday," she said pleasantly. "And I should tell you, Mr. Broome is now Mr. Sunday. He has changed his name."

Finding Mr. Sunday

With that she ushered them into William's office.

William was standing near the door to greet them, a big smile on his face.

"Hello, Poppa," said a smiling Will.

"Hello, son," said an equally happy William.

"Poppa, I want you to meet the woman I am madly in love with. We are going to be married next week. Poppa, this is Mary Nel."

William reached for both of Mary Nel's hands. He stared at her for a moment.

"Hello, Mary Nel. You are the most beautiful woman I have ever seen."

He shook his head slowly back and forth in sincerity as he lifted both hands to kiss hers.

"Hello, Poppa. I'm so happy to meet you," she said, her dazzling smile lighting up the room.

She gave him a warm hug.

"Please, please, sit down and let's talk," said a glowing William.

They sat for more than an hour. William was alive, animated, beaming with joy.

Will watched the delight in his father's blue eyes as he spoke with Mary Nel.

"Poppa," said Mary Nel. "This is for you."

She handed him an envelope. He opened it and read an engraved invitation to their wedding.

Tears fell from his eyes.

He stood and hugged the two of them.

"You couldn't keep me away," he said.

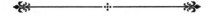

Five years later, Judge Will Sunday and his beautiful wife, Mary Nel, could be seen walking in the park. They were followed closely by a proud grandfather, Mr. William Sunday, who was holding the hands of his twin grandsons, William Caleb Sunday and Thomas Nelson Sunday.

The End

Dick Ward

Dick Ward is a retired marketing executive who lives in Bermuda Run, NC with his wife Betty. He is a native of Virginia and a graduate of Virginia Commonweatlh University.

He may be reached at: *findingmrsunday@gmail.com* or
dickward.findingmrsunday@yahoo.com

CPSIA information can be obtained
at www.ICGtesting.com
Printed in the USA
BVHW081627031218
534638BV00003B/88/P